Tilly's Song

To Jan,

A dear sister of mine in Christ.

You are a blessing in my life!

CAROL WELTY ROPER

Carol Welty Roper

May 2, 2010

Copyright © 2009 Carol Welty Roper.

All rights reserved. Written permission must be secured from the author to use or reproduce any part of this book, except for brief quotations in critical reviews or articles.

Cover photo layout by Dan and Bernice Williams.

Cover created by Brianna Anaforian.

All Scripture quotations are taken from the King James Version.

Printed in the United States of America

Table of Contents

1	Choose Life	13
2	Letting Go	29
3	A Trip Over Troubled Water	38
4	So Close ... Yet So Far	59
5	We Are Free!	88
6	A New Life in a New Home	97
7	Never a Dull Moment	116
8	What Do You Do?	122
9	Back to Normal	135
10	Light After the Storm	158
11	Romance Is in the Air	183
12	The Phrasing of Every Song	209
13	Love Goes On	225
14	In Everything Give Thanks	255
	Epilogue	271

This book is dedicated to the memory of my

Great Grandmother
Mathilda Martha Baumann Bogda
and
My Nana
Marie Martha Bogda Bartholomew

"And I will restore to you the years that the locust hath eaten …
And ye shall eat in plenty, and be satisfied, and praise the
Name of the Lord your God that hath dealt wondrously with
you; and my people shall never be ashamed."
(Joel 2:25-26)

Acknowledgements

I am in awe of the inspiration that makes up the creative process. The inspiration for this story came to me in two forms: First, my grandmother told me the skeletal, factual portion of the story, and then the Holy Spirit helped to flesh out the dialogs and remainder of the story. It has been said that all first novels are autobiographic. This is true only in the emotion used to infuse some of the scenes that was pulled from some of my personal experiences. The majority of this story is fiction based on factual events.

I wish to acknowledge my heartfelt gratitude to my Heavenly Father, my husband, Philip, and my children: David, Bonnie, Jennifer, Andrew and Christina. Philip has been my research assistant, cheerleader and breadwinner and has allowed me the leisure to explore my long someday list of things to do. Thank you, Phil! Jennifer Bowers, my daughter, has listened to the story from the very first sentence scratched down on a yellow pad. She has been my coach and fan all in one. Thank you, Jennifer!

In addition to the above, I wish to thank Freddy Sue Lee, my English teacher, who encouraged me to write and to finish what I wrote. Linda Fode receives my gratitude for showing me how to live free of fear in God's perfect will.

I have received much strength from the prayers of my buddies in our intercessory prayer group: Victoria Gotthardt, Cindy Plumb, Debi Watson, Beckie Coles, Kim Voehl and Mary Remole. Much love and gratitude goes to Tommy and Barbara Davis and the students at Far North Bible College, who helped me take the leap in faith to write this story for God's glory. Thank you to Brenda Sanborn and Eleanor Liddell for helping me with the technical part of this novel and for their friendship. I am also grateful for Daren Lindley, Michelle Cuthrell and Peter Bell, my publisher and editors.

A very special thank you goes to two organizations: The Salvation Army and the Lutheran women who support missions in their churches. Both groups have remained true to the cause of advancing the Kingdom of God. They have had a positive influence in thousands of families, my family being one. Thank you, and may God continue to richly bless you.

Carol Welty Roper
Deuteronomy 30:19

Chapter 1
Choose Life

Mathilda listened to the soft creaking rhythm of the chair as she slowly rocked back and forth. This motion was a habit her body had learned from years of rocking babies to sleep. It had always soothed her, but today was different. Her body and mind were numb as she rocked with no sense of time. From an unknown distance, she heard a voice. The word did not register. She heard the voice again; this time it was very close. The shrill tone hit like the tip of a spear. Mathilda recognized the word "Mama" that demanded her attention and turned her face in the direction of the sound. It took a moment for her eyes to focus. A small girl ran toward the rocker and stopped, extending her arms toward Mathilda. It took all of her effort to recognize her daughter.

"Marie," she heard herself whisper. The child quickly climbed onto her lap and clutched her mother's neck. They held onto each other, touching their cheeks, wet with tears. Rocking and patting her daughter's back gave as much comfort to Mathilda as it did to Marie.

Not everyone is dead, she thought. Renewed energy allowed her to breathe in and force out a sigh. Her darling little girl was still alive, and she was, too. *Was this a horrible nightmare or was she awake? Had exhaustion robbed her of all consciousness? Was it morning? How long had she and Marie been weeping in the chair?* Mathilda's body was sluggish, heavy with despair. The room remained uncomfortably silent. No, she was wrong, there was a noise. She opened her eyes and searched in the direction of a buzzing. A fly was trapped at the window; its little sound grew to be quite deafening. Her eyes searched for other recognizable sights and sounds. She knew this room because she cleaned it daily; however, something was not right. The smell was not the same. No welcoming food aromas lingered in the air, as normal. Instead this smell filled her stomach, not her lungs, and she felt weak, panicky and sick. Without thinking, she pulled her handkerchief from her sleeve and covered her nose. Still holding Marie, she rose from the rocker and took a few steps toward the front door, which opened effortlessly; light and heat poured from the morning sun into the house. Suddenly hot and sweaty, she felt so dizzy that she thought she might fall. She left the house and staggered toward the village.

"No!" she shouted, not knowing whether she had done so aloud. "I must go to the stream." She turned and ran downhill toward it.

Marie's body was also hot as she continued to sleep with her head on Mathilda's shoulder. She passed the dead milk cows without seeing them. The gurgling sound of the stream revived her spirit, enough for her to run faster. She stopped abruptly, then gently laid Marie on the cool grass. Mathilda waded into the waist high water and sat down. Cupping her hands, she drank in the frigid water that washed away that acid burn in her throat. The nausea subsided. A slight breeze caused her to shiver. Mathilda stood up from the water and walked over to join her sleeping daughter. With the sun and breeze drying her clothes, her mind came alive, though her body still felt heavy and slow.

What happened? When did it start? What am I to do now? Mathilda's mind jumped from one thought to the next. She put her hands over her ears as if this could stop her from hearing her own thoughts. She wanted to run away. If she opened her mouth, she would surely scream. She felt her heart pounding in her head and throat; the tightness in her chest caused an ache. Through all the pain, she sensed a small calm voice speaking from within her racing heart. Mathilda responded to this voice with a demand.

"Heavenly Father, send guardian angels to help my daughter and me in our hour of need." There, it was said — but to her ears, her tone sounded much too demanding. Her voice softened. "Please, God!" she whispered.

The sound of the stream and a bee singing in the clover returned to her ears. She looked at the clover and saw that Marie was awake, sitting and looking up at her.

"Mama, I'm thirsty." Marie yawned and rubbed her eyes. Mathilda looked at Marie's sky-blue eyes and stroked her blond ringlets. Marie was alive. This was no dream, and her little girl needed water. Mathilda's numbed brain quickened to the need of her child. Taking Marie by the hand, she led her into the stream. Cupping her hands together, she dipped out icy water and let her daughter drink. This single action sapped her energy. Exhausted, they returned to the grassy knoll and lay down. Mathilda forced herself to breathe because her body might just forget how. Once her breathing slowed to normal, she made herself think. Nothing came to mind but the haunting question, *What must I do next?*

The world around her was lifeless, like a framed oil painting on the wall; one could stare at it over and over, yet never see the details. Like an observer of the scene, she heard herself speak and listened intently to what she had to say. "Marie, I must go from house to house to find help for us, but I don't want you to see any more death. Please come back with me to our home and play with your toys. I will return to you," Mathilda spoke gently.

"Oh no, Mama, don't leave me. Please, Mama, I'm scared. Don't leave me!"

"What can I do?" Marie winced in fear as her mother raised an angry voice. "Oh, I'm sorry. I don't want to frighten you." Mathilda's voice quickly changed from anger to remorse.

Marie looked at her mother's eyes. They reminded her of the rabbit that Papa, Mary and she had trapped in the woods. Mama's eyes were usually sparkling and happy, but now she had those scared, desperate rabbit eyes.

"My Love, you may come with me, but I cannot carry you. You must do as I say. I must try to find someone to help us." Mathilda could not keep from weeping. "Papa is dead." Both Mathilda's hands and voice shook. "It is time to bury him next to Mary and the baby. I can't do it alone, My Love. I need help. Do you understand, Marie?"

Marie looked up and nodded yes. In a whisper, she answered, "I will help you." Marie grabbed hold of her mother's

Tilly's Song

leg. Mathilda's chin quivered. Holding hands, they walked to the nearest neighbor's house. Mrs. Günter was seated in a chair next to the bed, slumped over her husband; both had been dead for several days. A big rat running out of the door startled Marie as she peeked across the threshold. Mrs. Günter had been Mathilda's best friend, and Marie thought of her as a grandmother. But Mr. Günter was no grandfather to Marie; he had frightened her. The Günters' cottage was untidy and unwelcoming. Food had dried on the plates, still on the dinner table from their last meal. Flies were cleaning whatever the rats had left behind. Too shocked to grieve, Mathilda grabbed Marie by the hand and headed down the grassy knoll to the cobbled walkway leading to the village square.

The rest of the evening, mother and daughter went to every house and shop. All the villagers and their animals had perished. Relatives, friends and neighbors were all dead. Their last stop was the church, where the dead pastor and his wife were lying together on the bed. Mathilda remembered what the pastor had taught his parishioners: "Your old earthly bodies will someday be replaced by new celestial ones." Leaving them in peace, Marie and Mathilda left the parsonage and stepped into the sanctuary.

Mathilda kneeled and poured her heart out to God. Wiping her eyes, she rose to sit on the pew and let her mind carry her back to the last time the church was full: It had been at her son's christening. Her mind's eye could still see the smiling faces of those who had been at her wedding and each of her children's dedications. Mrs. Günter and even her husband had been there last month to give her baby his first Bible storybook. The Bürgermeister and his wife had given baby John a silver spoon that matched Marie and Mary's spoons. The pastor's short wife had been perched on pillows to reach the keys of the church organ; the memory of that music touched Mathilda's heart and gave her a moment of peace. The trance faded as Mathilda decided to remember these happy faces and not those she had found tonight within their homes, bloated and barely recognizable.

Moving from the altar area, Mathilda bumped the lectern and knocked the Holy Bible to the floor. She knelt down to pick it up and spied the familiar scripture that lay open, Jeremiah 29:11. John loved this scripture and would read it to the children at bedtime. With a sigh, she picked up the worn Holy Book and carried it to the door of the church. Mathilda then emptied the alms box and filled both of her apron pockets with money intended for widows and orphans, knowing that they were qualified to receive it. Outside, next to the shed by the parsonage, she noticed the pastor's wheelbarrow; she placed the valuable Bible in it and rolled it to the harvest garden plots behind the village, where she and Marie found vegetables ripe for picking. Then she pushed the full wheelbarrow up the knoll, all the way back to their house.

"Mama, I don't want to go into the house."

"Very well, then. Lie down on the grass near the stream. I will come for you when I am finished." Tears rolled down Mathilda's cheeks as she anticipated the difficult task of burying her husband. He was still and waxy. Enormous energy shot through her body in the form of anger.

John, it was not supposed to happen this way. It was enough that Mary and the baby died, but I don't know what to do without you. I don't even know how to get you from here to the grave you dug for yourself. I need you, John. I am not a strong person. I'm not! I can't think what I am supposed to do. What am I supposed to do? You would know. Now you're dead. You are dead, but I can't die. Marie needs me. I don't want to die, and I don't want you to be dead, either. John, I'm too angry and tired to cry anymore, so I'm just going to have to sit here a minute and think what I should do. I guess you already know by now everyone else is dead. I took the money from the church and the vegetables from the gardens. I'm not hungry. Hmm ... Marie should eat something ... We can't stay — the smell is getting strong, and soon there will be wild animals ... I can't think about that right now. She burst into sobbing that shook her entire body. Again her body was drained of energy, so the sobbing ceased to control her. *I guess I lied: I'm not too tired and angry to cry. Oh, John, I love you.* She paused and looked at his corpse. With no affection in her face or voice, she said, "I'm talking to a pile of your clothes. You are not here anymore.

Tilly's Song

Well, of course not, you and the rest of the village are rejoicing in heaven right now ... and, and ... I'm not!" She sighed and then returned to her shoveling.

After the last shovelful of dirt, Mathilda looked down at the three mounds, the graves of her beloved children and husband.

"I will always love you. We had a good life." Tears choked her words. "I wasn't finished yet! I wanted ... more! I wanted you all to live for a long, long time. John, I'm not really angry with you; I am scared without you." The pain in her chest seemed unbearable. "Forgive me for yelling at you before I buried you. It is not my strength, but God's strength that I must have right now. Do You hear me, Lord?" The words roared up from her belly.

The autumn colors of the provincial setting grayed through Mathilda's teary eyes. All the passion of life drained out of her as she used the shovel to caress each mound. Her only thought was that of sleep, deep sleep ... so as to never awaken. Then another thought flashed through her entire being like a bolt of lightning piercing through a dark storm cloud: *Who would care for Marie?* With this thought of her daughter, Mathilda felt her heart beat again within her; even though her chest was heavy and full of pain, it pumped life back into her body and with it, strength to move. She walked from the graves to a place under one of their apple trees. She stood on the fallen leaves and looked up. Two leaves still clung to a tall branch. As she watched, a sudden gust severed them from their branch and carried them up and into the air, taking them quickly beyond her sight.

As in a trance, Mathilda made her way down to the stream. Marie was sleeping under a bright pink sun that cast its hue onto the whiffs of clouds suspended in the azure sky. Mathilda sat down beside her daughter and gazed into the most beautiful sunset she could ever remember. Color had returned to her vision.

Out of her spirit emerged the song, *Nachtlied.* *(Night Song):

Choose Life

Over all the hilltops it is quiet now;
In all the treetops hearest thou hardly a breath.
The birds are asleep in the trees:
Wait; soon like these thou, too, shalt rest.

Peace took over where fear had filled her mind. Worry ceased. She lay there and listened to the song of her youth sing within her spirit, until her eyes grew heavy. Together, Mathilda and Marie slept under the stars as angels watched over them.

***

When Marie awoke near the stream, she looked over at her mother, who was lying beside her with her arms under her head, looking at the sky. Without turning to face her daughter, Mathilda spoke: "Marie, My Love, we are going to be all right. I have asked Jesus to help us. His Spirit comforted me. We must start a new life, one filled with blessings, in America. Now we shall get up and burn the houses in the village. Be quick because the smell is getting stronger, and I have already seen many rats and swarms of flies." Mathilda sat up and pulled Marie into her arms.

"Look at me now." She touched Marie's face with both of her hands and stared directly into her daughter's eyes. "I know you are little, but you must be my good helper. You must be a big girl now. We shall stay in this world a little longer before we join our family and friends in heaven. Don't be afraid, and I will try not to be afraid, also. Do you have any questions?" Mathilda asked, hoping she had none.

Marie wanted to ask her mama when they would die. Looking into her mother's sorrowful eyes, she only shook her head and said, "No." She knew her mother needed her help, and she needed to obey whatever her mother told her to do. Marie had always helped with chores — especially with the younger children. Sometimes her mother and father would scold her because she was not always quick to obey. Now she had only her mother to help and decided not to cry, whine or annoy. She also knew they were not going to die, at least not for a long time, not until they arrived in America and received the blessings Jesus had promised.

The next moments became surreal as mother and daughter went from house to house, lighting fires until the entire village was ablaze. Running from the flames back to their own house, they gathered the necessities that would fit into their cart. They took the vegetables out of the wheelbarrow, cleaned them and placed them into a bag, then tossed them on top of the cart beside as many precious valuables as they could pack. Their house was left unburned; all who had died there had been buried. Mathilda and Marie bathed in vinegar water to remove the stench of decay and smoke, then quickly dressed in their traveling clothes. It was late morning when the two departed for Hamburg, Mathilda pulling the cart behind them.

***

"Mama, I'm so very thirsty. May I have a drink?" Marie broke the silence for the first time since their journey began. Mathilda dipped out some water from the large crock they usually used to make sauerkraut. They both shared the dipper and drank until satisfied. The crock made the water taste a little like vinegar. Marie started to complain, then quickly decided to pretend that it was wine and she was a princess traveling to a beautiful castle. After her thirst was quenched, she skipped ahead of her mother and danced in the road, as if she was already in the grand castle at the fine ball. But moments later, her legs were tired, and her mother let her ride in the cart.

Once Mathilda was far enough away from the village that she could no longer smell smoke, she stopped to rest and stood with her face to the wind and sun. Both strengthened her, as did the acidic water and exercise of walking. She began to feel less numb, and her mind seemed to take in things that her eyes saw, as if recognizing them for the first time. As the sun approached the horizon, Mathilda realized she had not eaten that day. In fact, she could not remember when she had eaten last. Her stomach grumbled. The first words she spoke were, "Marie, I'm hungry!"

"Oh, Mama, I am so hungry! I didn't know if we were going to wait until we got to Hamburg to eat anything," Marie responded with the sound of a pout in her voice.

"Oh, you poor thing, let's see what we can make into a meal, shall we?"

Together, they carefully looked over the food, trying not to rearrange the items they had hastily but mindfully placed into the cart for the ease of moving. They found cheese and cabbage and shared an apple. Both ate hungrily. Although the light had not yet left the sky, there were a few stars visible as the two fell asleep under blankets knitted as wedding keepsakes by Mathilda's mother. In Mathilda's opinion, these precious labors of love were never intended for the bare ground. Always kept for special company, her mother's work of art now served a new purpose. Mathilda and Marie wrapped up in the comfort of their warmth and smell of cedar from the old chest they left behind.

Morning came and went. Neither of them stirred from their sleep until the sun was directly overhead. Mathilda wondered if she would have the strength to move. Every muscle in her body ached. The day before, they had walked all afternoon, almost until dark. They had seen no one on the road, nor had they seen any houses or animals. A fearful thought shot through Mathilda's mind: *What if what happened to her village had happened to other villages, like long ago when the Black Plague spread throughout her country?*

God help us! Mathilda gasped at the thought.

Marie spoke, causing her mother to jump with alarm. "Mama, why isn't Jesus helping us?" At first the words stung her spirit, but to Mathilda's surprise, she heard the words she used to respond, with surprising calm, to her daughter's question.

"My Love, Jesus is helping by making us stronger in our faith. He gave me a promise, and He is always faithful to do what He says He will do. Now we must do our part and believe Him!"

Marie smiled and then rolled over and gave her mother a big hug.

"I believe Him, Mama."

Mathilda got up and looked in the bag of food. She pulled out some beets and peeled them to eat. Marie had never eaten raw beets for breakfast before.

"Mama, I shall pretend this beet is a hot potato pancake with lots of applesauce," she announced, proud of her cleverness. When she looked for approval, Marie caught her mother hastily wiping tears from her eyes. It was then she knew her "pretends" were not to be spoken.

As the two continued their journey, they played a game of seeing how many plants they could name. If Marie did not know the name of a plant, Mathilda would tell her. If Mathilda did not know the name, they made one up. Marie's young legs grew tired all too soon, so she often rested in the cart. Mathilda told her stories, any and all she could remember. Some were Bible stories and some funny tales from her childhood. They stopped for the night near a brook, more hungry and tired than the night before. Both slept soundly in the uncut hayfield away from the road and brook.

***

A cold wet nose sniffed Mathilda's face. Startled, her eyes popped open. The brightness of daybreak blinded her so she had to shield her eyes with her hand to recognize a dog and farmer standing over her. The farmer stared down at Mathilda with a curious look on his face.

"What are you doing in my field?"

Mathilda sat straight up. "Good sir, my daughter and I walked as far as our legs would carry us, and we drank from the brook and found rest in this hay." The farmer reached down and helped her to her feet.

"Where are you going?"

Marie answered before her mother could. "Mama and I are going to America!" He smiled at the child and then looked back at Mathilda who was pulling grass out of her hair.

"Madam, where is your husband?" Mathilda moved to stand by Marie.

"My Love, let me talk with this good gentleman." Marie redirected her attention toward the dog sniffing the ground in search of a rabbit or bird.

Mathilda briefly told the farmer of their plight.

"Come with me; my wife has food prepared. You both are welcome to share." He pointed in the direction of his home. Mathilda and Marie followed him as he pulled their cart to the house. His wife was standing in the doorway, waving to him a warm greeting. She welcomed the mother and daughter with a smile.

"Please, come into our home."

The aroma of freshly baked bread engulfed their senses as they stepped inside.

"Hot water is on the stove if you wish to bathe."

Mathilda bathed and put on fresh clothing while Marie ate several pieces of hot bread with butter and apples. It was now Marie's turn to use the water warmed from the stove for her bath.

Mathilda offered the farmer and his wife some money for their kindness. They refused. "It is an honor and a privilege to help in such a small way," the farmer assured Mathilda after hearing more of her story.

"Good gentleman, I need direction to Hamburg. Ships leave there and go to America. Is that correct?"

"Yes, yes. We know a clergyman and his wife in Hamburg who help people with their travel arrangements to America. They know how you can find help once you arrive in that distant land." He instructed them if they stayed on the main road, not straying to the left or right of it, this very road would lead them straight into Hamburg. While they talked, the farmer's wife gathered food for their journey the next morning. Mathilda and Marie left with bread, jam, cheese, sausage, eggs cooked in their shells, apples and prunes. Marie decided that day that she wanted to be like the farmer's wife when she grew up.

The farmer and his wife asked God to grant them traveling mercies. Then he warned them, "Do not enter the city at night. It is far too dangerous for a woman and child pulling a cart with

23

all their earthly possessions. We have asked God's protection, but you also need to be wise."

***

Mathilda walked much faster after they left the farmhouse. From what the farmer and his wife had told her, it would take them probably three more days before they arrived in Hamburg. In Mathilda's hand was the paper with the name and address of a Lutheran pastor who knew how to get to America.

Mathilda's restored hope was apparent in the spring in her step and the desire to sing. Marie requested songs her mother had taught her, and Mathilda sang as many verses as she could remember. Marie also felt more energetic now that she could sing with her mother. Together, they walked along the bumpy road as Mathilda pulled the cart.

In the past, the family horse pulled this cart to deliver hay to feed the milk cows and to carry milk and cream to customers in the village. Now it held food, blankets, clothing, toiletries and the song book *Myrthen* (Myrtles) by Robert Schumann. This book had been a wedding gift from John. However, her most prized possession was a small tea set of fine china with a cobalt blue background and delicate pink roses illuminated with gold paint. This had also been a wedding present given to her by her grandmother.

Mathilda had said repeatedly to her children: "No one is to touch this, except for me. This was given to me by my grandmother, before she died, as a present when Papa and I got married. No one is to touch it, pour tea from it or wash it, except me. Do you hear me?" Her speech was always given to the children while she wagged her finger at them, followed by the "I mean it" look. The tea set was the most beautiful thing she owned, and it looked expensive. Mathilda had wrapped it so it would not rattle or break during the journey. Whenever Marie got into or out of the cart, she was warned not to sit on the tea set.

Marie was trying to sit carefully in the cart while singing with her mother the first verse of Martin Luther's great hymn,

"A Mighty Fortress Is Our God." During the second chorus, she spied a yellow tabby cat walking out of a field. The cat sniffed the air and turned in the direction of the cart, then quickly began to follow it down the road. Marie stopped singing and began talking to the yellow cat. The tabby took that as an invitation to join her and jumped into the cart, rubbing against Marie, begging to be petted. This affectionate feline allowed Marie to pet her for only a moment and then started nosing around the food bag. The pushy pussycat was after the sausage and communicated this message in loud kitty words. Mathilda stopped the cart.

"That cat is more interested in our sausage than in our friendship," she announced, as much to the hungry cat as to Marie. The clever animal instantly jumped down and began rubbing Mathilda's legs. Mathilda's mood softened toward the kitty. She fed the little beggar a good supper from the food bag, since the farmer and his wife had so kindly shown grace to Mathilda and Marie. That evening, all the sausages were eaten. In the morning, the cat was gone. She had loved them only for their sausage, and since the meat was gone, so was she.

Mathilda and Marie started to see other farm animals in the pastures and to encounter other travelers on the road. Mathilda took this as an encouraging sign that they were getting closer to Hamburg. It was mid-afternoon when she pulled the cart off the road near a stream and changed into their best clothes with their Sunday aprons. Mathilda combed her own hair and braided ribbons into Marie's. They shared an apple and drank cool, fresh water from the stream.

Mathilda found herself humming *Widmung** (Dedication), her favorite from the songbook. She pulled out the book John had given her as a wedding gift and sang courage into her soul as she made ready to enter the city. With solemn resolve, she whispered, "John, this was always my heart's song to you. I sing this as a prayer."

> You are my soul, you my heart, you are my joy,
> oh, you my pain;
> You are my world I live in, my heaven that I soar in,

Tilly's Song

>Oh, you are the grave into which downward
>I for eternity my grief gave!
>You are my rest, you are my peace
>and the heaven granted to me.
>That you love me makes me worthy;
>your gaze has me transfigured.
>You raise me lovingly above myself,
>my good spirit, the better me!

"You are my rest and peace; you are the heaven that has been granted to me," she whispered. After a long moment of reflection, she then kissed the cover of the book and carefully rewrapped it into her clothing bag and tucked it away for safekeeping. Wiping tears from her eyes, she took in a deep breath.

"Marie, you have never been to a big city before, so listen. Be very quiet, look but don't stare and smile sweetly, but do not talk to strangers. If we are separated, run as fast as you can to the church with the tallest steeple and ask the people inside for help." She gave Marie one of her "I mean it" looks. Marie knew by her mama's tone and look that she needed to be especially obedient. She did as she was told.

The smells in Hamburg were different from those on the farm. The aroma of freshly baked bread mingled with other sweet smells that whiffed past Marie's nose. Saliva almost dripped from her mouth as they walked down the street lined with shops. Neither Mathilda nor Marie had ever seen a bakery before now. Through the windows, they saw many delicious baked goods and shoppers lined up for their daily purchase. Next door, a butcher shop emitted heavy smoked and salty aromas that followed them down the street. Mathilda licked her lips and heard her stomach growl.

The narrow street opened up to a market with vendors calling to shoppers to buy their merchandise. There were pots, dishes, cutlery, utensils, clothing, pretty beads, toys, soaps and linens. Mathilda's eye caught the sight of some wonderful tatted lace. Marie strained her neck to see around customers standing in front of a booth displaying beautiful dolls. Marie's senses were overloaded with new food smells that hung in the air;

these quickly gave way to the sounds of horses' hooves against the cobblestone. Children's voices rang out along the grassy area next to the canal where they were playing tag. Somewhere in the distance, music from a violin gaily joined the feast of sights, sounds and smells. Her attention was then directed toward carts overflowing with colorful ripe vegetables and fruits.

"Mama, may we look at all these things?" Marie had a look of delight upon her face.

"Oh, I wish we could, but we must find the church or the pastor before it gets dark," Mathilda answered, looking from left to right to spy as much as she could while still moving. Twice they stopped to ask for directions, and then they found the church. It was almost time for vespers, and the pastor was outside greeting parishioners as they entered the side chapel to pray. Seeing unfamiliar faces, he moved quickly toward Mathilda and Marie while motioning to a young man to help them with the cart. Mathilda looked quizzically at the pastor and thought to herself that he seemed to know they were coming. The young man locked the cart in a stable next to the church. The pastor invited Mathilda and Marie to join him and his congregation.

After the worship service, they shared dinner with the pastor's family at the parsonage. When nightfall came, the family gave them bedding so that they could sleep on the back pew. Upon waking, Mathilda and Marie returned to the parsonage for breakfast. The young man who had helped with the cart was the eldest son. He stood from the table and offered his seat to Marie while his younger brother offered Mathilda his chair. Two young daughters quickly passed bowls with hot milk and toasted sweet bread to their guests. The youngest girl was just two years older than Marie. While Mathilda talked about going to America, the girls invited Marie to play with them and let her hold their dollies. The family had two large watchdogs, which Marie didn't like very much. Mathilda called them to her, and they playfully competed for her affection.

That night, Mathilda and Marie stayed in the children's room in the parsonage while the pastor's children took their turn sleeping on the back pews. Mother and daughter shared a bed, cuddling together, kissing each other's cheeks, scratching each other's back and softly singing hymns. They joined to pray and gave thanks to their Heavenly Father.

"Tomorrow is the Sabbath. You guided us to this safe haven, and now, filled with anticipation and expectation, Marie and I will join others in song and prayer to, Oh Mighty One, You who hold us in the palm of Your hand. Thank You. Amen."

Marie fell asleep while her mother played with her hair.

* *Nachtlied, (Night Song)* Music by Robert Schumann and lyrics by Johann Wolfgang von Goethe. Translation into English was by Henry Wadsworth Longfellow.

* *Widmung, (Dedication)* Music by Robert Schumann and lyrics by Friedrich Ruckert. From Schumann's book *Myrthen* (Myrtles) that he created as a wedding present for his bride, Clara Wieck, on their wedding day, September 11, 1840.

Chapter 2
Letting Go

The beautiful music of Felix Mendelssohn filled the sanctuary as the small congregation found their seats and entered into worship. Mathilda and Marie sat by the window near the back of the sanctuary, trying not to draw attention, since they were strangers to the community. Marie was fascinated by the morning light as it shone through the beveled glass and created small rainbows on the floor, the wall and the lectern. She began to play, moving her fingers to create breaks in the refracted light. Her mother soon took her hands and placed them, ladylike, in her lap. As the music came to its dramatic finale, Pastor Matthias took his place at the lectern. He spoke in a deep baritone that had an almost musical cadence.

"Good people of the Lord," he opened, "I bring to you this morning a woman and her child who are in need of your prayers. They have come a great distance on foot to reach our church and are being sent to America to advance the Kingdom of God.

"Let us pray:

"Almighty Heavenly Father, we thank You for the mercy and kindness You have displayed by bringing this mother and child to our parish, that we may show love to them as You have shown Your great love to us. Our petition this day is that great love will rule and reign in both their lives, casting out all fear. Gracious Lord, You have inspired Mathilda, through Your Holy Spirit, to seek a renewed life in America. Calling upon Your goodness, mercy and grace, we now ask, dear Lord, that You anoint this woman and her child to accomplish all that You desire for them, in Your abundance. You are a covenant-keeping God; for this reason, we ask for added strength for them to obey the guidance You have given them. We trust and claim Your promises, and with the authority given to us by Your precious Son, our Lord and Savior, Jesus Christ, we send forth this mother and daughter to be Your Children of Light to those children still in darkness. We ask on their behalf that when they meet temptation, You will kindly show them the way, so that they will not sin. Bless them, Lord, with health, purchased with Your shed blood, and deliverance from evil all the days of their lives. In all ways, we give You our worship, thanksgiving and praise. Amen.

"Now let us remember our Lord by eating at His table. Take this bread as His body and this wine as His blood, His very life force. Let God's Holy Spirit continue to guide, instruct and comfort you. Go in peace, living righteously and filled with Christ's joy. I beseech our Father that you may dwell in the peace of His presence. To this we join together and say Amen."

When Mathilda and Marie moved forward to receive communion, the pastor laid his hands on their heads, and looking first directly into Mathilda's eyes and then down into Marie's, he said, "We shall continue to pray for you to receive traveling mercies from God's guardian angels. Go now. If we meet again, what a delight! If not, we have assurance that we will meet again in our eternal home in heaven. God blesses you; live your life as a blessing to Him!"

Marie had never taken communion; she was always told she was too young. She had wanted to and had even asked her mother. Today, she looked at her mother and then at the pastor, and they agreed to give her first communion.

In her spirit, Marie heard, *Marie, my beloved, you are my friend. There is a time for everything, and I am with you through it all.*

Marie was so happy, she wanted to sing and dance. She bowed her head in silence, but in her mind, she ran free shouting, jumping, singing and laughing. She knew instantly that she could talk to Jesus, her friend, anytime, and He would talk with her in many ways about many things. For a long time, she shared her secret with no one.

Pastor Matthias and his wife, Beatrice, accompanied Mathilda to help her arrange for passage on a ship sailing from Hamburg, Germany, to Antwerp, Belgium. There they would board a steamer for New York City.

Letting Go

"Mrs. Baumann, do you have documentation of your birth and that of your daughter?" Pastor Matthias asked. The pastor read the panicked look on Mathilda's face. "The authorities will require such information."

"I have the church Bible. In it, the people of our village recorded the names and dates of their births, marriages and deaths. Will this be acceptable?"

"Yes, yes, very acceptable. I will write letters of introduction to some of our Lutheran friends in America. I will send them today. I shall also give you a letter to carry with you — take care to keep it with you at all times."

"Thank you, yes. I will do as you say."

"Do you have any money?"

"Yes, I have money. Do I pay you?"

"No, not me. We will go to the docks, and you can purchase your passage to America from a ticket agent. It is not far from here. Our son Peter will drive us."

"Thank you, thank you."

Pastor Matthias left Mathilda, went to his study and wrote the letters. He posted them that afternoon, as promised. He had done this same kindness for three other families, who had arrived safely in New York. There was a specific church group in America who assisted immigrants from northern Europe to find jobs, as well as housing: the Lutheran Ladies' Aid Society.

At the docks, Mathilda followed the pastor to the ticket agent's office. He stepped aside to invite some sailors to the evening vespers service. Mathilda counted out the money in front of the ticket agent.

"Madam, I am sorry to inform you that this is not enough money for two fares to America. Do you wish to leave the child here in Germany?" the ticket agent asked with a smile, trying to appear helpful with his solution.

Mathilda was stunned by the very thought of leaving her daughter behind, and in a flash of anger, she answered, "No, never! My child will not leave me."

"There are gentlemen willing to take women to America if they will, in turn, perform wifely duties for them while they travel. Would this serve your purpose, madam?"

"Oh, my, no! Is there not any other way for my daughter and me to travel on your ship?"

"You must go to another building to apply for a legal note that promises payment in full, in exchange for servitude."

"Sir, what is this agreement of servitude they wish me to sign?" Mathilda asked the pastor as she fought off disappointment and fear.

"Mathilda, the officials of the shipping company are extending you credit for the full price of the tickets to America. When you sign their agreement, they expect payment within a certain time or you and your daughter will be deported from America back to Hamburg. Do not worry, you will become employed and soon be able to be free of this debt."

As she waited for the official to give her the papers to sign, Mathilda lowered her head and prayed silently. *Heavenly Father, I love You, and I praise You, for You are my fortress, my ever-present shelter from the storm. Please hear my prayer. Except for Marie, all I have known in life is gone, and still I bless Your holy name. You know my every need, so I trust You, God, for a trip to America. Lord, I have a question — how shall we get there? I trusted that the money from the alms box would be enough, yet the people who provide passage on the ship tell me I do not have enough money. Help me, Father! Help me, please! Help my unbelief! Through Your Spirit, reveal to me what I am to do. I want to live in Your presence. You promised never to leave me nor forsake me! Oh, God, I feel so alone. I am not smart in the workings of such worldly affairs. Father God, Marie and I are Your daughters; remember us now, please, oh please, oh please ....*

There was nothing else to do now but wait. Unknown to Mathilda, an economic depression was affecting many countries in Europe at this time. Families throughout her homeland were leaving for America, lured by the promises of employment and freedoms not enjoyed in their part of the world. While the pastor left her to post the letters, another man working in the ticket office made advances toward her.

"You look like you need some help," he slyly commented. "I see you have no husband. I can help you. If you give me the money, I will book your passage for half the fare and provide you with better quarters. This, of course, requires some ... 'special favors'... from you. You are a beautiful woman, and you do look so lonely. You will not be lonely with me by your side to protect you."

"Sir," she returned, "I honor my deceased husband's memory too much to entertain such thoughts!"

"Very well, then." He shrugged his shoulders. "If you refuse my kindness, I must inform you that you will have to wait 10 days longer for the required documents to book your passage to America." He looked her straight in the eyes, and his smile faded.

Mathilda turned away from the agent and rushed to the pastor, who was walking toward her. She quickly stepped into the buggy. As they drove away from the pier, she looked back to see the two ticket agents watching her depart.

While they waited for the documents to be processed, Mathilda and the pastor's wife, Beatrice, shared household chores and took food and clothing to poor families in Hamburg. Most of them were widows and orphaned youths. They distributed food daily to those in need, and any food remaining fed the pastor and his family.

Mathilda sold the family silverware, some handmade linen and most of their clothing in order to raise more money for their journey, cleverly sewing her traveling money into a pouch near the waist of her skirt.

Two days before they were expected, the documents arrived, and the pastor surprised Mathilda by handing them to her. Everyone marveled how good God was and how perfect His timing. Mathilda and Marie could now depart on the next day's ship for Belgium. They would arrive just in time to make the passage from Belgium to America.

"I rejoice! We are going to America. I thank you. Marie and I give you all our gratitude for your most wonderful help. Please, let me help you in my very small way. Beatrice and the children need something to haul much-needed supplies to the parishioners. Take the cart. It is a good cart. My friend Beatrice, I also give to you these treasured hair combs, as a special thank-you." Mathilda watched Beatrice's eyes light up as she put the two beautiful combs in Beatrice's red wavy hair. A lump formed in Mathilda's throat as she remembered when John had removed these combs from her hair right before her long blond tresses caressed the pillow of their wedding bed. These combs had been his gift to his bride.

I am not yet ready to part with my wedding ring, she thought. She touched it to reassure herself of its presence. *My hope is that I will never become so impoverished that I will have to sell it.* Her proud thoughts pushed back the fear that, in the future, this last possession might also be required of her.

The remainder of the day culminated with a whirlwind of emotion, as last-minute preparations, made in haste, filled their final day in Hamburg.

"Marie, my little love, it's Mama!" Mathilda called as she entered the bedroom looking for her daughter. She and the Matthias girls were playing on the floor on the other side of the bed, out of sight. "My Love," she called again. Marie always knew her mother was happy when she called her by that endearing name. "I have wonderful news. We leave on a ship tomorrow from this port to sail to Belgium." The excitement was building in Mathilda's voice, and her eyes were dancing with hope. Her excitement was contagious: All three girls began jumping up and down, giggling and clapping their hands. "We have reservations on the Westernline Steamer in Antwerp, Belgium, but we must be there on October 12th so the ship can sail to New York and arrive by October 23rd. Oh, it is really happening! The good pastor is taking me to the port with our completed documents so I may pick up our tickets. Hmm, now let me think. I shall need to make a list of everything we must do before we leave for the ship. There is so much to think about. 'Oh, please, Holy Spirit, will You remind me of all I must do?'"

Marie did not hear her mother leave with the pastor. She was still jumping, dancing and twirling, caught up in merriment with the anticipation of the adventure.

Mathilda had been so brave through all the paperwork procedures. Upon returning to the pastor's home with her handful of documents, she dissolved into tears. She went back into the bedroom and sat down on the floor, rocking back and forth. Marie was still happily playing with the other girls when she heard her mother's sobs. She didn't know why her mother was crying and didn't know what to do, so she sat down next to her. One of the pastor's daughters handed Marie a dolly, and with sad faces, the girls left their room. Marie listened to the crying until she could no longer stay awake. Sometime in the evening, Mathilda moved her to a bed; Marie awoke the next morning looking at her mama, wondering about her weeping. It worried Marie that even as she slept, her mother's eyes were red and swollen from the day before.

She probably misses Papa and Mary and baby John, just as I do. God put America into Mama's heart, but we don't know anyone in America, Marie thought. "Jesus, I just know it will be better, I just know it!" Marie whispered to her friend. She remembered the farmer and his wife and the pastor and his family. She had not known them, but she did now. Her spirit soared. "We will meet more people to love, I just know it," she spoke in a louder whisper. Marie looked over at her mother's face. Her swollen eyes were open, and a sweet smile was upon her lips. She pulled her daughter to her for a big hug.

"I love you so much, my brave girl. I shall try to be brave as well. However, if from time to time I weep, remember you and I are sad because of our great loss — but not today — for this is a new day, and I shall wash the tears from my eyes, because you and I are going to America!"

That morning, Marie left the pastor's house wearing one of his daughter's hand-me-down coats. It looked new. Beatrice had knitted a hat and a matching scarf for her daughter to wear with this coat. They were now Marie's, to keep her warm on the ship. The gloves, almost too small for her growing fingers, Marie had brought from home.

Beatrice handed Marie two white bags filled with ginger cookies, which she instructed Marie to save and eat while on rough water. Mathilda's gift was a box of tea to go with the cookies.

Long steep stairs awaited the restless line of people boarding the ship. Once on board, both mother and daughter stood by the railing and waved goodbye to the people on the pier. A swift breeze blew salt into the air and stung Marie's eyes and cheeks. Seagulls were searching for any morsel available to eat. Loud noises made it hard to hear even their own voices as they shouted goodbye to the strangers below. Sailors on board stared at Mathilda, ignoring Marie. Marie noticed and did not like it. Her mother didn't seem to notice their looks; her mind seemed to be somewhere else as her eyes looked out past the crowds.

Mathilda did not cry that day, nor did she smile.

As Mathilda and Marie stepped off the ship in Antwerp, Belgium, a large crowd engulfed them and pushed them in different directions. Disoriented, they searched for the ship named Westernline, sailing under the British flag of the Red Star Line.

Marie called on her friend, Jesus, in her heart. *I can't see anything except people. They bump into me with the bundles they are carrying. The body odors and babies' dirty-diaper smells are so thick in the air, I can hardly swallow. I can't breathe, Jesus! We don't seem to be moving. I'm trapped. Mama is holding my hand so tightly that my arm is tingling. I'm thirsty. My head has a drum beating in it. My tongue is stuck to the roof of my mouth. I hate being little! I hate this place! Everyone is talking, but I don't know what they are saying. Oh, ouch, someone just stepped on my foot! And they didn't even say they were sorry. Mama always makes me say I'm sorry if I do that. Mama won't do anything to make them stop. All she does is hold my hand tighter, look straight ahead and tell me to stop fidgeting. I'm trying to be good, but I can't! I want to go home to Papa and play with Mary and baby John. I want to sit on Papa's lap and hear him laugh and sing and look at Mama and see her cheeks turn red. I don't want to go to America with these stinky strangers!* The more she prayed, the more she cried. *Mama is not being nice to me. Jesus, where are You? I need You now!*

Marie heard fluttering sounds of birds overhead. It caused her to look up. A whole flock of pretty little birds was flying in a pattern. As they turned, she could see their light bellies; when they turned again, they showed their dark feathery backs. Again and again the pattern changed. It was as if they moved as one.

"How do they know to do that, move all together?" she wondered aloud.

Marie was startled as her mother pulled her hand. The whole crowd began to move as a loud voice spoke instructions to the crowd in several languages. Marie understood her language when the man said everyone needed to get his or her documents ready. Her mother finally let go of her hand, and in that moment of freedom from the grip, Marie was able to relax.

"Thank You, Jesus. Thank you, birds. I feel better now. I'm still thirsty, though." Marie looked forward. Looming ahead of the crowd stood another tall ship with another long line, another set of steep stairs and another long wait before she could get a drink of water.

Chapter 3
A Trip Over Troubled Water

They were no longer in Germany; no longer did everyone speak German. Everything was confusion as Mathilda and Marie were pushed along with the crowd. People were yelling at Mathilda in words she could not understand. What she did understand was their demanding tone to hurry. The more she tried to hurry, the more her legs felt like lead, weighted down with the heavy load. She had to transport everything except a small bag she gave to Marie to carry. The crowd was hot, tired and eager to get on board. Mathilda could not physically carry Marie, so she did her best to pull or drag her up the gangplank steps.

They chose not to wave goodbye to everyone on the pier. Mathilda showed the papers to a man in uniform who spoke in German. Without looking at her, he pointed in the direction of their room, down many stairs into the belly of the ship.

"I feel like Jonah in the belly of the whale!" Mathilda said lightly, trying to be funny. Marie did not laugh. That was exactly what it felt like, only everything was cold metal; no life to the ship at all. When they found the number on the door, they opened it, only to find it was just a room full of beds. To save money, they had to share a bed. No sooner had their bags been stowed under it than they felt the ship move and heard the horn blow.

"Mama, I'm still thirsty."

"I am, too, My Love," Mathilda answered without looking at her. Sitting on the bed, she began to pray. On the other side of the room were a woman and her three little girls. All Marie noticed was their faces staring at her. Though she smiled sweetly back at them, they did not return the smile; their big, hollow eyes just stared back at her. Marie looked up at her mother's face to find encouragement, but Mathilda was crying again.

A Trip Over Troubled Water

Mathilda did not open her eyes after crying and praying. Nausea filled her head and her throat, created by the rocking motion of the ship. This sick feeling generated a flashback ...

Mathilda saw herself standing at the head of a small hole — the grave for her baby John. Every emotion was relived: holding her perfectly shaped lifeless baby in her arms, rocking and singing a farewell lullaby, then finally kissing his cold forehead. Covering his face with the same baby blanket she had used with her daughters, she laid him in the ground. Looking at her husband for comfort, she found none; he was too sick, too weak. After standing for the longest time, she reluctantly took the shovel from John's hand and began to gently place the dirt over her little boy.

The ship's horn sounded, and her mind returned to the present. When she opened her eyes and looked around, she saw Marie and then noticed, for the first time, the other people in the room.

"Mama, I found some water for us to drink. I drank, and I'll get you some." Marie jumped to her feet and returned to her mother's side with a dipper full of cool, fresh water. There was a water bucket and dipper in each room for all to share. Mathilda drank three dippers full until she was satisfied, and then she crushed a ginger cookie and ate some of the crumbs. She offered some cookies to Marie, but she shook her head no. Mathilda quickly ate a few more crumbs, washing them down with two gulps of icy water.

The ship had hardly cleared port when Mathilda began feeling dizzy and nauseated again. Several chamber pots were placed in each room with instructions to the passengers to empty them daily. Mathilda discovered that she should have brought many more bags of the cookies to relieve her seasickness, but she rationed them, only munching on hardtack, butter, a little cheese and tea.

Marie had been exploring the ship and had discovered the dining area. There she found a nice lady that would make tea for her, free of charge. Marie took some of it back to their room for her mother to sip while she rested.

The first night, as they entered into the North Sea, a severe storm met them, as predicted. October and November were the stormiest months at sea — everyone on board learned firsthand what that meant. The ship rocked from side to side, making all the lights in the lamps go out. The force of the wind created giant roaring waves. All sat in the dark, hearing only the sound of retching, totally consumed with sickness, smelling the sour air. Marie was the only one in her quarters who did not get seasick and was actually a good nurse to her mother throughout the storm. By pretending she was on a swing, going high into the trees, making her toes touch the leaves on the highest branches, Marie was able to deal with the rough movement of the ship. She couldn't see anyone with her, and yet she knew she was not alone as she fell asleep.

When she awoke, the light was back on, and the ocean was calm. The covers of the bed were damp, and there was water on the floor. Everyone was still asleep, so she left the room, tiptoeing through the water to find the stairway leading to the upper deck. Each step she climbed, the air became fresher. It smelled rather salty but good. Licking her lips, she thought how the briny flavor tasted strong and pleasant. Others were walking about, stretching their legs and recovering from the rocky ride of the stormy night. Three times she returned to check on her mother.

The woman with the three daughters was going to have another baby. She had worn big clothes so no one would notice. At her last check-in, Marie found the woman in bed, groaning. Hastily, Marie got a dipper full of water and offered it to her. She refused.

"Do you want some tea? Mama will share some of her tea and cookies with you if you are sick."

"No, nothing!" she barked, grimacing in pain and gritting her teeth. The little girls sat frozen next to her.

Marie broke the silence. "Where is your papa?"

The oldest one answered, "He is in another room with our brothers."

Mathilda opened her eyes to see what was happening. As weak and sick as she was, when she saw the situation, she immediately took charge.

A Trip Over Troubled Water

"Marie," she directed, "we need several blankets, a teapot with hot water only, one of your hair ribbons and my scissors."

"Mama, I can't get all those things!"

"Oh, very well, then; go get some buckets." Looking at the eldest daughter of the woman in labor, Mathilda asked, "Do you know where your father is?"

"Yes, madam. He is in room # 20."

"Then go fetch him and tell him the baby has decided to be born today." Mathilda then looked at the middle daughter. "Do you know where the dining area is?"

"Yes, I do, madam." She looked as if she was about to cry.

"Then go ask that nice lady to give you a pot of hot water. Tell her your mother needs it; she'll understand when you tell her a baby is coming."

Mathilda asked the littlest girl, "Do you know how to pray?"

Her big blue eyes answered *Yes*.

"Then pray that God will send angels to help your mama and the new baby. Will you do that, please?"

Again, her big eyes agreed to the request. There in the bed, with her mama in labor, she folded her hands and prayed exactly what Mathilda had asked her to pray.

When Marie made it back with the buckets, she saw her mother putting her mouth over the baby's nose and mouth, then spitting the mucus into the chamber pot. The tea water had cooled enough to wash the baby and clean up the mother. A screaming, tiny, well-formed baby boy was put to his mother's breast while Mathilda cleaned up.

The door burst open at the sound of the baby crying. The father of the newborn had rushed in to see his son. Since men were not allowed in the women's quarters, he quickly closed the door so no one would see him in the room. He covered his wife with kisses and then looked over his new son carefully. Bowing to Mathilda, he thanked God for her. Mathilda's cheeks flushed; she told him to give all the glory to God. She then asked what name his son would be given. He said "Johann" — John.

Marie gasped, "Baby John!"

"What a fine name," Mathilda said, biting her lip. She took the baby and swaddled him in a special blanket his mother had brought along for him, knowing he would soon be born. Mathilda rocked him and sang to him as he slept. While she held him, she saw his little mouth move. "Look, he is talking to the angels!" She made sure the littlest girl saw this, so she would be assured God had heard her prayers.

Mathilda's milk had not dried up from nursing her own baby John. In the presence of this infant, her milk began to flow, and she felt it soak her blouse. She reluctantly placed the baby back into his mother's arms.

"How old was your baby?" the new mother asked Mathilda.

"He would have been 1 year, last week."

The lady did not ask any more questions, and Mathilda went back to her bed, physically and emotionally exhausted.

Marie stood watching, feeling very small. She held the door open as the new papa removed the full buckets from the room. He returned with a clean chamber pot. Smiling at his girls, he hugged each one, then kissed his wife. He looked at his newborn son with pride, smiled again at his wife and left the room so all the women could rest. The girls invited Marie to see their perfect little baby brother. Marie didn't remember ever seeing such a small baby. She exchanged smiles with the little girls. The oldest girl tiptoed to Mathilda's bed and whispered, "Madam, are you asleep?" Mathilda rolled over to face her.

"No, no, my dear, not at all; I am just resting."

"Madam, I believe God sent you to be an angel to help my mama. Thank you."

"I am no angel. God's Spirit guided my every move. I am so very thankful to be of help; however, it is God who should receive the praise. My hope and prayer is that this little Johann will live a long and healthy life and prosper in his new home in America. Now, my sweet child, this has been a very busy and happy day. I will close my eyes to sleep, and you and your sisters need to do the same. We all need to sleep while the baby sleeps."

"Yes, madam, I hope I can sleep. You sleep well, also, kind lady."

Mathilda rolled back on her other side to avoid looking at the happy scene. Her heart ached. Red-hot jealousy rose from

A Trip Over Troubled Water

deep within her being, and she tasted bile. Bitterness, aggravated by the sour smell of her blouse, gripped her. Mathilda sat up on her bed and looked at Marie. "You have explored the ship! Is there anywhere I can bathe and change my clothing?"

"Yes, Mama, there is a place to wash everything, even clothes, and lines to hang them to dry, but no tubs to bathe. Do you want me to show you?"

"I'm not sure I have the balance to walk on the ship yet." She clenched her teeth; it took every ounce of control to act civil. Her whole body seemed to be aflame. She felt trapped in the tiny room, yet more than anything, she had to get away from the mother and new baby. Mathilda was surprised how quickly she was able to gather her soap, towel and clean clothes, even though she was exhausted. Marie led the way. The washroom was around the corner, very close to their room.

"Marie, will you go back to the room now? I need a little time alone right now to clean up. I fear my odor will overcome all of us in the room." She tried to say it lightly, with good humor, but failed. Marie hesitated. Mathilda shot her a look that said, "NOW!" Marie obediently returned to the room.

Mathilda was glad no one else was in the washroom, and she ducked under lines of laundry while she made her way to its farthest corner. Removing her sticky blouse and camisole, she saw that her engorged breasts were red. Both were throbbing with pain. She poured some cool water into a washbasin, then removed her other garments. Her arms were weak; she had noticeably lost weight. Washing her body seemed to comfort her only for a moment. Emotions flared again into bitter jealousy, and in anger and self-pity, she cried out.

"Lord, You know I am Your servant. Don't You know I love You?" Hot tears began to run down her face. "I want to be happy for this family who is struggling right now, just as we are, but honestly, don't You think that was cruel to have me deliver that baby, whom they named John? And …" Her voice broke and she sobbed until she was sick to her stomach. No longer could she push down the bitterness; it erupted out of her mouth onto the floor. She sank down onto the floor again, wet in her own milk and vomit.

43

"Heavenly Father, I need Your help in the worst way. I feel so scared, so lost and so miserable and so, so … I don't even know what. I don't need to know why You do all You do, because I truly know all of this suffering will produce something good in my life. Oh, but the despair I feel this moment is more than I can bear. I miss my husband. God, do You hear me? He would know what to do; he always took such good, wonderful care of me. He loved me. He would touch my body and hold me through the night, and in the morning, he would make love with me, but … but … he is gone. I know You love me, but I can't feel Your arms wrapped around me the way I could his. Oh, Lord Jesus, please be my husband. Will You let me be Your bride? If I am to live celibate, help me with my need and take that bitter jealousy from me, please. Please!"

When her hysteria subsided, she slowly rose to her feet and washed her body again. She rinsed out the bowl and filled it again to wash her hair. It was then she realized she had forgotten her comb, so she just let her hair fall down her back to dry. She carefully removed the stitching in her skirt and retrieved the money, which she slipped into the top of her stockings. It felt more secure to know where it was, even though there was very little money left. Her mind wanted to worry about it, but she just didn't have the energy to spend on worry right now. Hurriedly she dressed and, using her soap, washed her dirty clothes and hung them to dry in a spot away from the other clothing. Mathilda stood motionless for what seemed a long time. Not ready to go back to her room yet, she walked down the hall, following the sweet smell of something baking. No one was in the dining area, so she helped herself to some hot water. The tea box was back in the room with her comb. She sat down and began to sip the hot water, unaware she was being watched, when out of nowhere a lady appeared with a tea ball and dipped it into her cup.

"You must be Mrs. Baumann," the woman greeted her.

"Yes, I am. How did you know my name?" Mathilda looked surprised.

"Oh, I'm the one who gets hot water for your daughter, and I noticed the resemblance. You have had quite a busy day delivering a baby, washing and having tea!" she said, smiling. "Goodness! Let me introduce myself. I'm Margaret Pelto; I just go by Marge. Since I seem to know a little bit about you already, let me share a little about me. Do you mind if I join you? You see, I'm just so lonesome, it appears I have lost all my manners." Marge suddenly looked shy. "I just took some crumb cake out of the oven; would you share some with me?'

"Yes, yes, please join me. The crumb cake smells delicious, but I am starving for conversation."

Marge and Mathilda sat there talking like long lost friends, drinking tea and eating half the pan of crumb cake. They had much in common. Marge told her she was from the Bavarian region of Germany and had lost her husband during the War of Unification serving in the Iron Chancellor Bismarck's Army. Her husband had left for the Army soon after their wedding day, and she had not conceived a child, which grieved her almost as much as his death. Both of her parents were dead, and the rest of her family lived in America. She explained to Mathilda that she was working in the galley to help pay for her passage. The plan was to meet her family in New York City and begin a new life. Mathilda noticed that Marge still wore her wedding ring. When Marge saw her looking at the gold band, she touched it with her finger. "I keep it on so the sailors won't bother me. But to some, it doesn't matter." She laughed nervously.

Marge made it her business to know what was going on in the lower deck and was eager to share without sounding gossipy. Excusing herself for a moment, she returned with some clean cloth to bind Mathilda's breasts; this would help her dry up more quickly. Mathilda pushed herself up from the table, suddenly feeling weak. Taking the bundle of cloth, she thanked Marge and said good night. Mathilda walked slowly down the hallway and then turned around to look at Marge.

Marge walked to meet her, not wanting the visit to end. "I feel like you are my dear friend, Mathilda. Sometimes I think God gives us people to be His arms so He can hold us. Come here and let me hug you!" They embraced for only a second. Mathilda turned to go, then turned back and hugged Marge again. This was another assurance that God was still on the throne, as He had also been with her on the washroom floor. She said good night again to her newfound friend and closed her eyes for a moment to whisper a prayer of thanksgiving for God sending her perhaps a real angel.

Tiptoeing quietly into the room, she moved Marie over so she could crawl into bed. Marie pretended to be asleep. Relieved that her mother had returned, she decided to talk quietly with Jesus. She knew He would be waiting to speak with her. "I thought Mama would be sad after all of this that happened today, but just the opposite happened. She seems full of hope again. Life must go on, isn't that right? I remember Grandmother would say that to Mother whenever she was sad. It is true, Jesus. Thank You for all Your help today. I'm sleepy now. I'll talk with You tomorrow. Good night, my dear friend."

***

The next day, Mathilda let the girls go up to the top deck under the supervision of the oldest girl, who was only a few years older than Marie. All were given strict orders to stick together, to walk around, to get some sunshine and fresh air and then return to their quarters. This break, in the early hours of the morning, would give Mathilda time to help the mother and infant and not have all the children underfoot in the crowded space.

The sun was hot and bright, so Marie took off her little coat and sat down on a pile of ropes in a shaded area. One of the little girls came running up to her and showed her a peppermint stick that a man playing a harmonica had given to her. Marie remembered having peppermint candy only at Christmas time, but she wanted some of that candy, too. Leaving her coat, she walked over to the man who was giving candy out to several children around him. He saw Marie and followed her with his eyes as she drew closer to hear him play funny little tunes and to receive her share of the sweets. He reached out his hand and motioned for her to come closer, so she did. In very poor German, he offered her a stick of candy, and when she reached for

A Trip Over Troubled Water

it, he pulled her onto his lap. He had ugly teeth and his mouth smelled like Mr. Günter's when he drank too much beer. She jumped to her feet, but he held onto her hand. In a soft whisper, he said, "You are the prettiest girl I've ever seen, as pretty as the sirens that lure sailors. If you come and sit on my lap, I will tell you a wonderful story and give you some more candy. Come now, be a good girl and sit here on my lap."

He held her body closely to his, kissing her cheek, while he placed his hand on her leg and eagerly rubbed it where her stockings ended. His face and hands were rough and scratchy. When she tried to stand up, he pulled her with such force that he hurt her arm. Her heart was beating so hard and fast, it felt like it was in her throat. She tried to scream, but no sound came out. He spoke a few words to her that she could not understand. He sounded angry, and this frightened her. Then he changed his tone and began speaking in German again, telling her she was lovely and soft and how much he liked her. She froze stiff with fear. Every bit of light was enveloped by the darkness that overcame her as he touched her body.

"Hey, what's going on here?" A man appeared and yelled at him. The sailor let go of her arm. Now that she was loose, she ran and ran to get to the safety of her mother. Like a scared kitten chased by a pack of hounds, she flew to the door that led down to the stairs, the door with the blue number on it. She had been running so hard she could hardly catch her breath, so she stopped at the door and waited until she calmed down. From above, she now heard men yelling and then a thud. Her face was hot, and her hands were sticky from the candy. *Where are the other girls?* she finally thought. *Oh no, where is my new coat?* She knew she would be punished, but she didn't care; she needed to get back to her mama. *Mama had gotten better,* she thought, *but what would happen if she got sick again? Would she leave, too, and go be with Papa in heaven?* She was scared of the thought of being alone and needed to return to the protection of her mother.

"I want my mama!" she heard her voice scream as she continued to run down the stairs to the lower deck. When she opened the door, everyone stared at her. She looked at her mother, who was nursing the baby.

"Mama, what are you doing?"

"Gretchen asked me to try to nurse little Johann, since she is too weak." Her mother had a look of satisfaction on her face. That was not the look on the faces of the little girls, who stood motionless, staring back at Marie. She looked at the oldest girl, who looked away from Marie. Marie looked in the direction the girl was looking and saw her new coat.

That night, when everyone else was sleeping, she came to Marie and whispered, "Shh ... I asked that big man to help you. I told him that sailor had given us candy and was being mean to you."

"Thank you," Marie whispered back.

"Did he hurt you?"

"A little, but I didn't cry."

"You are brave, but we must not do that again. Papa warned us that not everyone will be nice on this ship. Go to sleep and thank God for sending His angels to keep us from harm." The oldest girl then found her way back to her own bed through the darkness.

The baby was crying, but Marie managed to fall asleep anyway. She dreamed that she was in her home in Germany, licking a peppermint candy from the gingerbread house her aunt had made for Christmas day. It seemed odd to Marie to see there were little milk cows outside the gingerbread house. The cows grew bigger and bigger, and they had huge human lips that tried to kiss her. When she saw their lips and smelled their foul breath, she jumped awake.

"Jesus," she prayed, "thank You for sending that big man to help me get away from that mean sailor. It was bad to disobey my mama. I'm sorry." She fell back to sleep, this time with no strange dreams.

The sea was rough again, and Mathilda was seasick. No one in the quarters felt good, except for Marie. She was wide-awake and hungry for breakfast.

"Mama, may I get some food? Would you like some tea and toast?" When she mentioned food, everyone groaned. Mathilda didn't even open her eyes but nodded her head yes. Marie

A Trip Over Troubled Water

quietly opened the door and bounced from one wall to the next as she navigated down the corridor to the galley. Marge greeted her.

"Hello, little miss."

"Good morning. I'm the only one who feels like eating this morning."

Marge asked a woman who was helping in the galley if she would please carry a tray of tea and toast to Marie's room, while she made Marie a bowl of porridge. Marge talked to Marie as she ate her breakfast.

"You are such a good girl to wait on all those seasick folks; I have added some steamed milk and cinnamon sugar to your porridge." She looked at Marie for a response and was rewarded with a big smile. "Marie, yesterday I had a lovely visit with your mother. She and I ate half the crumb cake I baked for the crew." Marge laughed at her own confession. "Your mother said you will be traveling on to Chicago after we arrive at New York City. I'll be getting off the ship in New York City to join my family … what's left of it. My brother already has a husband lined up for me, but I'm not going to agree to marry this stranger, sight unseen."

Marie listened, not really sure what Marge was talking about, marrying a person sight unseen; all she knew was that Mamas and Papas got married and had children. She knew about sisters, brothers, aunts, uncles and grandparents; other than that, she knew nothing.

Seeing that Marie was not interested in what she had to say, Marge turned her attention toward Marie and away from herself.

"Marie, where were you born?"

"I don't know the name of the place, except we just called it home. It is a long way from Hamburg, because Mama and I walked there to find a ship to sail to Belgium, so we could get on this ship." Marie spooned the last bite of porridge into her mouth.

"Do you want more?" Marge asked, looking at the empty bowl.

"Oh, thank you, no, my tummy is full." She patted her

49

stomach to show Marge. "What do you put into porridge to make it taste so good?" She wiped her mouth with the back of her hand and then finished her milk.

"You must mean the cinnamon. I find it to be a lovely treat to make the sugar go farther. In Belgium, people bring spices from the East Indies and from South America, chocolate and coffee. Belgium is known worldwide for its very exotic chocolates. Have you ever tasted something called 'hot cocoa'?" she inquired, with her eyebrows lifted and an inquisitive smile on her lips.

"I don't know; I'll have to ask my mama. Sometimes for Christmas we get lovely sweets wrapped up in pretty paper. Mama doesn't let me eat many because she says they are just for grown people." Marie was trying hard to remember the celebrations and the sweet treats eaten at such occasions.

"Hmm, just for grown people, you say? How very interesting. I shall have to remember that when I have children." Then Marge laughed out loud.

When Marie finished her milk, she thanked Marge for a good breakfast. "Do you have any of that hot cocoa I could try sometime?"

"Yes, I do, but tell your mother to get well and all of us can have some."

The door opened when Marie neared her room. The girls were going to wash up after a night of seasickness.

"Mama, that nice woman you talked to last night, Mrs. Pelto, is going to America. She is getting a husband as a present from her brother. She told me all about it as I ate my porridge this morning. She put cimmum — I don't know how to say it, but that brown powder — in it, to make it taste really good. She also told me to tell you to get well, and all of us will drink hot cocoa together. Can we do that, Mama?"

"Bless her." Mathilda closed her eyes, then slid down onto her pillow and removed the washcloth. She handed it to Marie so she could wet it, and then she put it back on her forehead.

"Thank you, My Love. Sometimes it is the simplest things, like a cool washcloth, that make a person feel so fine, just as cocoa makes things seem better than they really are. Yes, I will

A Trip Over Troubled Water

do my very best to get control of my stomach and head, and then we can have some delicious cocoa." Her quick smile faded; then she closed her eyes again, covering them with the cloth.

"Mama, you always have a way of making me happy with your kind words. I love you, Mama!" Marie reached over and kissed her on the cheek.

Her mama went back to sleep, and Marie daydreamed to pass the time. In her mind, she began talking to herself, as if hearing the words would somehow make it more realistic.

I can see Mary and baby John and the flowers in our window boxes. Mama is baking bread, and I am rolling yarn into a ball for her. The laundry is hung outside, blowing in the breeze. Mary and I are running and covering ourselves with the sheets that are still hung on the line. Every morning we eat our first meal together, then Mama feeds the chickens and Papa milks the cows. The eggs, cream, butter and some of the milk are all taken to the market and sold. Papa works outside growing grain and hay. Mama grows the vegetables, fruit and flowers. Papa tends to the bees, and Mama says she feeds them with her fruit and flowers. "We live in the land of milk and honey, just like in the Bible," Papa says. We are happy. I am happy. I was happy. Marie's daydream began to fade, and the pain of reality changed her happy thoughts into sadness. She struggled to maintain her monologue. *On Sundays, we go to church and have someone come over for dinner; then we promenade into the countryside. Mary and I play, and sometimes Mama lets me push the baby carriage. Baby John loves it. I think I can hear the sound of the stream running near our house.*

Boom! Boom! Boom! The loud knocking startled Marie back into present reality. Mrs. Fischer opened the door. Marie didn't even know her name until now, when the man standing in the door wearing a ship's uniform called her by name. He introduced himself as Mr. Schmitt and spoke in German that sounded different from what everyone in the room spoke. He announced that all the children were to gather in the dining area where, as a group, he would teach them English. Even though he made the German words sound odd, she could still understand what he wanted the children to do. Marie thought

51

to herself, *In America, doesn't anybody speak German the way we speak German?*

Children between the ages of 4 and 10 were to follow him to the dining area. Their mothers helped them put on their shoes and brush their hair before they started this new adventure. These children were first to learn the new language, practice speaking it and then instruct their parents.

The smallest children sat in the front of the room on the floor, and the larger children sat or stood behind them. Mr. Schmitt now stood in front of the children and showed them large pictures.

First was a simple drawing of a child smiling. He spoke the words, "Good morning" — in German, "Guten morgen." Now he instructed them to repeat after him, "Good morning," and then turn to another person and smile. They were then to say, "Good morning."

The next picture was of two people shaking hands and smiling — the word was "Hello." The word wasser was "water," danke schön was "thank you" and bitte shörn was "you're welcome." The children had name tags pinned to their clothing, and Mr. Schmitt introduced each child to the group. When the lessons were over, Blanche, the oldest Fischer girl, who shared their room, took a cup and handed it to Marie. "Vatter?" she giggled.

"Tank zoo, Blanche," Marie giggled. The girls hurried back to their room to share the new knowledge with their mothers. Blanche and Marie entered through the door together and said, "Gut moornin!"

The next lesson included the words bread, butter, tea, meat, salt and pepper. Many English words sounded similar to the German words. Blanche learned very quickly and helped the rest of the girls remember the words by using them over and over in sentences she would make up. Marie was excited because this activity made the time pass quickly. She learned to count to 10. She also learned that, in America, the money was called dollars rather than marks. Actually, she didn't even know what money was called in Germany. Her papa had taught her to count, and her mother had taught her the colors, but she

A Trip Over Troubled Water

couldn't read or write, except for her name, which she proudly displayed on the cloth pinned to her dress. She also learned her mother's name, Mathilda Martha Baumann, which her mother displayed on her own blouse.

During their final English class, they were all told that when they arrived in New York City harbor, everyone on the ship would see a statue of a lady holding a book in one hand and an uplifted torch in the other. This lady statue was placed in the middle of the harbor to welcome them to their new home.

Mr. Schmitt told them they would no longer be Germans, but now would be Americans who would speak English and enjoy freedom from tyranny. None of the children knew what that meant; however, it was supposed to be a good thing. *Why were they no longer Germans?* Marie wondered. Whenever he said Germans, he said it as if it was a bad thing. She knew her mother would be very happy to be an American. She guessed perhaps she was happy, too. It was important to be happy.

The final day arrived when the ship entered the waters of the United States of America. A uniformed officer came through the halls instructing the passengers to collect all their gear and to come topside.

"Mama, will you come upstairs with me to see the statue?"

"What statue?"

"The lady statue Mr. Schmitt told us about in our class."

Mathilda felt better today; the sea was calm, so she agreed to go up top with her daughter to see the lady statue. They put on their shoes and coats and took their bags with them. Mathilda put what little money she had left in a handkerchief, tied it with string and concealed it under her blouse. Marie glided up the stairs without any effort. She then had to wait on her mother who slowly carried her load. Mathilda was still weak from her seasickness, but the fresh air was invigorating.

This was truly a day to remember. A beautiful, cloudless October sky greeted them on deck, but a cool breeze robbed them of the warmth from the sun. Seagulls, busy looking for any spare scrap of food, squawked loudly in complaint upon finding none. Marie found a place by the railing, and she and her mother gasped as they saw the skyline of New York City for the first time. Suddenly a hush came over the crowd as the ship came into the harbor. It was quickly replaced by an explosion of joy and roaring merriment.

"HIP, HIP, HOORAY!" rang out from the crowded deck as the splendor of that Lady of Liberty came into view. More shouts and whistles followed, and Marie and Mathilda were caught up in the whole celebration. Everyone was still shouting when smaller boats arrived to ferry them over to the port of entry into the great country of America.

As they stepped off the boat onto the dry ground of Ellis Island, they still felt as if they were walking on the ship. It took a while before they felt like they were walking normally. They took their place in the long lines that formed to get into the buildings, inching their way toward the doors. No one seemed to know what was happening or where to go.

The noise was deafening. New lines formed by countries, so everyone was scrambling to find the sign with the name of their country. An older German couple, looking quite lost, reached out to Mathilda, and she helped them find the line with the sign labeled "Rhineland." Of course, Marie was hungry, then thirsty, then she had to go to the toilet. The older woman had to go to the toilet, also, so together they searched for one. As soon as Marie was out of sight, Mathilda began to fret.

Whatever have I done? she thought. *I do not know this older woman.* She felt herself start to panic. She began to talk to herself. *Calm down, she will be right back. She is being helpful to this elderly woman, and she is in God's protection.* Her body relaxed a bit. The line was at a complete standstill. There was no air; the panic returned and became a chant.

"Oh Lord, oh Lord, oh Lord."

She heard a child's voice call "Mama!" Mathilda turned in the direction of the voice and saw Marie skipping ahead of the older woman. Mathilda's chant changed to, "Thank you, thank you, thank you."

"Marie, I need you to be very good right now. There is such a crowd; we must not be separated. Please be good for me." Marie's face lost its smile, and she resumed her dutiful place beside her mother, saying nothing. A man came by pushing a

A Trip Over Troubled Water

large wheelbarrow with a water container on it. He looked at Marie.

"Do you want water, my fine lady?"

"Yes!" answered Marie in English. He handed her a dipper, but she dug down in her bag and pulled out a metal cup Marge had given her on the ship. She handed it to him, and he filled it with cool water. Marie smiled at the water vendor and said, "Tank zoo."

He looked at her proudly and commented, "That's good!"

Mathilda drank some water from Marie's cup, and the man filled it again. Others were calling to him, "Wasser!" and he pushed his wheelbarrow on through the crowd. Mathilda was refreshed and smiled with approval at Marie.

It seemed to them they were in that long line all day. People here and there began sitting down on the floor. Marie took that as permission for her to sit down, too. Mathilda started to protest, but then she let her sit, since there was nothing to do and no benches or chairs available. Out of courtesy, they left the last spot on the bench near the German line open for the older couple to take. As unruly as the crowd could be, some simple manners remained for the elderly, the pregnant and families with small babies.

Finally, Mathilda and Marie arrived at the table where a man sat directing them to an office. When they entered the office, another man behind a desk stood up to greet them. He offered Mathilda a chair, and Marie stood by her mother listening to him speak in very understandable German, even though it did not seem to be his native tongue. He introduced himself as an intake medical officer and began asking Mathilda questions about their village and the area of Germany they called home. Mathilda seemed nervous, and her voice quivered as she spoke; trying not to cry, she bit her lower lip. She thought carefully before answering, which made the process slow and arduous.

The officer told her that upon entering this country, she and Marie would require an examination by a physician. Looking at her documents, he learned that Papa, Mary and baby John had died. He was now interested in knowing about the rest of the village and whether other villages in Northern Germany had had people die from the same kind of sickness. German officials had contacted immigration officials in the United States about this problem, so all Germans coming from the northern regions were questioned and sent to wait in another line for a physical examination.

The doctor was an old man with a long white beard, yet almost no hair on his head. He offered them some tea and cookies out of a canister on his desk. He seemed to know this was the first food they had had since the bread and butter on the ship. As he spoke with Mathilda, Marie looked around his office.

What a strange place, with lots and lots of books, she thought. Then she saw the biggest book she had ever seen. There were books on shelves that went all the way to the ceiling. She noticed a cabinet with glass doors full of all sorts of blue, brown and clear bottles. Marie was curious as she observed something funny looking that the doctor wore around his neck. Later, he used it to listen to her mother's heart. Marie noticed that the tips of the fingers on his right hand were black. The doctor was writing down everything her mother was telling him, and he kept dipping his pen into an ornate glass bottle of India ink the shape of an elephant. She had seen a picture of one in a book and guessed this was what the bottle was supposed to look like.

"Mama, is that an elephant?" Her question startled Mathilda.

The doctor answered for her mother. "Yes, it is. You are smart to know what an elephant is." He quickly resumed his interview and asked Mathilda how she was feeling.

"I am well. Seasickness is my only complaint."

"Mrs. Baumann." The doctor cleared his throat and looked at Mathilda with great concern and then over at Marie, who was staring with her mouth open and reaching to touch the thickest book she had ever seen.

"I am so sorry for your great tragedy. I am also sorry to inform you that I must detain you from your journey for a while. Our staff at this immigration facility on Ellis Island must become absolutely convinced that you and your daughter are not ill. Sometimes people are sick, yet have no symptoms. I know you would never wish to do harm to others upon entering a new country. Therefore, madam, I must put you and your child into quarantine for three months to observe you and see if you develop symptoms of diphtheria."

"What is this word, 'diptha'?" Mathilda asked with great concern.

"Diphtheria. It is the disease that caused your family and village to perish," he answered coldly, not looking up from the notes he was still writing.

"How will we live? I have little money, and I planned to get a job as soon as I could. A Lutheran pastor wrote a letter of introduction for me, and our final destination is to be in a place called She-kah-go. It has all been arranged. I have been promised work, and I must still pay back my debt to the travel company. Oh, dear doctor, what am I to do? If we were going to die from the disease, wouldn't we have already died?"

"Mrs. Baumann," he said, looking up from his writing to speak to her now comfortingly. "I don't know why you and your daughter did not die with the others. You must know I agree with your logic; however, you must also know that it is my sole responsibility to make sure you do not get sick now or infect others with this terrible disease. I will have an office worker who reads and writes German help you with a letter that will be discreet so it will not banish you from working. I must, however, be quite clear with you that if you are sick, you may not enter America and may have to be deported. That means, my dear Mrs. Baumann, sent back to Europe. You marked 'excellent health' on your paperwork, Mrs. Baumann. That was not quite true, was it now, my good woman?" His kind tone had turned harsh.

"*Herr* Doctor, I must protest." No longer nervous, she spoke out boldly. "I did mark 'excellent' when asked about our health. God spared my daughter and me from the dreadful disease, and my sickness on the ship was only from the rolling of the sea. Please examine us both; you will find I answered that question truthfully."

He agreed to examine them and behaved like a gentleman.

The nurse came through with a fine comb and looked at their hair and scalp for lice. She gave them both nightgowns to wear while she sent their clothes to be washed. Mathilda realized this was the first time people looked at her with pity and with disdain. She knew that it was just their job to help; nevertheless, from that moment on, she wanted no one's pity — ever again.

Chapter 4
So Close ... Yet So Far

Out of extreme precaution, the authorities quarantined Mathilda and Marie Baumann for three months in a dormitory that stood apart from the other buildings on Ellis Island. From one window in their room they could see the Statue of Liberty, and from the other window they could see the skyline of New York City.

The first day, Mathilda was in a mood Marie had never seen. Marie noticed her mother's eyes were bloodshot. Her face was pale, except for her cheeks, which were bright crimson. These two new immigrants had been stripped of all their clothing and were given nightgowns and robes to wear day and night. Their other belongings were put into storage. Nothing was left that they could call their own.

However, they were thankful they were provided a bed. Some well-meaning church folk had left an English Bible under each pillow. Mathilda began pacing back and forth praying aloud — something her daughter had never witnessed. She was angry, and she was telling God all about it. One minute, she would thank Him for life and His great protection; the next, she would cry out for being mistreated by being put into quarantine.

Mathilda could see no good coming from being a prisoner in the "Land of the Free." The words of her despair were spoken through clenched teeth.

"Haven't we been tested, tried and punished enough?" She broke into inconsolable sobs. When she could cry no more, with her voice almost hoarse from weeping, she sang to herself as a dirge the song, *In der Fremde,** (In a Foreign Land).

> From my homeland, which is hidden by red lightning,
> Clouds are coming this way.
> But Father and Mother died long ago,

and nobody knows me there anymore.
How soon, very soon, that quiet time will come
when I shall rest, too,
And the solitude of the forest will surround me,
And no one will know me here anymore.

The grief expressed in this song was too much for little Marie. She was tired and did not know what to do for her mother: tired of watching her mother being sad and sick, tired of hearing her cry at night, tired of everything! She walked to the threshold of the door to their room and looked down the hallway. There she noticed an older lady looking outside through a large window; beside the woman was a bowl of smoke. Curious, Marie walked down the hall for a closer examination.

The lady had a condition that made her cough, so her treatment was sitting three times a day with a towel over her head breathing in steam from a bowl of camphor water. Marie, recognizing the strong smell, remembered visiting her own grandmother who had smelled like that whenever she was sick with a cold.

The smell made Marie's nose tingle, and the air she breathed in felt cool. The closer she got to this older woman, the more she felt an attraction to her rather than the curiosity of the smelly steam bowl.

I wonder if this lady is somebody's grandmother? she thought. *I will ask her and make a new friend.*

With her back to Marie, the woman asked in German, "Nurse, have you brought the knitting needles and yarn I requested?"

"Grandmother, I am not a nurse," Marie replied sweetly. The woman whirled around in her seat to see this beautiful small blond child approaching.

"Well, my goodness, forgive me. No, you are not a nurse, but you are a more welcome sight to me than a nurse!" She smiled from ear to ear.

"My name is Marie Martha. Are you somebody's grandmother?"

So Close ... Yet So Far

The woman opened wide her arms and invited the child in. "Do you need one right now?"

Marie ran to this stranger as if she had known her through eternity. She began crying, and the woman held her and stroked her little head and hair silently.

The moment was interrupted by a nurse bringing the older lady some supplies that church folks had sent specifically to help the sick pass the time until they could leave Ellis Island. Inside the large bag was some loose wool with a drop spindle, a few tatting shuttles, various-sized knitting needles and crochet hooks and many brightly colored balls of yarn.

The woman, still holding onto Marie, took the bag and thanked the nurse. "Shall we look inside, darling, and see what the people have sent us to help pass the time here in our quarantine?" Marie choked down her tears and nodded her head in agreement.

"Oh, what lovely things! So many items can be made from all these materials. Aren't we blessed to now have something to keep us busy?" The words were as much to comfort her own heart as they were to comfort the child. "You told me your name, little miss; my name is Mrs. O'Donner."

"Hello!" Marie greeted, wiping her eyes with the sleeve of her nightgown.

"Reach into this big bag and pull out your favorite color of yarn, and I will make you a scarf with it. Would you like that, Marie Martha?" she inquired through teary eyes. Marie had not caught her breath after crying, and she hugged the woman just for talking sweetly to her. She received the kindness offered from Mrs. O'Donner's heart with more joy than the promise of a scarf. Sniffing and wiping her eyes again, Marie reached into the paper bag and pulled out a bright royal blue ball of yarn, which she shyly handed to her new grandmother friend.

"Oh, this is nice. It will match your eyes and make your hair seem even more yellow. I like this color." Mrs. O'Donner released her hold on the child as she looked into the bag and pulled out a pair of knitting needles.

Mathilda looked around the room and did not see Marie. She heard voices coming from down the hall, so she walked to the door and looked down the hallway. There she spied her little girl with an older woman; they were both looking down into a big bag.

"What is she doing now?" she spoke aloud to herself. They looked up at her as she approached them.

"Mama, look! This nice woman is going to make me a scarf out of this blue ball," Marie said excitedly, sniffing back tears.

"Hello, my name is Mrs. O'Donner. We received some treasures from some church folk in New York City. Aren't they lovely? I've been so bored with nothing to do but stare out this window. Your daughter and I were in need of some conversation. Please come and join us."

"Thank you. My name is Mathilda Baumann. We arrived on the ship today. We were just told we will have to be staying here for three months for observation."

"Well, now, let me ask you: Do you know how to knit, crochet or tat?" Mrs. O'Donner asked.

"No, I am ashamed to admit that my aunt offered to teach me to make lace, but I thought my hands were too large for such delicate work. I never took the time to learn," she answered with a nervous laugh.

"You have three months now to learn, and I am willing to teach you if you like!" Her request was also a solemn command. Mathilda took no offense because she could feel the kindness exude from this kind woman.

Mrs. O'Donner not only kept Mathilda and Marie from going insane from idleness by teaching them to spin, knit and make lace, she also taught them to speak conversational English, rather than just a word here and there. Mathilda asked one of the nurses if she could have her tea set brought to her out of storage so they might have afternoon tea together several hours before the evening meal. The nurse was quick to respond, and they were drinking tea within the hour. It was amazing how much tea was still in the box that Beatrice, the pastor's wife from Hamburg, had given Mathilda as a departure gift.

Using the English Bible, Mrs. O'Donner first would read a verse and explain its meaning to them in broken German. She would then read it to them in English. They would echo the words over and again until they memorized them. This became a daily routine.

Mrs. O'Donner had been reared as an Anglican (Church of England). Later in her adult life, she reported, she had been baptized in fire at a revival and was quite happy to call herself a Methodist now. Mrs. O'Donner told them at their teatime that originally her family had come from the Highlands of Scotland, but due to political unrest, they had sailed to Northern Ireland and had lived there for two generations.

All the men in her life had fished the North Banks; each of them now lay in an icy grave. Her second husband had been a German sailor, washed ashore after his ship sank off the coast of Ireland. She had learned his language, and he had learned hers. They had married and lived in wedded bliss for three years before he fell to his death off the cliffs near their cottage.

"You may think I'm cracked in the head, yet it is God's own truth," she began. "When I first saw this beautiful specimen of manhood, covered in seaweed with his belly full of sea water, I thought he was dead because the sea gulls were hovering over him, but as I walked toward him I saw his hand reach out to pull himself closer to land." A big smile came to her face. "We laughed years later that I would be willing to pick up just any old thing on the beach, even a half-drowned sailor." She laughed aloud at their private joke; then her smile slowly faded.

"He was a good man. Like a newborn babe, he came to me with nothing but himself; like a child, he left this world with no earthly goods. The only thing he did acquire was a heart of loving I gave to him! A sweeter, kinder, more fun-loving man I've never met, but I still have not forgiven him for falling and dying. Well, my dear Lord will not let me stay angry, because He let me live happily with him for 38 months and two weeks. He was never sick or cranky — he was just happy and free. You should have seen all the things he could make with his hands! Why, this man carved figurines of wood, sewed fishing nets, built a room onto our cottage and made new cupboards for the kitchen. He worked about the area fixing up other people's homes and sheds. What amazed me the most was the wonderful roses he could grow! Our neighbor's roses were poor and puny, but his were the size of saucers." She made gestures with her hands as she looked first at Marie and then at Mathilda. Slowly she put her hands down into her lap and sat silently reflecting. After a long pause, she continued with her story.

"I had been a widow for 23 years, and he made me feel like a young girl. Well, I won't be saying any more about that with a young one listening in." She and Mathilda giggled like teenagers sharing a secret. Mrs. O'Donner's story changed from happy to sad. Marie had grown tired of all the adult talk and of trying to untangle her blue ball of yarn, so she walked over to the window to watch the icy rain fall, distorting the lights across the harbor.

"Yes," Mrs. O'Donner continued, "after I buried this good man, my true love, I decided to leave that place of death and go to the land of the living. Ten years ago, my sister came to America and now has a modest but happy home in Kentucky. She has been begging me in her letters to come and be with her family and live out the rest of my years." Mrs. O'Donner spoke solemnly, wiping her eyes with one of her own tatted-lace handkerchiefs.

"After all these years, what made you decide to join her?" Mathilda gently asked.

"We Scotch-Irish are a sentimental lot." Taking another handkerchief out of her sleeve, she wiped her eyes and nose, then reached into her pocket with her other hand and pulled out a letter. "Let me read to you my sister's words that gave me such a yearning to be close to my only blood relative." Mrs. O'Donner opened a crumpled envelope and pulled out a piece of stationery that had been folded and refolded many times. Clearing her voice, she read:

To the most darling person I have ever known.
Dear sister,

It is the pain of human suffering, the sheer joy of loving life and the pleasure of knowing that God is with you through it all that form the wool threads that weave people together in this world. Now what gets woven into this large tapestry is everyone's indi-

So Close ... Yet So Far

vidual uniqueness, their strengths and weaknesses, their talents and traits; some dark and some light, some soft and smooth, some coarse and rough. If anything is to matter at all, there needs to be all of it; that is why the Good Book tells us to be thankful for it all. This is the very will of God for us. Let me remind you, my beloved sister, that there is no hurt that Jesus cannot heal, no trial He cannot carry you through, no disappointment He cannot use for good and nowhere you can hide from His love. I need you, sister. Come be part of my life again. Enclosed is money for your passage.

Love from my heart to yours,
Emma

Mathilda put her arm around her new friend and moved closer while she wiped the tears from her own eyes. Before they left to go to dinner, they all prayed for one another. Mathilda prayed that Mrs. O'Donner would be healed. Mrs. O'Donner prayed that Mathilda and Marie would be able to learn English quickly. Marie prayed that no one would have any scary dreams.

That night, each in her own bed prayed again and thanked God for this divine appointment. Mathilda also prayed a special prayer of thanksgiving: *Lord God, my grandmother had me memorize Philippians 4:4-8 for times when the mind just wants to go wandering. Thank You for my grandmother who long ago helped to prepare me for this time in my life. Amen.* Mathilda turned on her side to see Marie looking at her.

"Mama, I like that old lady, don't you?" she whispered to her mother.

"I do, too, Marie. We will see her tomorrow. Close your eyes and get to sleep. I love you." She blew her daughter a kiss, and Marie returned the kiss.

"Mama, I love you, too. Will you tell me what your grandmother taught you?"

Mathilda recited the scripture to her sleepy little one as Marie's eyes closed and she fell into a peaceful sleep.

"Rejoice in the Lord always. Again I say, rejoice. Let your

gentleness be known to all men. The Lord is at hand. Be anxious for nothing, but in everything by prayer and supplication, with thanksgiving, let your requests be made known to God; and the peace of God, which surpasses all understanding, will guard your hearts and minds through Jesus Christ."

As Mathilda lay in bed staring into the darkness, she remembered that the Lutheran ladies had left stationery and stamps for her in the bedside table. Her heart was full, and she decided to rise and write her friend Beatrice in Hamburg. She wanted to thank Beatrice and her husband for caring for them and helping them reach America. Pulling out a sheet of fine linen stationery, she wrote:

My Dearest Friend and Sister in Christ, Beatrice,

I greet you with thanksgiving that God brought you and your family into our lives. Marie and I have completed the perilous journey across the Atlantic Ocean, but we have been detained at a hospital on Ellis Island. The doctors have to observe us for three months to see if we get sick with the illness that took the lives of our entire village. I explained to them that God, in His immeasurable mercy, had spared us; if not, Marie and I would have died with the others. They did not agree with me, so here we are — confined to a prison filled with people who have every kind of sickness. Marie and I are the only people, other than the nurses and doctors, that do not have some sort of infirmity. Please pray for us. I have never been confined before, and I confess I find it maddening. The only break from the oppression of being confined here is the freedom to write you this letter and hopefully receive one from you in return. However, our Lord Jesus will not tolerate any self-pity. Please pray for me. I feel such heaviness come over me that it makes it hard for me to move. My heart is heavy, and the pain makes breathing difficult.

But all is not sadness here; don't let me mislead you. We have met an older woman who is teaching us to speak proper English from the Bible given to us by the Lutheran Ladies' Missionary Aid Society. We study and then have tea. Your tea canister miraculously still has tea leaves in it, even though I shared it with others on the ship. I do thank you for the tea but more importantly for the ginger cookies, which served as medicine to combat the seasickness I had aboard the ship. They are all gone, but the tea continues to bless us. After teatime, we learn to knit and tat with yarn and needles provided by the Lutheran Ladies' charity. The kindness shown to us has humbled me and yet blessed me so that I weep now as I write to you. These kind deeds are medicine to me. I can see how my healing is not of the body as those around me, but rather

So Close ... Yet So Far

healing of a broken heart and spirit. I feel the presence of God's Spirit. His light penetrates the blackness of my despair. I cannot stay sad. I remember Saint Paul said he could be content in any circumstance. Beatrice, my beloved, I do believe this experience is that lesson of contentment about which he spoke. Please pray for me to pass this trial. Pray that Jesus' great love will continue to cast out all fear, doubt and worry. You are so important to me, and I thank God for you. I hope to see you again in this life, but if not, I cling to the hope of seeing you in our home in heaven.

*Blessings and Honor and Praise to the King of Kings,
Mathilda Baumann*

Mathilda's eyes were heavy. Tomorrow she would reread the letter, find an envelope and stamps and ask one of the nurses to mail it to Hamburg. She slept without bad dreams this night.

On November 2nd, the staff brought in flowers for a special service celebrating All Soul's Day. This day was set apart to remember loved ones who had died. In the past on this holy day, Mathilda had sung at her church Richard Strauss's song, *Allerseelen**. The words now flowed out of her heart as the others in the room looked on and listened.

> Put fragrant mignonettes on the table;
> bring in the last red asters,
> And let us talk about love, as once in May.
> Give me your hand so that I can hold it secretly,
> And even if people see, I don't mind.
> Give me just one of your sweet glances, as once in May.
> There are fragrant flowers today on every grave;
> One day a year is devoted to the dead.
> Come and embrace me, so that I again possess you,
> as once in May.

Mathilda's voice was clear and strong. It served as the benediction because everyone left the room wiping their eyes and seeking a place of solitude to finish their private prayers and reflective thoughts. Marie was surprised there were no tears in her mother's eyes after she sang such a sad song making others cry. Born into a home filled with music, she loved to hear her mother sing.

Marie's mother and father enjoyed music and had beautiful voices. Both were drawn to nostalgic lyrics used in Northern German songs. The Bürgermeister and his wife were musicians who would travel to Hamburg and Bonn to purchase pieces of music to share at church and to entertain friends. Occasionally, they invited the Baumanns to learn a piece of music and perform as a duet for a holiday or festival. The villagers enjoyed the couple's lovely voices and the affection they showed to each other as they sang.

Singing was not just for show. In daily life, Mathilda and John hummed and sang as they performed their chores. Marie smiled remembering her father leaving the house humming a tune and then hearing that same tune hummed later in the day by her mother. Her parents were connected by music that just naturally and melodiously flowed out of their love for each other. Today her mother sang like an angel, but she missed hearing her father's voice.

Mathilda received sweet treats and a red aster for the holiday; the aster was just like the ones she had planted in her window boxes in Germany. Looking at the beauty of the flower, in her mind she spoke to her beloved John: *My heart is only yours, my husband. I love you. I shall always love you.*

A week before Christmas, Mrs. O'Donner was discharged from Ellis Island and was able to travel by train to Kentucky. All the prayers of that first meeting had been answered: Mrs. O'Donner was healthy again, and Mathilda and Marie were speaking English in simple sentences. Mathilda had soaked up everything she could learn from her motherly friend.

"This is the address where I will be living with my sister and her family. If things do not work out for you in the Chicago area, come to Kentucky. I promise my sister will love you two as much as I do."

Mathilda threw her arms around Mrs. O'Donner's neck and kissed her wet cheeks. "I have no German or English words to express how grateful I am to you. You have been my mother, my friend, a perfect angel. What will we do without you?"

So Close ... Yet So Far

"I know, I know. I love you, too. This lifetime is a series of hellos and goodbyes. Don't fret; you are a young woman. You have a whole lifetime ahead of you. Oh, you will witness your child become a young woman, marry and have babes of her own." Mrs. O'Donner gave Mathilda a big toothy grin and kissed her again.

"Now, Marie, I want you to listen to this grandmother you have claimed. You are a blessed child. I love you, and I will think of you every day from this day forward." They embraced and held each other for a long time. Together, Mathilda and Marie watched as the nurses walked their friend out of the building. Mathilda thought there was always a bit of mystery about her name. If she had indeed married that German seaman, why did she keep her Irish name? *Oh well, some questions are best not answered,* she thought to herself.

As she thought of her dear friend, she had to laugh at how much Mrs. O'Donner loved potatoes. While on Ellis Island, Mathilda and Marie learned to eat potatoes every way they could be prepared. They also learned to eat turnips and oats. Before this experience, Mathilda had only given oats to the horse. However, the Lord received thanksgiving for the horse food, as well as the people food. Occasionally, they would receive chipped beef or corned beef with cabbage, or even a few sausages. The menu always included bread and butter. Sometimes the nurses would bring in sweet breads for the patients, and Mathilda would save a slice for teatime.

Christmas Eve finally came, and Mathilda knitted several gifts for Marie and the nurses, but Marie had nothing to give her mother. She asked her favorite nurse what she could give her mother for Christmas, since she doubted her mother would receive any presents.

"What does your mother like?" the nurse asked.

"Everything."

"I know!" The nurse had an idea that excited her. "Follow me to the apothecary, and I will give you a beautiful cobalt bottle of simple syrup." Marie did as she was instructed and waited outside the door for the nurse.

"What is that?"

Removing the cork, the nurse put a drop on Marie's finger. "Taste it."

"Oh, that tastes sweet! She will like it. Thank you." Marie made a small curtsy.

"It is sweetness for your mother's tea." The nurse was quite pleased with herself. She reached into a drawer and pulled out a piece of string, a small piece of colored paper, a pen and a bottle of Indian ink. In beautiful penmanship, she wrote:

MERRY CHRISTMAS
TO MOTHER
FROM MARIE

"There now," the nurse said. "This is from you, and your mother doesn't have to know where you got it. Marie, whenever you run out of this syrup, I'll fill up your bottle with some more. Do you understand?" She bent over and handed Marie the beautiful blue bottle with the fancy cork on top.

"Tank zoo! I mean Tank uuuuu," Marie said very forcefully.

The nurse patted Marie on the top of her head and wished her a Merry Christmas, then reached for her coat.

"Where are you going?" Marie was curious.

"I am off work the rest of the day, so I must go meet the boat that goes to New Jersey. That's where I live. Our family would die if I didn't go there and eat like a horse and tell them I'm getting married." The nurse smiled and gave Marie a wink as she started to say goodbye.

Marie interrupted her. "You're getting married?" She looked at the nurse with her mouth wide open.

"No! Listen, you are a sweet little girl, but you are too young to understand a woman my age. I'm almost 20, and if I don't get a husband soon, I'm looking at being an old maid. God knows my parents and family bring it up to me all the time." She bent over, and cupping her hand to Marie's ear, she whispered, "I made up a little white lie to tell them what they want to hear. That's all." She stood up and waved at Marie. "Bye now, sweetheart, I'll look in on you tomorrow."

Before Marie could respond, the nurse was out the door. Marie ran to the door, but it was already locked. Marie called to

So Close ... Yet So Far

her mother and found her propped up with pillows in bed reading the Bible.

"Mama, do you know what a little white lie is?"

"It's a lie, Marie," Matilda answered, not even looking up from her reading.

Most of the staff went home to be with their own families on Christmas, so Mathilda and Marie had almost the whole building to themselves. They went to the bathing room and filled two tubs with hot water. Both enjoyed a long, hot soaking bath. Mathilda washed her long hair. Next she leaned over the tub and washed Marie's hair. She rinsed their hair with some lavender water that one of the nurses had given them for Christmas. The lavender gave the whole room a lovely fragrance that was very relaxing. Mathilda's hair was long and wavy, but she wore it braided, twisted and pinned up on her head. Sometimes at night, Marie would ask to brush her mother's long honey-colored hair; this seemed to calm Mathilda so she could sleep better.

The staff had left the patients a wonderful supper of sliced ham and sweet Christmas breads with an assortment of other dishes none had ever seen or tasted. Every morsel was delicious! Surprisingly, something was missing: There was not one potato dish. Imagine that! Potatoes served every day except on Christmas. The ladies from New York City who brought the holiday meal also brought Christmas pictures, holly, candles, mistletoe and ribbons so the patients could make their surroundings more festive. Mathilda helped decorate the halls and around the ends of each person's bed. She then found some matches and lit a few candles. All the quarantined patients joined together in singing Christmas songs they could remember. The melodies of these songs were the same, but each person sang the lyrics in his or her native tongue. It appeared everyone was in good cheer. The group gazed out of the frosty windows toward the lights of the New York City Harbor. They all seemed to look across the water with wonder in their eyes, not so much because of the lights, but more of a wonder what it was really like in New York City. None, thus far, had stepped foot on that shore, the real America.

It began to snow, soon resulting in whiteout conditions. Even the Statue of Liberty was blotted from sight. Slowly, people moved away from the windows that no longer provided scenery. The comfort that held these patients together tonight was warmth, safety and the knowledge that this day was Jesus' birthday.

Mr. Giovanoti pulled out a bottle of Italian wine to toast a Merry Christmas to all. Mathilda sipped some as a toast of good cheer, then saved a little in her cup so that later, just before bedtime, she and Marie could celebrate communion. She noticed that her little girl appeared small and thin. Rather than letting this sight steal her joy of the day, she chose to be happy.

"My Love, we have no pastor to serve us the elements, nor do we have any unleavened bread. Deep in my heart, I know that all that is required in this place, at this time, is what Jesus taught His disciples when He said, 'This do ye, as oft as ye drink of it, in remembrance of me.'"

Marie was very quiet. She clung to her mother, and even as they were making ready for bed, she squeezed in next to her so they could sing softly and feel each other's warmth. Mathilda played with Marie's hair; both were wide-awake.

"Mama, I'm not sleepy," Marie said softly into her mother's ear.

"I know; something just doesn't feel right," Mathilda spoke aloud.

When heaviness of sleep overcame Marie, a loud *pop* came from down the hallway. Both Matilda and Marie sat straight up in bed.

"That sounded like a gunshot." Mathilda pulled Marie to her and said, "Quick, take the blanket and get under the bed." Marie did as she was told.

"Mama," she whispered, "what are you doing?"

As Mathilda stepped into her cloth slippers and pulled on her robe, she commanded, "Marie, listen to me now. I must see if we are in danger. Stay hidden under the bed. I will be right back. Oh, and Marie, start praying!"

Marie spoke aloud in the darkness of the room. "Oh, Jesus, we need Your help. I'm so scared. I'm scared for Mama, too.

So Close ... Yet So Far

Mama says that Your perfect love casts out all fear. Please, I need some of Your perfect love right now. I don't know what is out there, but if it is danger, please keep it away from Mama and all the patients here: Mr. Giovanoti, Olga, Mrs. Withers, that old man whose name I can't remember, the nice man in the white coat, our nurse in New Jersey, our friend Mrs. O'Donner and, and, also me, too. Please, please, please help us."

Over and over she prayed until she heard her mother calling from the hallway. The light from the hallway made her form into a silhouette so Marie could not see her face.

"Marie, we are not in danger, but something dreadful has happened. It appears the doctor has shot himself. There is no one here in this building, so I must go get help in the next building. Listen carefully, Marie. You must stay here in this room. I don't want you to see any of this. Promise to obey me. Do you promise, Marie?"

"I do, Mama," she said with a little cry in her voice.

"Get back into bed and look at the treasures you received in your Christmas stocking. Please don't be frightened. I'll be back soon. I love you, my sweet." Her voice trailed off. Marie heard her run down the hallway, and then the door slammed shut. Muffled voices of those who were awake were asking one another what made the noise. Olga was crying. The old man Marie had just prayed for was cursing in German. Marie thought to herself, *I guess his mother never washed his mouth with soap for saying dirty words.* She remembered what had happened to her for saying dirty words. She sat in her bed with her Christmas stocking and began to daydream.

The scene she saw was outdoors watching Mr. Günter hammer a board on top of his roof. "What are you doing, *Herr* Günter?" she yelled up at him. He was old and a little hard of hearing and always smelled of beer.

"Oh, child, I'm just sitting up here farting and fixing this damned leak. If I don't fix it, my woman will nag me to the grave. She thinks I'm a shithead and a drunk, so I shall stay on the roof all day just to worry her." He sounded drunk and cranky.

"Well, goodbye, *Herr* Günter. I'm going to play now," she

73

said, waving goodbye.

She heard him grumble, "Damn, children play all day while I have to work!"

That evening when she came into the house to eat the evening meal, Papa asked her how her day went. "Oh, I played with the children in the meadow and watched *Herr* Günter fix his damn roof. He said his wife thought he was a shithead and a drunk. Papa, I think he was drunk!"

"Marie Martha!" her mother gasped.

Papa stood up from the table. "Daughter, never speak those foul words again. *Damn* and *shithead* are bad words. To teach you a lesson, your mother will wash with soap that filth from your mouth." She had never seen her mama or papa so angry. As she followed her mama to the washing basin, she heard the door slam and her papa talking to *Herr* Günter, who was still on top of his roof.

"*Herr* Günter, you have caused trouble in my household today. What you do with your life is your business, but whenever your actions affect my family, especially my children, then it becomes my business. I am a fair and peaceful man, for if I was not, I would climb that ladder and beat you soundly. I want to make myself perfectly clear: Never speak vulgarly to my daughter, Marie, ever again. Must I say more?"

Herr Günter hung his head in shame and said most humbly, "*Herr* Baumann, accept my apology."

Papa came inside the house and slammed the door hard. Soap had washed the filth from Marie's tongue. Her father asked her mother, "Have you finished with our daughter washing?" Mathilda nodded yes. "Then, Mother, let's eat!"

It had been a long time, and Mathilda was still gone. Marie tried calling to her.

"Mama, where are you?" She tried again and again.

What is taking so long? she thought. There were still faint noises, like people talking, but Marie could not make out their words. She thought if she could get just a little closer to the voices, she could hear. Her bare feet hit the cold cement floor. *Brrr — this floor is so cold.* She ran back to the end table by her bed and pulled out a pair of wool socks. She saw some sweet

So Close ... Yet So Far

bread wrapped in brown paper lying next to her Christmas stocking. "You mean old rats, you are not getting any of my Christmas goodies," she said aloud so all the rats could hear. She grabbed her wrapped bread and tiptoed to the doorway. While she was eating it, half dropped to the floor. She knew her mother would not let her eat anything that was dirty, so she asked Jesus to bless it, then picked it up and ate it. When she finished wiping the crumbs from her mouth, she crumpled up the brown paper. It made more noise than she thought; the voices stopped, and she heard footsteps moving toward her. Fast as a bunny, she dashed to bed and hopped in. The door squeaked, and the light shone in onto the bed.

A voice that was not her mother's spoke to her. "Marie, are you all right in there?"

"Yes, thank you," she answered, using her best English. "I just got out of bed to eat some more Christmas bread — it is so very good," Marie added nervously.

"Well, now, you try to sleep. Your mother is here and will be with you soon. Good night, sweet princess!"

"Good night!" She closed her eyes and fell asleep. Suddenly she awoke with a start. Her mother was still gone. "I am so tired, but I want my mama," she cried out, but no one heard her. She slipped out of bed again and went to the doorway to listen. The door was partially open, just enough for her to slip through without making the door squeak. Hugging the wall, she made her way down the hallway toward the voices. She recognized her mother's voice.

"Yah, there vas a letter on his desk," Mathilda said to a man who was writing down everything she said.

"Is it there now or did you move it?" he asked her, leaning low to hear her soft voice.

"Nein, I mean no, I read vhat little I could, his writin' vas so poor, vithout touchin' it I read zat ze red demon off morphine vould not leaf him alone, and he vas a disgrace to him's own profession. He couldz not face ze Christmas alone. Zaire vas more written, but I couldz not understand. *Herr* Doctor, he vas makin' strange sounds and movin' jest a little vhen I finds him. I touched his shoulder, und his head fell unto mine hands.

There was much blood. I moved him back to sit in da chair. I hope, I mean, I vas wanting much to help him; I did not know if he was dead or maybe life was still in him."

"Oh, Missus, he was dead. A shot in the brain does that. Can I ask for someone to sit with you tonight? This has been most tragic." He showed genuine concern.

"Tank you, no. I hoff been around a lot of death zis year. Tank you for yourn kindness."

He bowed to her and then put his hat back on. "If you will be all right, I will leave you now so I may finish my job. You are a fine woman." Both of their faces turned crimson when he said that.

Marie was just about to call to her mother when another man who worked in their building came up to Mathilda. He looked as pale as his orderly jacket. "You found him?" he asked.

"Yah," she replied. "Ve were goin' to sleep when I heard ze shot. I didn't know vhat vas going on, but after no other shots vere fired, I vent to see vhat vas vrong."

"I am so sorry. Some of us went to the main building to continue our Christmas cheer since all of the patients were fed and going to bed. There is just a handful of us staff left over the holidays, so we were playing music and some of us dancing, you know. Oh, God, I never thought anything like this would happen. I mean, we all knew he had a problem with taking his own medicine, but how awful." He lowered his head and put his hand to his mouth.

Mathilda looked at him with compassion. "Vell, he is free of tis life now, but I don't know vhat he has done to himself for ze rest of eternity."

"Madam, it is a terrible thing to live in such despair. It is a terrible thing to be so alone in life, and it is absolutely horrible that I never shared with him that there is hope. I mean, here we are, all celebrating God's gift at Christmas — we are all Christians, even though we transgressed by drinking a little too much — but here is a doctor I work with every day, and I never thought to invite him to party with us in the other building. What is worse, I never even shared the gospel with him. Come to think about it, I didn't really know him that well, if at all."

So Close ... Yet So Far

Marie looked at the man, who was now weeping and leaning on her mother's shoulder. Mathilda was stroking his hair, as she did her daughter's, to try to comfort him. Mathilda spoke to him as he regained his composure. "I am sorry, too. I nefer saw him as anythin' but *Herr* Doctor who vas to help me. Oh, Lord, have mercy on his soul and mine, too, for not seein' him as a man who needed a kind vord and help for his own troubles."

"Mama, what happened?" Marie said, rubbing her eyes. At once, they both turned and looked down at Marie.

"Don't come any farther," Mathilda said in German, with great alarm.

"Stop!" the orderly said at the same time.

Mathilda rushed to her daughter, as she wiped the blood from her hands on a towel.

Once all the people left, it seemed uncommonly quiet. Marie was almost afraid to close her eyes. Mathilda came back to join her daughter. They had taken a long Christmas bath earlier, but now Mathilda needed another bath. She came into the room humming one of her favorite hymns. Marie loved her voice and thought she sang like an angel; even Mrs. Günter had agreed. Again, Marie visited a memory. It was the time when she was pulling weeds out of her neighbor's flowerbed, and Mrs. Günter was talking to Marie about her mother's beautiful singing voice.

"My dear, I so love hearing your mother sing as she works in her garden; and even in the evening, her voice carries into our bedroom as she sings to you children at night. Marie, your mother sings like an angel."

Her memory was interrupted by her mother handing her the comb and sitting at the edge of the bed.

"Mama, what is the name of that song?" Marie asked as she combed her mother's wet hair.

"A Mighty Fortress Is Our God," she answered. "Don't you remember singing it with me? It was written by Martin Luther. The words are so powerful and so very real to me, especially tonight."

She sang out the lyrics of the third verse with great conviction and deep emotion.

Tilly's Song

> And tho' this world, with devils filled,
> should threaten to undo us,
> We will not fear, for God hath willed His truth
> to triumph thro' us.
> The prince of darkness grim, we tremble not for him —
> His rage we can endure, for lo, his doom is sure:
> One little word shall fell him.

Her voice grew softer but filled with resolve as she sang the last verse.

> That word above all earthly pow'rs,
> No thanks to them, abideth;
> The Spirit and the gifts are ours
> Thro' Him who with us sideth.
> Let goods and kindred go, this mortal life also —
> The body they may kill; God's truth abideth still:
> His kingdom is forever.

In silence, Marie combed her mother's hair, both busy with their own thoughts. The sacred silence was finally broken when Marie whispered into her mother's ear.

"What happened to the doctor? Why did he want to die? This is supposed to be a happy time. Christmas is happy, Mama, it is Jesus' birthday. Remember in church the pastor taught us the greatest gift from God was His son, Jesus. He brought us life. You told me when we left our home that death in this world was not the end, but each day we were in this world we were to choose life. Remember, Mama? I do. You read it to me in our German Bible. Remember, you told me you were planting the words of God into my heart and that someday, when I was older, I would understand. Mama, I'm older now. I understand Jesus told us we must be like little children in order to enter the Kingdom of God. This man was old; he would have died soon, anyway. Why did he want to die on Christmas?"

Marie had stopped combing her mother's hair and put her arms around her neck. Neither cried, but sadness came out of both of them in sighs and groans.

So Close ... Yet So Far

"Oh, My Love, I am asking those same questions. I can't begin to know all the things that led up to this man feeling such despair. What I do know is that this event must never rob you and me from the wondrous joy that Christmas brings. You and I must tend the light within us daily so it will never go out. I don't think the doctor knew he had a friend named Jesus, or else he would not have let his light go out." Mathilda took the comb from Marie's hand and continued to comb her long hair until it was dry.

Marie really didn't understand. She knew her mother wanted her to, so she kissed her on the cheek and crawled into her bed. She fidgeted until she found a comfortable place under the bed covers. Marie knew her light was still on because she could feel it inside her body; it was what kept her warm. It was almost dawn when both of them finally fell asleep.

Marie was cold and awoke shivering. The bed covers were up around her head, but her bare feet were uncovered. While rearranging her covers, she noticed her mother slip out of bed and kneel down beside her own bed. Mathilda began praying quietly aloud. It sounded more as if she was talking than praying. For a moment, Marie was confused and wondered to whom her mama was speaking.

"Oh, so much has happened; my mind is full, and my heart is heavy. Through all that has happened, the main thing my mind keeps going back to is the way that officer looked at me. He had hungry eyes, and I enjoyed the look. I am ashamed for responding to his look. My husband and two children are dead, and I'm still grieving. This night has been horrific, and my dear Marie — oh, please protect her mind from all this sorrow. I repent of these vain imaginations my mind wants to rehearse and explore. Please, let me not linger there so I will not sin. But, Lord, I don't want to be afraid, either. My heart is breaking. Give me Your words to comfort me this very hour. I can't feel Your presence. I know Mrs. O'Donner said that Your Holy Spirit did not just make us have strange feelings; however, right now, I am feeling like something is running faster than a horse inside my heart."

Mathilda lay down on the bare floor, the morning light

shining in on her through the high window. After a while, she got up off the floor and sat in the chair next to her bed. Reaching into the drawer, she pulled out the Bible and turned to Joshua 1:9 and read aloud.

"Haf I not commanded you? Be strong and courageous. Do not be terrified; do not be discouraged, for ze Lord your God will be vith you vherever you go." She closed the Bible and leaned back in the chair.

"Mama," Marie interrupted her mother's meditation, "what are hungry eyes?"

"Oh, Marie!" Mathilda sighed with embarrassment. She turned from her daughter and didn't answer.

***

The medical staff had returned to Ellis Island after their short holiday, and the place was buzzing with people talking about the night before. People who had never come close to either Mathilda or Marie were suddenly very talkative and wanting to know all the details.

"Marie, we are not going to gossip. People just want to hear all the gruesome details so they can go tell others, as if they knew all about it. You just say if anyone asks you, 'My mother doesn't want me to talk about it.' You be polite, but don't let them pick at you. Remember when our chickens would pick at one of the hens until her feathers were gone and — oh, well, don't talk to anyone about it."

"Does this mean we have a secret?" Marie was thrilled to know something that other grownups didn't know.

"Look at me, Marie. It is not a secret. People know he shot himself. We do not have to add to that fact. You and I may talk, but I don't want you to talk to anyone else about it. I'm very serious about this, Marie; you need to obey me — it is very important that you do."

"All right, Mama, I'll do what you say."

"Thank you. Marie, you are the most important person to me. I love you."

Marie responded, "I love you, too, Mama."

So Close ... Yet So Far

The day was a blur, and nighttime seemed to come quickly. Marie didn't feel very good, so Mathilda put her to bed early.

"My Love, are you awake?" Mathilda bent down and kissed Marie's ear. Seeing the wiggling under the covers, she knew Marie was awake.

"It is a bright new day. Get up and look out of the window at all the snow falling."

If Marie had been at her home in Germany, she would have skipped breakfast just to get outside to make snow angels and break off icicles. Her sister would pick them up and suck on them as they melted. Marie would then scold her sister, just as her mother had scolded her, about how dirty icicles could be. Together, they would meet the other kids their age and go sledding down the hill near their meadow. They enjoyed sliding down that old hill again and again without growing tired.

The painful reality was that there was no more home, no more kids, the sled was *who knows where*? and she was stuck inside for *how many more days?* She pulled the covers over her head and burrowed down into her warm nest.

I don't want to get up. What is there to do? There was just one problem: If she stayed there, she would wet the bed. She entertained that thought, but remembered that what was wonderfully warm soon would become freezing cold. Quickly she sprang out of bed and sprinted to the chamber pot. Then the unthinkable happened. She fell backwards, everything spilling on her and onto the floor. She was stunned! Humiliated! Tears came and she couldn't move. The crying began to crescendo when her mother quickly arrived to rescue her.

"It's all right, Marie, get up, Get UP, GET UP!"

Mathilda finally pulled Marie to her feet, stripped her nightgown off her and wrapped her in a towel. Marie received a second bath in two days, but this time, she wailed throughout the whole ordeal.

"Marie, darling, hush; you are not in trouble. You must stop crying. I am not angry. Please, My Love, calm down!"

The more her mother pleaded, the more Marie sobbed. She could not breathe through her nose, her vision was blurred and she had a headache. Her mother helped her out of the tub, wrapped her in a large towel and just held her. Together, they sat on the floor and rocked back and forth until Marie didn't have the strength to cry anymore.

Mathilda let Marie sleep until noon and then woke her so Marie could drink some tea with warmed milk and simple syrup. She used the syrup sparingly out of her tea supplies. Marie sat up and sipped the tea. *Crying can be hard work sometimes,* she thought. "I'm hungry," Marie confessed to her mother.

"Good, I'll get you some breakfast. Oh, my goodness, I'll get you some lunch. You've been a little sleepyhead — it is already past noon."

Mathilda began to sing: "Get up you little sleepyhead. Get up and out of bed. Get up, get up, my little sweet. It's time that you should eat."

Marie knew her mother was trying to cheer her up — and it worked. Her mother returned with a tray of food, and after Marie ate her lunch, her mother let her stay in bed.

Marie napped throughout the day. When she began dreaming, she had a series of nightmares. Her dreams jumped from one picture to the next.

First, she felt trapped and ran down a long hallway without doors. Next, she stood at the window watching ships sail in and crowds of people waiting in long lines. In the next scene, the window had no glass in it, so snow fell on her while she watched others talking and laughing. No one seemed to notice she was frozen in the snow. Then she saw her mother singing and laughing, hanging out towels on the clothesline; suddenly she saw her mother crying, wiping blood off her hands onto a clean white towel. Next, a man in the doorway, silhouetted by the hall light, reached out his hand to give her a peppermint stick.

Marie awoke gasping for air. She was perspiring; her mouth was dry. She saw that she was alone. She lay there for the longest time feeling nothing, seeing nothing, saying nothing. The pounding in her head caused her to call for her mother. Mathilda entered the room with another tray of food.

"Marie, I want you to sit up and eat something. Listen to

So Close ... Yet So Far

me, and do what I tell you. Get up now, My Love. That's a good girl."

Marie sat up and asked, "Mama, I need to use the chamber pot. Will you help me?"

Mathilda set the tray down on her bed and helped Marie get up. "Yes, I will. You are all right. You are doing just fine, My Love."

Marie got dressed. Eating a little food made her headache go away.

The nurse from New Jersey was back to work and bustled into the room with presents and cookies to share. There were all kinds of buttery sugar cookies cut out into shapes of bells, animals and birds. Each patient was given a little cloth drawstring bag with Christmas ribbon candy in it; Marie's favorite nurse's family had made up the treats for her patients to enjoy. One of the tins had Italian anise cookies in it for *Herr* Doctor. When the nurse heard the news of his death, she tore the nametag off the tin and took the cookies into the office, where the doctor from Baltimore was going over the details of the previous evening. The young doctor looked up from the desk and smiled at her, welcoming the distraction.

"Come in, come in," he said respectfully and motioned with his hand as he rose from his chair to greet her.

"Hello, I am Nurse Figeloni, umm, Miss Marlina Figeloni," she said, suddenly feeling shy.

"Well, Miss Marlina Figeloni, what may I do for you?" the doctor asked, almost too cheerfully.

"I have brought you some Christmas anise cookies. It is a tradition in our family to make them each year and share them with others throughout the holidays. Since this is the Feast of Stephen, I have brought these for you to enjoy." She handed him the large tin of cookies, then made a slight curtsy.

"I am grateful for your kindness. My grandmother is from Naples and always makes cookies like these for our family at Christmas time. I had to leave Baltimore and travel all day on Christmas, so I missed our holiday gathering. If you want to know the truth, I missed my nana's cookies the most. Miss Figeloni, no one could possibly appreciate your kindness more than I do right now!"

"Doctor, what is your name?" she asked, feeling less shy.

"Oh, my goodness, forgive me — ah, I know your name, but I have poor manners and have not introduced myself: Georgio Vianette, I mean, Dr. Vianette, MD. I am a pathologist. I am the doctor sent to be the interim for the late Dr. Wallace. I have been teaching at Johns Hopkins in Baltimore. That's in Maryland, but, of course, you know that, don't you? I received the telegram about the tragedy and was on the first train to New York. You see, I'm a little tired and I seem to just keep babbling on. So ..." He stuck out his hand, then pulled it back to remove his rubber glove. He stuck it out again. The nurse took his hand. He bowed and withdrew his hand. Both felt awkward. He sat down in his chair as if forgetting himself, then stood back up, since she was still standing.

"Do you have a break now so I might share these cookies with you?"

"Dr. Vianette, I just began my shift, but in two hours I could take a short break and bring you some hot tea for your cookies."

"That would be lovely. Oh, by the way, you don't need to stand on formality and call me Dr. Vianette. You can just call me ..." He paused, since he had not thought through what he was going to say. "You can just call me ... ah ... ah ... Doctor." He leaned forward and she leaned back. She turned slightly and noticed that all the patients were standing in the hallway looking into the office at them. He immediately pulled back and put on a more serious professional face. Clearing his throat, he announced to the onlookers, "Everyone can share the holiday treats at break time." Then he turned back to Nurse Figeloni. "I must speak with you about Dr. Wallace."

She suppressed her temptation to laugh and was able to curtail it into a smirky smile and answer sweetly, "Yes, doctor."

He put the cookie tin under his arm and walked quickly down the hall. The nurse turned and looked down at Marie.

"You stay right here, Marie — I have something just for you. I am so excited. You are just going to love it; I sure do. Wait right here, honey."

So Close ... Yet So Far

"Something just for me?" she questioned in disbelief. "Just for me?" Marie loved surprises, especially good surprises. She started dancing around.

Marlina returned as quickly as she promised with both hands behind her back. "Close your eyes," she commanded.

Marie obeyed. "Now open them!"

"OH! AHHHH!" There was the most beautiful doll. "Is she for me?" Marie asked, not taking her eyes off the doll.

"Yes, she is," Marlina said with great pride in her voice. On the way to the train to her home in New Jersey, she had seen this little dolly in the window in a shop in Newark. *It just had to be Marie's for Christmas,* she had told herself. The giver of this sweet treasure was as excited as the receiver, if that was possible.

"Mama!" Marie called. Her mother stopped talking with some of the patients and saw the nurse, the doll and Marie. She knew what had just happened without hearing the conversation.

"May I hold her, Marie?" Mathilda smiled in gratitude to the nurse who was watching every movement. Marie carefully handed her new doll to her mother.

"Fraulein Nurse, 'tis is such a vonderful gift for mine daughter. You are so kind to remember her like tis, and tis ist a most generous gift. Tank you."

Mathilda handed the doll back to Marie. Marie kissed it and started rocking it like a real baby. She blew a kiss, and with a big grin, forgetting all her English, said, "Fraulein Marlina, danke schön, I mean tank you." Off she ran to her bed to tell her friend about the most exciting present she could ever remember.

"I am so happy, Jesus. This is Your birthday, and I am the one getting the great presents. I am going to name her Hildegard. She can share all my secrets with You and me. She shall have tea with Mama and me, and she can come with us on our journey."

Mathilda had followed her daughter into the room and had seen and heard the whole precious scene.

She interrupted Marie's privacy when she asked, "Marie, you don't have any secrets that you haven't told me, have you?"

Her voice sounded worried.

Marie had not heard her enter the room, so she was startled to hear her mother's question. She didn't answer right away.

"Well, do you?" her mother asked a little more persistently. Marie knew she had a secret.

"My Love, I want you to come to me and tell me if something is bothering you, and together we shall seek God's help. We can handle any problem. Do you understand, My Love?" She kissed Marie on her forehead.

Marie knew the only real secret she had was the bad man on the boat. The sweet syrup for Christmas and birthday secrets were not what her mama was talking about. But still, how could she tell her mother about it? She decided she would just tell her what happened.

"Mama," she began. At that very moment, they were interrupted by the new doctor.

"Marie, wait, please. The young doctor seems to want to talk with us." Her mother now turned her attention to the doctor.

"Mrs. Baumann," he called, waving some papers at her as he approached. "Oh, I am so glad you are right here. I just found your paperwork, and I have a good report. You and your child shall be leaving Ellis Island right after the first of the New Year. This gives me time to submit your paperwork and summon the Lutheran Ladies' Missionary Aid Society. I shall be most honored to escort you and your daughter to Manhattan on the ferry and then see you to Grand Central Station to meet with some ladies of this group. I shall be returning to Baltimore at that time. I am informed that the ladies just received an unexpected letter of introduction from a pastor in Hamburg about you and your daughter. It had been sent all the way to Chicago and now back to New York City. I find this to be a most serendipitous event, don't you?"

Mathilda did not understand his big words, but she did understand the words LEAVING ELLIS ISLAND. Her mind had stopped hearing him after that, and her spirit was singing!

So Close ... Yet So Far

In der Fremde, Opus 39:1 (In a Foreign Land) Music by Robert Schumann and lyrics by Joseph von Eichendorff. The essence of the song is "I shall die here, far from home, and no one will miss me." The word *Waldeinsamkeit* is an invented compound word carrying the idea that solitude in a forest is different from elsewhere. The singer expects to be buried in a forest, like an animal, rather than in a cemetery. This song expresses the carnal groaning of extreme despair.

Allerseelen, music by Richard Strauss and lyrics by Hermann von Gilm. All Souls' Day, November 2nd, is the occasion for this song. The meaning of the song is "Our love was long ago, but let us remember it, just for today."

Chapter 5
We Are Free!

"Mrs. Baumann, may I ask you candidly how you were treated during your confinement at Ellis Island?"

The waiter arrived with a cart full of pastries and refilled Marie's cup with hot cocoa. The Lutheran ladies waited for their teacups to be refilled. Mathilda swallowed her bite of cake and answered.

"Madam," she began, thinking carefully how to use the very best English she could muster, "I hoff no complaints. Ve vere showed many kindnesses. Tank you for askin." She smiled shyly, quickly sipping her tea.

Another woman spoke up. "Mrs. Baumann, you are most gracious, but I just do not know if I could be confined to one place as long as you were."

Mathilda reached out and touched the lady's gloved hand. "Mine gut voman, at firs' I thought I shoult go mad. I luf zee out-of-doors, even in ze vinter, but after I surrendered mine self-pity, I saw in many ways God's plan in all of zis. May I share vhat I hoff learnd from our stay at Ellis Island? Pleaz forgife me, mine Anglish is not so gut."

The ladies nodded their heads in agreement.

"Mine child und me hav been frew zee whole sorrow of zee death off our beloved family und friendz and never hat zee time off mournin, because ve hadt to movf so speedily, und, vit no beast of burden fur so many dayz, I had to pull zee cart to Hamburg. Vit zee boat ve sail to Belgium und getz aboart a ship to America. Dis whole trip vas sickness from da sea, und mine Lord Jesus knowed I vould not rest on mine own, zo He allowed zis time to be such dat mine had gut rest." Her mouth was dry, so she sipped the now cold tea.

The lady who was the leader of the group spoke up while Mathilda took her drink. "My dear, your English is very understandable. Please continue."

We Are Free!

Marie was eating her third pastry, and the sweetness was causing her to feel a little lightheaded. She knew that her English was better than her mother's, and she could see that her mother needed a break. She leaned over to her and asked, "Mama, may I tell them about our friend who taught us English?" Mathilda looked surprised, but quickly gave a smile of approval.

"My mother and I met the nicest woman sent by God to help us. She taught us English from the Bible. She also taught us how to knit, tat and crochet so we would not get bored. Nurses were kind to us and brought us Christmas presents, and we had tea and even sang. One nice lady gave me my dolly, Hildegard, and another gave Mama some sweet syrup for her tea." Marie held up her doll so all the ladies could see.

"Oh, how lovely!"

Mathilda smiled at Marie with adoration and continued to speak, regaining her courage and composure. "Dis kind voman prayed vith us dat zee Holy Spirit vould come und change us. I see mine troubles being turned into gut, vhich is God's promise. Mine dear sisters, I am blessed vit your friendship and generosity and all because of God's grace and mercy in all of zis. I confess to you dat God, Jesus und His Spirit are so very real to mine life, und Christ ist mine strength und joy, in knowing His great love to me." Mathilda finished and wiped her eyes with her napkin. All the ladies sat quietly, except for the occasional sniffle.

The leader of the group rose to her feet and announced, "I should love to stay and hear more of this testimony, but, my dear, the call for your train has been made. Oh, before I forget, I also have a letter for you from Hamburg. It was sent to you in care of my address by way of Chicago. I pray it is full of happiness and encouragement. Now, do you have all your necessary papers and your tickets?"

"Ja, I do. Tank you, madams, all you nice vomens, for your gracious hospitality," Mathilda said, smiling and giving a quick curtsy. Marie blew kisses to all the women as they huddled around the two and walked them out of the tea shop toward the tracks marked for the Chicago departure.

Tilly's Song

Grand Central Station was full of immigrants from, it seemed, every country of the world. The ladies moved like a military shield, protecting their two very important companions. The conductor called out, through the noise of the crowd, "ALL ABOARD!"

The eldest woman took Mathilda's hand as they reached the designated train car. "Blessings upon you as you start anew in this country and in your new home. We have given you the names and addresses of those in Wilmette, Illinois, who have promised to give you employment, room and board. Go now; 'Let your light so shine before men, that they may see your good works, and glorify your Father, which is in heaven.' You are in our prayers."

Mathilda took Marie by the hand and helped her onto the steps of the train. Mathilda kept wiping her eyes and saying "Tank you" over and over until the train started to move. Both waved one last time and finally disappeared into the coach car to find their seats on the train. Looking out of the window, Marie blew kisses until the ladies were out of her sight. She busied herself looking at the city as it began to move past her in increasing speed. The gentle movement and the sound of the train whistle began to make her drowsy. She snuggled close to her mother and fell asleep. Mathilda stared out the window while she played with Marie's hair. She was finally on her way to the place she would call home for the rest of her life.

It was now her time of privacy so she could read the letter. Opening the envelope, she already knew it was from her dear friend, Beatrice.

Dear Mathilda,

May this letter find you and Marie within the freedom of the perfect will of our Heavenly Father. We received a letter from Mrs. Carlisle, telling of your severe circumstances of confinement at Ellis Island. Oh, my dearest Sister, be of good cheer, and do not give up hope. You must remember that you were given specific instruction to go to America, and God is always faithful to His promises and guidance. We are holding you in our prayers and asking that the Holy Spirit will continue to minister to you and give you comfort. Whenever I am tempted to be afraid, it always helps me to read some of the Psalms. You must look them up in your Bible and take these scriptures as food for your heart. In Psalms 27, 31 and 37:3-8, David confesses his fear. You must remember all Jesus has brought you through, and know He is not finished with you. You must help advance the kingdom of God, as only you can, for your Savior. Use this time of confinement to rest and heal. Take every opportunity to learn about this new country that God has brought you to, and serve others that may truly be ill. My love, do not lean on your own understanding, nor your own strength. Lean only on the Lord, and all will improve. Suffering is part of life that must be endured. Remember that no baby can be born without suffering by both mother and child. Our life here on earth is much like this; we suffer for a while, but what is that to eternity? Let your suffering be an act of worship, and share in the suffering of our Lord Jesus Christ, so that you shall also share in His great joy and His abundant life.

Oh, there is so much to tell you. The cart you gave us for carrying food to the widows and orphans, the children painted a gay yellow color and have named it the "Sunshine Wagon." Our youngest son, Herman, says it will be used to bring light into the dark lives of so many who need food, clothing and friendship.

The girls still pray specifically for Marie at bedtime and also in our daily prayer time. Mathilda, each day I wait to see the miracles that God has for our little flock. Many of our brothers and sisters are trying to go to America to meet their families who are already established. Many wicked men steal from these poor souls who, like you, sell almost everything to pay for passage to New York City. The money seems to always come, no matter what the rate is raised to be. The miracles of food are continuous, and my husband says that as long as we are willing to take time to visit those in need, God *will use us to meet that need. Mathilda, I saw this with my own eyes. We had little food to take to our lonely elderly women, but all received a portion, yet at the end of the day there was enough food left for my family's evening meal. We were all so very tired. Joy overcame our fatigue, giving us strength to prepare our meal with laughter and song. I even had enough strength to clean our home and scrub the floors. That night, the fragrance of the Lord was everywhere within our home.*

Gretchen and Hans, who provide us with milk and butter, send their greetings of love and prayers to you. Kristen and Paul ask about you; they have eight children and yet faithfully pay tithes to the church in currency. Herr Mueller asked me to tell you he has a nephew who owns a grocery store in the Chicago area. The Mussons' son, who you prayed for while you were here, is well and back to work. So many good things are happening, even though these are perilous times in Hamburg. We had such a wondrous time when you were here, and I miss you. I know we shall be the best of friends in our home in heaven. I do so look forward to Christ's return and continuing life through eternity. Know you are never alone, always loved and in our thoughts and prayers. "I can do all things through Christ who gives me strength."

Your sister in Christ,
Beatrice

Mathilda treasured this message of reassurance as she resumed the journey. When Marie awoke from her nap, the city was far behind them. She sat up and looked out the window to see big tufts of cotton-like snow falling slowly from the sky. The only sound was the rhythm of the train.

"Well, hello, sleepyhead. You slept a long while," Mathilda commented, smiling at Marie. "I must have snoozed along with you. I'm hungry; are you?" She folded the treasured letter and placed it back into its envelope. Marie snuggled back into her warm cozy place next to her mother and rubbed the sleep from her eyes.

We Are Free!

"Yes, Mama, I'm so hungry. What do we have to eat?" she asked with a yawn and a stretch. She quickly recoiled to her mother's side to await the answer.

"Well, let's see what the kind ladies packed for us to eat." She opened the oilcloth bag and began pulling food out of it. "Oh! We have two red apples, some summer sausage, two kinds of cheese, six hard-cooked eggs, two large dill pickles, some sliced pumpernickel bread, a dozen cookies, oh, and look — some tea in a small tin and another tin of chocolates. Oh, merciful Father, this is a grand feast!"

Mathilda had no sooner said that when out of nowhere appeared two little boys standing in the aisle with big sad blue eyes looking first at Mathilda, then at the bag.

She took a cookie and broke it in half and handed one half to each boy. They disappeared to wherever they had come from, without a sound. There was an amusing unspoken moment between Mathilda and Marie after what just happened. They gave thanks for the wonderful bounty; their hearts were glad to share this good blessing.

Mathilda offered a little bit of everything to Marie, but for herself, she ate little. She was unsure how many meals this bag would provide for them.

Moments after they finished their food, the train began to slow, then, with a bump came to a complete stop. People were getting off the train, and others were getting on. A rotund woman whispered into Mathilda's ear, "My dear, there are toilets in the depot, so if you have need of one, quickly get off and then back onto the train. We should be here for a short while."

Mathilda gathered her things, and with Marie by her side, she followed the woman into the depot. In the washroom, they freshened up, and before they boarded the train, each enjoyed some tea from a vendor's cart.

"It feels good to walk and stretch and get some fresh air. Go and run to the end of the depot and then come back to me, Marie."

Marie was thrilled to have permission to run and skip. When the first whistle blew, however, they scrambled back onto the train. Awake and refreshed, the two sat in their assigned seats and greeted the new passengers as they looked for the numbers on the empty seats.

The train made several stops, and they disembarked each time. It seemed wise to move about and to freshen up whenever they had a chance. Washing some of the dirt from travel off their faces and hands made the trip more enjoyable. Each time they boarded the train, a man would come through and check the new passengers' tickets. Each time he passed Marie, he gave her a wink.

"Mama, may I give that nice man half of my cookie?" Marie asked politely.

"That would be nice!"

The next time the conductor came through the train car, he winked again at Marie.

"Mister, would you like to share my cookie?" He looked surprised when she spoke to him; then, smiling so wide that he showed his teeth, he asked, "Little lady, you want to share your cookie with me?"

"Yes, I do. Here." She handed him the bigger portion she had broken off. He took the cookie and with one bite it disappeared into his mustached mouth. Chewing vigorously, he nodded and tipped his hat first to Marie and then to Mathilda.

"Missus, she is not only a pretty one, but she's charmin' as well. Thank you." He smacked his lips and made yummy sounds as he walked away. Marie started to giggle as she heard him talking to himself. "I sure do like my job, yes, sir, I do, in a mighty way, like my job!" Marie looked over at her mother, and together, they burst into laughter.

The next stop was to add sleeper cars onto the train. Mathilda and Marie shared an upper bunk. Marie was careful to make sure Hildegard was dressed in the washcloth gown made by her mama. They reviewed their whole day with gratitude.

Marie couldn't remember falling asleep while talking to Jesus, but she awoke when she felt the train stop again. After Mathilda, Marie and Hildegard dressed, they gathered their things and headed back to the coach car to reclaim their assigned seats. The nice conductor was there, taking tickets while the sleeper cars were being uncoupled from the train. He stopped and whispered something into Mathilda's ear. She smiled at Marie and said, "We are going to the dining car." They followed the man as he showed them to their table and held the chair for each to be seated. A waiter, the color of chocolate, showed up with a pot of tea for each of them. However, when Mathilda poured from Marie's teapot, there was no tea. Instead it was hot, delicious cocoa.

"Goodness! What a treat! Blow on it — it looks really hot," Mathilda cautioned Marie.

Next the waiter brought warm hard rolls, butter and strawberry jam. Feeling like fine ladies, they sat up straight, looking around at all the royal service. Mathilda looked at the nice conductor, a question in her eye. He read the question and said simply, "One good deed deserves another." He and the waiter both smiled and left the ladies to their dining enjoyment.

"Mama," Marie began with bread and jam in her mouth.

"Marie, finish swallowing before you try to talk."

After Marie enjoyed several sips of warm cocoa and half the bread and jam, she finished, saying, "Mama, I like America. Don't you?"

The scenery changed every day as the train snaked along the tracks, steadily moving westward. Thick black smoke belched out of the engine, forming sinister clouds. Yesterday much of the pastoral terrain was covered in a blanket of snow and dotted with dairy cows. Suddenly, today's journey took them through rich flat river-bottom farmland where crops would be growing in the springtime. Towns and cities along the way soiled with coal dust contrasted with the pure white snow of the countryside.

At each stop, passengers came aboard. All kinds of freight was also loaded onto the train: livestock, furniture, machinery and every other imaginable thing that people in Chicago would want. Muscular railroad men worked quickly to load everything on the train and keep on schedule.

When Mathilda came to fetch Marie, the men started whistling and snapping their fingers. Never in all her life had Mathilda experienced such behavior, not even at the Autumn Festival when the whole village had seemed to drink up far too much of their fermented harvest.

The coach car, where they spent all day, varied between two temperatures: stifling hot and freezing cold. When the passengers complained the coach was too cold, one of the porters would come and add coal to the wall heater. The heater would get so hot the metal grid would glow red. This devil, it seemed, would eat up every particle of breathable air. In order to breathe, one of the passengers would open a window for a moment or two, letting in cold air along with coal ash and the awful smell from the train's engine. The coach car would then grow cold, and the hot/cold cycle repeated.

Eventually they were traveling through an area where, even when the windows were closed, the smell seemed to leak into the cars. The cold wind carried the dense smell of Chicago's cattle and pigs from the well-known slaughterhouses. These were all at the edge of town close to the railroad tracks for convenient loading. The awful stink blew right through the closed window into Marie's nose. Whenever she thought the smell unbearable, the north wind blew, sweeping the stink away. The rocking train moved to a new section of the city with smells from factories and businesses.

The conductor entered into the coach car. In a loud voice, he announced, "CHICAGO, FINAL STOP! CHICAGO DEPOT, ALL OUT WHEN THE TRAIN COMES TO A COMPLETE STOP! CHICAGO, FOLKS, FINAL STOP!"

Mathilda and Marie just looked at each other. There were no words.

Chapter 6
A New Life in a New Home

Surrounded by the confusion of a hurrying crowd, Mathilda realized she needed to communicate in English. All the words she had spent so many hours learning seemed to escape her memory. She had never used a map before, and the directions to get from the Chicago Railroad Depot to the Carlisle residence in Chicago's North Shore community of Wilmette seemed more impossible than sailing across the Atlantic Ocean to New York City.

Mathilda sat on the depot bench with her sleepy daughter's head in her lap and all of her worldly goods at her feet. Again, fear put his icy fingers on her mind. Her body trembled so much she could not even read the directions from the paper she held. These directions were to the house where she would be employed. So far the whole journey seemed like a blur, but she still had not arrived at her final destination.

The hordes of people milling about were oppressive to her. She was cold, tired, hungry and nauseated at the same time. Her clothes smelled of body odor and train smoke. Her arms felt like lead, and her feet needed special encouragement just to move. A sinking feeling sucked her down into a dangerous whirlpool of fatigue.

"Nonsense!" she spoke in perfect English.

This is just fatigue, and I shall not give into it, she thought. *It is only by God's grace that we are here, and His grace is sufficient to get us all the way to our destination. Listen to me, Mr. Fear, you old enemy of my soul, I shall not give up so easily. Now, my comforter, my strength in time of need, my counselor and friend, I call on You this very moment to help me find the place You have planned for Marie and me.*

A voice from behind her spoke; she jumped in alarm at having her thoughts interrupted. "Madam, do you need some assistance?"

Mathilda turned around and looked up at a young man. He stood with a clipboard in his hand; he had a mature air, even though he looked barely 20 years old. "May I introduce myself? I am Carl Schultz, employed by the City of Chicago to assist travelers. Forgive me for my boldness, but you looked as if you might need some assistance. May I help you somehow?" He bowed slightly and almost smiled, then quickly caught himself and remained quite sober.

Mathilda asked him in German if he could tell her how to get to the Carlisle home. He answered all her questions in her native tongue and listened to why and how she had come to the Chicago area.

Young Carl knew Chicago's North Shore area very well. He instructed her to board the Chicago and North Western Railway to Wilmette, and then explained the best route to the Carlisle home. After he had rehearsed the directions with Mathilda and saw that she had confidence to make the journey, he bowed slightly again and gave her some tokens for the C&NW Railway, then bade her farewell.

"Pleaz forgif me, I am not sure vat to do. Do you require some monies fur dis helping me?" Mathilda shyly asked.

He answered her in perfect English. "Good woman, I get paid for this service. You owe me nothing."

Reaching into her oilcloth bag, she pulled out some cookies left from the trip and offered them to him.

He declined her offer, instead wishing her Godspeed. She watched him move quickly to another German-looking family who were weighed down with bundles and bewilderment.

Marie was unaware of any of this as she slept peacefully on the depot bench. Mathilda woke her gently. "Marie, you must wake up, My Love — we are taking another train."

Rubbing her eyes and stretching her arms over her head, Marie yawned. "Where are we, Mama?"

Mathilda motioned to her. "Come quickly." Marie followed obediently and held onto her mother's skirts as they boarded the crowded train.

The train stopped at Lake Avenue, just short of the Wilmette depot, where they disembarked. Carrying all they owned, they walked to the Carlisle home. Mathilda rang the bell at the back door.

A tall, cheerful woman with red cheeks and sparkling eyes invited them into the kitchen.

"Come in, come in, and welcome to ya both. I am so happy ya are finally here. God bless ya both. My, my, ya look so cold! Come, come and warm yurselves. My name is Mattie Johnson." She turned and, with a volume that startled both Mathilda and Marie, yelled at the top of her lungs, "AGATHA!" Another woman appeared instantly.

"Yes, Miz Johnsun?"

"Agatha, I would like ya to meet Mrs. Baumann and her daughter, Marie." Agatha curtsied, bumping her knee on the floor, and then jumped back up straight with a flush of embarrassment on her face.

"Oh, we have been a-prayin' ya'd get here soon. Let me help you with your bags." She smiled at the weary travelers. Marie smiled back, noticing one of Agatha's front teeth stuck out whenever she wasn't smiling.

Hmm ... Agatha ... funny tooth, Marie thought.

Miz Johnson was looking them over with a critical eye to see if they needed to freshen before meeting the mistress of the home. "Let me show ya to your room. Come now, follow me. Miz Carlisle wants to meet ya both, so I'll take ya to her next. Oh, goodness me, I'm forgettin' me manners. Would ya want to have a warm drink or to use the toilet?" Mathilda just nodded in agreement. Miz Johnson was talking so fast it was hard to understand everything she was telling them.

Mathilda was tired and felt dizzy. Soap, water and a washbasin were in the bedroom assigned to them. After they freshened up, they joined Miz Johnson in the kitchen for some tea and sandwiches. Marie was so hungry she ate two whole sandwiches. Mathilda seemed more thirsty than hungry. Marie and Miz Johnson both noticed that Mathilda's hand shook when she held her teacup, but no one mentioned it.

"Let's meet Miz Carlisle, so ya two can come back to yur room and rest a bit. I can't imagine the trip ya two have been on, it wearing to the bone and all. Now, don't mind me, I just chortle on and on whenever I gets the least bit excited like, and, well, I'm just so excited ya are finally here, well and in one piece an' all! Are ya ready to meet Miz Carlisle?"

"Yes, madam, we are!" Mathilda answered, finding a short pause in Miz Johnson's rambling.

Miz Johnson turned and looked at the two standing in the hallway. "We'll be climbin' some stairs to get to the second floor where the study is located. This here house has four floors, not countin' a basement where Mr. Carlisle works on things. The bedrooms for the family are all on the third floor, and the music room and studies are on the second floor. First floor is the formal living room, parlor, dining room, kitchen and pantry — and, of course, your room. Miz Carlisle has her sewin' room in the little room on the top floor. Oh, I know ya won't remember it all, but you'll soon learn; it's not hard. Oh my! Listen to me talkin' your ears off. Well, now, here we are."

She stopped at the open door of the study. Marie looked up the next flight of stairs and saw three children's faces peeking at her through the slats of the banister. Two of them were boys, and the littlest was a girl. A lovely sounding woman's voice came from inside the study in response to Miz Johnson rapping on the doorframe.

"Mattie ... ah, Mrs. Johnson ... are they here?" the voice asked excitedly.

"Oh, yes, ma'am," Mattie answered with such exuberance that Marie thought she might fall forward.

A petite, neatly dressed woman appeared at the door and rushed to shake Mathilda's hand. "Hello and welcome! My name is Mrs. Carlisle." She then bent over and put her hand under Marie's chin to look at her face. "Hello, are you Marie?" Marie smiled at her.

"Mrs. Baumann, our family and our housekeeper, Mattie Johnson, have prayed you and your daughter would arrive here safe and without harsh circumstances. I do know your travel was long and arduous. I wanted to meet you, but not keep you. Now go with Mrs. Johnson and bathe, eat, relax and rest. I shall see you tomorrow, and then I shall introduce you to my husband, children and staff. You shall hear our needs, and we shall learn of yours, and then we shall arrange a most satisfying working relationship. We offer you and your daughter a Christian haven and will pay you a proper salary. Please know you are welcome; I bid you a good evening." She turned and disappeared back into her study.

Mathilda did feel welcome, but she was so tired and relieved to finally be at the end of her journey that she was unable to feel anything else. Twice that evening she almost fell asleep in her bath. She looked at Marie, already sound asleep in her very own bed, in their very own private room. Mathilda's prayer was short but genuine. *Thank You, Heavenly Father.* She was asleep before her head hit the pillow.

The next morning seemed to come early. Mathilda and Marie dressed, ate a bite of breakfast and made their way to Mrs. Carlisle's office. As they mounted the stairs, they overheard a loud conversation.

"Franklin, you know the smell of that cigar upsets me. Would you be kind and not smoke around me before this child is born?"

"Ellie, don't start scolding me!"

"Oh, Franklin! I wouldn't scold if you were more considerate. You seem to receive some sort of cruel pleasure by tormenting me with that smelly cigar. Why must you push me to the point where I lose my temper?"

"My God, Eleanor, I'll put out the damned cigar!"

"Shhh! The children will hear you swearing."

"Eleanor, my sweet, sweet, Ellie." He grit his teeth. "It is really difficult to be around you when you are like this."

"Franklin!" she yelled, her anger escalating. That flash of anger quickly changed to hurt feelings. Not willing to accept defeat, she whimpered. "Oh! Very well, then." With a long sigh, she continued. "I hope your old stinky cigar and brandy keep you warm tonight, since I'm so hard to be with when … when … I'm so miserable."

The tears began to stream down her cheeks as she reached up her sleeve to retrieve her handkerchief. Her distress from misplacing her hanky was compounded by her inability to find a towel or anything else to use to wipe her eyes and nose. More than angry about the absence of a handkerchief, she was disappointed that she could not have a simple disagreement without tears. Eleanor was confident and knowledgeable enough to argue, debate and intellectually grapple with most educated men ... except when she was pregnant. It was then that her emotions ruled.

It is so hard to be a woman sometimes, she thought.

Franklin reluctantly accepted defeat, again. His conscience revealed there was a barb of truth in her whining. It pricked his heart to acknowledge that he continued doing the things she asked him over and over not to do. He didn't believe he was a cruel person; however, he did feel somehow strangely powerful to see his wife, normally strong and self-controlled, in a weakened condition. *What a disgusting thought. Tell her you are sorry, Frank!* he told himself.

"Ellie, darling, I'm sorry."

"No, you're NOT," Eleanor snapped, "or you wouldn't keep doing it over and over. Franklin, this is our fourth child. With each of these babies, I have told you the smell of alcohol on your breath and the smell of cigar smoke in the rooms MAKES ME VOMIT! You know this, and yet you keep doing it. WHY?"

"I don't know, Ellie, I don't know. Just stop crying. I hate it when you do that."

He moved closer to reach out and touch her. She bristled at his advance and moved away from his reach.

"I hate it, too, but I just get so angry. If I don't cry ... I'd, I'd ... I don't know what I'd do!"

"Would it help to go for a walk?"

"Franklin! It is blowing snow outside! It is freezing out there! No! NO! NO! I don't want to go for a walk! I want to be able to breathe in my own house!"

He turned his back to her and her angry voice. As he quickly headed for the door, he mumbled, "There is no talking to her whenever she is like this." In his haste, he didn't even see Mathilda and Marie. Franklin bumped right into Marie and knocked her off her feet. Shocked and embarrassed, he bent over to help her up. "Oh, good gracious, did I hurt you? Please forgive me!"

A New Life in a New Home

Hearing the commotion, Eleanor rushed out into the hallway and was horrified to see her husband helping the child to her feet. She shot him a disgusted look, but did not say a word.

Franklin looked sheepishly at Mathilda and spoke to her. "Madam, forgive me for my careless mood and boorish actions. My wife and I were … um … well, you no doubt heard some, if not all, of our argument. I assure you this is not our normal discourse. Well, um … I hope you will accept my sincere apology." He avoided looking at her. He then turned to his wife, walked toward her, took her hand and kissed it. "Mrs. Carlisle, my dearest Eleanor, I give you my sincerest apology. Can you … will you forgive me for being such a brute?" He looked directly into her eyes.

"Yes, yes, of course!" She was unconvincing. After an uncomfortable pause, she turned to Mathilda, placing her hand gently on her shoulder, and announced, "Franklin, may I introduce you to Mrs. Mathilda Baumann and her daughter, Marie. They arrived late yesterday afternoon. They have come to us all the way from Northern Germany."

Doing his best to show good manners and overcome his embarrassment, he bowed slightly to both of them. "I am very pleased to make your acquaintance, Mrs. Baumann, and yours, also, Marie!"

Mathilda, shocked by the whole scene, failed to meet him with a smile. She finally gave him a quick curtsy. After his awkward welcome, he turned quickly, descended the stairs and was out the front door.

Eleanor Carlisle asked Mathilda to come into her study and sit down while she began explaining to her the duties of the job. Marie found the domestic drama entertaining, but now that it was over, she wandered over to the window and looked down at the driveway. The weather was cold, and it was snowing. She noticed Mr. Carlisle standing by the street. He was hailing a horse-drawn cab and smoking his cigar.

Eleanor Carlisle was an educated, disciplined and creative woman. She was first generation American, and her family ties were in the meatpacking industry, one of the industries to put Chicago, Illinois, on the map. Her father and uncle had come from Munich, Germany, and had become resourceful romantics by marrying sisters whose father was a railroad tycoon. In addition to inheriting a fortune from their father-in-law, the brothers became very wealthy on their own. When their children were old enough, the brothers sent them abroad to Europe to study the fine arts.

Eleanor was gifted with natural beauty and uncommon intelligence. She had met Franklin in London and, after a whirlwind romance, had announced their engagement to the higher society of Chicago.

Franklin Carlisle came from old money that had been all but spent. His family was overjoyed with his marriage to Eleanor. She was beautiful, yet not vain; brilliant, yet not conceited; wealthy, yet not showy; and generous to a fault. Her faith was genuine and was revealed in her attitudes and consistent behavior. Her most endearing quality to Franklin was that she dearly loved him and considered him her best friend. She was longsuffering with his mother's unending bragging and his father's unfounded advice giving.

Eleanor was even overly tolerant of Franklin's prodigal brother, Lawrence Carlisle. Lawrence had a reputation for gambling, drinking in excess and having a wandering eye for the ladies. Yes, dear Uncle Larry, as he was known by the Carlisle children, was quite a character.

Sweet Eleanor had no trouble giving attention and affection to all the members of her beloved's family. However, Franklin oscillated from being incredibly embarrassed to being quite annoyed with his parents and younger brother.

Even though the in-laws had a home of their own in Chicago, each had their own bedroom in Franklin and Eleanor's home. Grandma Carlisle would come and stay for weeks, and then whenever she missed her covey of friends and their hen parties, she would leave for home at a whim. Franklin would go for days without even interacting with his mother, except at dinnertime, and then only because he saw no way to avoid the situation. Eleanor covered for him in those situations and truly was the blessed peacemaker.

Brother, or rather Uncle Larry, was quite another story. He

A New Life in a New Home

seemed to always be in trouble with his brother, who found him to be a constant embarrassment. Lawrence went out each day, as one would go to work, but no one was really sure where he went or what he did to make a living. The man had but two moods: up, meaning very happy, loud and outrageous, and down, meaning sullen, crabby or totally incommunicado.

Eleanor took Uncle Larry on as her major prayer concern. Her hope and reasoning was that, at another time in history, a man called Brother Lawrence had given his whole body, mind and spirit to Christ. She believed that God is no respecter of persons and that what He had done then, in that man's life, God was equally able to do now, in her own brother-in-law's life.

Her second major prayer concern was helping German immigrants see God's love. Eleanor saw both concerns as her life work, but the work with the immigrants had become her mission. She helped develop an extensive network between the Lutheran ministers in the German motherland and the American Lutheran Ladies' Aid Society. She was successful in finding employment that paid well for German families arriving from a depressed economy in Europe. Although Franklin was not involved with this mission as much as his wife, he fully embraced it and gave constant encouragement to her. Together, they had agreed to open their own home to train new immigrants and provide them a safe haven.

The goal for the Germans who received training in their home was to retain the customs of Germany while becoming completely American. To obtain this goal, a specific set of objectives was established for each immigrant. All were to learn a workable skill, to meet other Christians, to form friendships, to learn English and to earn money. Eleanor and Franklin believed it providential to do these things at this particular time in history. They took this mission very seriously and claimed the scripture, Matthew 25:34-40, to validate their deep commitment.

Eleanor loved reading aloud this scripture to each family that came through her home. In a tender and melodious voice, she read to Mathilda and Marie what had been etched on her heart for years:

"Then the King will say unto them on His right hand, 'Come, ye blessed of My Father, inherit the kingdom prepared for you from the foundation of the world; for I was hungered, and you gave Me meat; I was thirsty, and ye gave Me drink; I was a stranger, and you took Me in; naked, and ye clothed Me; I was sick, and ye visited Me; I was in prison, and ye came unto Me.'

"Then shall the righteous answer Him, saying, 'Lord, when saw Thee hungered, and fed Thee? or thirsty, and gave Thee drink? When saw we Thee a stranger, and took Thee in? or naked, and clothed Thee? Or when saw we Thee sick, or in prison, and came unto Thee?' And the King shall answer and say unto them, 'Verily, I say unto you, inasmuch as ye have done it unto one of the least of these brethren, ye have done it unto Me.'"

Brushing a tear off her cheek, she cleared her throat and announced, "This scripture explains why my husband and I have opened our home to you."

She then motioned to Mathilda to join her at her desk that had a calendar and a stack of paper, neatly placed, for correspondence with the members of her network. She shared with both mother and child her schedule, Monday through Thursday.

WEEKLY SCHEDULE

1. Breakfast is shared with her husband and children.
2. The children see their father to the door as he goes off to work at the bank.
3. The children spend three hours with their mother, playing and reading; then they all rest for one hour.
4. Lunch is shared with the workers so Mrs. Carlisle may fellowship with them.
5. From 1 p.m. to 3 p.m. the children are cared for by their nanny, while Mrs. Carlisle, in her office, is not to be disturbed. She works on her necessary correspondence, community work and church projects.
6. At 3 p.m. Mrs. Carlisle has refreshments with her children and then bathes them, to make ready to receive

A New Life in a New Home

their father. He returns home from the office anywhere from 5 p.m. to 5:15 p.m. Once the children have greeted their father and have played with him, they are fed and watched by their nanny.
7. Mr. and Mrs. Carlisle dine alone or with houseguests from 7 p.m. to 8 p.m. After supping, they pray with the children and tuck them into bed.
8. Visitors are never received Monday through Thursday until 9 p.m. The visitors are to leave no later than 10 p.m.

The weekend schedule was filled with entertaining and church attendance. At least once a month, especially those months with holidays, the home was open to friends and guests. This meant additional planning, cleaning, decorating and food preparation. Sunday, of course, the household was encouraged to attend church, and transportation was provided to Bethlehem Lutheran Church in Evanston. A cold lunch was prepared Saturday for the following day, and every Sunday evening a different family from the church was invited to dine with the Carlisle family. This was the only evening the children ate with their parents.

Mathilda began to feel Mrs. Carlisle's orientation was more like a military briefing. Overwhelmed by all the strange new activities, she found it difficult to stretch her mind to meet the demands of this very busy and overly organized large household. She felt her mind wander, while she still heard Mrs. Carlisle talk about dishes and linens and the polishing of silver.

Mathilda's mind floated back to her home in Germany. It had only two rooms. She kept it tidy, neat and orderly. Most of her chores she completed out-of-doors, weather permitting. She realized how simple her life had been compared to that of the Carlisle household. They grew most of their own food. Entertaining was not usually held inside their home; instead it was with all the parishioners of their one home church. The finest china — the only china — was her treasured teapot set, given to her as a wedding present. The idea of living amid such opulence was frightening to her. All this scheduling seemed like too much work. Children scheduled with one parent and then with the other seemed very odd to her way of thinking. In her own family, the children were either in the house with her or running in the meadow playing with their father. How were she and her young daughter, Marie, going to fit in with all this busyness? Mrs. Carlisle's voice grew louder, interrupting her thoughts.

"Mrs. Baumann, it is important that you remember that we have three sets of china. One is for everyday use, Monday through Thursday. Another is used for large parties, and the finest dinnerware is used on the Lord's Day."

Although the house was lit with lamps, requiring oil, Mrs. Carlisle went on to say that she insisted that Sunday dinner be eaten by candlelight. Even though it was not customary for children to come with their parents to such social gatherings, Mrs. Carlisle enjoyed the old European hospitality when guests were honored as "just one of the family" and made to feel comfortable with food and conversation.

"I must tell you (I am so amused by this) when Franklin and I first started inviting church members over to our home for Sunday evening dinner, many of our guests felt somewhat awkward because they had never eaten with their own children. Doesn't that almost seem comical to you, my dear?" Eleanor laughed as if she had heard a funny joke. Looking at Mathilda to observe her reaction to an attempt at humor, she met a face that looked stunned and without expression. Eleanor quickly changed her mood and became aware of the needs of her new arrival.

"Mathilda, may I call you by your first name?" she asked.

"Oh, jah, pleaz. I shall be here wiz you as your servant, and I need not be treated wiz formality," Mathilda shyly responded, bowing her head. Eleanor looked at this dear woman, who was clueless as to the workings of any large household, and read the look of bewilderment upon Mathilda's face.

"One thing Franklin and I feel strongly about is that the people in our employment are to be called and thought of as employees, or workers, not servants. You see, Mathilda, you and I are both servants. You work here because I need your help, but I work for you to see that your goals are met and that, in God's perfect will, your dreams come true. All of our employees are temporary. This is your starting place where you can learn. It is our hope you will save money to buy things of your own. Ultimately, you should save enough to purchase property. It all is up to you how fast you learn English and domestic skills. In this area of Chicago, there are affluent families who can pay you for your skill. Mathilda, when I look at you, I see a lovely, proud woman, who has nothing to be ashamed of and much to offer this whole household. You come to us with letters of introduction, informing us of your great courage and Christ-like humility — traits I can neither train you to have nor give you. I sense you have a great deal to teach us while you are here, and I submit to you to be one of your most loyal students." Eleanor took Mathilda's hands in hers and gave her an affectionate smile.

"Tank you." Mathilda smiled. She then moved one of her hands to brush a tear away.

In the Carlisle household, most of the workers were widows or older orphans. The men of the families were offered jobs in the meatpacking plants, or as livestock workers in the stockyards. The more skilled and educated men were groomed for work in the bank where Mr. Carlisle served as First Vice-President. It was an accepted fact that upon the President's forthcoming retirement, Franklin Carlisle would step up to replace him. Frank was quick to claim he was not superior, only greatly blessed. This seemed to cause even more envy in the circle of acquaintances he held, as no one could find fault in him or his wife.

The only gossip that held any truth was about his wayward brother. The Carlisles' family, his mother said, had come over on the Mayflower, but his German ancestors had come to fight the British during the Revolutionary War. None of the bloodlines meant anything to Frank; he had been blood-bought by his Savior Jesus Christ in his early 20s, and helping others, whatever their bloodline, was the greatest concern now in his life. He supported his wife's passion for the German immigrants, but most of the charity work he did no one ever saw or knew about, not even his wife. He was not really a religious fellow. He was more a devout believer.

Even though Eleanor tried, she could not make Frank feel ashamed for leaving the house during the Saturday women's Bible study. The ladies arrived at the very hour he left for Wrigley Field or scheduled polo with the boys. If he didn't leave the house, he would devote the day to puttering in the basement. One of the traits Eleanor respected most about her Franklin was his need for solitude, which, she clearly knew, differed from loneliness. He needed time alone "just with his bride," as he called his private time with Ellie. He enjoyed time with his affectionate children. But none of that could or would replace his undisturbed time of solitude. Mathilda noticed this trait in Franklin Carlisle after getting to know him and recognized it as being Christ-like. In prayer, she asked the Lord if she, too, might be given this gift.

As Mathilda and Marie got to know Mr. and Mrs. Carlisle, of course they also got to know their children. There were three Carlisle children: Michael, the eldest, was 7 years old; Foster had just turned 5; and Edna was almost 2. The next child was to be born in late spring sometime. The whole family seemed to be hoping for another girl.

Michael and Foster were tall for their ages and looked like their father, although Foster had his mother's kind eyes and gentle gracious manner. He admired his older brother and did whatever Michael told him to do. Foster was also fiercely protective of his baby sister. Everyone knew why: Edna was adorable.

With long blond curls, rosy cheeks and large azure eyes, she was everyone's baby doll. Marie and Edna loved each other from the very start. It was amazing Edna ever learned to walk, with Marie carrying her everywhere they went. Foster appreciated Marie as their new companion because it freed him from the duty of watching his little sister so closely. Michael took advantage of his lot in life as the oldest and kept his little following in tiptop shape. It was good for all the children that Michael showed no guile. He was, perhaps, just a little bossy, but other than that, he was quite responsible and mature for his age.

A New Life in a New Home

Mrs. Carlisle asked Mathilda's permission for Marie to be included with her children during playtime and story time. The offer was not just for social interaction, she explained, but rather another effective way to help improve Marie's English. To have peers to play with as part of her day, in Mrs. Carlisle's opinion, was a healthy, normal component for childhood development. Mathilda knew that children needed other children to play with and learn from, as had been the design throughout history, so she was happy to agree to the proposal. Mathilda prompted Marie to thank Mrs. Carlisle for her many kindnesses.

Mrs. Carlisle was extremely involved in parenting her own children, but she also employed a full-time nanny. Everyone, including the children, called her Nanny, but her real name was Blanche Randolph. Her pudgy frame and youthful face disguised her age. Two auburn braids crisscrossed on top of her head, and her ruddy complexion created permanent redness of her cheeks and nose. She was in her element with young children but shy and awkward with adults. Everyone observed she loved sweets particularly and food in general. It seemed odd that, as much as she liked to eat, she neither cooked nor seemed interested in learning how to cook. No one was able to pull her away from the children whenever help was needed in the kitchen. If she had any hobbies, no one ever seemed to know what they were. All her time, energy and focus was watching over the Carlisle children and now Marie.

She was never seen without her uniform, even on her days off. Eleanor and Franklin Carlisle had insisted that she take time off away from the family, but she never would. Nanny never spoke of family or friends. In fact, she actually never spoke unless spoken to. Mathilda tried many times to make conversation with her but to no avail. Most of the time she just seemed to be invisible. Nanny showed no interest in male companionship. She appeared to be more of an observer of life than a participant.

Of all the employees in the Carlisle home, Mattie Johnson was the biggest enigma to Mathilda. Agatha, the youngest worker of the crew, was Miz Johnson's main helper. She told

Mathilda little bits and pieces about her boss. Agatha was moving on to another home that gave her a chance to become head housekeeper, once Mathilda and Marie became oriented to the workings of the Carlisle house. Agatha told Mathilda about the housekeeper more as an orientation than as gossip.

"Mattie Johnson's history is sort of sketchy," Agatha began. "Her family came to America from Trier, Germany. She married Ivan Johansson, a sailor from Denmark who sails to various parts of the world through the Great Lakes. To become more Americanized, he changed his name to Edward Johnson. Many of the longshoremen are Irish, and Mattie learned English from an Irish girl her same age when her family settled in Chicago. Since that time, Germans and Irish have flooded into this country. No one knows how Mattie met her husband — Eddie, as she calls him. She never tells anyone about her past, and no one ever asks. Mattie and her husband have a small apartment nearby, but seldom does anyone from the Carlisle home ever see him."

Mathilda had observed that Mattie Johnson was a German who spoke English with an Irish accent and looked like she was French. She had coal black hair with an olive complexion. She was taller than most men. Her hips were broad and filled out her skirts, but her chest was small and did not fill out her blouse. She had an enormous appetite, yet she was the thinnest of all the workers. She never wore any powder or rouge, because there was redness in her face. Although her features were homely, there was a light shining from her that drew people to her. Mathilda was amazed and intrigued by her and instantly liked and trusted her. As talkative as she was, she never really talked about herself or her husband. Mathilda found all the characters in the Carlisle home fascinating and was eager to get to know them each individually.

That evening, Mathilda asked Miz Johnson for some stationery, a pen and some ink. She knew that Mrs. Carlisle corresponded with many pastors from Germany, so she felt confident that her letter would reach her friends in Hamburg. When the stationery and pen arrived, Mathilda sat at the breakfast table and began her letter.

A New Life in a New Home

My dearest Beatrice,

This letter is sent to you as one that will give God much honor, great praise and my wholehearted gratitude. I am so thankful to have a moment to sit and write to you about the many events in my life. Please forgive me if I appear too proud or boastful for my many blessings. Our Heavenly Father is to receive all the glory.

We have arrived in a place named Wilmette, which is near the very large city of Chicago. With much help from those God sent to us, we were able to come right to the house of Mr. and Mrs. Franklin Carlisle. Eleanor Carlisle is the woman your husband wrote to, and she made all the arrangements through the women of the Lutheran Ladies' Missionary Aid Society.

This place was an Indian Reservation called Ouilmette; I live in a wonderful land, surrounded by a forest of large trees near a magnificent lake that looks like an ocean in size. We may gather berries or butternuts in the forest, or walk on the shore of the lake and look at beautiful sunsets. Some of the German folks here call this place New Trier.

Marie and I miss our old life, but I must assure you our new life is very good. America is so big, and the people seem so happy. Whenever we walk down the street, even people I have never seen before smile and greet me. The others that work in the Carlisle home were praying for us while we were detained at Ellis Island. I am overjoyed with such kindness. It is that same Christian love I received from your family. Please give my greetings to your husband and all your wonderful children. Send my greetings to all the widows you introduced me to in your parish.

Everyone goes to church in this community, and almost everyone here has recently arrived from Germany. There are several families that lost loved ones and shared my peril but have remarried and are exceedingly happy. This knowledge is a great encouragement to me. My sweet Marie needs a father, as all children need both Mother and Father in order to grow into normal adults. Please understand that this is not to say that our Heavenly Father is not sufficient to meet all our need, for I have found He is our friend in every way, as well as our provider. The Lord Jesus has now become my husband, my friend, as well as the lover of my soul. I remember, before we left Hamburg, while you and I delivered food to the widows, you told me, with great confidence, that the Lord would restore to me what had been taken. You said it was just as He promised the Jewish people of long ago, through the prophet Joel. I embraced what you told me as if Jesus spoke it directly to me. The words of comfort and encouragement still nourish my spirit with the holiness of communion. Our Lord said, "This do ye, as oft as ye drink of it, in remembrance of me." In every new challenge, and in every new victory, I remember Him, and He is faithful to me. Even now, Beatrice, in my lonely times, in my moments of extreme grief and despair, I cling to the knowledge that He suffered for me, died for me, rose again and is alive

Tilly's Song

today for me. This is why, in deep and wondrous thanksgiving, I can believe what He says in the Bible and choose to live not for any other, but only for Him. He holds my future. You and your family helped me learn to trust Him again. I do not think I told you that when I left the flames of the village behind me, I was so gripped with fear that I did not think anyone else was alive. I was afraid to die and afraid to live. The farmer and his wife were there to point us in your direction, and you were there to point us in the direction of America. When I did not know what to do, the Holy Spirit showed you just what to do and say to help me and my child.

My child! Oh, Beatrice, my Marie is growing and speaking English very well. A wonderful lady named Mrs. O'Donner, who was confined with us at Ellis Island, prayed for us to learn English, and we are learning it! Marie is better at understanding than I am, but I continue to improve.

At the Carlisle home there are children, so Marie has good company. The Carlisle children are beautiful and well-behaved. It is good for Marie to be around others close to her age. She can be overly responsible for her age, and, at times, wants to get bossy with me and act too old. I find myself reluctant to scold or punish her, because Marie has been through so much trouble, yet I do not want my lenience in these matters to cause her to become spoiled or willful.

Whenever I have to make decisions for Marie, this is when I miss John the most. I confess to you, my sister in Christ, that I have strong daydreams at times because I also miss our marriage bed. I must frequently take these daydreams and thoughts into captivity, especially whenever I catch the scent of a manly man. Please pray for me that I will not fall into sin. Also, please pray that I will be led, by the Spirit of God, to be a good mother to Marie and an honorable worker to the Carlisle family.

Sweet Beatrice, I am so glad you are my Christian sister with whom I can share my heart, even if parts are black as coal. Please write soon and tell me everything that you are doing, thinking and hoping. My promise is to be more diligent in my correspondence. I received your letter in New York that you sent to the Carlisle home, but the lovely Lutheran lady had it for me to read on the train as I traveled to Chicago. It is funny to me that your letter has traveled farther than I have.

Beatrice, until we meet again, may our Father God continue to richly bless you. Farewell.

Your sister in Christ,
Mathilda Baumann

Somehow, talking to Beatrice through letters seemed to calm her spirit, even if it was one-sided. Now that the letter was

A New Life in a New Home

finished, it was time to review her day with her Heavenly Father. She gave Him her gratitude and quickly fell into restful, dreamless sleep.

Chapter 7
Never a Dull Moment

"Industrious! That is the word I would use to describe most of the German people I have met, in this country or in Germany. Most just seem busy doing things with great energy, whether work or play." This was the introduction of Eleanor Carlisle's little sermonette to her new employees.

The new arrivals' industry was not just to learn new skills, but to put into practice the excellent skills they had brought with them from Germany. Now that they were in America and had no plans to live elsewhere, they were American. The official language for the United States was English, so it was English they would speak. Other nationalities might speak only their native language among themselves. That behavior seemed somehow disloyal to their new homeland, in the opinion of Franklin and Eleanor Carlisle.

Mathilda put her whole mind and heart into learning and speaking English. However, at church, the hymns were still being sung in German, and from time to time, the minister would forget himself and with great zeal pray aloud in front of the congregation in his mother tongue. Marie noticed that both men and women would wipe the tears from their eyes after hearing these prayers. Although it didn't make Marie want to cry, it did make her feel closer to the minister and the congregation.

Sunday marked the beginning of the week. It seemed hard to believe they had been at the Carlisle home for a whole week. During that time, Mathilda and Marie both worked diligently to learn their duties.

Monday, after the first week of orientation was completed, Miz Johnson felt closer to Mathilda. She approached her with a proposition.

"Miz Baumann, I do wish we could be less formal-like and more friendly-like with each other. Why, ya are so cordial and friendly-like to me, I would, from here on out, appreciate you callin' me by my first name, Mattie. It's a nickname for Madeline, but everyone just calls me Mattie. I wish ya would, too." Mathilda's spirit relaxed, knowing something really significant had just happened to make her feel more accepted with the head housekeeper.

"Oh, yah, um, yes, I like dat idea wery much. Pleaz tell me, vhat ist da nickname fur Mathilda?" she asked politely.

With a long sigh, Mattie thought — and then suddenly it came to her. "Well, now, I think it might be Tilly! Yes, yes, I'm sure of it. Tilly Baumann. That has a nice American sound to it, don't you think? Hmm. Tilly! I like it!" Mattie playfully started dancing around the kitchen, making up a little ditty using the new name.

> Oh, don't ya call me silly
> When I call you Tilly
> 'Cause that name seems just right for you.
> And don't ya call me chatty
> When my name is Mattie,
> Even though I talk way more than you do.
> Oh, looky here and see
> That your little girl, Marie,
> Thinks the two of us have lost our minds.
> But I shall call you Tilly, dear
> As long as I am with you here
> That is, of course, if you don't mind?

Everyone burst into laughter; they were still snickering as they watched Marie skip around, twirling and dancing to the gaiety. It was as if the heavy gray clouds had parted and sunshine flooded through the windows of their hearts right there in the kitchen. Marie whispered to her friend, "Thank you for Mama's laughter."

New country, new home, new name and now finally a new heart. Yes, things were getting better. With every new day, Tilly was getting stronger, feeling better. In the midst of all the playful fun, the oddest thing happened.

"Mattie, vill you cut mine hair so I coult look more stylish-like fur to be a real American Chicago voman?" she asked quite seriously.

"Oh, Tilly, I'll just get my scissors right now, and in a short while you will look like …" Mattie stopped short and thought how she was going to finish her sentence. "New woman" had almost carelessly flown out of her mouth. No, that was not what she wanted to convey. "You will look just like a proper Chicago lady," she said, delighted with herself for thinking so fast.

Mattie was a good barber and liked to think she had an eye for fashion. She put a towel around Tilly's neck and shoulders, took down the long tresses and unbraided the thick, heavy honey-colored hair. Around her face and neck new soft hair grew, forming small ringlets. Tilly sat on the kitchen stool with a look of resolve upon her face. Marie, however, covered her mouth in shock and remained speechless throughout her mother's transformation. Mattie took the shears, measured between Tilly's shoulder blades and made one chop. The golden tresses fell to the floor. Mattie looked over Tilly's shoulder and asked, "Have you ever had your hair cut before?"

"Never," was Tilly's soft answer.

"Well, then, with this first hair cut comes a beautiful set of hair combs for ya."

She went to the top drawer of her chest of drawers and retrieved the Christmas present given to her by her husband, which she had never used. It would be her little secret, and she hoped her husband would be happy once he heard the story. The hair combs were made of ivory from walrus tusks and were the finest she had ever seen. Tilly had given the pastor's wife her hair combs as a thank-you gift. The sacrifice of giving her wedding present away didn't seem so bad now. Like all things on this earth, the combs were just temporary. What a lovely surprise to receive these combs that were even more beautiful than hers. Tilly started to cry, but fought back the urge. Instead, she allowed her new friend to place the cut hair into a net and place it as a rat to form her new hairstyle. Her lovely new combs adorned the whole creation. Other workers seemed to appear out of nowhere, gawking at the transformation. Their reaction was summed up in one expression, coming from them in unison: "Wow!"

"Mama, you look beautiful. You always look beautiful, just a different kind of beautiful now with your hair different." Marie smiled, approving of the big change.

Mattie had appeared with a handheld mirror for Tilly to see the results of the new hairdo. She looked at her reflection critically and looked up at Mattie. "Yah, dis is vhat I vanted you to do. I am pleased. Tank you for this, my friend, and for dis most beautiful hair combs. I had some once." She stopped herself from going into the story of her own combs because it didn't matter anymore. She was pleased with her blessing, so in her opinion, enough was said about the matter.

"Miz Johnson, Mama had some beautiful hair combs once, but she gave them to the nice lady in that place in Germany where we stayed before coming to America. Mama cried after she gave them away 'cause Papa gave them to her. Now she has some that are even prettier than Papa's."

"Marie, that is enough said. I vant you to be quiet now; you need to go to our room. Go now!" Tilly was clearly embarrassed by the whole situation. The joy of the moment was somehow gone. The other workers silently returned to their work, and Mattie busied herself with things in the kitchen. Tilly placed the mirror on the work table and retreated to her bedroom.

The first Monday of every month coal was delivered. A Negro man came to the back door and spoke with Mattie Johnson. She put her signature on a paper he had clipped to a signing board. As he turned to leave, two other men began to put the coal down the chute that went to the boiler room in the basement. Marie looked at the man, then looked at Miz Johnson and said, "Oh, my goodness, that man has coal dust all over his face and hands!"

Mattie looked shocked, then motioned with her index finger over her lips and said, "Shhh, he might hear you!" She loudly whispered, "He is a colored man, Marie. He doesn't have coal dust on him — well, yes, he does have coal dust on him, but that's not what makes him black. Have ya never seen a person who has black skin before, Marie?"

"Yes, ma'am, on the train. Why do you call him colored, Miz Johnson?" She looked confused.

With a sigh and a shrug, Miz Johnson answered, "Marie, I'm not sure."

"What do you call me? If he is black and you call him colored, do you call me colored since I am pink?" Marie questioned innocently.

"No, Marie, you are white," Miz Johnson corrected.

"So if a person has freckles, Miz Johnson, do they call them spotted or brown and white? Mr. Giovanitti was really brown, but they didn't call him colored, they called him Italian. This English is hard for me to understand. Why don't people just call each other by their names instead of what they look like? My name is Marie, so don't you call me pink or white, or I'll get mad."

"Marie Martha!" her mother shrieked. She had just walked in on the end of their conversation and only heard the insolence in her child's voice. "Marie, yu apologize to yur elder fur dis rude kind of talking." Tilly was so angry the veins stuck out on her face and neck.

"No apology is needed. Marie has just been puttin' it straight to me about one more foolish thing we all do to each other. Besides that, I like the child's spunk. I never need an apology from someone who speaks the truth to me. I'll tell ya all about the conversation later, but right now, I best be gettin' the teapot warmed and treats on the plate since Miz Carlisle and her brood will be down shortly."

Mattie winked at Marie and then smiled as she spoke to her. "I'm thankin' ya, my sweet Marie. The very next time that coal man comes deliverin' to this house, I'll be usin' some proper manners and ask him his name. I shall not be callin' him by anything other than his proper name from now on."

She reassured Tilly, "It has taken yur child, Tilly, to open up me mind's eye to see life properly in this instance." She began a spontaneous hum, grateful for the correction because she felt it came straight from the heart of God.

When Marie left for story time with the other children and Tilly and Mattie were alone in the kitchen peeling potatoes,

Tilly confided in her new friend. "Pleaz tell me the truf. Was my Marie disrespectful to yu? She sometimes makes me vorry. She is still little but acts and speaks too grown up. Vhat do I do vith that?"

"Oh, Tilly, all mamas worry about if their youngsters are offendin' other people. But no, to answer ya, I took no offense. But let me be plain with ya: If she ever does, ya'll be hearin' from me, I promise. Tilly, listen darlin', Marie has gone through more hard livin' than most grownups have. Oh, don't get me wrong, it is not anyone's fault. This couldn't have been helped. I think she is doing fine."

Tilly stopped peeling the potatoes and looking at Mattie, fretfully asked, "Are yu really sur?"

"Now let's just reason here a bit. God loves her, ya love her, this whole household cares for her, and she knows this, correct? She prays, I know 'cause I've heard her. You talk with her and answer her questions. She hears your prayers and knows she is safe. My friend, you cannot do more for a child than all you are already doin'. She's a girl, just a child, Tilly. She's good most of the time, but sometimes she will be naughty and not act according to how ya like it. But now, really, don't we all do that from time to time with our own Heavenly Father? Don't be fretting so much."

Tilly nodded her head in agreement. Mattie frowned at her and gently scolded, "Girl, can't ya work and listen at the same time? If it's something you need to fret over then it's this meal we're not getting cooked. We have to finish these taters and put those rolls in to bake before they fall and are no good to eat. Oh, goodness me, I got to be checking the roast. Totally forgot the roast. These vegetables have to go in now to be done before the roast dries up to leather. Your child is turning out better than this meal is so far. Now get on with ya; time's a wastin'."

Both knew the meal was right on schedule and all of it would be delicious. Tilly also knew her daughter would turn out just fine. She could trust God with her life and with her daughter's life. She always had and always would.

Chapter 8
What Do You Do?

Marie played with the Carlisle children and took lessons from Mrs. Carlisle. Soon Marie was addressing Eleanor Carlisle as Mama Carlisle, which pleased both of them. Mr. Carlisle paid Marie a wage for the chores Miz Johnson assigned her. He deposited this money into an account he opened for Tilly at the bank. This arrangement was, of course, pure kindness from the Carlisle family to help Tilly pay off the traveling debt. Each day, Marie's duties would include the following: folding napkins, helping in the kitchen, polishing the silverware, dusting the banister, collecting the shoes for polishing and delivering them back all shiny. On pressing day, it was Marie's job to sprinkle the clothes. Whenever the back doorbell rang, Marie would run and open the door to greet the delivery people. Within the first month, she knew everyone by name. Not only did she have a good memory for names, she had a good memory for all kinds of things. Soon after Tilly and Marie's arrival at the Carlisle home, Mattie discovered Marie was quite talented at finding things others had misplaced. Often she would overhear this kind of interaction between mother and child:

"Marie, My Love, do you know where I put my clean apron?"

"Yes, here it is, Mama."

Mama Carlisle knew Marie as the "Big Helper," and soon the whole household was calling her by that name. However, Mattie also knew Tilly was a good helper to her daughter. Mattie saw the light still on in Tilly and Marie's room. As she drew closer, she could overhear their conversation.

"Marie, I am so very proud of you for being such a 'Big Helper' to all the workers here and especially to me. Marie, I want you to learn something at your age so it will follow you throughout your life: What other people think of you is always subject to change; the only thing that never changes is God.

What Do You Do?

What He thinks of you is all that is important. Marie, God calls you His beloved. The thoughts He has for you this day are more numerous than the sands in the ocean. My dear, be secure knowing God is always faithful to you, even if at times you may not be faithful to Him."

Mattie was at least 10 years Tilly's senior, but she was continually learning from Tilly's wisdom. When the letter had come from the Lutheran Ladies' Missionary Aid League stating that the Baumanns were detained for three months at Ellis Island, Mattie had earnestly prayed for Tilly's safe arrival in Chicago. She knew those prayers had been answered, and now, after overhearing this conversation, was sure Tilly was a special gift sent by God to this entire household. Tilly was a good mother, and Mattie wished she could have been like her. Tilly taught Marie to trust and have great hope in spite of life's difficulties. Mattie admired their close relationship. She was confident that as Marie grew into womanhood she would not lose her way but would remain strong, knowing she was loved by God and her mother.

It was time for Mattie to head home, feed her cat and write her daily letter to her seafaring husband, who by now was on his way to England through the Northern Lakes. She pulled her hat on over her ears, put her coat on and turned down the lamp in the kitchen. Noiselessly she stepped outside, pulling the door closed behind her.

Within the first month, under Mattie's supervision, Tilly had mended some clothes, cooked some meals, overseen the children at play and cleaned the house from top to bottom. Mr. Carlisle taught her the American currency values, and she practiced what she learned when she went shopping with Mattie. Tilly's progress was evaluated under the critical eyes of Eleanor and Mattie to determine which area Tilly was best suited to work. Eleanor was quite pleased with all the skill Tilly possessed; none of the chores posed too much of a challenge, and she completed them with a cheerful heart. Eleanor and Mattie both agreed that she was definitely a candidate for a head housekeeper position. There was just one more test she must pass: Laundry was the biggest chore for the entire household.

There would be no doubt in anyone's mind about Tilly's abilities if she passed the laundry test. Each week, everyone knew how much Mattie hated laundry. Today, Tilly had the privilege of hearing her weekly complaint.

"Tilly, the very first woman I worked for was a stickler about laundry — never could abide anything with dirt on it unless she was in the garden, where she would sit right down in the middle of it all and weed or till or pick until she was covered with dirt. However, laundry, sake's alive, now that was very different. I guess she taught me all too well, 'cause when Mrs. Carlisle saw me doing laundry back when Michael was at her breast, she said she'd never send her laundry out again, since I did such a superior job. Now, everyone knows — and today that includes you — I am not so very fond of doing laundry and even less fond of pressing. My reward comes in puttin' all the clean things in their proper places; I always pretend it is brand new, like it was when it was first purchased. Oh, Tilly, I suffer from vain imaginations. But I don't think my little oddities hurt anything. Well, well! Now, tell me, dear, how do *you* feel about laundry?" Mattie asked, with great hope that this chore was Tilly's all-time favorite.

Tilly knew quite well where this was leading, and she really didn't mind at all, because laundry was not a dreaded chore to her. Her mind drifted off to when she would do laundry at her home. She smiled, remembering how Marie would put Mary and baby John in the laundry basket and pull them all around while she hung out the sheets and towels. She almost laughed out loud reliving the time when she went wild over the birds that left droppings on her clean clothes. When she saw a bird come close, she shook her broom at it to drive it away. Her neighbor, Mrs. Günter, laughed so loud it woke up her ol' drunk husband out of his stupor. It embarrassed Tilly to hear Mrs. Günter, but she also had to laugh at her folly. Both women were laughing so hard that John heard them and came out of the barn to see what was happening. When he yelled out to question what the matter was, she took the broom and danced around with it all the way over to him. He gave her that look that made her want to melt. John then reached out, pulled her to him and kissed her. Marie came running, carrying the baby, and Mary ran up and took hold of her papa's leg. They both picked up their children and gave them kisses.

Mattie looked at the tears rolling down Tilly's cheeks and asked, "Have I upset you so, my darlin'? I don't know as I have ever been to the point of tears over doing the laundry, but I certainly know how you feel."

During the cold winter weather, laundry was washed indoors and hung to dry in an area of the basement near the boiler. As the weather improved, the wet clothes were hung out-of-doors so the sun could dry and bleach them. A clothing brush was used to remove any soil or built up lint. Monday was laundry day so Sunday's woolen clothing could air on hangers for a week.

Accommodations for churchgoing also depended on the weather. In cold or rainy weather, those who attended church rode in a horse-drawn wagon. On Sundays, as the weather improved, many would walk to church, but on the way home, they would promenade, as it was called. This was not just walking for exercise or getting from one location to another. Promenading was a social event with the goal of seeing and talking with others, as well as being seen coming from one of the local churches. Many times parishioners shared box lunches following the Sunday service. Promenading was another way of walking off the fullness of overeating. Some used this opportunity to show off their new stylish clothing, but the Baumanns had only two types of clothing: church clothes and work clothes.

By definition, church clothes consisted of a simple dress accented by a beautiful lacy apron, hat, gloves, dark shoes and stockings. In springtime, fresh flowers made into corsages adorned the dress, but in the winter, silk flowers replaced the fresh ones. The daughter's clothing was a miniature version of the mother's attire. The main difference was that Marie did not wear a hat or gloves.

Work attire included two simple dresses with a daily change of apron. It was important to keep these clean and neat, since it was expected to always look presentable. Therefore, when dress "one" was worn, dress "two" was being laundered. In order for the aprons to look crisp and unwrinkled, they were bleached, blued, starched and pressed. Only new aprons were issued every six months, not dresses, shoes, stockings or undergarments. Each Christmas, all the new employees received a warm functional overcoat with rubbers and an umbrella. Someone usually would knit gloves or mittens as an additional gift for them. Marie received a new dress from the women in New York City as a Christmas present, but out of respect for the time of grieving, it was black. Tilly also wore black. They both wore white aprons, except for Sunday, when they adorned their dress with beautiful and colorful embroidered satin aprons.

One year was customary for wearing black as a sign of mourning. Marie was tired of this custom and asked her mother for a different dress. Instead of acknowledging Marie's request, Mathilda gave her a lecture on appreciation and gratitude for the many blessings she had already received.

All right, I will try to be grateful for this ol' ugly black dress. When I get older, Jesus, will You please bless me with a pretty dress and some colorful aprons? Marie prayed this same prayer for what seemed to her a very long time.

In Tilly's opinion, time was passing very quickly with so much to learn and so much to do, but for Marie, a week seemed like a year. She had asked her playmates what their favorite time was and they unanimously shouted "Christmas!" She told them about Christmas on Ellis Island, and they were astonished.

One Sunday, after Ash Wednesday, two single men approached Tilly and her lady friends. One man tipped his hat and asked if he and his friend might join them on their promenade. Both men attended the same church, and Marie remembered one man looking at her mama. Whenever she saw him looking, he would quickly look away. An older lady spoke up in English but quickly changed to German.

"Good Christian gentlemen," she began, "please do not forget your good manners just because we live in another country now. As respectable ladies, some of us widowed with children, we must guard our virtue very closely. We also require a proper introduction from a person we mutually trust and respect. Perhaps next Sunday the pastor may introduce you to these dear womenfolk and to me. This is, of course, if you wish to be seen in our eyes as fine gentlemen. I do trust I speak for you, dear lady friends?"

All the women nodded. "Yah, Yah!"

With that response, the men tipped their hats with a quick bow, and the one with the mustache that had looked at Tilly said, in German, "We shall honor your request, good ladies. We say farewell for now."

The ladies all watched as the men turned and left with a spring in their step. No sooner were they out of hearing range than the women began to giggle and talk all at the same time, pleased with the attention these young men had showed to them. They were still aflutter when they arrived back at the house ready to change clothes and begin preparation for the Sunday dinner.

Mattie seemed to know all about everyone in the community. To show off this knowledge, at breakfast she spoke loud enough to demand everyone's attention.

"You see, me brother is a constabulary on patrol, and he warns me about things happening round about these parts. People are seldom what they seem unless you tarry with them long enough to see their true character. Now you take those two gentlemen yesterday who asked if they could go a walkin' with you ladies after church. Both are widowers; both have seen their fair share of sorrow, but they are going about their life in a true and honorable way to find good women for marryin'. They know happiness can't be found chasin' trollops and drinkin' their sorrows away every night of their life. No, these here are good men folks, with jobs and self-respect. Only God knows their heart, but they behave like Christians — not perfect, mind ya, but lovin' life and stayin' law abidin'. Remember, Mrs. Mathilda Baumann, God said only, 'Til death do us part' … it would be unnatural to go through life havin' your physical needs unmet and never knowing the tenderness only lovin' can bring. I've seen that fellow, surname of Bogda, tryin' not to stare too hard at ya. If you haven't noticed his looks … I dare say you are the only one. Well, now, enough said, I've most probably said too much. Let's get to work, my beauties; it's Monday, and laundry won't wash itself."

Tilly's face was beet red after Mattie singled her out from the others. She felt particularly vulnerable since others had noticed her noticing the young man named Bogda. She scolded herself for being so open and careless with her looks. After all, she was a one-man woman, and any stirring or urges just had to be subdued. She must be the model of good moral behavior for her child. She would take the teasing because it was harmless, but she would not let her mind dwell on the idea of other men. She felt a bitter taste form in her mouth and the heat of anger radiate through her body. In her mind, she began to lecture her poor deceased husband. *John Baumann, why weren't you stronger? You were always stronger than I was. Always wiser, smarter, happier, better than I was. People say the good die young, so is that it? Well, maybe Mattie is correct. John, I am just so angry with you right now — and what angers me the most is I can do nothing about it.*

She was distracted from her tongue-lashing when she felt her fingernail scrape the rub board. When she looked down, she saw her finger sticking through the shirt she had been scrubbing. "Well, now, how am I going to be able to mend that?" she complained.

The next day, her anger seemed temporarily washed out of her thoughts along with the laundry. It was now Tuesday: pressing day. While Tilly pressed the clothes that Marie had sprinkled, she asked Mattie about Mrs. Carlisle.

"Mattie, Mrs. Carlisle has asked Marie to call her 'Mama Carlisle.' Does that seem proper to you?" Tilly knew she would receive an honest answer.

"It is not my opinion that matters about what is or isn't proper when it comes to your own daughter. Do you have a feelin' that makes you uncomfortable about her request?" Mattie countered the question with a question.

"I have never thought of my daughter calling another woman 'Mama.' Marie is learning so much from Mrs. Carlisle, and the other children call her 'Mama,' so it doesn't seem disrespectful. I guess it just takes a little getting used to before it sounds all right to me. I must sound silly to you talking this

way, but I am her mother, and she is my only child now. I'm not sure what I really feel right now. Mrs. Carlisle is good and kind, and I know that she loves my little girl. I want her to be loved by all who know her …"

Mattie stood still, listening to every word she spoke and all the words unspoken. She was not a "know-it-all," after all. She had no advice to give, only a listening ear.

Tilly, to those who knew her, was normally quiet, polite and reserved, but there was a boldness in her character that would cause her to speak bluntly, often when no one else would. The chatter among the employees of the Carlisle house was the concern for the way Eleanor Carlisle looked as she carried her fourth child. They commented on how swollen her face and hands had become. Mostly, however, they were amazed at how very large her belly seemed to have become overnight. No one said a word to her; instead, they acted overly cheerful whenever she was around them. Tilly had had enough of the deception, so at lunch, she approached Eleanor.

"Madam, I speak for all of us here. We love you, dear, and are most concerned about your health. It is a good thing that you do, working with the church and civic projects, but there is a season for everything. Please take counsel and rest more. You know we are here to help one another. I request that you lie down or at least get off those swollen feet, stop wearing your stockings and comfort yourself, as well as the child within you." The lecture was over, so she sat down and continued eating her lunch.

Eleanor Carlisle looked like a little girl and flew to Tilly with her arms wide open to embrace her. "Oh, Tilly, I adore you. I just needed some mothering right now of my own. I will not be contrary but will obey your counsel, because I know what you request is for my good." Smiling at the children, she proclaimed, "Children, I shall be resting instead of going to my study today." Excusing herself from the table, she rose quickly to her feet and then swooned. The chair was close, breaking her fall, as she sat back onto it.

"Something is not right. Summon Dr. Stolp at once; if he cannot come, ask if his son, Rufus, is able to help us right now.

Her time is not yet complete, but she is too large," Tilly said to Mattie.

"Tilly, you are right, darlin'. I see it in her face. Let me get my hat and coat, and I'll soon be back with the doctor. I leave you in charge, Tilly. Bless you!" Mattie was still putting on her hat as she rushed out the door. She flew down the street to Mr. Sexauer's store to use his new telephone to call the doctor. Several others assisted Tilly as she helped Eleanor to her room.

"Come with me, Marie!" Tilly commanded.

"Where are we going, Mama?" she asked, frightened by all the commotion.

"Marie, I want to gather the children together so we can pray for Mama Carlisle." Her voice had returned to a calm low tone, less stern and more comforting. She led Marie into the playroom. The door was open, and all the Carlisle children were just standing with their heads lowered. They looked up and seemed startled when Tilly and Marie entered the room. Michael spoke as Edna ran to Marie.

"Mrs. Baumann, is Mama going to die?" he asked, in a calm and matter-of-fact voice. Foster walked over to Tilly, put his arms around her waist and hung on to her. She reached out and touched Michael's hand to hold it. He snatched it away and folded his arms across his chest.

"Children," she spoke with great conviction, "I must apologize to you and to God for not placing my faith in the right order: I sent for the doctor before praying. You all have been taught that Jesus is our healer; His blood was shed to forgive sins, but also to heal every illness and brokenness. Let's go to your mother's room and quietly pray for her and the baby."

The children were grateful that they would be included and with great reverence entered their mother's bedroom. Her eyes were closed, and she lay perfectly still, except for her shallow breathing.

Foster knelt down by her bed, folded his hands and looked up to the ceiling as if expecting to see all the way to heaven where Jesus was sitting on the right hand of Father God.

"Father God, please help my mama and our baby live. Amen."

What Do You Do?

Edna was next. Little Edna's prayer was more of an affirmation. "Mommy, live ... live ... live!"

Michael tried to act older, although he was little and frightened, like the rest of them. His grownup prayer was no less sincere. "Lord, my mommy has told me how great You are. I've heard about miracles, so, please, God, I am asking You for a miracle for our mother. Thank You very much. Amen. Oh, yes, and help our baby, please. Thank You, I mean, Amen."

Mama Carlisle's eyes opened just a little as a smile formed on her lips. Marie stood at her head petting her hair. She prayed, just as her father had, saying "Thank You" over and over from a heart filled with assurance that Mama Carlisle and all her children were going to live a very long time in this world. Long after the children were tucked into bed, sometime in the middle of the night, Tilly tiptoed into the room and quickly crawled into bed. Marie awoke and called out to her mother, "Mama?"

"Yes, Marie, it is Mama. My Love, God gave us that miracle we prayed for this afternoon. Twin girls were born tonight. I'm so sleepy. I'll tell you all about it in the morning. Good night, my simple *honekayh*." She reached over and kissed Marie on the forehead.

Marie stared into the darkness of the night. *Mama hasn't called me "simple honekayh" since, since ... I can't remember,* she thought to herself. This nickname came from the word *little curl*, those that formed from new hair around the face and hairline on the back of the neck. To tease Marie, her mother would put her little finger in one of the little curls and pull it softly, just enough to make her protest. It had been a long time since her mama had been so playful. *I'm sleepy, too, but I am also excited. Thank You, Jesus! I now have two babies and Edna that I can love. Little babies, hmm, I can play with these little baby girls and dress them and bring them toys and ...* She yawned, then rolled over and dreamed of baby girls dressed in pink lace.

The orderly, scheduled home of Mr. and Mrs. Franklin Carlisle was in total chaos when Marie awoke at her normal time of 6 a.m. The children were still in their nightgowns running here and there, talking to everyone, hugging and being hugged.

Tilly's Song

Frank Carlisle had never changed out of his work clothes, except somewhere in all the excitement his suit coat and tie were off, as well as his socks and shoes. He was parading around the kitchen with a bundle of baby girl in each of his arms and a fat unlit Havana cigar stuck in his mouth — grinning from ear to ear, stopping for this one and that one to take a peek at the miracle babies.

The children saw Marie and pulled her toward their father to show her the new little ones. Mr. Carlisle bent over, and standing on her tiptoes, she saw two beautiful, perfectly formed babies that looked exactly alike. What hair they had was so blond that their scalp showed through as light pink. Their eyelashes were long, and their lips formed a perfect heart shape.

"Well, my little Miss Marie, what do you think of my two newest girls?" Mr. Carlisle spoke with difficulty, managing to hold his cigar without using his hands.

"Oh, sir, I just want to kiss those little cheeks," she giggled in reply.

He smiled and gave her a wink, then turned to show another person, who continued to make a fuss. Marie looked at Michael and asked, "How is your mother?"

"Wonderful!" he almost shouted. "She told me this morning that she heard our prayers, and she felt strengthened. Mother said she knew that everything was going to be all right and that the babies would live. Papa said he already has names for them: Victoria and Gloria. Aren't those just the best names for our little miracles?"

Marie nodded her head in agreement and repeated the names. "Victoria and Gloria — they sound like angel names!"

Mattie came walking up to the children, as proud as if she had had the twins all by herself. She stood over them inspecting each of them while she wiped her hands on her apron. "Who all wants potato pancakes?" She made her appealing inquiry with a twinkle in her eye and mischief in her voice. "Ooh, I've got hot potato pancakes with cinnamon sugar and applesauce; any takers?"

"Yes," they all yelled.

"Yes," Frank Carlisle yelled, mocking the children. "I could

What Do You Do?

eat a hundred of them. You all better hurry to the table before all those 'tater cakes end up in my tummy!"

He was in an awfully good mood, playful and fun, happy with his family. He had only dreamed, before now, that life could be so good. He handed the babies to Tilly, who put them together in a large basket in a protected area near the warmth of the oven. She hovered over them, watching every little antic they made.

The twins were replaced by Foster and Edna, who insisted on being carried upside down under each arm of their father. Michael and Marie raced to the table. Michael won. All the noise and boisterous behavior was not normally tolerated, but those rules were not enforced today — there were just too many reasons to celebrate. Everyone had an enormous appetite; even little Edna ate three big pancakes all by herself. All thanked Miz Johnson for the delicious treat but also complained they were too stuffed to move. Frank sent word to the bank with all the vital statistics and notified them he would not be back to work until the following Monday. During breakfast, Tilly took the babies back to their mother so they could have their breakfast. Upon returning to the kitchen, she reported that babies and Mother had all been fed and all were now sound asleep. Everyone seemed amused at this good report.

"Mrs. Baumann, I mean, Tilly," Frank spoke up. "May I have your permission to take Marie with my children and me today? This is such a special day. It is spring; we can go to the park, ride some ponies, eat at a restaurant and buy some gifts."

"Yes, of course," Tilly answered, smiling. Then in jest she put her hand on her hip and wagged her finger at each of the children. "Now listen to me, children. Your papa is being very brave to take all of you shopping and dining and playing, so be kind to him and be obedient and — oh, yes, very important — have a wonderful time!"

She giggled and blew kisses as she finished helping Foster and Edna with their sweaters and shoes. On the front porch, Frank waited as a hansom cab pulled up to gather his happy gang. He picked up Edna, and she laid her head adoringly on his shoulder.

Many happy memories were formed as the children grew up in the Carlisle home, but the day the twins were born and Franklin Carlisle took off work, just to be with them, created the fondest memory all the children kept of their father.

Chapter 9
Back to Normal

Normalcy returned to the Carlisle home, as best it could with two babies. The good thing was that they shared the same schedule. Mama Carlisle fed tandem, which allowed her more rest and kept the babies happy and contented. However, when the babies cried, they did so with such gusto it penetrated every nook and cranny of the house. Marie found their crying almost intolerable. All the children asked to play out-of-doors; the days were getting warmer, and it was a way to escape the noise from crying babies.

Spring had at last arrived. Mama Carlisle bundled up the children in sweaters, hats, scarves and mittens and shooed them out into the garden to play. The children loved to watch Mr. Boehl, the gardener, as he cleaned the gardens and the flowerbeds. Even though he was extremely busy, he always made time to teach the children out-of-doors games: blind man's bluff, tag, kick the can, hopscotch and jump rope. He even took time to show and explain his job, using the out-of-doors as his classroom.

There was a rumor that Mr. Otto Boehl had not always been a gardener. Mattie had overheard Mr. Carlisle talking with him about the university in Berlin; she had deduced that Otto Boehl once had been a professor of law. Now, in America, he was leading a simpler life and one he totally loved. He never spoke of life in Germany, nor of family or friends. He would mysteriously leave every November and December; not even the Carlisles knew where he would go — or at least they never told anyone.

Mr. Boehl had a workshop beside the greenhouse. It had copious amounts of tools and numerous books about botany, landscaping and construction of gardens. The children believed Mr. Boehl knew everything about life. His persona was that of Pied Piper.

The children would follow him as he worked, continually asking him every question they could think to ask. He loved to see things grow, and watching the children grow was his greatest delight. He was tolerant and never scolded them for leaving toys in the yard, but he did warn them that special toys might become broken if left outside overnight.

Heeding his warning, Marie told Hildegard she had to stay indoors so she would not get dirty or broken. Marie's precious dolly never joined Edna and her while they were making mud pies or playing ball with the boys. All the children had indoor toys and activities, but whenever the weather permitted, they preferred to be out-of-doors with the gardener. It was so much fun to be around him when he hid treats for the little ones to find in the garden. The children named this game "The Hide and Find Game." The rule, according to Mr. Boehl, was that whoever found the treat had to share it with the other children. Marie, however, seemed to be the only one to find any of the hidden treasure. She did not seem to think anything strange about it and always shared with the other children. Her expertise was probably due to all the prior training she had finding things for people inside the house. Mr. Boehl hid a copy of *Grimm's Fairytales** up in a tree. Once it was found, he read to the children as they sat in a pile of freshly raked leaves. Each day for a week, he read a different story to them, and he always ended it with the statement, "And the mouth of him who last told this story is still warm."

Another time, he hung a cloth bag of sassafras stick candy on a twig in clear sight, but Marie was the only one who noticed. As the weather became more spring-like, the treats became garden tools; the gardener hoped to spark interest in the wonderful nature that was present right there in their own backyard. He hid a small pouch of flower seeds one day and, the following day, a hand trowel. The seeds were sprinkled and covered by working the soil with the hand trowel. Within a week of planting, little sprouts appeared. A watering can magically became the next big surprise of "The Hide and Find Game."

Mrs. Carlisle loved flowers. She had Mr. Boehl landscape her front flowerbeds with several varieties of tulips, hyacinths,

Back to Normal

daffodils, jonquils, rampion and narcissus bulbs shipped to her from Holland. The hedge was bridal wreath, with blooms that lasted into the summer months. Two majestic lilac bushes stood guard at the corners of the house, one a light lavender color with a wonderful fragrance that lingered in the air; the other a rich, majestic purple hue with almost no fragrance at all. At the south of the house was a sunroom where Mr. Boehl kept many tropical plants, transforming them into enormous, sumptuous houseplants. In addition to the gardens and sunroom, there was a greenhouse where he started the plants early in the spring and then transplanted the flowers and vegetables outside after there was no longer a danger of night frost.

Mrs. Carlisle needed to have a dutiful gardener who kept the grounds of the house lush with vegetation because she loved splendid lawn parties. The care of her garden was as important as the care of her house. In the garden, she enjoyed reading the Bible with some of the ladies of the church. They complimented her on the beauty of her flowers, and she replied to this praise, "God's ideal home for mankind has always been a luscious garden full of every good thing to look upon, to smell and to eat. I believe that is why it is so important to share this lovely spot with others; it can minister to them in a more powerful way than words. Franklin and I are so blessed to have such a godly man as Mr. Boehl to take this land, work it and reveal God's magnificent art."

No matter where Mr. Boehl was in the yard, she always made a point to acknowledge him and show him her gratitude for his excellent work. He shyly nodded his head and then disappeared to an undisclosed part of the garden.

Tilly loved to hear him whistle while he was puttering around in the workshop and greenhouse. She would recognize the hymn and burst into song to accompany the distant whistling. Tilly just naturally loved to sing as she hung out the wash or gathered in the dried clothes from the warm sunshine.

In the evening, Tilly claimed the garden as her personal sanctuary. Once she had tucked Marie into bed, she rushed out to the garden to commune with God. Many times, Marie pretended to be asleep and then quietly tiptoed outside to listen to her mother's prayers. Tilly would sit and relax at the end of her workday, enjoying her solitude by looking up at the moon and stars. Tonight she replaced humming and singing with pacing back and forth and praying aloud. It was Saturday night; Tilly was already dreading the regular Sunday promenade after church tomorrow.

"Oh, Lord! I do not know what to think or feel. Should I feel indifference? No, I am nervous. This man is showing his attention to me. Oh, goodness, I should be ashamed. The love of my life, my darling, darling husband has not been dead a year," she sighed. "I like the attention of this other man — I confess it to You. Mattie is right. You know I was faithful to my wedding vows. Jesus, please help me right now. I keep thinking about him, wondering about things, hoping for things, but I do not even know him! Yes, he has a good reputation, but men are not always kind to their wives once they marry. I am also concerned about Marie. Ugh! Listen to me. I am being so foolish, silly, outrageous and maybe even proud. He just asked to walk with us, nothing more. How do I know what he is thinking? Florence probably embarrassed those two men by demanding the kind of proper introduction a courtship requires. She probably scared them off."

She paused in her prayer, distracted by a random thought. *Bogda, hmm, now where would his people be from in Germany? I wonder if the Carlisles would know ... hmm.*

"Oh, Lord, I am doing it again with my vain imaginations. If I am to marry again, You pick, Jesus. You know best; I am just one big ball of urges and lusts. I don't trust myself with any of this, Lord, but I put my complete trust for Marie and for myself into Your capable hands." After a long pause, Tilly spoke aloud again. "There now, I feel better. Thank You, God." She stopped and turned in the direction where Marie was hiding. Marie had tried to be quiet, but she could no longer hold back her sobs. Her crying seemed even louder than the roar of the two babies.

"Marie? Is that you?" Tilly rushed over and found Marie lying on the ground crying. She sat down and pulled her onto her lap to comfort her. "Marie?" she asked again in a calm tone.

Back to Normal

Marie was crying so hard she was unable to speak.

"My Love, do you hurt somewhere?" Tilly continued to probe. Marie's heart was hurting, but she did not know how to tell her mother.

* * *

"Bill, have you asked him yet?" Fredrick Herzog (Fritz) asked his friend while he took his church shoes out of the wardrobe.

"Fritz, maybe he won't do it," Bill said shyly.

"William Bogda, he surely will not do it if he doesn't even know anything about it! Until you explain to him that we want to act appropriately in our manners in order to meet Christian women, nothing is going to happen. You know that is true."

"Fritz, I really want to meet Mathilda Baumann, but I feel strange asking the pastor to be my go-between. When I married Helenea, I had known her from childhood. Fritz, don't you see? I do not know how to talk to women. I do not know what is customary. When I went to sea, marriage was not on my mind. Oh, yes, I looked at the women in the different port towns, yet I had no thoughts of settling down because I would ship out in a few days. Things were so different when I came home. Helenea was a girl when I left, but when I returned, she was a fully-grown woman, beautiful! She told me that she wanted a husband — she wanted me. I shared her feelings and pledged my love to her. Our parents, even our grandparents, were good friends. The women on both sides of the family did everything. All I did was go to dinner at her parents' home and announce my love for their daughter. Overnight all the wedding plans were made, marking one year to the day of announcing our courtship. Her father led me to their barn and retrieved some type of dust-covered bottle out of an ancient truck. It was so old the cork had to be pushed through to get any liquid out of the bottle. Cherry schnapps was what it was, and it was so sweet and strong it tasted like my grandmother's cold remedy. What was worse, he had another one of those bottles hidden away for our wedding day. That was the worst drink in the world, Fritz, but everyone in her family seemed to drink it with great gusto and then proceed to laugh all evening. Oh, please don't misunderstand, we had a grand time. The celebration was wonderful! Everyone in the village came, and our house was completely filled with linens, dishes and candles. It is funny to me, Fritz — her parents even gave us a horse! Can you believe that, a horse for a wedding present? Her father told us if we produced him a grandchild in the first year, he would give us a cow." Bill paused a moment, rubbed his forehead as if it hurt, gave a big sigh and continued his oration.

"Her father never gave us that cow. Year after year, we prayed for a child. The sorrow began to rob the beauty from my darling bride's face. Each month, when her time had come, I would find her crying. The older women of our village were always having me drink something or other that tasted almost as bad as the schnapps her father had given me. Fritz, it has been four years now that my darling Helenea came running to find me in my workshop. This fragile flower of a girl smothered me with kisses all over my face and hands. She had been afraid to tell me for fear she would lose the baby in the first few months. She would not let herself get excited until she felt the life within her. That day, I felt my daughter's movements within her body. However, before the end of that year, I buried my wife with this perfect little girl in her arms." He stood with his arms folded over his chest, blinking back the tears.

"I came to this country as a German widower, and I am stupid. I never paid any attention to parties, weddings, funerals or any such occasions. Helenea took care of the food, the clothes, the presents, the notes of gratitude; I just arrived, ate the food, drank the beer or the wine, came home and made love to my wife. Fredrick, I have faced many frightful events in my life and was never afraid until now. You probably think of me as a coward. Well, you are right! I am frightened of this person, Mathilda Baumann. Do you know what is so absurd? I really do not know a thing about her except her name, her daughter's name and the place of her employment. If it appears I am asking to court her, she may find me too forward and obnoxious. She is not bold as my Helenea was. Yet, Fredrick, I never saw

Back to Normal

her before I asked God to choose a wife for me. Right after my prayer, there in church last January, she came into the sanctuary, and my heart just about beat out of my chest. Fritz, my heart is about to burst right this minute as I talk to you about her. She and her daughter are still dressed in black; that much I do remember. That means she is a widow and is still in mourning." He paused again and for the longest time was deep in thought.

"Whoo," Fritz whistled, "Billy boy, I think you are in love."

Not listening to his friend, Bill asked a question that no one needed to answer. "But have you heard her sing? When the congregation sings, it is but a roar of voices that are muted by her clear, crystal voice. She closes her eyes and sings to God. There just are no words to describe how lovely she is to me."

"Talk to the preacher, Bill!" his friend replied to the "lovesick" puppy.

Fritz could hear Bill talking to himself in a whisper. "Why am I so nervous?"

He called to Bill from the other room. "Hey, Bill, do you have some shoe polish I can borrow?" There was no answer. Again, he yelled from the other room. "I'll shine your shoes if you let me borrow some polish." Growing a little annoyed that there was no response, he walked to the doorway and looked at his friend who was still in a trance. Fritz smiled and muttered to himself, "Oh, boy, I hope she won't be in mourning too much longer."

***

"Marie, I washed and pressed my collar, but I can't find it anywhere. Do you know where —"

"Mama, look in the mirror," Marie answered disgustedly.

"Oh, yes!" Tilly giggled. "I am just a little nervous today. Marie, are you feeling well? Do you need to stay home from church today?" She suddenly quit fussing with her collar and turned her attention to her daughter.

"I feel good, Mama," she answered truthfully. She was, however, also feeling annoyed at all the needless primping and

Tilly's Song

fussing going on with her mama's grooming. It was pointless to mention this aloud, but she thought it all the same: *Mama is never like this.*

The truth was that Tilly was always ready on time and hurrying Marie. "Get ready, Marie!" she would say. "We do not want to be late. Hurry and finish your breakfast. Stop dawdling!" This morning, there was something wrong — Marie just knew it. It had started last night in the garden when she had overheard her mama talking to God.

All of a sudden, Marie felt ill. "Mama, you are right, I don't feel very well," she whined and made a face, trying to look sickly.

Ignoring Marie's comment, Tilly continued. "I think I shall wear the hat I received from the ladies in New York City."

Marie changed her mood from sickly to indignant. "Mama, I thought you were going to save it for Easter Sunday!"

Absentmindedly, her mama continued to chortle, "Oh, yes, I forgot. I'll save it for Easter."

Mattie had hot crumb cake and cold cider ready for a quick Sunday breakfast. When Marie and Tilly entered the kitchen, Mattie was ready for them.

"Tilly, what a lovely morning it is outside. I suspect it shall be an even lovelier afternoon out there promenading up and down the streets where single women walk alongside single men. Oh, what can I say? Tilly, did you know you look quite lovely when your face is all red like it is right now?" She giggled and pretended to be promenading around the kitchen with her potholder holding onto the crumb cake pan. Mattie was such a rascal and loved to tease.

"Miz Johnson, remind me to do something clever to get you back for your cheekiness," Tilly retorted, trying hard to get a word in and still finish her crumb cake.

Taking her last swallow of cider, she continued. "Oh, thank you for the delicious breakfast. I need my strength to promenade, you know. Oh, goodness," she giggled, "I hope I can walk with my knees shaking like they are right now!"

Mattie smiled and gave her a knowing look and said, "Oh, me luv, like new lambs you'll be wantin' to frolic soon enough.

Back to Normal

Have fun!" Mattie saw the solemn look on Marie's face. She smiled and gave her a wink.

"I'm just a teasin' your dear mother — don't be such an ol' sour puss. See ya at church, Marie."

Marie gave her a pouty stare and thought, *Oomph, I will be an ol' sour puss if I want to be.* She ran to catch up with her mama, who was already on the front porch waiting for her ride to the church building. Marie took hold of her mother's gloved hand and asked, "Mama, what's a sour puss?"

***

The pastor ended his Sunday sermon, titled "Bondage to Our Past," with the following statement: "I am overjoyed to witness the Holy Spirit working in our lives. He is interested in every detail. He delivers us from the hurt and shame of our past and gives us liberty."

Then he proceeded to announce from the pulpit, "There are many newcomers attending our church. In order for people to get to know one another, there is a special soup and dessert luncheon provided by the ladies of this parish. All are welcome."

The congregation stood for the closing blessing and then funneled their way to the tables that had been set up for the luncheon. The new attendees had their names written on cards and placed on the tables. The assignment for those staying for lunch was to meet and greet one another, to remember everyone's name and to be able to recall at least one thing about each person. The children went to eat and play games in another room while the adults stayed to get to know one another.

Tilly looked feverishly to find her name on a place card. She found it next to the Brahm family, who owned the bakery. She did not know their first names, but had seen them often at the bakery and at church. Right across from her stood William Bogda. His seat was next to Mr. and Mrs. Max Mueller, who owned the local grocery store. The Mueller family seemed to know everyone in the community, either from church or through their local business. As everyone was standing around waiting for the blessing of the meal, Mr. and Mrs. Mueller took Mr. Bogda by the arm and stood in front of Tilly.

"Mrs. Baumann, it honors me to introduce my lovely wife, Hilda; also, let me present to you our new friend, Wilhelm Bogda."

All gave a slight bow to Tilly, which she quickly returned with a polite smile and a slight curtsy. Bill Bogda stated that he was delighted to make her acquaintance, and then he helped her to her seat. Thomas and Elsa Brahm knew Bill Bogda as well. They had met Tilly several times at church and frequently at their bakery when she picked up orders for the Carlisles' parties. Bill very conveniently seated himself next to Tilly, hoping no one noticed that he moved his name card. Max already knew the answers to the questions he asked Bill Bogda, but they were for Tilly's benefit.

She learned he had been a Merchant Marine as a young man and had traveled to many ports in South America, Africa, Dutch West Indies and Siam. He had grown up east of Berlin and had been an apprentice to a butcher, but the economy grew bad, and he and some friends had left to see the world. After three years, he returned home to become a clocksmith and to marry his childhood sweetheart. They were married seven years when she died in childbirth. America was his place to make a new beginning. This coming summer, he would be in America for two years. Bill worked in a meatpacking plant, where he received a handsome salary based on his previous experience as a butcher.

It was now Mrs. Baumann's turn to share about herself. She was suddenly shy. *What should she tell these nice people? What did she want to become common knowledge, and what was to remain private?*

There was a long, uncomfortable pause. Hilda Mueller spoke up to break the silence.

"Both Elsa and Thomas Brahm and Max and I were all widowed and met one another at this church. This has been a new start for all of us, and we are proof it can be done. We had nothing, yet within seven years, our life became blessed. We enjoy a good business with many loyal customers. This church has become our new family, in a way. Ha! Ha!" She suddenly felt awkward. "That is why in church we call one another brothers and sisters. Mathilda, may I call you Tilly?"

Tilly nodded her head, and Hilda continued speaking. "Tilly, we wish to welcome you so you, too, might feel someday this church is your family and we are your new relatives." Hilda laughed nervously and looked at her husband for reassurance.

Taking a deep breath, Tilly relieved the awkward tension by giving a brief account of her trip to America, emphasizing the many kindnesses shown to her. The group at the table sat eagerly listening. After the sharing assignment was over, everyone relaxed and began to enjoy one another. Hilda invited both Bill and Tilly to an Easter Sunrise Celebration that included breakfast. The Brahms and the Muellers hoped their newly made friends would help them set up the festive decorations in the church on Saturday afternoon, the day before Easter. A small party would follow at the Muellers' home. Tilly was careful not to accept the invitation until she spoke with her employer. This was a polite way to decline without looking unfriendly or unappreciative. The truth was that she did not know all the rules demanded of widows during the one year of mourning. She would ask Eleanor Carlisle about this. She did not wish to bring condemnation upon herself or upon the Carlisle household.

These couples were lovely people, and she felt their genuine friendliness. William was a very handsome and strong-looking man. She thought he would be what others referred to as a manly man. He was stout, and his complexion revealed he worked outdoors. His hands were large, but not bulky; he had artist's hands. She was curious what the clocks looked like that he made — or did he just repair them? She was not sure she had heard which he did: build or repair. He certainly did have a good appetite. She thought that was good; it meant he was healthy. The clothes he wore were modest, not too showy, but they looked expensive — not like the ones rich people wore; more like those that would last many years. That meant he was frugal. He showed good manners; he had helped her into her chair. He acted interested when she spoke — in fact, when anyone spoke. She liked that in a person. She also liked his smell; it was clean and manly. This made her heart beat in her throat. Her mother had warned her about such heart throbbing. She had instructed her daughter not to be alone with a man whenever she felt that way about him unless he had given her a wedding ring.

"Do not be a napkin when you can be the tablecloth," she whispered to herself. What an odd little saying! Her mother was purposely vague about those things that go on between men and women. She hoped she could be more direct with Marie, but she really did not know how. Suddenly anxiety swept over her like a breaker wave. She had so much to learn about life. Today made her realize how simple and sheltered her life had been in Germany. Yes, she knew much about birthing and dying, but everything in between seemed so complicated, so confusing, so difficult. Sitting with these strangers, she suddenly felt vulnerable and frightened. She looked at Hilda, who gave her a reassuring smile. Next, she looked at Elsa, who caught her eye and smiled. When she looked at Bill, he, too, smiled. He then looked at Max and began talking about getting another bowl of soup.

When the fellowship meal was over, Marie came with the other children to find their parents. She had made a picture for her mama and wished to show it to her immediately, but she saw her at the table sitting next to *that man.* Marie came to the table and stood between Bill Bogda and her mother.

"Mama, look what I made for you!" Marie said with her back to Mr. Bogda.

"How lovely, Marie, thank you! Marie, this is Mr. Bogda. We saw him once before. I have had the privilege to meet him today. My Love, please say hello."

"Hello," she said without looking at him.

"No, dear, turn around and greet him to his face." Tilly's mouth was smiling, but her eyes were demanding.

Marie gave her mother a dirty look. Her mother gave her a "do it or else" look in return. Marie reluctantly obeyed. Turning to look at Mr. Bogda, she gave a small curtsy and said, "Hello, how nice to meet you, sir."

He smiled and returned the pleasantries.

Back to Normal

She thought to herself, *I deserve a big reward for that performance, and I am going to be sure to ask for it later.*

Mrs. Mathilda Baumann awkwardly took her daughter's hand and said goodbye, then joined the others going back to the Carlisle home. When they got back to their room, Tilly changed clothes and curtly informed Marie she needed a nap. Then closing the door behind her, Tilly went into the kitchen and began to work on the Sunday evening meal.

"Mama, do you love me?" Marie asked as she awoke from her nap.

Tilly had opened the door to check on Marie. She found her daughter awake and offered her some dinner. "Yes, I love you Marie. I have loved you before you were born, and I shall love you for all of eternity. Do you know what eternity means?" Marie sat up in bed, wiping the sleep from her eyes.

"It means forever and ever and ever," Marie answered, jumping to her feet on the bed. Her mama grabbed her around the waist and swung her to the floor.

"That's right, My Love!" Tilly kissed Marie on the tip of her nose. "Did you know that you were Papa's and my miracle baby?" She knew all too well that Marie had never heard the story. Tilly sat down on the bed and pulled Marie onto her lap. She nestled her nose into the back of Marie's neck. Marie squealed but then came back for more. Tilly began the story.

"Your papa and I were married many years before you were born. Papa had fallen off a horse ... oh, well, it is not necessary to know all about that. I was convinced life would be just lovely without children. But secretly, I never really lost hope of having a child." She paused and fought the tears welling up in her eyes. "Well, then you came into our life, and I am so thankful. I love you, Marie. You, My Love, have a place in my heart that belongs to no other person. However, Marie, your mama has a big heart with lots of room for others as well. You have your place, but you do not have a right to anyone else's place. The same goes for you; you have a special place just for me in your heart, but you also love Mama Carlisle. I cannot be jealous of her having a place in your heart. There is room for both of us and many others as well."

Tilly's Song

"Yes, Mama." She knew all this was really about Mr. Bogda. She looked at her mama and asked, "Is there any dinner left for me? I'm hungry, Mama."

***

Easter was approaching, and springtime was in full bloom. The twins were thriving, and everyone was at last able to sleep through the night. Mama Carlisle was extremely resilient and almost back on her household schedule. The church ladies were meeting weekly in the garden. Each time they arrived, they were greeted with a new bulb flowering at its peak of fullness.

Tilly had put off talking to Mama Carlisle because she did not exactly know what to say. Time was running out, and she needed to respond to the invitation to the Easter activities. After everyone left, Mama Carlisle stayed in the garden and watched the children play while the babies enjoyed some fresh air. Tilly was collecting the used teacups and putting them on the tea tray when she stopped to speak with Mama Carlisle.

Approaching her and the babies, Tilly asked, "Mrs. Carlisle, may I speak with you, please?"

"'Mrs. Carlisle,' is it?" she looked up, surprised. "This must be something serious. Of course you may speak with me, 'Mrs. Baumann.'" Eleanor pretended to act formally and replied with a tease.

"Sorry, Mama Carlisle, I do have something serious to speak about with you," Tilly replied.

Mama Carlisle turned her full attention toward Tilly. "What is it, my dear?"

"Will you help me with the customs of this country in regard to the period of mourning? I heard that a woman must not socialize with men folk for one year. I need to know if it is inappropriate to go to church socials. You know I would never want to bring any shame to this family, my daughter or myself."

Eleanor interrupted her and asked, "Does this have to do with the gentleman who wishes to promenade with you and the other ladies?"

"Yes, it does — and not just that. On Sunday a few weeks

Back to Normal

ago when the pastor invited all the newcomers for the luncheon, the Muellers made a formal introduction of him to me. You see, I don't think I am ready to, well, I'm not sure what, um …"

Eleanor broke in again. "Are you afraid you are moving too fast since the death of your husband?"

"Yes, madam," she answered with her head lowered.

"Tilly, I can't advise you about such things. You must let the Holy Spirit guide your heart in these matters. By now, everyone here knows your character and respects you. Please don't think anyone will snicker or talk bad about you if you fall in love, no matter what time in life it happens."

"Thank you; you are kind to say such nice words to me. The year of mourning will not be over until September, and any time before that I just do not feel is right. Of course, this attention causes the ugly head of pride to rise within me. To have the attention of such a fine man, who would be a fine husband and father, honors me and yet it … also frightens me. I am so silly to think this way. Mr. Bogda has never been anything but cordial and a perfect gentleman. You see how my mind leaps ahead of me?"

"Nonsense, your instincts are accurate. The man is clearly attracted to you, and it is not silly to think he would want to take you as his bride. I do think he is also timid because he does not want to frighten you in any way. He may also still feel loyalty to his departed wife. Tilly, I can only imagine what the two of you must be feeling right now. However, I sense it is better to err on the side of waiting, rather than to rush into any relationship at this time. If you would feel more comfortable, I will talk with Max and Hilda Mueller and ask them to remember you at another social gathering sometime this autumn. Would that be to your liking?" Eleanor spoke to her as a very close confidant.

Tilly nodded her head in agreement. She trusted that Eleanor would be discreet and Hilda Mueller would understand Tilly's predicament and explain it to her husband. She most definitely did not want them to misunderstand her on this important matter.

Mattie was humming a tune and busying herself around the

kitchen when Tilly brought the tea set into the house. She knew Mattie had the gift to see all and hear all, so she started right in on her.

"What do you think about all this, Mattie?" she asked, regaining her nerve.

"So you wants to know what it is that I think on this, do you now?"

"Yes, I do. You know a lot about the goings on in this community, so tell me, how do I ignore this man — and even more, how do I ignore my feelings?"

"Well, darlin', the good Lord told us straight that while we were here on earth we would have troubles. However, in the same setting, He also told us not to despair for He had overcome this world. Tilly, our Lord has gotten you through many troubles; He can be trusted to carry you through to the end and you can be an overcomer yourself! Besides, there be lots of fish in the sea. If this one gets away, you'll catch you another and be happy, I know that to be God's truth."

"Thank you, Mattie!" Tears formed in her eyes.

"Now, now, don't start getting teary on me. You needs to be a washin' them cups with soap and water, not those tears coming out of your eyes." Abruptly she turned and resumed her humming and busied herself with the crust for the coconut pie.

Marie left the kitchen and went in search of Mr. Boehl. She found him with a mama cat feeding her seven little kittens. He was gently petting the mama's head. Marie heard her loud purring and saw the contented look on her face. Mr. Boehl told Marie that he kept cats around to keep rodents out of the garden. Rabbits ate his vegetables, and mice ate his seed. Cats were good about keeping the bird population low as well. Birds were pretty, but they made messes after eating the strawberries, raspberries, gooseberries and currants that Mama Carlisle counted on each year for pies and jams. Cats hunted all these critters. The Carlisle family had a love for animals, but they also respected a balance in nature.

Mrs. Swartz Kats was the name of the black mama cat that had two litters of kittens each year. All her babies learned to be good hunters, just like their mother. When the kitten population grew too large, Mr. Boehl would take the weaned kittens to the feed store where they earned their living by keeping mice and rats out of the grain.

The children loved to explore and use their imagination to pretend. There were kittens, baby goldfish and frogs. They would gather up the frog eggs and watch them change into tadpoles. While playing by the pond one day, Michael and Foster found a garter snake, but before they could pick it up, Mrs. Swartz Kats jumped on it, grabbed its head in her mouth and shook it until she severed its head from its body.

When Edna and Marie saw the cat chewing on the head, they ran around the yard screaming. The boys just stood there with their mouths open in disbelief. Marie was overwhelmed by the sight, but little Edna would go over to the snake body and poke it with her shoe, then run away screaming. After running around, she would go do it again. Mr. Boehl finally took a stick and carried the limp body off somewhere out of sight.

During the summer months, the children spent almost every waking moment outside in the garden. Often their lunch was in the form of a picnic. Sometimes they played so late into the evening that the lightning bugs would be out to entertain them. Since it was often hot in the house, the twins would join the other siblings in their buggy or on a quilt spread on the soft grass under the large oak shade tree.

Edna was just starting to talk and could not say Victoria or Gloria, so she called the twins *Vic Vic* and *Glo Glo*. The household embraced these cute baby names, which eventually became their nicknames. Marie would make believe she was the mama and tell Edna what to do and say. Vic Vic and Glo Glo were her babies. The twins were happy that the girls carried them around the yard and showed them special attention. Edna loved Marie and played well under her sometimes-bossy demands. When the kittens were old enough, Marie and Edna would dress them up in doll clothes and put them in the baby buggy with the twins. Mama Carlisle supervised the play, and in her absence, Nanny paid close attention so neither babies nor kittens would harm one another. Both Mama Carlisle and Nanny found the whole dress-up scene adorable.

Tilly's Song

It was mid-afternoon on an exceptionally hot July day in the Chicago area. The boys were catching frogs in the goldfish pond, and the twins were taking their nap in the buggy. Mama Carlisle took Marie and Edna into the house to gather some old clothes to play dress-up. This activity was usually reserved for rainy days, but it was a whimsical idea to dress up for a make-believe tea party in the garden, just as the grownups did. The two girls followed Mama Carlisle into her bedroom. To everyone's surprise, there was a man with his back to them taking jewelry out of Mama Carlisle's musical jewelry box.

"Lawrence?" Eleanor asked with alarm. He was caught red-handed. As he turned to face her, he saw the two little girls. In shame, he put his hands up to cover his face.

Edna ran over to him and hugged his leg. "Don't cry, Uncle Warry."

Marie, in shock, looked at Mama Carlisle. The look of horror was all over Mama Carlisle's face, and her eyes immediately filled with tears. No one spoke or moved for what seemed a long time. Finally, Mama Carlisle regained her composure. Clearing her throat so she could speak, in a rough whisper she asked Marie, "Will you take Edna outdoors and play, please?"

Without answering, Marie took Edna's hand and led her out of the room. Before they made it to the stairway, they heard the door slam; then they heard the yell, "Lawrence, you are in trouble!"

Both girls ran down the stairs and out the back door as fast as they could run. Without acknowledging Tilly and Mattie, who were peeling potatoes in the kitchen, the girls ran right past them.

"Marie, stop!" Tilly shouted. Edna and Marie stopped and turned around just as Mattie and Tilly caught up with them. "What is going on, Marie?" Tilly's voice demanded.

"Mama, I'm not sure I'm supposed to tell!" Marie pleaded, trying to catch her breath.

"Marie Martha Baumann, you answer me right now. You don't keep secrets from me, remember?" her mama barked at her.

"Mama!" she protested. "It concerns Mama Carlisle and

Back to Normal

what Edna and I saw. I don't think we were supposed to see it."

"Marie, tell me this minute what is going on!" Tilly commanded.

Mattie eased up to Tilly and said calmly, "Tilly, you're scaring the child."

Edna looked at everyone and said, "Uncle Warry was in Mama's music box. That made my mama really angry."

Tilly and Mattie looked at one another strangely and did not ask any more questions. They turned and walked back into the kitchen and continued preparing the evening meal. When Marie and Edna turned to go back to where the twins were, they saw Mr. Boehl, the boys and the nanny staring at them. All had heard Edna's account.

Frank Carlisle came home early that day, and with him were his mother and father. No one sat down to dinner until nine o'clock. Before the meal began, Eleanor excused herself to her bedroom, complaining of a headache. Frank walked her to their bedroom, then went down into the basement. Frank's mother, father and brother silently ate their meal; when they finished, they left the house together. An hour later, Frank emerged from the basement and ate alone in the kitchen.

The next morning when Marie came into the kitchen for breakfast, everyone stopped talking. The children were not included in any of the conversations about what was going on, and they seemed to know to stay out of the way of the grownups. Over the next few days, Frank and Eleanor Carlisle met with different groups of men during the day. Each group received a tea tray with an assortment of orange cookies, brownies and butter cookies.

Mattie Johnson was not her normal jolly self, and Tilly tried acting very busy. Nanny kept the children from being underfoot by reading to them and having them paint pictures of flowers from the garden. Michael's pictures were the only ones that slightly looked like flowers. When they came inside for lunch, the men were still in the parlor; Frank was talking loudly, but no one could understand what he was saying.

Marie looked at Mattie and asked, "Miz Johnson, who are those men and what do they want?"

Tilly's Song

"Oh, Marie, darlin', you seem to know what's goin' on around here more than the grown folks. We cannot be talkin' about these things to anyone outside this house. Uncle Larry is a bein' 'vestigated by the Constabulary and these insurance people for some very bad things they claim he has done. The other day he was a stealin' while Edna, Mama Carlisle and you walked in on him. Now it seems he has been a stealin' from a whole bunch a people to pay off his gamblin' debts. He's just 'bout broke poor ol' Grandma and Grandpa Carlisle. They are such fine folks and all; yes, indeed, it's a hurtful time for this household."

Tilly came up and said to Mattie, "She doesn't need to know everything — it will only burden her."

"You're right, Tilly, but she needs her questions answered or else she'll suffer from bein' excluded."

"I know," Tilly agreed.

"Marie, just know this is serious, and the whole Carlisle family has been put to shame. We need to help them through this time by respecting their privacy. Do you understand?" Her mother gave her the look she always gave when something was very important. Marie knew everyone was very serious, but she still had to fight back her giggles as she watched her mother's eyes quiver back and forth. Her mother's look somehow lost its impact because the eyes went crazy. This was no laughing matter, but if she did not leave, she was going to burst with laughter. Marie looked away from her mother and nodded her head in agreement, then ran to play with Hildegard on the front porch. She loved playing with the other children, although sometimes she just needed to be alone with her two other friends, Jesus and her dolly.

Hildegard was seated next to the railing of the porch while Marie leaned back to soak up the warmth of the sunshine. Mr. Carlisle stepped out of the parlor into the hallway and lit his cigar. Remembering his manners, he opened the front door. Frank did not know Marie and Hildegard were on the front porch.

"Why, hello!" Marie greeted him with a smile.

"Well, hello to you, my little friend." He smiled back at her.

Back to Normal

Marie struck up a conversation with him while he sucked on his cigar.

"When Mama and I were made to stay at Ellis Island for so very long a time, I didn't have anyone to talk to except Mama and Jesus. Sometimes Mama was too upset for me to talk to her, but Jesus never got upset, and I always felt better whenever we would talk. You see, most of the time, it is just me doing all the talking, and He does all the listening. Sometimes He talks to me, and I hear Him in my head. He says things to me, just like out of the Bible, you know, words like, 'Do not worry, I will take care of you', 'I love you' and 'You are my friend'. Now that I have Hildegard, I can hold her while I talk to Jesus, and it is as if she is hugging me while we talk. My dolly, Hildegard, never says anything. She just listens to us. Well, Mr. Carlisle, I was thinking if you need to talk to Jesus sometime about what's going on right now, you may borrow Hildegard to help you, if you want to, I mean."

Mr. Carlisle threw his cigar down, then reached down and picked Marie up and hugged her hard. "You little angel, you wonderful messenger, of course, that is exactly what I must do. I have been so angry, worried about my own reputation, I haven't even prayed. Marie, my darling, I am going to have a talk with my friend Jesus."

Marie looked at him and motioned to Hildegard.

"Not this time, but you are most gracious to offer Hildegard's special blessing to me. You have blessed me, Marie. Thank you, my darling child." He let her down and she took Hildegard up into her arms. Together with her dolly, she skipped around the corner of the house toward the garden to join the other children at play. As she turned her head to look back and wave goodbye to Mr. Carlisle, she saw her mama and Mattie watching through the curtain by the doorway.

The next morning, Mama Carlisle and all five children said goodbye to their father at the front door. Business was as usual. Marie joined the children for their lessons, and Tilly came upstairs to call everyone to lunch. Eleanor asked Tilly if she would stay a moment while she talked with the children.

"Children," she began, using her most formal tone of voice,

Tilly's Song

"I need to speak with you about Uncle Larry. Remember when all of you prayed for me when I was about to give birth to the twins? Your prayers were full of faith. We know from scriptures we are unable to please God if we do not have faith that He will do what He says He will do. Well, we all need to pray, believing for Uncle Larry right now. He made a decision to put his faith in luck rather than God. He started taking chances and gambling on games and horses and I don't know what all. Anyway, he lost a lot of money, and the men he owed it to said they would kill him if he didn't give them the money.

"Now, Uncle Larry made another decision. Instead of confessing his wrongdoings to God and asking for help, Uncle Larry took matters into his own hands. He started stealing things and selling them, hoping he would get enough money to pay these men. The other day, Uncle Larry was in the middle of stealing more of my jewelry when the girls and I caught him. The men who came to our house told us other wrong things he did. Uncle Larry is going to prison because he broke the law. Grandma and Grandpa will be coming to live with us because they have to sell their house to pay back the money he stole."

"Mama," Michael spoke up and asked, "is Uncle Larry a bad man?"

"Michael, Uncle Larry has done some very bad things, and he has hurt the people that love him. We need to pray for Uncle Larry."

"I love Uncle Larry," Foster spoke up and then began to cry.

"Come here, son," she motioned to Foster. He ran to his mother and sat on her lap.

"We all love Uncle Larry," Mama Carlisle said, comforting her son.

"Mother, Daddy doesn't love him!" Michael retorted.

"That's not true, Michael!" She stood up while still holding onto Foster. "Daddy is embarrassed, but more than that, he is frightened for him. He has been angry with his brother for taking advantage of your grandparents. My darling, he loves Lawrence — and together, as a family, we will get through this time of testing. Do you remember when we were studying the book of James? This is what he called tests and trials. We are going to count this pure joy because our faith will not diminish; instead, it will grow stronger. I have claimed Uncle Larry for the Kingdom of God, and I shall stand firm. Michael, let's sing a song and praise God for His mercies and grace."

"Mother, may we sing the song, 'Christ Our Solid Rock'?"

"Lovely! Let's begin, Michael."

They sang with great gusto all five verses, and then they sang all five verses again. This little band of believers sang with their whole hearts and prayed for Uncle Larry.

---

* *Grimm's Fairytales* is a collection of fairytales written by the famous German brothers, Jakob and Wilhelm Grimm.

Marie's favorite Grimm's story, "The Fisherman and His Wife," is about being content with the things you already have and the dangers of being greedy for things you do not need.

Chapter 10
Light After the Storm

It was well past the children's bedtime when the prayer meeting for Uncle Larry ended. As Marie and Tilly prepared for sleep, Marie asked her mother to pet her hair. This was a favorite way for both mother and child to relax before sleeping. Tilly played with her daughter's golden curls while they both spoke in whispers.

"Mama, you said I must come to you with anything that bothers me," Marie said, trying to fight off her sleepiness.

"Yes, My Love, I do want you to come to me. Is there something bothering you about tonight?" Tilly asked hesitantly.

"Mama, it is not about tonight; it is something different. Mama, I cannot remember Papa's face. I try, and I try, and I just cannot see him in my rememberer! Mama, it scares me because I do not want to forget. Mama, it scares me that you might forget him, too." Her voice was soft and sad.

"Oh, my sweet child, I shall always remember your papa. I miss him so much and the life we had together. Whenever I look at you, I see your papa's crystal-blue eyes looking back at me. So many of the little things about you are the same as his: your smile; your little nervous habit of biting the inside of your cheek; the way you tilt your head when you are listening intently to someone talk; the attention you pay to everyone's moods; the gift you have to see beyond the obvious." Tilly spoke tenderly; then with a giant sigh, she tried to relieve the heaviness within her chest. "Marie, you are so much like your papa. He also felt protective of me and never wanted me to cry or be upset. You know how much I love you, don't you?" Tilly paused for what seemed a long while. Marie wanted to know what she was thinking, but resisted the temptation to break her mother's reflective mood.

"You have many of my qualities, too," she said, now looking into Marie's eyes, "but, Marie, mostly you are unique with

qualities all your own. God designed you to be you, and He wants us all to be more like His Son. I am happy with His design, and Papa and I want you to be all God birthed you to become." Her voice was no longer a whisper. "Marie Martha Baumann, I like who you are!" she declared, almost jolting Marie by her exuberance.

Marie turned and hugged her mama, and together they wept.

"Marie, I don't know how to address the loss you feel because you cannot remember your papa's face. I just do not know what to say. We have no pictures or paintings of Papa and the children. We just cannot let ourselves be sad about all the things we do not have; we must embrace life and delight ourselves in all the good we do have, with no regrets or bitterness." Tilly looked down at her daughter, who was asleep in her arms. "That's all right. I needed to hear myself say these words!" Tilly reached down to kiss her beautiful girl and gently release the golden curl from her finger. "Sleep well, My Love, and dream of your papa. I hope you can remember."

The next morning as the children were learning their memory verse, Mrs. Carlisle asked Nanny to stay with her children while she talked with Marie alone.

"Marie Martha, you have such a lovely name. Did you know Marie is another name for Mary?" Mama Carlisle was hoping to impart some new information.

"No, Mama Carlisle, but Mama has read me the story of the two sisters, Mary and Martha, who were good friends with Jesus. She told me she named me after those sisters because she hoped that I would have the best of each of their qualities and that I would always be good friends with Jesus."

"Well, then, you remember that those friends called upon Jesus to come and heal their brother, Lazarus; they were very disappointed when He didn't come right away and their brother died." She looked at Marie to see if she understood.

"Yes, but Mama told me that was not the end of the story. She said sometimes we ask Jesus to do things for us, but He has something even better for us that we don't know about." Her words sounded wiser than her years.

Tilly's Song

"What do you mean, Marie?" Mama Carlisle asked, testing Marie's knowledge.

"The story in the Bible says that Jesus cried when He found out Lazarus was dead. Then He called His friend's name, and Lazarus came back into his body and walked out to Jesus, still in his burial linens."

Mama Carlisle was genuinely impressed. "Very good — you know this story well!"

"I love that story. I wanted Jesus to call Papa back from the grave, but He didn't," Marie reflected sadly.

Mama Carlisle pulled her onto her lap and rocked her back and forth. Marie felt her warmth and love. They did not talk for the longest time. "Marie, what I was going to talk with you about can wait. My dear, go back to the playroom now; I need some time to pray." They looked at each other and smiled.

Marie jumped off her lap, then turned and asked, "Shall I shut the door?"

"Would you, please?" Mama Carlisle quietly responded. Marie closed the door but listened outside the door to the prayer.

"Gracious Father, Your ways are so much grander, wiser and lovelier than my ways. I am so grateful You send those You have chosen to come through our home to stay for a little while. My friend, Jesus, help our friend Marie. Guard her mind, please. She carries burdens that only You can bear. Oh, Lord, in this time of change, have Your way in Marie and Tilly's life. I pray believing, Father. Thank You for hearing my petition, Lord. Amen and Amen."

Marie scrambled off to the playroom. Mama Carlisle started singing and moving about in her study. A song that she had learned while studying abroad in Germany had come into her mind — a song to all her new immigrant friends who felt very much alone, just as her little friend Marie must be feeling right now. Marie must, no doubt, have felt misunderstood, just as the mysterious waif named Mignon had in the novel by Johann Wolfgang von Goethe, *Wilhelm Meister's Lehrjahre (Learning Years* or *Apprenticeship)*. In the novel, which was put to music by Ludwig van Beethoven, an apprentice is called a *Lehrling* and a master craftsman is a *Meister*. The story is how an apprentice in the art of life becomes a master through years of life experience.

>Only one who has felt longing
>Knows what I suffer!
>Alone and isolated from all joy
>I gaze at the sky to the south
>Ah, he who loves and knows me
>Is far away.
>It makes me feel dizzy;
>It burns my inner parts.
>Only one who longingly knows
>Knows what I suffer!

The lyrics, *It burns my inner parts,* expressed the inner self revealed in Martin Luther's translation of the Psalms into German. It was Mama Carlisle's innermost self that burned with compassion for her people, her ministry, her life's work. The rest of the afternoon she talked to Jesus about her prayer and the song in her heart.

Marie heard this grateful prayer as she ran off, and it helped her remember one thing she thought she had forgotten about her papa: how he had prayed.

She could see him in her mind standing outside their barn looking at the children running through the bed linens Mathilda was hanging on the line. Marie could hear him thanking God. It seemed that all he ever said was "Thank You," over and over, as he named off his long list of blessings. Mama Carlisle prayed like her papa prayed.

"What do You think, Jesus? Is this what You want? Do You want me to remember, or am I supposed to forget everything of my past?" Marie always felt better after talking to her friend, even if He did not answer her right away. However, He was very clever in answering her prayers, and that night, Marie received His help in a dream.

The dream began with Marie smelling cherry-flavored pipe tobacco smoke. She followed the sweet smell into a living room where her mother was sitting on the couch tatting lace for a handkerchief. Her papa was sitting with his back to her, smoking his pipe while reading the Bible aloud to her mother. Marie was so thrilled to see him. In her excitement, she ran to him, calling out the name, "Papa!" When he turned his face to greet her, it was William Bogda. He laid the Bible down and took her into his arms, swinging her around in the air. Though surprised, Marie was genuinely happy to see him. Her mother looked on with joy on her face; she dropped her handwork on the floor and rose to join them in their merriment.

Marie was giggling and rolling around in the covers of the bed when she opened her eyes to see her Mama looking at her and smiling.

"Wake up, sleepyhead!" Tilly opened the curtains in the bedroom to let in the morning light. Marie jumped out of bed and ran to her mother. She threw her arms around her mama's waist and kissed and hugged her.

"Oh! My goodness! I wish you would wake up every morning like this." Tilly acted a little startled, yet pleased.

"Mama, I want to wake up every day and give you kisses!"

Later that morning as the children were playing and Tilly was pressing clothes, Mama Carlisle came into the kitchen for a cool drink.

"Good morning, Tilly! How is your day?" It was as if she sang the words to Tilly.

"It is a great morning, thank you," Tilly replied. "Do you have a moment that I could talk with you?" She suddenly had a serious tone in her voice.

"Of course. Do you want to go upstairs for privacy, or shall we talk here in the kitchen?"

"May I come to your office in five minutes? That will give me enough time to finish this shirt while the irons are hot."

"Very well, I'll heat some water, and together we can have a cup of tea and chat." Mama Carlisle smiled sweetly at Tilly.

A few minutes later, the two women climbed the stairs to Mrs. Carlisle's office. After both had finished a couple of orange cookies and most of the tea, Tilly began.

"My dear friend, I come to you not as an employee, but as

one mother to another. Please advise me about how I may help Marie right now. Last night, she told me she could not remember her papa's face. This really upset her, and she was also concerned that I would forget what he looked like. Oh, goodness, listen to me rattle on; I'm not too good with words, and I don't really know how to express what I am asking you to do or say. Does any of what I say make any sense to you?" Tilly was now on her feet, pacing back and forth in the office, wringing her handkerchief in her hands. Mama Carlisle motioned for her to sit down again.

"Memory is a funny thing. As little children, how much do we really remember, or how much do we remember people telling us about what happened? So much has happened since you left Germany. Marie has not just forgotten how her papa's face looked; she does not remember many of the everyday things she did while growing up in your home. If I may offer you a suggestion, I would take time to remember her papa's birthday and other special occasions that are important to you and to share with her what life was like in Germany. Tell her not only about her papa, but about her grandparents, the friends in your village, how your house looked — anything and everything that you want her to remember. Mathilda Baumann, this is not just your history, it is also Marie's history. The heart must heal, or the feeling of grief will never leave you or your child. Remembering life as it was does not keep you from living life as it is. However, if you bury those memories, they will never let you live in all the abundance Christ has for you." She looked at Tilly and then asked, "Does what I say help at all?"

"Oh, yes, yes, yes, it does. I thought if I talked about our past, I would cause her to hurt all over again. However, the way you said it, it will help her know who she is. I believe you are right! Yes, we must have a good talk; and as things come up, I will share from my heart the good times and the truth about the bad times. I don't want her to grow into a melancholy woman, sad and bitter in life."

"Oh, my dear, I do not think that will be a problem with Marie. She is in love with life and too much of a free spirit to ever become sour on life."

Tilly's Song

"Thank you for your advice and always for your great kindnesses you have shown my daughter and me." She rose to her feet again and gave a quick curtsy, then she took Mrs. Carlisle's hand and kissed it.

Eleanor Carlisle reached over with her other arm and pulled Tilly to her, hugging her and holding her for the longest time.

All Tilly could think of at that very moment was, "When two or more are gathered in my name, there shall I be also." She then took the tea set downstairs and returned to work.

***

Eleanor Carlisle began her daily lessons with all the children.

"Today, children, we are going to learn about the great nation of the United States." She pulled the globe out from the corner of the playroom. All the children huddled around it as she pointed to the country, then to the Great Lakes area and finally to the place on the map named Chicago. Mama Carlisle had an innate ability to make learning fun. Today she explained the facts about the big blue ball called Earth in such a way that even at their differing ages the children could grasp the amazing truth about it.

That night, Tilly asked Marie what she and the other children had learned in their lessons. Marie told her mother that they had been studying geography and they had been looking at a round globe that was actually a miniature of a planet named Earth.

"That is where we all live. I saw the ocean we crossed to get to America, and I saw New York and all the places we traveled to get to Chicago. Mama, we live on a very big planet." Her eyes were filled with wonder. She talked about the sun and the moon and even the stars. Marie was anxious to share her new knowledge with her mother.

"Did you know all that, Mama?" she asked, feeling really smart.

"No, I didn't, just some of it. I have known about the sun, moon and stars since my own mama and papa taught me about them. Well, let me ask you something you may not know. Did you know that God put the stars in the heaven so people could find their way to places and that some people plant the crops of the field or breed the livestock according to the seasons? Did you know that is how your own papa would farm? When we had a milk cow that needed to dry up so she could have a calf, Papa always checked the signs in the heavens," she told Marie, now thinking of herself as being really smart.

"Really? Please tell me more about Papa!"

"All right." She sat down next to Marie and began her story.

"Marie, your papa was a very strong, hardworking farmer who received the land near the village from his older brother. His brother acquired land for farming as payment for being a soldier in one of the many wars. Your uncle died while fighting in Chancellor Otto von Bismarck's Army long before your birth.

"I met Johann, your papa, at our village church. Johann had planned to go into the ministry to become a pastor. He was the third son of the family, and that was his lot in life.

"Things changed when both of his older brothers died, one in battle and the other in an accident. He then inherited the farm. Johann, now considered the eldest, could become a farmer, as he had always dreamed of being. Some of your papa's relatives lived near Prussia, close to Poland. Johann traveled there once to help them. They were very poor.

"However, throughout the years, these relatives no longer wrote letters, and soon we no longer knew their whereabouts due to many wars and too many changes in countries' boundaries. I do not know of any other relatives of your papa."

Marie listened and watched her mother's face as she spoke about her papa. When Tilly finished, Marie told her mama what she remembered.

"Mama, I've tried and tried to remember Papa's face, but all I can remember is his big hands. I can see him with his hands together in front of his face talking to God and saying 'Thank You,' over and over. I can see him in my mind standing by the barn saying 'Thank You, thank You' as if his whole prayer was just one big 'Thank You.' I remember falling asleep in his arms as he read to me and, better yet, sang to me. I don't remember any of the songs or stories, but I do remember loving the moment. That was where I felt safe and warm. See, Mama, I do remember some things, don't I?" She looked at her mama for approval.

"Oh, my, you remember so many good things. I am happy, My Love. Your papa called you his little bee. One reason was he said you were sweet as honey, and the other reason was you were so busy. You loved flowers, and you were always sticking your nose in them to smell their fragrance. You were his Miss Bee." She smiled as she remembered.

These memories were shared without tears of sadness. Smiles were on both of their faces as little bits and pieces of their past floated to the surface of their minds. Together, they said their nightly prayers and went to sleep. Tomorrow they would awake into a new day.

***

One new day was followed by another, and soon spring had turned into summer. All summer, the days were warm and fun. The entire summer seemed to pass quickly. It was those summer nights, however, that seemed to be long and often sleepless for Tilly. Sometimes when she closed her eyes, she would dream of the village in Germany and awaken with a start, smelling smoke and seeing her friends' homes burning. Her new life was good, but there seemed to be many ghosts of her past that would not let her rest. The blackness of her mourning clothes began to feel heavy and burdensome.

Finally, the dreaded day came, the day traditionally marked to end the proper period of mourning: September 22, 1895, exactly one year to the day since Tilly and Marie had buried John next to their other children and begun their journey to America. And on this day to remember, the Chicago area was experiencing one of its massive thunderstorms. This particular type of storm made the air heavy and humid, and the clouds were full of hail and torrential rain.

All day, Tilly had been uncomfortable from the heat.

Drinking water had not quenched her thirst; she had no desire for food. The mosquitoes and flies were pesky, and every noise seemed to make her more and more nervous. The static in the air had been building all day. These weather conditions matched Tilly's heavy mood.

Everyone within the house was making ready for bed; Marie was already asleep. Tilly was restless, not a bit sleepy. The house was hot, and her skin felt sticky. The sleeves on her dress were wet with perspiration and clung to her arms. Not one minute more could she be confined within her room or any room — she had to get out of the house. She barged out the back door into the blackness of the garden that would light up periodically with long twisting lines of lightning followed by the deafening crashes of thunder. The thunder sounded so close to the lightning that the storm seemed to be right over the house, moving from the direction of Lake Michigan. With one large boom of the thunder, the sky opened up and threw down small balls of ice onto the hot ground. The odd combination created fog that formed around her ankles and inched up her body to her waist.

Tilly would not be swallowed up in these elements of nature: hail, fog or storm. In the grand universe, this place and moment were infinitesimal. In her emotions, time or place did not exist. She did not *feel* anger — she *was* anger. The energy and might of the storm could be spoken to and silenced, but the incredible emotion within her could no more be subdued than lava spewing toward the heavens, melting the clouds in its path. Her body was numb, and the fury within her was blinding.

She screamed as she gritted her teeth. "Oh, this awful dream — what a horrible nightmare! I can't wake up. Who is this, this body, and what am I doing here? I am not alive; this is not living; I am dead and this is *hell*. I don't want any of this to continue. I can't breathe — there is no air. The light does not conquer the darkness. I'm being swallowed up by the darkness. Where is my Savior, and why has He forsaken me? This dress — its blackness has become my identity. Who am I if I am not Frau Johann Baumann? Am I Tilly? Who is she? An impostor! She is not real!"

She shook her fists at the violent heavens and fearlessly declared war. "I want my husband to come home to me and wake me out of this awful illusion. I want my baby to wake me in the night to suckle. And Mary — Oh, God, I want *Mary.*" The hot tears burned down her face and disappeared into the creeping fingers of the fog that clung to her. Her ranting continued as she screamed toward the angry heavens. "I have tried to do what You wanted me to do, but it is too hard, and I hate it! I hate it, I hate it, I hate it!"

The thunder, the croaking of the frogs and the sound of the rain pounding on the metal roof of the shed drowned out her screams. Tilly could not hear her own voice. She felt defeated, as if God Himself would not be able to hear her. She hung onto the trunk of the shade tree that was unable to block the downpour of rain. Her screams of travail, giving birth to this grief, suddenly transitioned into muffled sobs. Tilly's groans of pain rhythmically surfaced from a place deep within her, creating a primitive beat recognizable to every animal ever wounded or in pain.

Franklin and Eleanor Carlisle looked down into the garden from the second floor window, somewhat hidden by the drapery.

"Oh, Franklin, what should we do?" Eleanor pleaded.

"Ellie, she has been a hard one, so stoic, appearing to be just fine. She needs this catharsis, darling. I won't let her hurt herself. Mattie is also watching out for her right now. She knows what to do for her. Mattie's gift is helping hurting women who are like soldiers coming home with battle fatigue. Ellie, you always want to rush in and comfort, but, darling, she has to do this or she will never move on into her new life. Each of us must endure the dark night of the soul in order to break out of the old ways and into the new creation." He pulled his wife to him and held her as they gazed out the window. He could hold and try to comfort his wife, but there was no way to comfort Tilly at this time.

It seemed as though a long time had passed, and Tilly was still out in the storm. Marie was sound asleep and safe in the comfort of her bed. The temperature was much cooler; the house was no longer an oven. Mattie had heard the clock chime when she saw Tilly run out the back door. The clock was chiming again, letting her know an hour had passed. She decided she had waited long enough, so with teacup in one hand and umbrella in the other, she took a deep breath and charged into the dark, wet night.

"Tilly, here you are, darlin'. I thought you might like some nice hot tea as refreshment since you have been out here so long feeling sorry for yourself. I've added extra sugar to the tea to wash away some of that bitterness." Mattie's voice was impatient.

Tilly lunged at her friend like a hungry wild animal. "How dare you invade *my* privacy! How dare you talk to *me* like that! Who are *you*? I know, you think you are 'Queen Know-It-All.' You are always so quick with your 'God's own truth.' Well, how do YOU know what I'm going through right now? *You* have never lost a husband or children! You, *you!* Life is not all crumb cake and blessed cups of tea!"

In her rage, she slapped Mattie in the face and knocked the teacup from her hand. Tilly reached down and picked up a sharp piece of broken china.

"I have had enough. I hate this place. I have no life. Marie is just like one of the Carlisle children; she can stay here. I'm better off dead. I can cut myself, and I can cut you if you try to stop me." Her eyes were wild, but they suddenly changed, and she looked like a little scared child.

"Where did God go? I can't feel His presence anymore. I've been abandoned. Everyone is gone, too. I have no family, no village. I am so, so … *sad.*" Tilly's voice was hoarse, and she could only speak now in whispers. "I'm so disappointed. There must be some horrible mistake. What did I do wrong? Am I being punished?" she whimpered.

Mattie reached out to her. She could see Tilly was exhausted. Up to now, Tilly's emotions had been fluid, running to fill any low place in her psyche, but now they had solidified and become rock-hard.

Many Germans were described as being hard, emotionless, and this characteristic set them apart from other people from

Northern Europe. This was viewed as a quality of strength, yet it was treated with disdain by others to the point of stereotyping. Once the volcanic explosion of her anger had spewed its passionate magma out toward the heavens, it quickly cooled. It seemed now that nothing could move Mathilda to tears. This cooling of anger was the first warning of emotional depression of the deadly kind.

"Darlin', let's go inside, out of the rain, and get dried off. We can talk about all this inside." Mattie's voice was very calm and consoling.

"I'm not your *darlin*!" Tilly yelled back, letting out the angry beast once more. "I'm not anyone's 'darlin'.' This is a dark place. I am so tired of all this. DON'T YOU UNDERSTAND? I AM SPEAKING GOOD ENGLISH!" She turned away from Mattie and began to walk away from the tree. Suddenly, she turned and faced Mattie again.

"I can't remember how he smelled, Mattie. I CAN'T REMEMBER! So that's it? He dies, I forget him? I just go fishing in the sea of life 'cause there are so many of them out there and catching just any one of those ol' fish will make me happy? Well, I am here to tell you, I AM NOT HAPPY. I AM NOT HAPPY! Living in this foreign country where everyone eats far too many potatoes, I am not happy. No, I am not happy!" Tilly was pacing back and forth in front of Mattie. She had cut the tip of her finger with the broken china, and the blood was running onto her wet, not-so-white apron.

"Lov', look at yah! You are shakin' like a leaf. Come on inside and get warm. We can —"

Tilly cut her off. "My name is Frau Johann Baumann to you!" She started to sway, and Mattie ran to catch her before she fell. Mattie took the piece of china from her hand and helped her up the steps to the back door and then into the kitchen. Tilly was sobbing as Mattie removed her shoes and stockings, put her feet into a pan and then warmed them with water from the teakettle. While Tilly soaked her feet, Mattie quickly retrieved a large quilt from one of the beds and wrapped it around her. Then she took off the other wet garments.

Tilly was spent. Mattie prayed silently and constantly. Eleanor stuck her head in through the hall door. Tilly's back was to her, but she caught Mattie's attention. They spoke no words, but they exchanged looks to communicate concern and then to say it was better. Eleanor and Franklin prayed the night away in front of the fireplace in the parlor. Mattie put Tilly to bed in a spare bedroom so she would not wake Marie.

By morning, the storm was over, and bright sunshine filled the sky. Marie was informed her mama was not well and needed some time to sleep. Tilly slept almost two days due to the medicine given to her in her tea. No one offered her any food. The household was given minimal information, but all the workers knew firsthand the troubles in life and respectfully allowed Tilly her privacy.

Mattie was her full-time nursemaid and sat in her room reading the Bible while Tilly slept. Whenever she awoke, Mattie would help her to the chamber pot and then right back into bed to continue her rest. Although Tilly did not speak, Mattie could read her face and the look in her eyes. Both women stayed at the Carlisle house while all the others, including Marie, went to church. The pastor and other friends at church made concerned inquiries, but the members of the Carlisle household actually shared little of the situation.

**

Eleanor Carlisle, everyone soon discovered, was an excellent cook. She took charge of Sunday dinner for the household and the evening guests. Sauerbraten with spaetzles was the main dish. The fish entrée was fresh Sun Perch with a grated horseradish red sauce. The bread and dessert were ordered and delivered from the Brahms' bakery. The rolls were a hearty rye with caraway seeds, and the dessert was, of course, apple dumplings. Tilly received her first food in the privacy of her own room. The guests complimented the lady of the house for the fine meal, and everyone, including Tilly, devoured every morsel.

This menu Eleanor designed was clearly with Tilly in mind. She remembered Tilly claimed each dish to be her favorite.

Eleanor prepared the meal as food for her soul, and Tilly appreciated the comfort of the feast as soon as the fork met her lips.

When Mattie came to take the empty tray, Tilly put her hand on top of Mattie's. "Mattie, will you ever be able to forgive me? I am so sorry. My fear has always been that I would lose control. I did once on the ship coming to America, and I almost did again while I was confined at Ellis Island. I would like to say that behavior is unlike me, but it is too late; you have seen my ugliness. I really do want to live. I am so ashamed. If I want John's memory honored, I cannot go mad. You all have nursed me and loved me, and I do feel much, much better. Will you accept my apology? I said so many ugly things to you! None of them are true, none of them. I haven't forsaken God. I know with all my heart He has never, no not ever, forsaken me! I am a brat, Mattie, a big overgrown brat —"

Mattie interrupted, "Oh, stop it! Yes, Tilly, I do forgive ya. And do ya be a knowin' why I forgive ya? Ya don't need to be guessin', for I'll tell ya why. It is 'cause I have been forgiven much. I not only forgive ya for your mean words, I forgive ya for the false ones as well.

"Tilly, my dearest friend, ya have a contrite heart so I will tell ya who I was. Today, mind ya, I am a new creation because the Lord Jesus had mercy upon me and for no other reason. Tilly, ya said I did not know how ya felt, that I had never lost a husband nor little children and all. Well, that is not true. You judged me, Tilly, just by the things ya know about me today." She set the tray of dishes down on the end of the bed and turned toward the window and pulled back the drapes to expose the sunset. Turning back to face Tilly, she began her story.

"It has been not one year ago, but rather 14 years ago when life as I knew it came to an end. I was born a bastard child and, as far as I know, have only one living brother. My mother sold me into the flesh market, but Mr. Johnson took me in. We never had a proper wedding. By the time I was 21 years old, I had four children. Every day, I was drunk. I was a beggar and a thief. Oh, I wasn't stealing to keep my children from starving; it was to get one more bottle to keep me drunk. My youngest was born with the face of a child from a drunken mother."

Mattie stopped and looked out the window to regain her composure. After a short while, she turned back to Tilly and continued.

"One day — I guess it was bone cold, I was too drunk to know — I'd passed out in the alley shelter made out of shippin' crates. I didn't even have a blanket 'cause I sold it and even the baby's diapers. Me brother, the cop, found us. I woke up to him beatin' up on me with his billy club. When I turned from him, I saw all my little ones in a heap, tryin' to stay warm. They were all blue and gray.

"Another cop brought Mr. Johnson to see what I had done. The next day when he sobered up, he signed up to go to sea. Me brother took me to a place where the people called themselves Christians. Later, they called themselves The Salvation Army. They talked to me from the Bible. They said it was God's own Word recorded so we here on earth could get to know Him, you know, how Him bein' the creator of everything, how it was all supposed to work. He let us know over and over how we were His children and how He wanted us to act. Well, I didn't need any army to tell me I was not living the way He created me to live." She looked at Tilly, pointed her finger at her and continued.

"You know, Tilly, darlin', I cannot to this very day understand why the Creator of the Universe gave His son to die in my place. When I told the preacher God just couldn't love me, a murderer, thief and drunkard, he told me a story about a man named Saul of Tarsus, who was changed and even got a new name: Paul. Paul called himself a sinner of sinners. Well, that title described me. The preacher asked me if I wanted to be saved and washed clean and become a new creation. He also said if Jesus would save Paul, then Jesus could save a woman name Madeline. You see, I never knew who I was, either. I didn't even know if I had a last name." As she walked to the end of Tilly's bed, the setting sun poured through the window with light so bright it made her skin seem translucent.

"That was one of the miracles Jesus did in my life. The other miracle was with Mr. Johnson. When his two years at sea were up, he came lookin' for me. He found me working as domestic help at the Bonn home. That was Eleanor Bonn, who is the mistress of this house and the lovely wife of Franklin Carlisle. Her family is so rich even the rich look poor alongside them. Her parents had heard my story, and they told me all they would consider was how I lived after the day I believed. They took me in, fed me, clothed me, trained me, paid me and every day showed me what God's love really is.

"When Ellie married Frank, I mean, you know, Mr. Carlisle, they both insisted I come to be head housekeeper in their new home. Well, of course, I just love 'em both so much, I said yes.

"Well, about six months rolled by, and Mr. Johnson showed up at the back door asking me if I would marry him. God had totally changed his heart at sea. He said he even saw Jesus walkin' out there among the waves — and Tilly, honestly, he had never even once read the Bible, knowin' Jesus walks on water. He was so different acting, but in the same body. You see, God brought me a new man, a new creation. The old man never loved nobody! He told me it was him that killed the children 'cause he didn't care for them or me like a godly man does.

"Well, we got married the next Sunday in the Lutheran church that we go to every Sunday. Now that's it. You see me as I am today. My Lord is still workin' with me to be perfect as He is perfect. I suspect that is one of the reasons you are here: to help God with my perfectin'." She reached down and picked up the tray off the end of the bed and started to the door. Tilly called to her.

"Mattie, set the tray down, I can get it!" Tilly stepped into her house slippers and put on her robe. "Mattie, my dear, will you tell Marie and the Carlisles that Tilly is getting well?" She held her head up and took the dishes to the sink for washing.

As time went by, Tilly learned many people's stories. Some of her newfound friends had come from wealth and now had none. For others, the opposite was true: They had been poor, and yet now in America they were gaining wealth. America was a great equalizer with opportunity and liberty for all to seize.

The self-pity that Tilly had worn like a garment could no longer cling to her as she heard these stories. It was true that they all had their stories; at first, they drew her simply out of morbid curiosity. However, hearing the pain of others soon began to numb her to her own pain and form some sort of odd comradeship of suffering. Eventually she no longer needed to hear stories of the past; she was forming new memories of new life experiences. For Mathilda Baumann and her child, Marie, life took on a new rhythm much like the change in a song when the chorus follows the verse.

So it was in the early 1890s: More than 500,000 German immigrants flooded into the United States of America seeking a new start with God's blessing. The past was just that: *the past!* It was the glorious future that now offered hope. Without much thought, both Tilly and Marie knew they were finally in a safe place of happiness. People who had forsaken everything came together with others like themselves to form friendships, extended families and even communities.

Wilmette, Illinois, was this kind of community. Although originally an Indian dwelling, it had grown to approximately 1,500 and was now predominantly German. It took on the name New Trier after the city of Trier, Germany, an ancient outpost for the Roman Empire (where Roman ruins can be viewed to this day). This new Trier of America was built over the ruins of many people's lives. Somehow this served as a firm foundation that allowed the community to build a town rich in mercy; second chances were offered around every corner.

In the year that followed the anniversary of Marie and Mathilda's arrival in Illinois, they both adjusted to their new way of life. With the guidance of the Carlisle family, they slowly entered more and more into a social life of their own, making most of their friendships through the church and local businesses.

In the fall of 1895, Tilly attended the Oktoberfest at the home of the Brahm family. There were refreshments, games, music and much dancing. As soon as Tilly heard the polka music, it brought back memories of her youth dancing with her father and uncles — and, of course, all the young men her age. John had loved to dance. Sometimes in their small kitchen, he would hum a tune and take her in his arms and dance around the room. It always made her laugh; even now, the memory of it made her laugh out loud. Bill Bogda was in her periphery and took this moment as an opportunity to speak with Tilly.

"What's so funny?" he asked.

She had not seen him there at first, so she was startled by his presence and question. "Oh, just remembering how much fun I used to have dancing," she quickly replied.

"Well, then, would you do me the honor of dancing with me?" he asked as smoothly as he knew how.

"Yes," she answered and took his hand as he led her onto the dance floor.

"You look very pretty. Is that a new dress?" he asked, making polite conversation.

"Oh, yes. I have a new wardrobe. No more black," she said with a smile. Together, they held their gaze, broken only by the end of the music. Another man came up and tapped Bill on the shoulder and asked for the next dance with Tilly. She reluctantly accepted, but kept her eyes on Bill the whole time she danced with the other man. Bill was quick to tap in for the next dance and the next and the next. When the party was over, a group walked back to the Carlisle house, and Bill asked if he might accompany Tilly. Before she could answer, the others answered for her. "Come on, Bill, it will be fun." Bill waited and looked at Tilly for her approval.

"Please, walk with us; it will be fun." Her eyes were smiling at him. The others quickly entered the house, leaving Tilly and Bill to say their goodbyes. They both spoke at once and then started to laugh.

"You were about to say?" Bill politely let her go first.

"I was about to say, you are a very good dancer, and I had fun tonight." Tilly giggled.

His mind was running wild with all the things he wanted to say but decided not to right at this moment. Instead he returned the compliment and said good night. He waited at the door until she was inside.

She waved goodbye through the window at him as he walked back to his apartment. When he turned the corner, he ran as fast as he could to burn off his pent-up energy.

"Bill, ol' boy, I think she likes you!" he said out loud to

himself. As he turned to walk back to his apartment, he was whistling the tune of *Der Nussbaum,* The Nut Tree.* He hoped it was a prophetic message the Holy Spirit had placed within his heart and mind.

> A walnut tree is turning green in front of the house,
> Spreading out fragrant, airy branches.
> It has a lot of lovely blossoms;
> gentle breezes come to caress them.
> Two by two they whisper,
> bowing and bending delicately to kiss each other.
> They are whispering about a girl who would be thinking
> night and day about she knows not what.
> They are whispering (Who could make out such a quiet song?)
> About a bridegroom and about next year.
> The girl listens to the rustling of the tree.
> Longing, imagining, she smiles as she falls asleep and dreams.

The next morning was cooler than the day before, and Tilly was pleased because she had to finish pressing clothes. Marie was busy sprinkling clothes that had been starched stiff, and Tilly was heating up the iron.

"Mathilda, my sweet, someone is asking for you and your dear Marie at the front door!" Miz Johnson announced loudly so everyone could hear her formal request. It was something special, since Mattie Johnson almost never called her anything but Tilly — and besides that, people wishing to speak with the workers used the servants' entrance at the back of the house.

Tilly set the iron down onto the holder, wiped her hands, straightened her hair, smoothed down her apron and pinched her cheeks. "Do I look presentable?" she asked, looking for everyone's approval. She looked at Marie and smiled. "Well, come on, dear, let's see what this is all about!" She motioned to Marie to hurry. Marie trotted down the hall behind her mother, and both arrived at the front door as Miz Johnson opened it to reveal a deliveryman standing there with two boxes with red ribbons. He looked up and spoke to Tilly.

"Mrs. Mathilda and Miss Marie Baumann, I presume?" he

asked formally.

"Why, yes, yes, that is our names," Tilly replied shyly.

"Please sign here. This letter is for you as well." He handed her the pen and paper to sign and then retrieved a small envelope from a pocket in his uniform coat.

Tilly signed and received the boxes and the letter. The deliveryman tipped his hat and turned to go.

"Oh, forgive me, young man, I brought no money with me. Could you wait just inside here for your tip?" She turned and gave Miz Johnson a pleading look.

He smiled. "No need for one, madam; the housekeeper has blessed me with two bits, but thank you for your generous offer and kind manners." He tipped his hat again, then got on his bicycle with the delivery basket and rode off down the driveway.

"Mama, I'm so excited! What is it?" Marie whispered.

Tilly put the packages down on the floor and with trembling hands opened the envelope and read the letter. It read:

Dear Mathilda Baumann and Miss Marie Baumann,

I am writing to request the pleasure of your company for dinner this coming Saturday evening at 7 p.m. at the Cologne Bistro. I shall come to your address and collect you at 6:30 p.m., if you so agree. Please reply by giving your answer to Mr. and Mrs. Mueller at their grocery store, since I am away at work most of the day. It is my sincere hope you will join me, for I have wondrous news to celebrate, and I can think of no others I should want to share my happiness.

William A. Bogda

"Oh, my goodness!" Tilly handed Marie the smaller box with her name on it and watched her untie the bow.

"Oh, my, my!" she sighed.

"Oh, Mama, look!" Marie pulled out a lovely nosegay of violets. She sniffed them and then took a long deep breath. "Umm, they smell wonderful!" She held them up to her mother's nose for her to enjoy their fragrance.

Inside Tilly's box were four roses of red, yellow, pink and white. The roses, fern and baby's breath flowers were bound with a beautiful velvet ribbon. The two looked at each other and began to giggle. They saw all the coworkers come toward them to admire their glorious surprise. Eleanor Carlisle even stepped out of her study and leaned over the banister to see what all the excitement was. When she saw the flowers, she rushed downstairs.

"What is happening? Tilly, what is all this?" Mama Carlisle asked with excited curiosity.

"Look, look!" Tilly and Marie said together, and they both reached into the boxes to show off their bouquets.

"Here, read the letter. I am too shaky to read it aloud," Tilly said to Mama Carlisle.

Nanny had already gotten two vases filled with water and asked Tilly if she could put the bouquets into the vases. Tilly agreed and asked her to place them somewhere everyone could enjoy them. Nanny flashed Tilly a look she did not understand and immediately dismissed due to all the excitement.

"Madam Tilly, may I place them on the credenza so everyone may see them?" she asked Tilly, but then quickly looked at Mrs. Carlisle.

Eleanor Carlisle missed her look because she was devouring the short letter. She finished, clasped it to her heart and sighed to herself, "How wonderfully romantic!" Looking at Nanny, who was still waiting for a response, she brushed her hand with the letter toward Nanny in approval. "Oh, yes, place the flowers wherever Tilly wants them. It is so kind of you to share them with the household. Oh, Tilly, someone is more than just fond of you!" she said with tears in her eyes and a tease in her voice.

Tilly's face suddenly lost its mirth, and she soberly asked, "Oh, Mrs. Carlisle, what do I do now?"

"You do want to accept his dinner invitation, don't you?" Eleanor asked, already knowing the answer. Everyone in the hallway giggled. Tilly's cheeks turned bright red; then, forgetting her shyness, she boldly answered, "Why, yes, I do!" and then she giggled in embarrassment.

"Well, then," Eleanor motioned, "come with me. I have the perfect stationery for you to use in response. Come to my study, and you can compose the letter there. I will send Mr. Boehl to the Muellers' grocery store, and he can deliver it as soon as you complete it. Next, my dear, we need to look at your wardrobe and decide what you will wear to this special dinner engagement. Oh, Tilly, this is so exciting. Now, about your hair: Mrs. Johnson, I need your assistance."

Tilly and Mattie followed Eleanor Carlisle upstairs.

"What about me, Mama Carlisle?" Marie called after them. They all turned as one to face Marie. The smiles upon their faces were just the invitation she needed. Together, they all climbed the stairs.

***

Bill Bogda showed up at the Muellers' grocery store after he got off work. He rushed to the living quarters in back of the store and gave a rap on the door.

"Anybody there?" he called.

"Bill, is that you?" came the voice from behind the curtain.

"Yes, it is I!" he answered.

The lady of the house, Hilda Mueller, greeted him with an envelope in her hand and showed him his name written on it. "Don't worry, Bill, it is still sealed. I was very tempted to open it and take a peek."

He took it and stood as if frozen.

"What is the matter with you? Open it, open it — I can't stand the suspense!" Hilda squealed. He opened the envelope and looked at the even, artistic penmanship before even giving notice to what the message said. The words were as follows:

Dear Mr. Wilhelm Bogda,

My daughter and I most happily agree to accompany you to dinner on this coming Saturday.

Respectfully yours,
Mrs. Baumann

Hilda looked eagerly at Bill but could not read any emotion. "So, hey there, friend Bill, what did she say?"

She could not contain her excitement.

"She said yes," he answered, still showing no emotion.

"What's the matter? I thought you would act pleased." Hilda was confused.

"I am. I mean, I really am pleased," he said, snapping out of his spell.

"So, what is it?"

"Here, read her note." He handed her the note card and envelope. Hurriedly, she read the contents. He looked at Hilda, his friend, and stated, "It sounds so formal."

"Now, Bill!" She used the words most happily. "I think she is excited. She can't come across too anxious, you know; it might send the message that she is desperate. We women have to be a little coy, or you may think we are not being respectable. My guess is that she wrote a dozen notes before this one, which sounds like she was pleased you asked without appearing too eager. I like her response; it's lady-like. I like it, Bill, and you should, too. It's a good acceptance. Yes, a good note, Bill."

"Do you really think so, Hilda?" His voice stammered as he gazed at the tips of his shoes.

"Yes, I do!" She watched the smile form on his lips.

"Thanks, Hilda. Well, I better go. There are plans to make, you know." He left in haste and knocked the curtain rod off the doorframe. He bent over to retrieve it.

"Just leave it, my friend. It happens all the time."

"Sorry, I am so clumsy."

"Bill!" she shouted to him as he was leaving.

"Yes?"

"Flowers! Remember, Bill, she loves flowers." She felt very proud of herself for being such an encouragement to him. "Oh, my," she sighed, then quickly turned and prayed. "Lord, help them. Please!"

Max Mueller came in through the back door and saw his wife picking up the curtain off the floor that separated their living quarters from the store.

"Hilda, what are you doing, love?" Max asked as he walked toward her. She swung around to face him and rushed to give him a big kiss.

"Wow, I am glad to see you, also. You sure look happy!" He leaned in for another kiss.

"Oh, darling, romance is in the air, and you know how much I love romance!" she sighed.

"Are you talking about you and me, or are we talking about someone else here?" He looked confused.

"Oh, silly, it's Bill and Tilly! It is finally happening. I've been such a little matchmaker, and everything is falling into place." She smiled up at her handsome husband. "After all, I prayed God would send me the most perfect husband, and He not only heard my request, but He continues to answer it every day. I just put a good word in with the Lord for Bill and Tilly, and see, God is so faithful." She giggled and kissed him on his nose.

"I must admit, you and the Lord make a mighty good team!" They both laughed.

"So what's for supper? I have been working at selling food all day, and I am famished." He sniffed the air to guess what was in the oven.

"Oh, it is not quite done yet. You and I have some time together before it is time to eat." She gave him that look he loved to receive.

* *Der Nussbaum,* The Nut Tree, music by Robert Schumann and lyrics by Julius Mosen.

Chapter 11
Romance Is in the Air

William A. Bogda was a friendly, respectable man, well thought of by others. He had learned as a Merchant Marine that there were two kinds of women in this world: the marrying kind and the kind to avoid. Bill had but one weakness: beer. He would have a beer or two, not seen as excessive for a German; the problem was that the wrong sort of woman hung out in the local pubs or neighborhood bars. He could have had his loneliness abated nightly if he so decided. Instead, he longed for a lasting relationship with a woman who could honestly make the commitment he could count on for richer or poorer, for better or worse, in sickness and in health.

He had seen a sailor buddy go mad from years of brothel visits and had seen the unfaithfulness of bar girls. No, he'd tasted the good life of love and home, so he wanted a God-fearing woman — not just one that dressed up each Sunday to be seen. He desired one who displayed the fruits of the Spirit in her life. He was too old to be marrying a girl. Instead he wanted a spiritually mature and physically attractive woman, one with mirth and thrift. About to give up on the idea that God still made that type of woman, he saw Mathilda Baumann in church that Sunday late in January. There was a light shining through her that he'd seen only in his own sweet wife's presence. No, she didn't look the way his wife had looked, but she possessed the same gentle spirit and ladylike manners.

Mathilda Baumann, whom he had heard called Tilly, had a stout build. Stronger looking than his wife, who had always seemed fragile and weak, Tilly was the picture of wholesomeness. She was well groomed and tidy; her dress was conservative, although it could not camouflage her voluptuous figure. Though proper and modest, her movement conveyed a natural sensuousness that only men would notice. Her complexion was ruddy, yet smooth without blemish. Darkened with age, her

Tilly's Song

hair in the direct sunlight revealed blond from her youth. She wore it pulled back and confined in a thick bun that held the mystery of its length. He supposed this secret was revealed only at times of washing and brushing. The blueness of her eyes was the same intensity as alpine glacier ice. However, those eyes were not icy, but warm and compassionate. Her full and soft lips hid her wondrously straight teeth that were exposed only by spontaneous laughter.

Thinking of his wife made his heart heavy, while thinking of another woman made him fight feelings of guilt. Since he had trouble with his thinking when he drank every day, he had finally decided to only have a friendly beer occasionally and save his money for things in the future. His hope was that Tilly and Marie would be in his future. It had been almost a year since he had shown his interest in Tilly, but he had respectfully kept his distance. He felt her interest; he also knew he dared not go too fast or he might lose any hope of someday being with her. He asked God for patience.

His thoughts moved to Mathilda's daughter, Marie. For such a little girl, she was mature beyond her years in her thoughts, words and actions. She was fiercely loyal and overly protective of her mother. He admired these qualities, although he was not sure how to deal with them, since their object was to keep him away from her mother. He wondered about his own little daughter. Had she lived, how would she have acted if somehow the story had gone the other way? He decided she would have acted just like Marie, and that was a good thing.

He was not sure how to prepare for the challenge Marie posed to him. She clearly saw Bill as the invader. The happiness of his marriage to her mama, as he saw it, depended not just on getting along with Marie, but on somehow building happy memories among the three of them. Bill knew he had to be good to Tilly and never hurt her, though she would forgive easily. He knew, however, that he had no effective defense against the wrath of Marie. He realized this little girl had taken upon herself the heavy burden of her mother's happiness. He wished to share the burden so Marie could be freed up to be a child again.

Romance Is in the Air

These deep thoughts had been running through his mind as he cleaned his boots with saddle soap and allowed them to dry by the stove before putting polish on them. While he waited for them to dry, he opened his Bible and ate a dried apple ring.

"Lord, I have asked for a perfect mate for me, and You have sent me Mathilda. You know our love will grow. I know the good things You have started in me You will bring to completion, so, Father, help me to be the husband and the father I need to be. I can do nothing without You, and I am confident I can do all things with Your strength. Thank You for bringing love again into my life through my dearest Tilly. Help Marie and me to love each other. Amen."

He polished his boots and then crawled into bed. He lay there remembering his conversation after church on Sunday with his buddies, Carl and Charlie. Tomorrow was Saturday. His stomach tightened as he thought to himself, *The courtship has begun!*

***

Bill had requested the horse and rig as soon as Tilly agreed to go to dinner with him. He was borrowing it from Charles Hoth, who worked as a blacksmith for Richard Herbon, owner of the livery stable and the icehouse in Wilmette, Illinois. Charlie, as he was called by his friends, went to the same home Bible study as Bill.

When Bill had first arrived in America and gotten established, he had helped Charlie slaughter two hogs and had then helped him make smoked sausage out of the scraps. They became friends, and then Charlie introduced Bill to Carl Burgdorf, one of the chefs at the Cologne Bistro.

Bill did some butchering as a favor to the restaurant owner, and Carl became a fishing buddy to Bill through the years. Carl had recently purchased the restaurant from the original owner and with Charlie and Bill's help had redecorated the place. Now it was one of the finer restaurants in downtown Wilmette.

The two men had encouraged Bill to take Tilly out to dinner. Once they heard she had accepted, they planned the whole evening together. Charlie instructed Bill about the plans as Carl listened in.

"Bill, you will arrive at the Carlisle home in the hansom buggy. Give Tilly the flowers, and then take her to dinner at the Bistro. You think you can do all those things?" Charlie winked at Carl, and they both started to laugh.

"It will be an evening on the house for you and your sweet lady friend," Carl offered as an enticement to Bill to get the ball rolling. "She's not too large a woman with too large an appetite, is she, Bill?" Carl teased.

"No, no!" Bill laughed.

Charlie spoke up. "Are you going to tell her you're cheap or wine and dine her and just let her find out once you're married?" They all laughed.

"That's the plan; now you keep your mug shut on how cheap I am, or she may decide I'm not irresistible," Bill chimed in.

"I've wondered about her eyesight, Bill. It must be true, 'love is blind,'" Carl joked.

"Yah, but I'm a sweet talker, and the woman is not deaf!" Bill laughed at his own joke. Carl patted Bill on the back.

"Bill, you can count on me, no funny stuff — it will be nice. I planned chops and apple dumplings. Sound all right with a nice Mosel wine?" Carl bowed deeply like a waiter extraordinaire.

"Carl, it will be perfect!" He paused. "Bread? You must have a good bread and cheese. A nice nutty smoked cheddar and perhaps a chocolate with Kirsch brandy?" Bill was dreaming out loud.

"Well, I am certainly glad we are entertaining simple folk." Carl looked down his nose at his friend.

"I owe you, Carl!" Bill said, smiling.

"You owe me nothing. I am happy for you, my friend." He reached out and gave him a firm handshake and a pat on the back. "Saturday. I will see you then!"

Carl smiled at Bill. "Saturday it is."

Saturday arrived. Mattie looked at Tilly eating breakfast and said, so all could hear, "Well, Tilly, when is your face going to show how excited your heart is?"

Tilly looked down at her hands folded in her lap, and then she turned away from Mattie.

"Tilly?" Mattie walked over and put her hands on Tilly's shoulders. "Are ya nervous, luv?" Mattie's tone was gentle.

"Yes, I am! Thank you very much," Tilly snapped. Catching her tone, she quickly retorted, "Sorry! Oh, Mattie, my poor husband has been dead less than two years, and I'm jumping at another man!"

"Jumpin', jumpin'? You think yer a jumpin' at a man who is fine mannered and Christian, who wants to git to know ya and yer littl' girl? Tilly, he hasn't broken down yer door and thrown ya over his shoulder, nor has he made ya do anything. He wants to enjoy the company of a lovely woman, and he's so accommodatin' to anticipate your feelin's, he's included your littl' child. Please, Tilly, please don't say no to livin'. If the two of ya don't get along, well, then, that's that. Oh, well now, I can't be tellin' ya what to be doin' with yer life. Except a good Christian lady keeps her word and ya did agree to dinner this evenin'. If ya are indeed the lady I know ya to be, ya best be hurrying up with ya chores and leavin' some time for primpin'. Ya know, darlin', if ya have need of anythin', I'll help ya."

"Mattie, I don't want to be afraid or nervous, but honestly, I don't know what to do. I'm really just a farm girl. The things I am supposed to know, I don't think I know. What am I supposed to do? Do I pay for my food? Am I to write him a thank-you note for the beautiful flowers? When he comes, do I shake his hand, and when I walk, do I go before him or behind him? Oh my, what do I talk about?"

"Well, now, calm yourself. If ya offered to be makin' him dinner, would ya expect him to pay fer it? If ya gave him a gift, would ya appreciate a note of gratitude? Do ya normally shake men's hands? And tell me, what's wrong with ya walkin' beside him? Hm? Ya can tell him he looks nice, only if ya really think he does. Get him to talk about himself. Men love to talk about themselves. If you get him to talking, ya won't have to worry so much about what you are to be sayin'. This will also tell ya what kind of man he is. If ya do all the talkin' by the end of the eve-

Tilly's Song

nin', ya won't know any more than ya do right now. Think about it." She felt a little smug for sounding so logical.

"Thank you, Mattie. One more thing, since you offered. Do you have an evening shawl?" Tilly asked, regaining some of her courage.

"Yes! Now git goin'. I'll bring ya what ya requested after you and Marie bathe. An', Tilly, be yursef, that's what attracted him to ya in the first place. Ya look so beautiful when yur smilin', but when yur worried, you look so ... so ... just don't be a worryin'!" she said, acting somewhat worried herself.

Tilly had remembered a beauty secret her own mother had taught her about using rainwater rather than well water to wash her hair. After air-drying her long, curly hair in the sun, she cleaned and trimmed her fingernails and used whipped egg whites as a facial. She put fresh cucumbers over her eyes while the egg whites dried. When her face and hair were dry, she tied her hair back and rinsed her face, then washed it with heavy cream and rinsed it again with ice-cold water. After she finished patting her face dry, her complexion was soft and lovely.

Tilly stepped out of the bathtub and wrapped the towel around her body. She looked down at her stomach and noticed the small stretch mark lines that had increased in number with every pregnancy. She walked over to the mirror and looked at her face with her honey-colored hair cascading in long ringlets onto her shoulders. She examined her features as if looking at them for the first time.

She spoke out loud to herself while looking into the mirror. "I'm telling you this so you will know. Today is the day I am saying goodbye to you, Broken Heart. I have hung onto you because I thought it would be impossible to let go of you. But I've changed my mind. I'm talking to both of you two, also: My Sorrow, My Loneliness. Holding onto all of you is too difficult. I have nursed you every day and every night. You have demanded my attention with sleeplessness. You were important for a while; I think I even needed you. But listen to me. Now you have become unreasonable taskmasters. I have a life, and I intend to *live it!* If it makes you angry that I can laugh and play, even enjoy things, well, so be it. I shall no longer live with ghosts in my life. I am not honoring the dead by being melancholy or morose. Look at me! See this face? I am not the most beautiful, but I don't care. See this belly? It has housed new life before; it can do it again. John was, but like it or not, he is not now. I shall love his memories, all of them: good and bad. I was a good wife to him. If it is God's will for me to remarry, I shall love with all my new heart, not with my broken heart. So, I am here to tell you, Broken Heart, Sorrow and Loneliness, you can no longer stay. Leave now, and take your sleepless nights and gray moods with you."

She opened the wardrobe and gazed at the new dress. The smell of sizing was still in the fabric, not yet removed by numerous washings. She slipped it off the hanger and took a moment to feel its texture before finally dressing. Moistening her fingers, she made finger waves from the crown of her head to her forehead. All the primping, bathing, hair doing and dressing were finally complete. The last touch was a drop of rose perfume behind each ear. She looked at her reflection in the mirror again and stood back to take one last critical look. The face staring back at her was a happy face. She blew herself a kiss and, feeling quite lovely, greeted herself: "Hello, Tilly!"

Tilly had waited to the very last minute to dress Marie so nothing could possibly get spilled on her best Sunday clothes. Marie fidgeted with the bow in her hair. Tilly scolded her to stop touching it.

"Marie, leave the bow alone. You are making it look crooked. Now smile at me, and let me look at your teeth."

"This bow feels funny in my hair, and my teeth are clean, Mama," Marie reported.

When they emerged from their room at 6 p.m., Mattie was there for the final inspection. She placed the hair combs that Tilly had received after her first haircut in her soft hair. Mattie then opened the night shawl so Tilly could back into it and wrap it around her shoulders and upper arms. Mr. and Mrs. Carlisle waited in the formal parlor with them as the grandfather clock struck 6:30. At the stroke of the last bell, Bill Bogda knocked on the front door. Franklin squeezed Eleanor's hand as they exchanged smiles.

Franklin Carlisle opened the door quickly and greeted the suitor with a toothy grin. Bill bowed slightly to the head of the house, then to Mrs. Carlisle. He then shyly looked at Tilly and finally at Marie. Tilly gave a little curtsy and met Bill's smile with one of her own. She noticed his expression change as he looked at Marie, but she could not discern if it was disappointment or surprise. Tilly looked at her daughter to discover that the bow was out of her hair and the shoes were off her feet. Marie was bent over, fidgeting with the toes of her leggings, and the bow was nowhere in sight. Without a word, Tilly took Marie's hand and pulled her to a standing position. Eleanor Carlisle came to the rescue and helped Marie with her shoes, talking to Bill as if nothing was happening.

After the awkward moment passed, Bill presented each with a small corsage. Tilly's corsage had yellow sweetheart roses with daisies, whereas Marie's had fragrant lilies of the valley. Taking each by the hand, he silently helped them into the buggy. Marie sat between the two adults. As they drove away from the Carlisle home, he told Tilly and Marie how very lovely they looked and then proceeded to make them laugh.

"My goodness gracious, you two look like fairy princesses. Don't look now, but people over there on the sidewalk are looking and pointing at the two of you 'cause they've never seen beauties like you two, except in storybooks. Oh, we are going to have a grand time tonight," he said jovially.

Marie loved the ride and felt so very special and grown up. She looked at her mother. Tilly was not smiling; instead she had her eyes squinted shut, and she was biting her lower lip. They arrived at the restaurant and walked inside. All the women were wearing large stylish hats.

"Oh no! I think I should have worn my hat!"

Carl came forward to greet them and overheard Tilly's comment.

"Mrs. Baumann, your hair most certainly does not need a hat to hide under," he said politely, bowing to her and nodding to Bill. Carl's gesture included both eyebrows rising and a quick wink that communicated to his friend that he very much approved of his taste in women.

Romance Is in the Air

"My friends call me Tilly. Will you call me Tilly?" Her smile quickly turned to Bill Bogda. "And will you call me Tilly?" She giggled.

"Only if you call me Bill!"

"Very well, Bill. I seem to be informal in dress, so it seems acceptable to be informal in how we address each other." She smiled at them both.

"Tilly, I feel more relaxed already." Bill looked at her and smelled a faint scent of roses.

Carl did not miss a beat. Looking at Marie, he asked, "And, ma'am, how do we address you?"

Suddenly feeling shy, Marie looked at him with her big blue eyes and whispered, "You may call me Marie."

"Please allow me to introduce you fine ladies to my good friend, Carl Burgdorf." Bill reached over and patted him on the shoulder. Carl reached for Tilly's hand and gently kissed it.

Looking at her and then at Bill, he said, "Please, just call me Carl. Please, we are all friends here, right?" They all laughed and nodded in agreement.

"Very well, you are my friends, Marie, Tilly and Bill. I, Carl, the chef, owner and host of this fine establishment, will now show you to your table and take your order for the finest meal in town." He sounded very professional.

Tilly looked at Bill and then at Carl. "I don't know what to order." Suddenly she became quite serious.

"I have taken the liberty to prepare my favorite food for you tonight. Shall I serve it to you now?" Everyone was intrigued, filled with anticipation about what his favorite food might be.

"Yes, yes. We have all come hungry," Bill quickly stated.

Marie was served a child-size bowl of chicken and dumplings with a side dish of freshly grated applesauce and a large glass of rich creamy milk. She looked at Carl with such eager surprise that she could not keep her voice shy and quiet as before.

"Oh, good friend, Carl, how did you know this is my favorite food?"

His eyes twinkled as if he knew all kinds of secrets. He was very pleased with himself.

Tilly's Song

A familiar looking waiter arrived at the table and offered Tilly and Bill a glass of very popular German Mosel wine. Toasting to each other's good health, they took a sip. Next, another waiter brought an assortment of bread and cheese. The selection on a tray included hard rolls, dark pumpernickel and caraway seed rye bread surrounded by smoked cheddar, baby Swiss and French brie cheeses accented with pats of butter molded into various shapes.

Carl emerged from the kitchen with the main entrée of roasted stuffed pork chops amid a bed of cooked red cabbage. The first waiter poured them the last of the wine and then brought the dessert. Each was served a warm apple dumpling with top cream. The meal ended with a tray of fresh fruit and a piece of chocolate in a golden wrapper. A dessert liqueur of Cherry Kirsch was offered to the adults.

Everyone ate slowly, and Tilly kept the conversation going by asking Bill about his work, his travels and then finally about his big news.

"Tilly and Marie, I have such wonderful news. My parents will be arriving this next week in Chicago. They are going to live here in America. I have saved money to pay for their passage, and they agreed to sell everything and come and be with me. My older brother will be coming, also. My sister and her husband will not come — well, not my brother-in-law, at least, not yet. Isn't this just the best news? This pastry on these dumplings is delicious. But wait until you taste Mother's pastry; it melts in your mouth. And my father, he can do anything. He always wins prizes for his beer and sausages at the local fair near Berlin. They are good people, and they will adore you, Marie, and you, Mathilda, I mean Tilly. They will ... ah ... think you are ... well, wonderful, too. I've told them all about you — I mean the little I know about you — I hope you don't mind? I've written them." His voice began to trail off.

Tilly looked uncomfortable again, and Bill looked embarrassed.

I have said too much, too fast, he thought to himself.

Tilly sat there speechless. Marie looked at their apple dumplings and wondered if they were going to finish them. She had eaten all of hers, and she wished she could eat more because she liked apple dumplings very much.

***

Sunday morning came early to Tilly and Marie. Mattie woke them, and they quickly dressed and entered into an atmosphere of chaos.

"Foster, where is your other shoe?" Mrs. Carlisle asked as they all sat down for Sunday breakfast.

"I don't know," he answered. "Mama, where does snot come from?"

"What was that, Foster? I didn't understand what you said." She gave him a curious look.

"SNOT, WHERE DOES IT COME FROM?" he said loudly.

"Oh, goodness, I don't know, from your nose," she answered impatiently. "Marie!" she called.

"Yes, Mama Carlisle?" Marie emerged from the kitchen with hard rolls, butter and jam for the breakfast table.

"How many shoes did you bring down to polish for Foster?"

"Two."

"Foster, where is your other shoe?" she asked him again, forgetting she had just asked him.

"MAMA, I SAID I DON'T KNOW!"

"Well, don't yell at me, come with me upstairs and help me find it!"

"But I haven't had breakfast yet!"

"Neither have I!"

She got up from the table and took her youngest son by the hand, and together, they mounted the stairs.

"I know snot comes out of the nose, but where does it come from inside your body?" he continued.

"Let me see, did you look under your bed?"

"FOR SNOT?" He jumped in horror.

"Don't be ridiculous. No, for your shoe!" The irritation was building in her voice.

"Ellie!" Frank called to her from the stairs. "You both need to come down and have some breakfast, or we will be late."

"FRANKLIN, I CAN'T FIND FOSTER'S OTHER SHOE!" she yelled back to him.

"Well, where did he put it last?" He looked back at the other children, and with a sparkle in his eye, he whispered, "One, two, three …"

"FRANKLIN, YOU COME UP HERE AND HELP US FIND YOUR SON'S SHOE!"

Franklin went running up the stairs, leaping two steps at a time. "Daddy's here to help!" he said with a big grin, not able to catch a look from his wife.

"My goodness, I try to keep organized, but sometimes it just seems hopeless. I can't find that shoe anywhere," she mumbled to herself.

"Daddy, where does snot come from?" Foster asked his father who was busy looking under toys and blankets.

"Why, it comes from your nose, son."

"No, Daddy, I mean where in your body does it come from?"

"Well, let me think. You see, son, there is this special room inside your head and on the door it has a sign, <u>SNOT FACTORY</u>, and that is where it comes from!" He reached over and gave his son a noogy.

"Franklin, you are not helping here!" Eleanor scolded.

"Oh, well, I will just have to carry him like a baby in his little socky feet," Frank teased.

"No, Daddy, I'm not a baby!" Foster began to cry.

"Well, then, why are you crying like one?"

"I'm not a baby, I'm a big boy!" Foster pouted.

Frank pulled his son to him and gave him a big hug. "That's right, you are getting to be such a big boy. Do you know what big boys do? They keep track of things like their toys and their SHOES!" He laughed.

"I found it! Now what was it doing in the toy box with little soldiers in it?" Eleanor asked as if speaking to the wind.

"Great!" Foster responded as he took the shoe out of his mother's hand. He turned and started downstairs to get a bite of breakfast. His father stopped him.

Romance Is in the Air

"Wait a minute, Mr. Big Boy. Don't you think your mother deserves a big thank-you for finding that missing shoe of yours?" He gave him a semi-stern look.

"Oh, yes, Mother. Thank you for finding my shoe." He ran to her and gave her a big hug and a snotty kiss.

"Ooh, where is my hanky? Come back here and let me wipe your nose, Foster!" It was too late. Father and son had already made it downstairs to the breakfast table.

"Ellie, you better hurry or we will be late!" She heard Franklin call to her.

"JUST A MINUTE, I CAN'T FIND MY SUNDAY HANDKERCHIEF," she yelled down the stairs.

***

Getting ready for church that morning, Marie was very sleepy; it seemed everyone in the Carlisle house was running late. Bill was standing in the foyer of the church looking for them to arrive and waved hello as they climbed out of the wagon. Marie was hurrying to catch up with her mother when she tripped and the corsage from the night before fell off her dress. Before she could bend over and retrieve the little flowers, the wagon wheel ran over it and crushed all the beautiful blooms.

Marie stood there in shock, and Eleanor Carlisle was mortified. Tilly had missed the tragedy because she was eager to catch up with Bill to hand him a small note for him to read before the worship service began. Rather than read it at that moment, he stuck it into the middle pages of his Bible to read later. Marie and Eleanor were able to retrieve the pin and the satin bow before catching up with Tilly and Bill.

All the church members hurried to their usual pews as the organ bellowed out the morning hymn. Bill was one of the ushers, so he sat in the back of the church near the door. Marie looked back to wave at him, but he was busy reading the note that Tilly had given him.

The note read as follows:

Tilly's Song

A fond greeting this morning to you, my friend Bill,

Our friendly conversation, the delicious dining, the lovely gift of flowers and the entire evening spent with you were absolutely perfect. Thank you!

I am so happy for you that your parents will soon be here. Please understand that my reaction last night was inappropriate because I was overcome with envy: I no longer have any family other than Marie. I have asked our Lord to forgive me of such an unlovely display of envy, and I also ask you to forgive me. Bill, will you please forgive me? You must know I think it is wonderful news that your family is coming to America. Also, please know that you are wonderful to think of me so kindly and to share your great joy with me.

Very truly yours,
Tilly

His thoughts were interrupted by the opening hymn. All he could hear was the singing voice of Tilly, the woman he loved.

As soon as the service ended, everyone funneled out of the sanctuary and onto the lawn for the share-a-dish luncheon. Tilly looked for her friends from the bakery, and of course, Bill was there waiting for her. Elsa and Thomas Brahm brought a plate of fresh brötchen (hard rolls) with butter patties for the whole table to enjoy. The Muellers had furnished a large fresh ham cooked in sauerkraut that fed the entire church. Tilly brought her delicious potato salad that had now become a favorite at the church meals. Everyone ate as if they had never tasted food before and ended up going back for seconds. The pastor would take the bundled-up leftovers with him when he preached in the late afternoon at the prison. Now they all sat around the table drinking their last cup of coffee, feeling satisfied and enjoying one another's conversation.

Thomas Brahm was a natural-born comic and always entertained his friends with his outlandish stories. Both he and Elsa, his wife, were fun and funny people. Thomas began one of his stories, and they all turned their full attention toward him.

"You all know I hoff been tryin' to improve mine wocabulary so I voods learn a new vord each and every day. So I looks into the dictionary for da vord and its meanin'. Vell, mine teacher tells me to use dis vord many times in sentences. So I looks up da vord 'captivating' in the dictionary, and the sentence used vas: 'You have the most captivating smile.' Vell, dat day I vould say to da postman, 'Gut mornin', you have da most decapitating smile!' The postman looks at me with horror upon his face, and he runs out of da bakery and forgets to leave me da mail. I don't know vhat is vrong, is it something I said? Vell, again I try my new vord on this beautiful voman who comes in every two days for a fresh loaf of bread and two scones. I gaf her da order, and she pays me. Vhen I hand her da change back from her monies, I look deep into her beautiful blue eyes and I say, 'You have the most decapitating eyes.' And then I give her my biggest smile. But to my surprise, she looks at me and screams, drops her bread and scones and even her change. Nickels and dimes rolled all over the floor. She ran out of the bakery vithout even shuttin' the door, and I never sees dis voman ever again. You can tell I am most upset by all of dis. So I go home that evening time, look up in the dictionary, I see nothing vrong. The next day, I ask my teacher, and she looks confused. So she asks me to use dis vord in a sentence. So I do. I look at her with my most charming smile and say, 'I find you decapitating!' To this, she burst into laughter and told me I didn't say 'captivating,' I was saying 'decapitating.' She told me it meant to cut off someone's head." He made a face and shrugged his shoulders.

Everyone at the table laughed and laughed at his humorous mistake. Then his wife, Elsa, spoke up. "Yes, but what upset him more than losing a beautiful customer was trying to figure out if he could re-sell the bread and scones." Again, the group roared with laughter. Tilly looked at Bill, who was laughing heartily. Still laughing, she studied the faces of her new friends. Each was so free, so happy. Never could she remember having so much fun; never had she laughed so hard. Never!

***

The day finally came when Bill's family arrived by train. He had rented a horse-drawn cab and waited for them at the train depot. He had shared an apartment with Fritz, but with his parents coming to live with him, Bill had bought a new house.

Many things were running through his mind as he watched the passengers step off the train. The last time he had seen his family, they were standing at the depot in Berlin waving goodbye to him. His brother, Johann, and then new bride, Winifred, had said farewell to him, and he thought then that he might never see any of them ever again in this life. His sister was just a teenage girl when he left, but now she was married and had three small children. He wished she was also among his loved ones arriving. However, he would not allow one sad thought to interfere with the joy he felt at today's reunion.

When he caught sight of his family, it was his mother he recognized first. She seemed shorter, heavier and grayer than he remembered, but, of course, that had been years ago. His father looked the same until he got closer. Bill then saw how time was etched into his father's face, how the years had somewhat bowed his shoulders and how he walked a little unsteadily.

Motherhood looked good on his dear sister-in-law, Winifred, and his brother had never looked manlier. In his arms he held a beautiful little girl with a head full of blond curls. Winifred held the hand of a little boy who wished to run and explore. A wave of relief engulfed Bill; tears of gratitude welled up into his eyes as he watched them coming quickly toward him with arms open wide, smiling and calling out greetings of love. The first thought that came to his mind was Tilly, how she would love these people. Bill already knew they would love her and Marie. Soon he would have his family. This was more than just a fanciful dream; it was his most basic need in life. Whatever happened, he knew somehow it would work out now that he had loved ones with whom he could share his life.

The dream did come true. Everyone was so happy to meet one another and acted as if they had always known each other. Tilly felt very comfortable with Bill's parents, Peter and Elsa Bogda. John, as he preferred to be called, was just like a cousin who teased Tilly from the very first meeting, and Whinny, as Winifred was called, became her good friend. Everyone knew that Tilly and Bill were in love. How could they not? Love sparkled in their eyes and shined from their faces.

Romance Is in the Air

After the new arrivals settled into their new home in America, John and Peter were hired on at the packing plant where Bill worked. Peter, with his prize-winning recipes for sausage, was quickly placed in a position of sharing his skill in the sausage and wurst department. John and Bill, working together, were happy that their relationship as brothers was better than it had ever been.

"So, mine gut bruther, so handsome and debonair, vhen are yu plannin' on askin' Tilly to become yur bride?" John asked Bill as they walked from the train to the wagon.

The Engagement

"That was a very good service this morning in church, don't you think, Bill?" Tilly asked to break the silence as they walked back to the Carlisle house.

"Um, I beg your pardon? What was that you were asking?" Bill looked distant and then stunned by the question he had only halfway heard.

"You seem far away. I was just making conversation. It was nothing, really." Tilly picked up her pace, which made Bill jog a short distance to catch up with her.

"I was far away. Actually, I was into the future just now, thinking of you and me. Thinking about us being together every day and …" He stopped there on the street and took off his hat. Tilly kept walking for a few more steps, then turned and looked back. Their eyes met, and she slowly walked to him as he put his hand out for her to take.

"Bill?" she asked, much more with her eyes than her words.

"Tilly, you know I love you — you know that, don't you?" He reached for her hand and pulled her to himself.

"Oh, Bill!"

"Ha! That wasn't as hard as I thought it would be. I mean, if you didn't know, I am telling you right now: I love you, Mathilda Baumann."

"Yes, Bill. Yes, I know, I know. Then you must also know that I have loved you for a very long time. I just was afraid to admit it to myself or anyone. When you and Fritz first came up to all of us walking home from church that day, you stole my heart right then. But I was ashamed to have such feelings, and I dismissed them as just being lustful."

"I have waited for you a very long time — at least it seems a very long time. I want you to be my wife — you are already my friend." He took her other hand and faced her. Looking her straight in the eyes, he asked, "My dearest friend, whom I love with my whole being, will you be my wife?" There was a long pause. Taking her in his arms, he held her until they both heard a buggy driving by and separated until it passed.

"You are a good man, a patient man, a handsome man, and I love you. I will be most honored to become your wife." Her face was glowing with happiness. He reached over and quickly started to kiss her and then, suddenly remembering where he was, put her hand to his lips and gently caressed it.

With a spring in their step, they walked together back to the Carlisle house. As he walked her to the back door, he asked, "Should we tell everyone?"

"Oh, silly, everyone already knows!" she giggled as she stepped up to the door.

"Will I see you tonight?" He gave her a wink.

"Shall we say, 7:00 in the garden?" She smiled, feeling really pleased with herself.

"It's a date!" He was fighting the urge to kiss her. "Until then, I bid you goodbye." He tipped his hat respectfully as any good gentleman would do toward a beautiful lady.

"Don't be late!" She turned and opened the door. There in the kitchen was everyone who lived in the Carlisle house. As soon as she saw them, they all started clapping their hands and giving her words of congratulations. Her face ached from smiling so hard, but she didn't mind.

Later that week after Peter, mostly known as Grandpa Bogda, arrived home, his wife, Elsa, was waiting at the door for him.

"Welcome home, mine good husband." Grandma Bogda greeted him with a smile as her husband leaned down and kissed her cheek.

"What is cookin'? It smells like I want to eat it now." He

walked toward the kitchen.

"I made you a good supper of meatballs and gravy with fresh bread and butter and some berry tarts. There are some wilted beet greens just like you like them with some vinegar. We will eat the pickled part tomorrow after they have had a chance to set up overnight. Sit down; it is ready for you. I knew you would be hungry," she instructed him as she finished setting the table.

They enjoyed their meal together, and as they were finishing the tarts, Elsa began to speak what she had rehearsed all day to ask her husband.

"Peter, my love, Bill and Tilly are so in love and have been so good to us, I want to give them a special gift for their wedding. In this country, many of the women have a ring before they marry to show they are engaged. I would like to give Bill some money from the bonds we brought here from Germany to help buy Tilly this kind of ring. What do you think?" She had waited until now to ask, knowing he was in a good mood since his stomach was full.

"He already has a ring. Why does he need to buy her a ring when he has the ring that Helenea had?" he said, reaching for another tart.

"What are you saying? Do you mean the ring from his dead wife? Oh, I have never heard of anything so terrible!" She stood up with her hands on her hips and gave him one of her "looks."

"Oh, sit down and quit looking at me so hard. What is so different from that and me giving you my dead grandmother's ring?" he spoke, not even looking up from his plate.

"Peter, are you really so insensitive as to think there is no difference? He was married to another woman, who died giving birth to their child, and now you expect our William to give his bride a 'used' ring?" She picked up her dishes and took them to the sink, not really expecting an answer from her husband. He picked up his plates and followed her into the kitchen.

"How much is it going to cost?" he asked, knowing all too well that a specific ring had, no doubt, already been chosen and priced.

"I believe the one that is the most beautiful is no more than

$50," she said quickly to get the bad news out of the way.

"Very well."

"Oh, thank you. You are such a good man. This makes me so happy to be a part of all the festivities. They are going to have such a lovely wedding, and you know we are going to be watching Marie while they go on their trip after the wedding. This shall be such a great time." She rushed to him, put her arms around his waist and reached up to give him kisses. He felt the sting of stinginess subside and entered into the joy of the moment. He knew his frugal wife must feel very strongly about giving this gift, and in such matters he had never known her to be wrong.

***

Eleanor Carlisle was in her element. She just loved any reason to celebrate, and she always did so in style. Tilly and Bill had made an appointment with Franklin and Eleanor to ask permission to have their wedding in their garden. The Carlisle couple already knew what was coming and offered their home and garden as a possible setting, rather than a very hot church building in the month of June.

"Tilly, it appears they are one step ahead of us!" They all laughed and expressed gratitude, as well as congratulations. Now that they had decided to have the wedding in the garden, Eleanor seemed to be everywhere at once.

"Tilly, dear, what is your dream for this wedding? Tell me, and we can work together to make it happen."

"Well, the first part of my dream has come true, of course. God has chosen a Christian man who will love my daughter and me. He has great passion for life, and he is great fun. We laugh — oh, he is just wonderful. The other part is that my past debt is now paid in full, thanks to you and your husband's gracious generosity." Tilly sighed with great relief, looking first at Bill and then at Eleanor and Franklin.

"Tilly, you must not give us the credit. You worked for it. Also, Bill and his parents took care of the last bit so it would be completely paid off before the wedding. I just see God's hand in all of this, don't you?"

"You are so correct. For the last few years, my life has seemed so unreal. But not this — no, this is really real. It is so good to be in love and to be able to love again."

Eleanor had her hands on her heart and sighed, "Tilly, it is so magnificent to be in love, and you, my dear, are aglow because of it. Oh, this is so exciting. Now we must tend to the business part of this celebration. Who will be officiating?" Eleanor began her mental checklist.

"Well, the pastor, of course!" Tilly looked surprised at the question.

"All right, we have that decided." She pulled out a pen and a piece of stationery, ready to take down every one of Tilly's responses.

"Who is invited? Well, everyone in this household, of course, and I shall get a list of church friends. Oh, let me think." She was now talking as much to herself as she was to Tilly. She began again with the questions for Tilly.

"Tilly, do you want a private wedding or a deliciously wonderful, let-everyone-come-and-dance-and-be-festive kind of wedding?" Eleanor was now on her feet, lifting her hands in the air and whirling around her study.

In her merriment, she bumped the small table holding the pen and bottle of ink, which Frank caught just before spilling. Frank gave her a serious look, and she ceased her whirling.

"Eleanor Carlisle, you have such a wondrous way of promoting your most excellent plans. Hmm, now let me think." Tilly paused, playfully. "Oh, all right, I guess I shall speak for William and myself and go with the deliciously wonderful wedding!" She giggled at her own joke.

"Very well, now that we have that decided, flowers, food, dancing?" She was writing as fast as she could.

"Yes, yes! All of it!" Tilly was now on her feet wandering around the study.

"Now, what about the attire for the wedding party in your deliciously wonderful wedding?" Eleanor looked up and around the room for Tilly.

Tilly came and stood in front of Eleanor and announced,

"For this part, we must be sensible. Bill and I want to go on a small trip, what they call in this country a honeymoon. He wanted to take a boat trip to Michigan, but I really do not want to be seasick, so we have agreed to stay in a lodge on the shore of Lake Michigan for a few days. Marie will be staying with her new grandparents. So, the clothes must be nice garments we can wear to church or other special occasions. Eleanor, my friend, I must make it clear to you that William and I shall pay for this wedding!"

"Tilly, yes, yes, of course, of course! But you must be aware that Mr. Boehl is providing the flowers; the workers here are all bringing the food for your reception; I am giving you and Marie your wedding clothes; Franklin is buying Bill a suit of clothes; the Brahms are giving you the wedding cake and the church is giving you a shower. So you and William will have to pay for the rest." Her eyes were twinkling as a smug look formed upon her face.

It took a moment for all of it to soak into Tilly's brain, and when it did, her eyes filled with tears — happy tears, tears of gratitude and praise, tears of humility. When Mattie came to fetch Eleanor and Tilly for teatime, she found them holding each other and wiping their eyes; Mattie had to reach for her own handkerchief. Franklin knew the meeting had come to an end. Rolling his eyes, he looked over at Bill and invited him outside for a cigar.

Upon returning to the house, he said his polite best wishes to the engaged couple and continued upstairs to greet the children. Vic and Glo were dropping flower petals all over the room as Marie slowly paraded with a pillowcase on her head that served as a veil. Frank turned and headed to the basement to escape the wedding frenzy that had invaded his home. Although he was extremely happy for the betrothed couple, he knew his safest place was out of the way of the women and all their preparations.

That night, Bill stopped by and knocked on the back door. Tilly was waiting to let him in; she opened the screen door. He removed his hat and stepped inside. They stood there awkwardly for a moment while everyone in the kitchen looked at them and then left the kitchen.

"Tilly, I got your message that you wanted to see me. Is everything all right?"

"Billy," she said affectionately, so as to disarm him, "come out into the shade of the garden with me, please, so we can talk." He followed her lead to the fishpond.

"Oh, Bill, I'm sorry if I worried you, but before things get too big or too much — well, I wanted to tell you about the wedding plans and find out what you think about everything. Bill, I don't ever want to presume I can speak for you." She moved closer to him as she spoke.

He pulled her to him and kissed the long fingers on her left hand, one by one. Then he kissed her on the mouth. "This is the only part of the wedding ceremony that concerns me. But to get it just right, you and I must do a great deal of rehearsing," he teased.

"Oh, silly Billy," she giggled. "Really, Bill, you need to know that Mr. and Mrs. Carlisle are planning a fancy party for our wedding."

"Well, let them, Tilly!"

"Really, my dear, they have it all divided up so this one and that one is giving us part of the wedding expense as our present." She wanted to share the surprising blessing.

"How grand!" He looked up to the sky with hands lifted up. "Thank You, Lord, for Your rich blessings." Looking back at Tilly, he added, "Tilly, don't be so surprised. We know these are good people because they serve a good God. God is just keeping His word to us that the windows of heaven will open and shower down good things to those who love Him and obey His Word. Tilly, my beautiful bride, this is the abundant life our Lord Jesus spoke about. Not one thing have we done to deserve this much kindness, and yet that is what is so glorious about God's grace. Tilly, remember, the pastor spoke last week from Ephesians 2:1-9. My sweet, we must receive all He has for us!"

"Shall I tell you the plans?" Her eyes were wide with excitement.

"No, not now, let me be surprised. I want to hold you right now." He put his arms around her and held her close. They both felt content and loved. She pulled back just enough to look him in the face.

"Oh, Mr. Bogda, you will be surprised. You will be so surprised!" She gently kissed him, and they said their goodbyes. He left and walked to his home. Although the Chicago area had been experiencing an Indian summer with warmer than normal temperatures on these November days, the nights were becoming more chilly. Tilly stayed out in the garden and prayed for another hour, then suddenly felt cold and went inside for the night. She was still too restless to sleep, so she decided to write a letter to her dear friend and confidant, Beatrice.

My dearest Sister in Christ, Beatrice,

I greet you and pray that you and your family are well and happy. This letter is sent to you to share my uncontrollable joy with you and the pastor and children. America is a wonderful place for Marie and me. We are both happy and doing exceedingly well. Mr. and Mrs. Carlisle are perfect angels from God. They have welcomed us into their home and are paying us handsomely for the duties we perform there. They pay Marie, also, for the things she does, and the extra money helps to pay off the debit to the shipping company.

All of this is just to lead up to the most wonderful news. I am in love! A wonderful man named Wilhelm A. Bogda, known as Bill, originally from Prussia, has wooed and won my heart. It was not easy for him, though. I have grieved John and the children's death to the very depth of despair, and there was a time I did not even wish to go on living. But Marie needed me, and so I begged God to at least let me live long enough to see her grow into womanhood. At first, I thought I could never love another man and did not entertain the idea of marriage. Well, between you and me, I did think of him and what it would be like to marry him. I felt it shameful to have those thoughts so soon after losing my dearest John. My grieving has come to a place of resolution, and I can go on to live and love again. And, my good friend, I am in love, and it is wonderful, too wonderful for words.

First of all, he is a good moral man who cares for me and also Marie because he knows and serves the Lord. He knows how to be a real man: strong and bold, yet kind and tender. Second, he has a very good-paying job and is frugal, yet so very generous with gifts of kindness. Just to tell you what I mean, he knows I love flowers, so he picks me flowers whenever we go for walks or sends me flowers before we go out on special occasions. Isn't that just the most romantic thing? He speaks loving words to me that make me blush. Oh, and he is ever so kind to include Marie in our outings and only lets me say whenever she needs to stay in the care of others so we may have some privacy. But, oh, let me assure you, he is the best of gentlemen, and we are always in the company of a chaperone. Did I fail to mention he is also very strong and handsome?

He is such fun and has many good friends. We both go to the same church. He helped pay for his brother and family, as well as his parents, to come to America. Such a fine family, so easy to love — and they absolutely adore Marie. He proposed marriage to me, and I agreed. We shall be married in June, and I ask that you and the church would please pray for our marriage.

You have been so very kind and generous with your love for us, I just had to write and share my good news with you. I promise I shall write again and tell you all about the wedding and include you as if you were here with me. I so dream of seeing your family again. But if not here on earth, then surely we shall meet in our true home, heaven. I pray that God will continue to bless you and your family.

Your sister in Christ,
Soon to be Mrs. Wilhelm A. Bogda

After reading and rereading the letter several times, she finally addressed the envelope and placed the letter into it. She was now ready to sleep. She felt at peace with the world, but sleep was not going to be hers through the night.

Soon after falling asleep, she awoke from a nightmare feeling cold and clammy, gasping for air. She sat up in bed, and it took her a moment to remember where she really was. Remembering her dream, she saw herself pulling a cart away from a burning village. The fire seemed to contain a force that kept pulling her back toward the flames. Tilly felt weak and unable to move forward. A feeling of despair flooded her body; she felt as though her legs were about to give way. No one was alive. Smoke burned her eyes and choked her throat. She couldn't catch her breath. The familiar feeling of panic returned. Now that she was awake, she spoke to calm herself.

"That was then, and this is now. Go away, you awful feeling. There was nothing I could do to prevent that from happening!" she said out loud.

The voice of despair whispered in her ear. "Only the good died that day; you didn't die. The others died, but you didn't die."

"Enough! God spared Marie and me. Goodness had nothing to do with it. I am not good enough and never will be. My Lord loves me and protects me, so get out of my thoughts and get out of this room and get out of this house! DO YOU HEAR ME?" she yelled out loud. She got out of bed and changed her nightgown and washed her face in some cool water from the basin.

Again, she went to sleep, but at first light awoke with a start, gasping for air. This time in her nightmare she was inside the ship, and she could not open the door of the sleeping compartment because there was no door handle. There was no porthole to open and no air within the room. Panic had returned and gripped her in her sleep.

After this nightmare, Tilly did not go back to sleep. She quickly dressed and walked out into the garden, breathing deeply the cool air as she watched the sky grow light and then turn reddish golden. Snow began to fall and formed little prisms of light in the sky. She felt stronger now, knowing that somehow the sun would frighten away all the shadowy things that brought fear in the night. Tilly opened the back door and began her new day with a song of praise on her lips. Singing a wake-up song, Tilly roused Marie from the bed, took her daughter into her arms and began kissing her cheeks. Marie looked at her mama with surprise, and then she returned her mama's kisses.

Chapter 12
The Phrasing of Every Song

"Bill, what was your wife like? What did you love about her?" Tilly drew close to him and reached for his hand. His face lost its color, and he turned away from her before she could grasp hold of his hand.

Not looking at her, he answered. "Tilly, I don't want to dwell on the past. Whenever I think about her, it is as if it was all a dream, or a story told to me by another person. She was not like you, if that is what you are trying to find out from me." He paused, thinking carefully before he spoke again. "She loved me — and more importantly, she wanted me. I really needed her to want me." He stopped again, and there was a long uncomfortable silence between them.

"Did you love her?" Tilly asked almost in a whisper.

He turned on his heel, and all the color rushed back into his face. She could not understand the emotion on his face as it flashed from anger to sadness, then to shame. He walked toward Tilly and grabbed her arms with force, but without causing her pain. This startled her. Tilly could see tears well up in his eyes and the clench in his jaw as he fought them. She leaned toward Bill to comfort him or maybe even to be comforted by him. Tilly sensed she was stepping into the unknown of his emotional world, void of any light she could detect.

"Tilly!" he breathed as he took her into his arms. His heart was beating so hard it drummed into her ear as he held her to his chest. An eternity passed in those few moments of their embrace. Tilly trusted her instincts to remain silent and to give Bill time to form his thoughts into words.

"Tilly, I know I loved her, but it is so hard to explain for fear you will misunderstand me." He spoke this to her slowly and hesitantly.

"Bill, please make me understand whatever it is you want me to know." With her hand, she gently stroked his cheek.

"Helenea was everything I knew a woman should be: pretty, happy, fun, eager to please, wanting to live a good God-fearing life. She wanted a husband, children and a home. Family was her world. She had no life experience outside of the village. She was fragile and delicate, easily sickened by exposure to difficulty. This made me her champion. At first, I felt needed and very strong. I planned to take care of her all her life." He stopped at his last words and pondered them before he spoke again. "Well, I did just that. I took care of her all her life. I just didn't think her life would be so short."

Tilly could see the agony in his countenance as he spoke out thoughts of his late wife for the first time. There was a cry in his voice. "She wanted a child so badly. I think our major difference was that I wanted a wife more than a child. After trying so long to have a child, when she did give birth and our baby daughter died, Helenea just didn't have enough strength to live without the baby or enough love to live for me. I feel like I failed her somehow."

He stopped, and in a voice no louder than a whisper, he said, "But there is a part of me that feels that she failed me as well." He quickly bristled. "I should not speak such things about the dead. Tilly, she was a good woman, kind and charitable to everyone who knew her."

Tilly put her fingers to his lips.

"Bill, my love, don't apologize. Speak to me from your heart. I, too, was married to a wonderful person who was also flesh and blood. We had our human failings." She softly smiled as she took her fingers from his lips.

He looked her straight in the eye and proclaimed, "I just want you to know I feel differently toward you. I know I shall love you whether you love me, need me or want me! I don't feel particularly strong around you; I sometimes actually feel weak in the knees. You are not just a pretty woman with a beautiful singing voice. Your spirit and your passion excite my body, my mind and mostly my heart. You have experienced life with its challenges beyond the village, and I know I can trust you to be with me in whatever God has in store for us. Tilly, I am foolish in my desire for you. I am confident, however, that you would never require one foolish act from me. If I am away from you too long, I ache for your presence — and sometimes too long is whenever you are out of my sight. With Helenea, I drew pleasure from hearing her tell me she loved me. With you, I draw pleasure from telling you I love you. I don't question if I do. I do. I love you! I want you to marry me, and I want you to care for me as I care for you. You don't need me, I can see that, but I hope you will want me and love me." His eyes never left hers.

Tilly was shocked and pleased at the same moment. Possibly for the first time in her life, she was struck dumb. All she could do was hug him and pat him and caress his face with her fingertips. This was the first time in her life she could distinguish the difference between loving a man and being in love with him.

The Morning of the Wedding Day

Blanche Randolph, also known as Nanny, came to the door of Tilly and Marie's bedroom just as they were both getting out of bed. They heard the very loud knock on their door and looked at one another, wondering who it could be. Suddenly the knocking stopped, and the door abruptly flew open.

"Tilly Baumann, this is the day I have longed for since you arrived at the Carlisle house. You will soon be gone, and I will be glad! Everyone adores you in this house and at church. Not me! The children used to adore me, and Mrs. Carlisle used to confide in me, until you waltzed in here with your little princess.

"You might as well know it, Tilly: I wish with all my heart that William would have looked at me at church. In fact, I was so stupid as to think he *was* looking at me. But no, it was you sitting next to me that he could only see. I am two years older than you, Tilly, and still it is my lot in life to take care of other women's children." She burst into tears and stood there crying. Tilly looked so sad and helpless. Marie just looked shocked.

Silently, Marie asked Jesus for help. Nanny finally stopped sobbing and blew her nose. In horror, she looked at Tilly and then at Marie.

As if she was another person, she ran and knelt down in front of them.

"Oh, Tilly, Marie, forgive me," Blanche begged. "Jealousy is such an evil, wicked thing. This is your happy day, which you both deserve, you really do. I shamefully came spitting my selfish venom all over you. Oh, that I could take back every hateful thought and every vicious word. Oh, sweet Tilly, don't hate me, please. You must know how torn I am right now, and my moods can be so dark at times. Most of the time I just hate myself because there is no goodness in me."

Sobbing, she buried her face in her hands.

Mattie appeared at the door and gave Tilly a look of concern. Tilly motioned to Marie to leave with Mattie and gave both a quick smile as she closed the door behind them.

No one was sure what happened behind that closed door. Hours later, both women emerged with their arms around each other. It was obvious both had been weeping. Together, they sat down and ate a late breakfast, then parted and went about making ready for the important day ahead.

The Wedding

No one could have asked for a more perfect day. The temperature was mild with only a slight breeze and not a cloud in the sky. All of nature seemed to be in celebration on this June day. All the plans had been immaculately orchestrated: Flowers of every kind were arranged in large sprays; a large white arch had a colorful array of spring flowers woven in and out of the slats; white ribbons affixed on the aisle chairs also held a single red rose and a sprig of baby's breath; bouquets were placed near an outdoor altar beyond the arch and also on the reception table off to the side near the bridge over the fish pond. Chairs were draped with white cloth that matched the table linens. The beautiful cake and all the luscious food were on display, as well as fine china and crystal wine glasses.

Music for the procession was played by the violinist who would later be part of the wedding reception's dance band. Eleanor Carlisle was in her element, and everything was on a strict timetable. With a nod from her to the pastor and the violinist, her twin daughters with small baskets of rose petals began the march past the rows of guests, down the white carpet that led to the outdoor altar.

Although they had been drilled with the proper way to gently drop petals as they walked down the aisle, Victoria managed to dump all of her petals before she even reached the chairs, and Gloria was so mesmerized by the crowd, music and flowers that she forgot to drop any petals at all.

The next person to march down the aisle was Marie, smiling from ear to ear and looking adorable in her new dress, her blond hair styled in long curls. The matron of honor was next, smiling at her husband, the best man, as if she were living her wedding all over again.

Bill stood straight as an arrow with a sober face until he saw his bride, and then his eyes filled with tears of joy as he smiled so big he almost burst into laughter. All the guests changed their gaze from Bill to Tilly as they stood to their feet to honor the bride.

Franklin Carlisle escorted Tilly down the aisle with his chest puffed out with extreme pride. He quickly took Tilly's hand and placed it into Bill's, then assumed his seat next to his wife, who was already sobbing into her second handkerchief. He placed his arm around her as she cried and he smiled.

Mathilda and Wilhelm became husband and wife on that beautiful summer day within a garden paradise among a crowd of witnesses of family and friends. The sacrament of marriage was a celebration of praise and worship to the God who is continually restoring people's lives. Everyone enjoyed a good time, with much food, wine, music and dancing. It was the happy look on Tilly and Bill's faces that gave Eleanor and Franklin the ultimate thank-you for a job well done. This was a day that all who were in attendance would always remember.

The Honeymoon

It was the song of the loon calling to his mate on the moonlit lake that woke Tilly out of her blissful sleep.

Tilly's Song

She carefully left the warmth of her beloved Bill, trying not to wake him from his peaceful slumber. Looking at him breathe with a heavy rhythm made her content.

The breeze off the lake put a chill in the air. Her bare feet found the slippers without looking for them, and an afghan tossed over the chair found its place wrapped over her shoulders. Night sounds caused her to relax, but not grow drowsy. Walking into the kitchen area, she found a kerosene lamp and lit it, and then found the stationery box she had left out just for this occasion. She stared at the blank piece of paper and wondered to herself where she should begin.

My best friend, my beloved Beatrice,

I am writing to you from the honeymoon cabin on a moonlit night by a beautiful lake listening to the rhythmic breathing of my adorable husband. I am now Mrs. William A. Bogda. I must tell you every little detail because I can truthfully say it was the happiest day of my life.

First of all, the good church folk gave us a party they called a "shower," and we received linens, cookware, dishes, silverware, glassware, pottery, blankets and some crystal vases. Bill and his parents bought me a diamond ring to go with my wedding band. I can see it sparkle much like the stars right now in the night sky. Mr. Boehl manicured the garden to be a paradise of flowers. He even ordered more flowers: red and yellow roses for my bridal nosegay. Day lilies, iris, baby's breath, gladiolas, daisies and carnations were in large sprays at the outdoor altar. He had rolled out a white carpet for me to walk on, and the Carlisle twin girls walked ahead of me and dropped rose petals in my path.

It seemed everyone from church and the neighborhood was in attendance. I walked on the beautiful carpet to the altar and my awaiting beloved to the music of Ludwig van Beethoven's, DIE EHRE GOTTES AUS DER NATUR (Nature's Praise to God). There we pledged our hearts and lives to each other. It was as if all those who were married grew close to one another and renewed their marriage of love as we took our vows.

As we sealed our covenant with a kiss, doves were released and flew into the cloudless summer sky as a prayer sent to heaven. I felt the love and good wishes from your family that day as you had prayed for me so long ago in Hamburg and spoken God's words of blessing to me for a better life in this new country. Oh, my sweet friend, the power of prayer is such a delightful mystery and reality to me. Thank you, thank you.

The wedding party was a feast of every kind of delicacy. The wedding cake, prepared for us by our kind friends who own the bakery, was decorated with butter cream icing on all three tiers. One layer was filled

The Phrasing of Every Song

with vanilla cream, another hazelnut cream and the last layer with cherry kirsch filling. A figure of a bride and groom appeared atop the cake. The rest of the food was set on tables where everyone gathered and filled their plates. Friends of Bill's, Max and Fritz, rented a band, and we danced to many old German songs, as well as a few American tunes. Mrs. Carlisle had made a silk purse for me to wear as I danced, and those men who danced with me put money into the purse. I handed the money to Bill, and he had to sit down, he was so amazed at the generosity of our guests. I still do not know how much we received, but he told me not to worry about the expense of the honeymoon. Our friends who came to America from Friesland gave us a 30-pound ham, as is the custom among their people.

It is still so amazing to me how much fun our wedding was. My little Marie ate so much cake she got ill all over her new clothes. Grandma Bogda gave her some soda water to settle her stomach, and she seemed to be fine after that. She is staying with her new grandparents while we are on our trip. They love her so much, and Marie is so happy with them. Our future is filled with such hope.

Bill and I left the wedding party before it was over because we had to journey to the cabin and arrive before nightfall. We stopped off at his — our — house to gather up some clothing, and there in our bed we became one. Beatrice, he is so wonderful, so strong, virile and passionate. We needed each other so much, and now we are together. I am happy, really happy. My hope is that if the Lord tarries, Bill and I will have a long life together. However, life has taught me that in truth, life is but a brief moment in eternity, and I shall cherish every day I have with the man God has given me to be my good husband.

Oh, I hear him call me back to bed, and I must close now and go to him.

Your true friend,
Mathilda Bogda

P.S. I like the sound of my name, don't you? HA!

After all the goodbyes were said and the rice-drenched bride and groom had made their hasty exit, Marie stood between Mama Carlisle and Grandma Bogda.

"How long will they be gone, Mama Carlisle?" Marie asked, even though she had been told at least seven times whenever she had asked her mama. Before Mrs. Carlisle could answer Marie, Grandma Bogda answered for her.

"My dear, your mama and new papa will be gone for five days. Remember, we all talked about this, and you know that you will be spending those days with Grandpa and me. Marie, your things are already at our home, dear." Marie looked at Mama Carlisle with her big sad blue eyes for validation of these words.

"Marie, that is correct. This shall be a little holiday for you, also." She tried to sound convincing. Eleanor turned and in a soft-spoken voice addressed Grandma Bogda so Marie would not be able to hear their conversation.

"Frau Bogda, you do realize that in all of the six years this child has been on this earth, she has never spent a day or night without her mother?" This was more of a statement than a question.

"Oh, my, no, I did not realize that, my dear. Well, thank you for this bit of information. I shall be mindful of this and work hard at earning her trust," she said in German, smiling and giving a nod and looking down at Marie who was oblivious to what they were talking about. Now a little louder, Mama Carlisle spoke to Grandma Bogda so Marie would be privy to their conversation.

"If it would be permissible, Marie is invited to come here from time to time and play with my children, who through the years have become her playmates."

Grandpa Bogda by now had joined them and overheard their conversation. He answered for his wife, while looking for her approval. "I think that is a good idea and a gracious offer. Don't you agree?" He first looked at Eleanor, and then at his wife.

"Oh, yes, I do so agree, Peter. We thank you, Mrs. Carlisle." Together, they all looked down at Marie for her reaction. She, too, was smiling in agreement.

Though reluctant at first, Marie really had fun at her new grandparents' home. On her own bed on the screened-in porch was a pillow with her name embroidered on the pillowcase. She learned from her grandmother how to make rye bread, and her grandfather requested Marie's help stuffing sausage into casings. They all would sing as they worked. Grandma Bogda told interesting stories to pass the time. Marie helped Grandpa Bogda make sausages and hang them in the smokehouse; three days later, they all sampled a few of the smoked sausages with lunch.

Both of these new relatives seemed to always have fun things to do, and in the evenings, all three would walk to the beachfront of Lake Michigan and watch the sunset. Sometimes they saw storm clouds gather and watched for lightning from a distance. A game they often played was guessing how long it would take to hear the thunder after they saw the sky light up. On the way home from the beach, they would stop to have a dish of ice cream at the drugstore. While they ate their sweet treats, they watched a lamplighter turn the dusk of the evening into an illuminated walkway all the way to their house.

Grandpa knew a gentleman named Mr. Schlosses, who owned a pony named Buck. He let Marie ride his pony one afternoon. However, when Buck tried to bite Marie on the leg, Mr. Schlosses yelled at Buck and told her grandpa that it was probably best they not let little children ride him anymore. Grandpa seemed a lot more disappointed about this than Marie did. So instead, Grandpa made a swing to entertain her and hung it in the backyard on the biggest limb of the old elm tree. He would push her in that swing for hours, or at least that is what it seemed like to him. Marie always begged for more, but he always had an excuse for why they had to stop and go inside so he could lie down.

While he took a nap, Grandma Bogda would read Marie a Bible story or just talk with her about their life in Germany. She always included Marie in whatever she was doing and showed her how to cook many different and interesting dishes. She was the best cook — and it showed, too: Around her middle she wore the weight of tasting her own cooking. Her roundness was accentuated by her short stature. Grandma Bogda was no taller than 4 feet, 9 inches. Grandpa, a good 10 inches taller than she was, looked thin and wiry. Both were ruddy complexioned with silver-white hair. They had "happy marks" on their faces, which is what Marie called the wrinkles around their eyes and mouths.

On Wednesday, Marie's new cousins came to visit for the afternoon while their mother went shopping with a friend. They visited too often for Marie's liking. The first time she had met

Papa Bill's family was after they arrived from Germany. She and her mother had dressed up in their finest clothes and had prepared homemade sweets for the tired travelers.

Little Peter was 4, and Agnes had just turned 1 year old. That first meeting, Peter had pushed Marie down onto the ground, and she had gotten dirt and grass stains on her freshly pressed white Sunday apron. He was quickly punished with a spanking and then made to apologize to both Marie and Tilly. Peter did so reluctantly, and then when no adult was looking, he stuck his tongue out at Marie. She couldn't quite think what to do about Peter, so she would play with baby Agnes and avoid Peter as much as possible.

Peter seemed to always be in trouble. If he wasn't dangerously close to hurting his baby sister, he was making nerve-wracking noise with his mouth or anything he could find to pound on with his feet, hands or head. Once, at his home, Marie had walked into the room where he was playing, and he was on the floor banging his head. Aunt Whinny was beyond knowing what to do with him most of the time. She would spank him, and he would look at her with defiance and say, "It didn't hurt!"

Aunt Whinny would send him to his room, withhold his dinner, take away his toys, but nothing seemed to work. Whenever she was at her wit's end, Aunt Whinny would take him to Grandma Bogda's house, and there he was very good. His grandmother never had to spank him or withhold anything from him. All she did was look at him with one of her "looks." Grandma Bogda's "looks" were powerful. Even Grandpa Bogda knew the power of her "looks" and did whatever he could to avoid getting one from her.

The week finally came to an end, and Marie saw her mother and Papa Bill drive up in the buggy in front of Grandma Bogda's house. As she ran to embrace her mother at the front door, Marie tripped on the throw rug and fell, bumping her chin on the floor. Blood sprayed out of her chin like an explosion.

It seemed that instantly everyone came running to her aid. Marie was motionless and then started screaming, more in fright than in pain. Grandma and Grandpa scurried for towels or anything they could find to put on the wound to stop the bleeding. Marie cried inconsolably even after the bleeding had stopped. The happy homecoming had been thwarted. Tilly looked at Bill with great concern and met his helpless gaze. After Grandma Bogda bandaged the wound, she looked up at Tilly with an unreadable expression.

Grandpa Bogda picked up the crying child and carried her to her mother. Marie looked away from her mother and hid her face in her grandfather's arm.

Tilly felt a sharp pain in her heart from her child's rejection. Bill busied himself with collecting her bags and the food his mother had prepared for their homecoming and carrying them to the buggy. Tilly followed behind Grandpa Bogda, who set Marie in the back seat of the rig. He then joined his wife on the front porch and waved goodbye to the newlyweds. Bill and Tilly mumbled their goodbyes and left as quickly as they could for their new home.

Marie got over her upset, and her chin healed as if nothing had ever happened. She was pleased that her mother and new papa had brought her a bag of saltwater taffy from the lodge where they had stayed on their honeymoon. Peace once again reigned within their home; soon a nice rhythm was established as each person got into his or her own routine of life.

Summer was filled with lots of picnics, swimming and playing at Lake Michigan, band concerts in the park and almost every Sunday, a good Lutheran share-a-dish luncheon on the church grounds.

Marie and the Carlisle children learned to fly kites that summer. The twins were growing to be big girls. Edna and the twins would always run to Marie whenever they spied her at church or in the park. Michael and Foster treated Marie just like a sister, with love and much teasing.

Two weeks after they had settled into their new home, the postman arrived with a letter addressed to Mrs. Wilhelm A. Bogda. Without looking at the postmark, Tilly already knew who it was from, recognizing the handwriting.

Tilly's Song

My good, good sister and friend, Mathilda, and now Mrs. Bogda,

    I send you greetings in the name of our Lord and Savior. May your marriage be blessed with good health, much wealth, great happiness and abounding fruitfulness. Your wedding sounded like a dream shared in a book read to children.

    Please remember how kind people can be, because whenever you are happy, it will give others an opportunity to bask in the warmth of your good fortune. Happiness is such a wonderful thing to share. This joy comes from the very heart of God. It costs you nothing and so enriches others. I am enriched by your story and long to hear your good tales as your family grows. However, never, my friend, edit your life for me. I want to hear it all, the good, the bad, the dark, the light, the funny and the sad. You and I are intuitive, and that makes us feel deeply and strongly about events and how they affect our lives and those we love. But how else must we be but to be ourselves? After all, God chose to create us in His image, and I do know that our God feels deeply and strongly about everything He has created.

    As I write this letter to you and send it halfway around the world for your eyes to read, I think of you, possibly sleeping soundly after loving your man and dreaming sweet dreams about whatever it is you dream.

    I, too, am content, meaning that I have that great joy in knowing the Lord and being loved by a godly man. Happiness and sadness come and go, depending on the circumstances. I sometimes think fanciful thoughts of going to America and living next door to you so we can drink tea and talk while we fold clothes. But I know God has a plan and a purpose for my husband and me here in Hamburg. I do grow weary of doing "good" sometimes, I must confess, but your letters bring me delight. I can confide in you like no other, except for our sweet Jesus who knows my heart and every thought. I shall not pretend to know how to be a friend to you or anyone else, without Him. In all I say and do, the best I can

The Phrasing of Every Song

do for you, sweet sister, is to always point you in the direction of our Lord Christ Jesus. So take my counsel and consecrate your marriage to Him, and He will be your strong tower, your rock and shield. Thank you a thousand times for sharing your heart with me. You always have a place of love in my heart.

Christ's awaiting Bride,
Beatrice

Summer eventually gave way to autumn. Marie started attending school. She had her very own slate and chalk; she was speaking excellent English, soon began to love school and made many friends quite easily. Her favorite part of school was reading and writing, but Papa Bill had to help her with her math problems.

While Marie was in school and Bill was away at work, Tilly would go and help out at the Brahms' bakery decorating special cakes and making pastries. Most days, she was able to bring some unsold products home with her, and she always shared these items with Uncle John and Aunt Whinny.

The newlyweds were very happy and so grateful that the windows of heaven had opened up and showered down blessings upon them. Marie was happy that she now had a normal life and could just put her energy into exploring her childhood.

Bill seemed to always have a smile on his face, and he was always humming a tune. Drying the dishes after dinner as Tilly cleaned up the kitchen, he would begin to hum, and Tilly, who seemed to know every verse of every song Bill knew, would join in with the voice he had first heard in church. He had fallen in love with the woman to whom that voice belonged, and he never seemed to tire of telling her how beautiful she was and how happy he was that she loved to sing.

Though Tilly was happy, content with her life and very much in love with Bill, she would sometimes find herself comparing Bill with her late husband. John had been a reserved man who loved his solitude. He liked to read and meditate. His life as a hard-working farmer allowed him the freedom he needed to space himself away from too many people. He had no trouble talking to a person one-on-one, but he shied away from groups of people, causing some of the villagers who did not tolerate this type of behavior to leave him alone.

Tilly knew that John loved his God, his family and his land, in that order. She differed from him in that she needed social contact with friends and neighbors, but they seemed only to be her friends, not their friends. She loved John and knew he was steadfast and deeply in love with her and the children. He was proper and dignified and most definitely the definition of a gentleman. Often she thought how comfortable it was to be married to him.

Tilly had never heard John speak vulgarly or act inappropriately. However, sometimes she felt restless with him. She was always the one that made the first move to kiss or to show affection. She always had to initiate their lovemaking. He never showed her any passion; this made her feel odd whenever her friends complained about how their husbands wouldn't keep their hands off them. John was a hard worker, but he was often lost in his own thought world. Into this place she was never invited.

Bill was also a loving man, but a little bit of a flirt, which made her jealous from time to time. His hunger for love and affection matched hers with a passion she had never known, and she felt no restlessness around him. She truly felt they had been made for each other; Bill had said that to her just as she had been thinking it. Bill was not shy with her physically or with his words of affection. His talk was kind and uplifting and sometimes even made her blush. Nevertheless, he sometimes seemed to be underfoot. He had high energy and seemed to have an opinion about everything she was doing — or, even more unsettling, what she was *not* doing. His strength and drive left her exhausted at times.

As time passed and they grew to know each other's little quirks, what at first were minor irritations turned into mischievous, playful teasing, and the atmosphere changed from that of tension into bright sunshine again. Together, they learned how to play again, and laughter filled their home. Their hospitality as a couple welcomed in many strangers, who left their home as newfound friends.

Both were eager to have a baby together. Bill knew how healthy and strong Tilly was, and he was most certain that before their first anniversary a baby's coos and cries would fill their home. But as with his first wife, no child was born after the first or second anniversary. At first, there was a lot of planning and dreaming in their conversations, but after a while, the subject caused tension between them. They had prayed. The family had prayed. The pastor and the church had prayed. Tilly had seen a doctor; still no baby. She felt strange whenever she saw a pregnant woman or a baby buggy being pushed by a new mama and papa. Likewise with Bill, the jokes and teasing from the guys at work had died down, and the subject just wasn't mentioned anymore. Whenever Grandpa Bogda would periodically ask, Grandma would shoot him one of her "looks," and he would automatically go silent.

It was two weeks before Tilly and Bill's third wedding anniversary when Tilly awoke uncommonly early on a Saturday morning. Her last period had been irregular, but she had worked long hours in the garden and she excused it for that reason. This morning when she made coffee, the usually wonderful aroma of coffee perking made her vomit. Her suspicion was further strengthened when Bill awoke, found her in the kitchen and gave her a big hug. She squealed in pain as she pulled away from his embrace.

"Oh, my dear, what did I do?" he asked, looking surprised and holding his arms above his head.

"Nothing really, my breasts are just very tender," she explained, trying not to get her hopes up too high.

Each morning for the next week, food smells, laundry soap, body odor — all made her vomit. When she totally missed her next period, she was convinced. She made up her mind she would not tell Bill until she felt movement. After all, she reasoned, it would be mean to get his hopes up just to be disappointed. "That's what I will do," she spoke out loud to herself.

But on the morning of their third anniversary, she rolled over in bed and kissed him for a long time. As he responded and pulled her to him, she said, "Darling, I'm pregnant."

A big grin formed on his face. He kissed her, and they held each other without speaking a word, just feeling happy and content. Then he looked at her and said, "Get dressed, my bride; I'm taking you to breakfast!"

Tilly sat up in bed and responded to his command. "Oh, Bill, we really shouldn't tell anyone yet," she said with caution.

"You're right, but this is our anniversary, and I want to celebrate. Will you do me the honor, Mrs. Bogda, mother of my child, of accompanying me and daughter Marie to breakfast?" He was feeling very fine as he teased her.

"Why, yes, I accept the invitation, my silly Billy. Did you know I love you and am so happy? I'm glad you wanted to marry me all those years ago," she said smiling.

"See this grin on my face? Nobody could make me this happy but you. I wanted to marry you that first time I saw you in church. I'm glad you decided to say yes to me." She responded by throwing her arms around his neck and rubbing her nose against his. They finally got dressed and woke Marie so they could go to breakfast and then go to church. Bill and Tilly felt extremely thankful on their third anniversary.

Months passed, and they kept their secret. However, the morning sickness continued daily, and finally, Tilly began feeling little fluttering movements. Grandma Bogda's birthday in October was coming up, so Tilly decided to plan a party for her and use the occasion to share their good news about the baby with the rest of the family.

Chapter 13
Love Goes On

"Tilly, my love, I'm home, and I'm feelin' frisky!" Bill announced as he bounded in through the front door. Tilly hurried from the kitchen, wiped her hands on her flour-smudged apron and greeted her husband with a welcoming kiss. The aroma floating from the kitchen into the living room made his mouth water — as did the sight of his bride of three years.

"You settle down, Billy boy! We have your parents and your brother and his family coming for dinner, don't you remember?" She noticed his sweaty face. "You have just enough time to go clean up while I set the table." She spoke over her shoulder as she went to the hutch and began gathering the plates and silverware for the table settings.

"What's all the fuss?" He began rolling up his sleeves and heading for the kitchen to wash his hands and face.

"It's your mother's birthday, and I made a delicious cake for us to celebrate. I think this cake is my best creation since I have been helping at the bakery. The fuss, Mister, is that tonight I thought we could use this opportunity to give them our good news. What do you think?" Her eyes were sparkling.

"Well, I don't know! Tilly, do you think it might be too soon to tell anyone?"

"My love, if we don't tell them soon, my stomach will be so big they will guess, and that will spoil our surprise."

"Do you want to tell them, or shall I?"

"Well, you are their son. It will be best coming from your lips." She felt a little disappointed that his excitement did not match hers.

"Does Marie know yet?" he asked, returning to the dining area, rolling down his sleeves.

"Does Marie know what?" Marie asked, walking into the room rubbing her eyes. "Mama, what is the cake for, and what are you both talking about?" She yawned and stretched her arms over her head.

Bill interrupted the questioning. "Before another word is spoken, I need my 'Hello' hug!" He smiled at the 9 year old. Marie met his smile and quickly came to him, putting her arms around his neck and squeezing with affection.

"I missed you today, Papa."

"Thank you! I also missed my women, but I have to work to make a livin' so we can buy food to feed all our relatives. By the way, to answer your question, Grandmother is celebrating her birthday, and Grandpa and Uncle and his family are also joining us tonight for dinner. If your mother wasn't such a cook" — he paused, looking mischievously at Tilly — "I surely am glad she is." He laughed at himself.

"Marie, we are having a birthday party for Grandma Bogda. You were so sleepy after you came home from school, you didn't even notice I was baking a cake. Look, didn't it turn out nice?" She looked at Marie who had only glanced at the cake and was again rubbing the sleep from her eyes.

"Look at me, Marie. How do you feel?" Her tone changed from light chatter to concern as she looked at her daughter's face. Marie still looked tired, and her cheeks were red.

"I'm all right, Mama; I just feel hot. The room at school was hot, and when we went outside to play there was no shade, and no one felt like running or playing today. I thought if I took a nap I would feel better, but it just left me with a headache."

"Go wash your face while I chip off a piece of ice for you to suck on. Once you cool down, you can help me set the table." Tilly had a little too much command in her voice. With ice pick in hand, she opened the lower portion of the icebox, chipped some ice and put it into a glass, which she then filled with cooled tea water. The combination of washing her face and sipping on the cold water revived Marie somewhat, though she still felt drained and not at all in the party mood.

The company was to arrive at 6:30. They arrived early and hungry. Everything was already prepared, so the group came in and found their special places at the table. Bill opened the back door and the front door to let the air move through the house and cool down what the oven had heated up from the afternoon baking. Grandma Bogda gladly agreed to wear the Happy Birthday paper crown reserved for all birthdays. She was also given the honor of being served first, which normally fell to Grandpa.

"I hope you enjoy your birthday dinner," Tilly whispered as she reached down and kissed her mother-in-law upon the cheek.

"What a lovely, lovely party. Thank you all!" Grandma Bogda announced as big tears welled up in her eyes. She quickly dabbed them away with her napkin.

Grandpa chimed in, "I didn't know I was so hungry until I smelled all the good food here in your home. What's for dinner?"

With great ceremony, Tilly smoothed her clean Sunday apron, cleared her throat and, with hands together, announced, "Our first course is cabbage soup followed by a nice beef pot roast with oven-roasted vegetables. I know you like the potato rolls, so we have them with fresh butter and currant jelly. Our dessert is white kuchen mit peaches and cream. And now, I say to you all, Good Appetite!" She made a small curtsy and ladled the soup into the bowls.

Bill prayed the blessing for the food and also a thanksgiving for his mother. His brother, John, arose from his chair and gave a short speech on how blessed the family was, and from there the food and merriment began. It was hard to grasp that people could talk and eat so much and so fast. A happy buzz filled the house, and waves of laughter and words of praise to Tilly came with each course.

Agnes sat beside Marie, and Peter sat across the table facing Marie. His mother, Aunt Whinny, had to call him down twice for kicking the girls under the table. Finally his father, Uncle John, raised his voice, and Peter ate his dinner without further mischief. Agnes had to be coaxed into eating her vegetables with the threat she would not get any birthday cake if she did not take at least a bite of each one. She ate the potato, carrot and piece of onion reluctantly.

Marie was uncommonly quiet at the table. Normally with this crowd, it was difficult to get a word in; usually she tried, but tonight she did not. She enjoyed the food but was too full for dessert. Before the birthday cake was served, she asked to be excused from the table and retreated to the living room to read while the festivities continued in the dining area. Agnes asked for Marie's piece of cake, but her mother said, "NO!"

Once the dishes were removed from the table, John and Whinny gave Grandma Bogda a present of Mosel wine, imported from Bernkastel-Kues, to share with all the adults. They offered a toast to everyone's good health and good wealth and asked for wisdom to know what to do with both of them.

"Prosit!" they all said in unison, and then everyone laughed at the joke except for Peter, who wanted to pout because he was too young to be offered any of the wine.

"Oh, Ma, I just want a taste!" he whined.

"No!" she answered sharply and then gave a deliberate look at her husband as if to say, *I said no, don't you say yes.* He read the look and supported his wife's wishes.

Grandpa, however, was clueless, and in the merriment gave Peter a taste. The liquid fire roasted Peter's lips, tongue, mouth and throat. He pulled away, making a scene about how awful it tasted. All the adults stared at Grandpa as he laughed and then at Peter as he ran to the kitchen for some water. Both John and Whinny knew it would do no good to scold Grandpa, but Grandma just shot him one of her "looks." He stopped laughing and had two more glasses of wine before coffee was offered.

To cut the tension and to return to the party mood, Tilly pulled out a neatly made tatted lace handkerchief and gave it to her mother-in-law to admire. Whinny rose from her chair and claimed it if Grandma Bogda didn't want it.

"Tilly, where did you learn to make lace? This is absolutely beautiful. Please teach me to make lace ... oh, better than that, make me a handkerchief for Christmas. Oh, please, mine look like old rags compared to this one." Whinny admired how even and neat all the lace was, knowing in her wildest dreams she could never master such an art.

At this point, the women were together listening to Tilly tell about her friend at Ellis Island who taught her to tat and knit, and the men were together having their conversation. All the children were silent in the living room, playing separately from one another. After the conversations came to a lull, Tilly shot a look at Bill; he received the unspoken communication.

"Mother." He cleared his throat. "Tilly and I want to use this occasion to announce we are going to have a baby." The news was received with an explosion of happy sounds that caught the attention of the three children in the living room. All their faces turned toward the adults, who were laughing uproariously.

Marie sat there unable to move or react to the news. Peter and Agnes quickly moved close to Tilly and eagerly joined in the merriment. Without trying to draw attention, Marie got up from the couch and silently retreated to her bedroom where she crawled into bed. She couldn't move or sleep. Her mind felt numb, but her stomach felt sick.

Although an hour had passed and the second pot of coffee was being shared, everyone still sat at the table talking and laughing. Agnes had grown tired and curled up on the couch, where she fell asleep. Peter, bored with the adult conversation, sat in the living room playing tirelessly with a yo-yo he had won at the local carnival.

It was an hour later before Marie was missed. Grandmother Bogda noticed it first.

"Tilly, where is Marie?" she asked after looking in the living room. The two other children were accounted for, but there was no Marie.

"I'll go check her room," Tilly replied, distracted from her conversation with Whinny.

"No, dear, let me. Sorry for interrupting you and Whinny," Grandma Bogda said with a concerned look on her face. Neither woman spoke; they nodded their heads and without hesitation picked up their conversation where they had left off.

Grandma Bogda walked down the hall and gently rapped on the closed door to Marie's bedroom. Peter was suddenly standing behind her, wanting to see what was going on. She turned to him and gave him a "look" that dismissed him. He turned and walked back into the living room, still playing with his yo-yo. After she could see he was back in the living room, Grandma Bogda quietly cracked the door open to peek inside.

Marie sat on her bed fully clothed, holding a pillow, staring off into space.

"May I come in?" she gently asked.

With a sigh, Marie replied, "If you like." Her tone was void of her normal happy sound.

"I do like. I missed you, so I came looking for you. This was a lovely party. Thank you," she said, trying to invade Marie's mysterious mood.

"Oh, no need to thank me. It was Mama's doing. She didn't really involve me in any of her plans." Her statement had a bite to it, and her grandmother picked up quickly on the undercurrent of emotion and its deeper meaning.

"Marie, do you remember when we first met? You know, before my Bill and your mother married?" She paused to wait for Marie's response. There was none, so she continued talking. "I was so thrilled you were going to be a part of my life. I thought I loved you at first sight, but as I've watched you grow into such a lovely young lady, well, I must say, I love you more now than I did then and more now than words can say." Marie turned and looked her in the eye. A small curve formed at each corner of Marie's mouth; she then moved to embrace her grandmother.

"Oh, my sweet, do you need someone to talk with right now?" Grandma Bogda asked, trying very hard not to intrude.

"Grandma, I have just been in my room praying. The more I talk, the more confused I feel. You know I love you, too. You are the best. I never really knew either of my grandparents in Germany, but I dreamed of having a grandmother like you." She held her grandmother tight, and then tears began running down her cheeks.

"Oh, now, is your heart so heavy you need tears?" she asked, patting and hugging Marie at the same time.

"Grandma, you know I love Papa. He loves Mama, and I know he loves me. I just don't know how things will be when … when, well …" She sighed. Her grandmother finished her sentence for her.

"When the baby comes?" she asked, knowing the answer.

"Uh huh." Marie nodded, and then she began to cry. They

held each other as Marie's crying turned to sobs. After she grew too fatigued to cry heavily anymore, her grandma began to speak to her softly.

"Marie, this will be a time of change for you. No doubt about it. There is a time for everything. You are almost 10 years old, and having a baby in the house will be a happy time and also a demanding time. You have had to share your mama with Bill, and now you will share her with your brother or sister. But you know what? Mama and Bill will love you and the baby. Love is a funny thing. We don't just have a certain amount of love to give, and when it's given, it runs out. No, no, love is different. It does not work that way. God gives us more and more love as he sets before us more people to love. Your mama and papa are not going to love you less; they will just have added love for this new child.

"Now listen closely to me. You should not confuse love with attention. A baby is totally helpless, so of course this little baby will need much attention. You and me, well, we are older now. We need less attention. But I still need love, and so do you, my dear. Peter needed my extra attention when Agnes was just a baby. He still comes over and stays with Grandpa and me whenever his little sister gets on his nerves. Marie, you always have an open invitation to Grandma's house and Grandma's heart."

"I know, I know. Thank you, Grandma," Marie said through her tears. "I really want to be happy. I don't want anyone to see me cry when everyone is so happy about the baby. I asked Jesus to help me, but sometimes when He helps me it doesn't happen all of a sudden, like I'd like it to. But He does always help." She paused for a moment, her mind running to various random thoughts.

"Mama had two other children that died, Mary and baby John. Did you know that? She still cries at their birthdays and almost every holiday. I have seen her look at other women with new babies and seen the tears in her eyes." Again she paused and pulled away from Grandma's arms, looking as though she had lost her way. Marie wiped the tears from her eyes. Grandma Bogda saw that Marie's nose needed wiping and pulled the lovely lacy birthday present from her sleeve to do the job. Marie showed no hesitation while Grandma Bogda wiped her nose.

Marie continued. "Did you know Mama is always so worried about me if I get a cold or headache? She just can't stand the thought of losing me, too." Marie sat up straighter on her knees and looked quizzically into her grandmother's eyes. "But, Grandma, what is going to happen when she has more children? What is going to happen to me?"

Marie's mood changed from curious to angry. "Grandma Bogda, I just hate change!" After making her declaration, she slumped down and put her head in her grandmother's lap. Grandma Bogda began petting her hair and gently wiped Marie's tear-stained face.

"Marie, my sweetness, our families have known much change throughout our lives. I can tell you there is no need to hate it, my dear. It will be best for you to make peace with change, because just when you think all is just the way you like it in life and you know what to expect from it, Ol' Friend Change comes to visit and stays so long he usually wears out his welcome." Grandma Bogda was gentle but spoke with a knowing that Marie trusted.

Marie sat up. "You talk about change like it's a person, Grandma. That's funny. Do you think my baby brother or sister is going to bring Ol' Friend Change to our home?" Marie brightened at her cleverness and smiled at her own joke. Her grandmother laughed easily, relieved that she had been able to communicate her message.

"Yes, Marie, you have it! When you get a little older, Ol' Friend Change will come and give you a grownup body. You'll see what I'm talking about then. But, Marie, let me tell you something else about Ol' Friend Change. There is something he cannot do. No, Marie, neither he nor anyone else can make you change the way you feel about things. You are the only one who can decide what you will do with the changes that come into your life. Only you can decide to be happy about what's going on rather than angry, or scared, or sad. You decide if you want to be giving when you'd rather be stingy. It is you that must decide to act lovely whenever inside you feel like acting ugly.

Love Goes On

Ol' Friend Change has to have your permission before any of that can happen." She smiled at Marie.

They both sat there for a moment, enjoying each other, and then Marie looked at her grandmother. "Is there any cake left from your party, Grandma?" she asked, suddenly feeling hungry.

"Yes, I saved you a big piece of that wonderful cake. I just knew you would want some later." She reached down and kissed Marie's forehead.

"Thanks, I love you." Marie smiled.

Their little talk was over, but they both seemed to know this was just the beginning of many more talks between the two of them. Marie took her grandmother's hand, and together, they stood up and walked into the kitchen. Taking two forks and two glasses of milk, they polished off the rest of the birthday cake.

The dishes were washed and put away and the company had long ago left for home. Both Tilly and Bill checked on Marie, who was fast asleep in her bed.

Just as Tilly and Bill were crawling into bed for the night, they heard a loud rap on the door. Bill called out to see who was knocking on their door so late at night. It was a messenger from the church telling them that Blanche Gerber, formerly Blanche Randolph — better known as Nanny — was in labor and had called for Tilly's help. Tilly quickly gathered up some things, dressed and hurried to the Gerber house to help with the birth of her friend's first baby. Bill rolled over and went back to sleep so he would be ready for work the following day.

Upon returning home in the early morning hours, Tilly was not ready to sleep, although she was very tired. Her heart was filled with praise and gratitude, so she sat down in the kitchen and wrote to her dearest friend.

My most wonderful friend and sister in Christ, Beatrice,

My prayer is always that my letters find you and your family in God's perfect health. I am writing this to you hurriedly so I don't forget to tell you every detail of how God is restoring lives. While in the employment of the Carlisle family, I had the good and wondrous blessing of being surrounded by loving and happy people — all, that is, save one.

Tilly's Song

This melancholy creature happened to be the nanny to the Carlisle children. Please do not judge me too quickly as I describe her, for it is not my intent to slander or defame her in any way.

The first time we made each other's acquaintance, I found her to be slow in thinking and shy in behavior. As I continued to observe her, she was neither of these in the presence of the children. She was cheerful without being demonstrative, quick to identify and remedy conflict, strict with manners and playful and fun loving with all the children, including my Marie. I was astonished to observe that around adults she acted almost invisible. Whenever she was in the kitchen with the other workers, I am ashamed to say, I found it difficult to know what to say to her. If I inquired about her wellbeing, she would look down at the floor and mumble only a word, such as "fine" or "all right." Mrs. Carlisle and Mrs. Johnson never seemed to have trouble engaging in conversation with her.

To avoid gossiping about her to others, I decided to confront her to determine why she was avoiding me and not speaking to me. The confrontation did not go as I hoped. Instead, she only looked sad whenever she was around me or left the room whenever she saw me. This type of avoidance went on up to the day of my wedding.

On the morning of my wedding day, the problem all came to light. Beatrice, I never understood that this dear woman was jealous and envious of me. I confess I was so absorbed in my own life that I never even considered someone else possibly wanting what I had. She was jealous of Bill's affection for me and envious that I had a child.

That day of my joining in marriage to William Bogda, my new friend was delivered from the monstrous spirit of jealousy. This spirit had joined the spirits of envy, grief, loss and lack to torment this poor woman almost out of her mind. She felt as though life had passed her by, and although she saw the blessings of God in everyone else's life, she could not recognize any such blessings in her own life.

Beatrice, that morning she and I held each other in our arms and wept once the truth was known about her feelings toward me. The Comforter came to us both, and He quickened my mind to remember our Mother Sarah, in the scriptures, and what shame she must have felt that she could not give Abraham the child promised to him. The comments about her beauty must have sounded hollow to her when other women her age now had grandchildren. Abraham had heard from God Almighty, and yet he still dishonored her by letting Pharaoh and then another king think she was only his sister and not his wife. She had gone from living in a large city to traveling by day tasting the sand from the wind to sleeping at night in a tent under the stars. Where was this wonderful God of Abraham when she needed Him? Sarah grew impatient waiting, and my friend, the nanny, had, also. But she knew the story as we all have heard it from our mother's knee. More importantly, she knew the end of the story. When I reminded her of this very story, she and I looked

Love Goes On

at each other and our weeping changed into uproarious laughter as we remembered all the miraculous things God had already done in our lives. I asked her what was too difficult for God. I also asked if she would be willing to put aside her jealousy of me and meet God at the altar in her heart and in His presence wait for the Isaac to come into her life.

Beatrice, God is so marvelous, so willing to make what seems impossible, possible! The most wonderful news is that my new friend met a remarkable man who delivers ice to the Carlisles' house. He just happens to be a friend of Blanche's brother. They met, fell deeply in love and were married in the Methodist church, just a short distance from where we live. Six months later, she was with child. She honored me by asking me to be one of her midwives, since she had seen me with Mrs. Carlisle and the twins. Oh, Beatrice, I have just returned home to scribble this all down on paper to announce that a beautiful baby boy was born in the early hours of this 7th day of October, 1899. Such joy and merriment was felt at his entrance into this world, surrounded with hugs and kisses and plenty of mother's milk. It was so dear. Her husband knew nothing of our earlier encounter, but he chose to name his son Isaac.

And all this to tell you another miracle has happened: I, too, am with child. God has showed me great favor through all of this. We just told Bill's family the news tonight before I was called to help deliver baby Isaac. I could not wait till morning to tell you this goodness and ask for your prayers for my little one to be born healthy and strong, like this little baby boy tonight. My new child will be born at the beginning of the new century, and my little Marie will be 10 years old. I pray she will love the baby and not fall into jealousy as I have just mentioned.

I am so sleepy. I shall write again soon, I promise. Kiss all your children for me, and give my offering of Christ's love to your good husband.

Singing praises to our King,
Mathilda

In five weeks' time, Tilly received an answer from Beatrice. A small parcel arrived containing white baby booties and many letters of congratulations from the widows. Each of these ladies who had met Mathilda in Hamburg sent a little handmade baby gift to her to show their great joy for God's sweet kindnesses.

Dearest Frau Bogda, good friend and fellow disciple of Jesus,

Your letter arrived today, and I am grateful that God has not allowed the Kaiser to interrupt our friendship or the delivery of your letters and parcels.

I have read your letter to the pastor and the children, to the ladies who help with the food distribution among the widows and to each widow who met you while you were in Hamburg. We all are so eager to hear word from America. Thank you, dear friend, for keeping us in your thoughts and prayers and including us in your life. Tonight we shall read the story of Abraham and Sarah and reflect upon the covenant of Abraham and upon the New Covenant that is now ours in Christ.

Remember, dear friend: God spoke to you to start a new life in America, and He is faithful to give you the desires of your heart. You have desired more children, and I am so happy to hear how God has answered your prayer. Yes, I shall continue to lift you up in prayer for the health and safety of this little one and also your big girl, Marie. We also shall pray for little Isaac and his mother and father. I am so amazed how God works.

You spoke in your letter of jealousy. Dear friend, this is a topic I know too well. Once you are delivered from jealousy, remember to fill your heart with gratitude. I confess to you that I did not always do what I now advise you to do. As a young bride to a most handsome young pastor, my heart would blaze with such flames of jealousy that at times my words would singe my dear husband's feelings. Again and again, his eyes would widen in disbelief at my accusations. My housework suffered because my mind was absorbed in seeing him being hugged and kissed by the women leaving the church on Sunday. He would always dismiss my complaint and explain these were only friendly gestures. He was always quick to reaffirm his affection toward me. But this had no effect on me because the very next Sunday, I became a fervently unfriendly wife.

A kind elder woman of the church confronted me about my coolness toward my husband in public. She could see my icy exterior covering the furnace within. Mathilda, I must say, it was my first experience being corrected in a true Christian manner. This kind soul did not scold me or shame me for being immature as a Christian or wife. Instead, she showed me Christ. The horror and hurt of my worst imagination she used to show me the heart of God. This was what God must feel whenever His own children deny Him love and carelessly give their lives, love and affection to other gods of their own making. She taught me that jealousy is not always wrong, but using it to falsely accuse is very wrong.

I saw within my own mind how it was not my husband being untrue to me but rather my own mind imagining him to be. I now understand that my sin was "vain imaginations."

The people in our community are overrun with vain imaginations. They are imagining their lives being doomed. The crops had a poor yield this season, and now on every street corner there is talk of loss and lack. Our dear widowed sisters have truly been in a position of not having even a farthing to buy day-old bread, and yet our Lord continues to be faithful to supply our daily bread. My dear husband, man of faith that he is, still will not take any of the food for our family until our sisters in the Lord first receive some food. My flesh cries out sometimes when we pull the cart down the street where the butcher shop is located. The other day, my stomach made such a noise it made my children laugh and point their fingers at me. Yes, we all laughed.

Pray for me, Mathilda. Pray that I may continue to laugh in the face of the enemy as he prowls around our neighborhood seeing whose joy he can steal. Please pray a hedge of protection around my dear little ones who see other children with plenty and look at me without words as if to ask, "Where is mine, Mama?"

Oh, now, I must not end these tidings on such a melancholy note, but please remember that the righteous and His seed never beg for bread. Let me confess that our Lord will not forsake us. Mathilda, please write soon.

In our Lord's gracious care,
Beatrice

Tilly's Song

Upon reading Beatrice's letter to Bill, she could read between the lines into the tension and misery that no words could express. Bill took it into his own hands to offer comfort to this good woman and her family by suggesting that Mathilda send some sausages to her as a treat that would hopefully arrive for their Christmas celebration. Tilly had already begun *Weihnachtsgebäck**, which is what they call the time of Christmas baking in Germany. Because she already had cookies prepared, she included a variety of them in colorful tins to keep them fresh and safe in the shipping. She used the ginger cookie recipe Beatrice had sent her, the same kind of cookies that had helped alleviate motion sickness while she traveled to America. She made them often and in large batches since she had grown very fond of the flavor and the calming effect they had on her.

Bill was able to send the package from his workplace at the packing plant.

In January, Tilly and Bill received a letter from Hamburg.

My Most Kind and Loving Friend, Mathilda,

Oh, what joy, what great generosity from our friends in America! When your enormous package arrived, the postman was surrounded by a pack of hounds hoping for more than just a whiff of the scent of delicious sausages. Oh, how disappointed they were when the door shut in their begging faces. The kind widows have enclosed their thank-you notes since, of course, they were given the first of this gift. I do so love that my dear husband and pastor are the same generous man that God uses daily to keep me from growing proud. Whenever I start to accept the gratitude others offer me for the good works, he is there to remind me all the thanks shall go directly to God.

We do give thanks to our Heavenly Father for remembering us and for prompting you to send us our one Christmas present this year. I kept the tin of cookies for our special Christmas Eve treat, since this year we had no rice to make the pudding or almond paste for our fruit-shaped candies. Thank you for your thoughtfulness; the cookies tasted so fresh!

Love Goes On

We shall have the remaining cookies for Dreikonigsbend*, as we celebrate the Feast of the Magi on the 6th of January.

My prayer has been for God to increase my faith. Your gift has done just that for me. This winter has been so hard. I best not complain to you, but, my dear sister, sometimes I think only you and I and God know my innermost thoughts. It is not so much for me, but for the sake of my children, I confess to you these things. I caught our youngest son digging in the rubbish bin behind the bakery, and I felt an ache within my heart that my own prayers cannot seem to quickly take away. Two of our dear sisters have gone on home to heaven, and my little daughter said she hoped God would take her home soon. I do not want God to honor that prayer.

In Hamburg, the fishermen are being paid so poorly for their catch, they are leaving the fish to rot on the pier. They shoot at those who try to take the fish, and yet my husband still comes home with fish scales inside his jacket so the widows can eat.

Oh, dear me, what was to be such a joyful letter has turned into a miserable funeral dirge. Please forgive me; I only wanted you to truly understand that the sausages were pure delight. Your kindness in sending them to us has nourished more than our bellies, it has been sustenance for our soul. Read Ecclesiastes 4:10. You are that friend to me.

Yours for eternity,
Beatrice

Mathilda and Beatrice's friendship grew through the years, and they were able to share their lives with each other. Beatrice read the letter of the birth of Wilhelm Bogda, Jr. aloud to the widows, and all cried with tears of joy. Everyone needed to hear words of hope and encouragement, since their lives in Germany seemed so colorless compared with the news from America. A cloud of darkness was gathering over Germany at this time, and it seemed everyone in the world would soon be affected by it. However, receiving the letters conveyed that if there was hope for Tilly, then maybe there was hope for them. Letters shared

Tilly's Song

the faithfulness of Christ in so many of the lives of the new immigrants, and they beckoned for others to come and join them in this "land of the free and home of the brave."

Added work of having a baby in the house made time pass quickly — added work but also added joy, since there was now a baby boy in the house. Tilly and Bill were so pleased with their handsome son.

Grandma and Grandpa Bogda acted almost embarrassingly silly over their newest grandchild. Marie was a big help — when she wanted to be. Billy was her baby doll, and she carried him outside and played with him, keeping the bugs from bothering him. All too soon, he was up toddling about, following her wherever she went. This annoyed her only a little. Her mama and papa were careful not to overload her with chores to interfere with her newly recaptured childhood.

However, after Billy was weaned, Tilly longed for another child. She hoped for a baby daughter but was reluctant to pray for one, feeling almost greedy. "God knows best!" she would tell herself, and then she would absentmindedly begin dreaming of pink baby clothes.

In the Muellers' store some soft pink sock yarn had just arrived. Tilly was tempted to buy some when she went to buy more yeast for her baking. Clara Mueller, Marie's friend, asked if Marie could stay and play and then go home after supper. Tilly agreed. Billy wanted to push his own buggy on the way home, so Tilly filled it with some of her packages, letting him push slowly with all his might. Less than a block from home, when he became tired, Tilly laid him among the groceries, where he fell asleep just minutes before arriving at home. She pushed him into the backyard and sat on the back porch to watch him sleep in perfect peace. Without realizing it, she was drawn into deep intercession and praise.

"Oh, Lover of my soul, You are to be praised for Your loving kindness, mercy and grace. I have two very healthy and strong children, a good husband and many dear friends. Thank You, thank You, THANK You! My life is full and happy.

"Oh, You know my heart. I would love to have another baby, but I don't want to sound demanding. I waited so long for my little Billy — I know it was not as long as Sarah waited for Isaac, but I still would be grateful for another child, boy or girl. Hmm, look at him, Lord. He is a delight with his little hands and his cute lips shaped like a heart. I ache inside, I love him so much." She was still deep in prayer when she heard little happy sounds and that one word that made her the happiest.

"Mama!" he called to her as he sat up in his buggy, crowded by the packages.

"Yes, darling, I'm right here," she spoke softly to reassure him.

"Mama, I hungry, Mama ... hungry ... Hungry!" he cried, reaching both his arms for her to take him.

"Well, my little man, let's get you a bite to eat, shall we?" she answered as she pulled him from the buggy. He instantly wanted down and began running around and around in the freshly cut grass. Taking the packages inside, she cut up an apple and some cheese and joined him on the back porch to eat their treat.

"Papa!" Tilly heard him squeal. She turned to see Bill walking home, looking tired. When he heard his son call his name, he came alive and ran to pick him up. Swinging him around and kissing him on the cheek, he asked his little boy if he had been a good boy today.

"Yes," Billy answered, shaking his head no.

"Papa, we went to da store, and I have apple. You want apple?" Taking a piece of apple, he turned and kissed Tilly, and the three of them hugged.

"Tilly, I can think of no greater pleasure than to come home to you and our children. This is such a happy time!" he said, smiling. Then he asked about Marie.

Tilly explained that the Muellers had asked if she could stay, play and have dinner with them. Bill acted pleased that Marie was forming good friendships with the children of their friends.

"Tilly, we are so blessed. After supper, if you like, I will walk over to the grocery store and fetch Marie. Have I told you today that I love you?" He winked at her as she gave him a big smile.

Tilly drank in the affection and felt content.

Tilly's Song

***

A salty aroma of fresh pork roast and sauerkraut permeated the whole house. The sweetness of the cooling cake, waiting for the final touches of raspberry jam filling and sugar glaze, mingled with the roasting meat aroma.

Sheets and towels were hanging on the outdoor clothesline soaking up the sun's rays and releasing their moisture to the warm Illinois wind. While hanging the last of the laundry to dry, Tilly noticed some nasty weeds among her prized Westerfield's cucumber plants and stopped abruptly from her laundry duties to bend over and pluck the invading weeds from around the young plants. These plants were her pride and joy, grown from the very seed Samuel Dingee, the Pickle Magnate, had personally given her to plant. If they proved successful and produced nice cucumbers, he promised to buy every one she would sell to him.

But right now, she was distracted by that all-too-familiar cramping, starting in her legs and then moving up into her belly with a steady rhythmic pain. She had been two weeks late with her monthly cycle, and she just knew her body held new life. But right now, as she raced to the toilet, her new suspicion was correct.

Oh, well, maybe next month, she thought, fighting back the tears of disappointment. Baby Billy was more than 3 years old now. Everyone was getting older. It seemed Tilly felt it the most.

How could she face Bill's hopeful questioning eyes one more time, to see his face fall and then quickly try to cover his emotions as he pretended it didn't matter? What about all those ladies at church who prayed for a miracle? She couldn't decide if she was mad, sad or depressed. She knew Jesus was near, waiting for their normal conversation. Lately, she wasn't talking, and neither was He.

She slowly made her way to the couch, feeling as if all the energy had been drained from her body and spirit. She wrapped the afghan over her feet and pulled it up to her chin. There in the quiet of the empty house, she fell asleep.

She floated in and out of dreams.

Love Goes On

First, she dreamed of knitting baby booties the color of the sky at dawn when the clouds take on a subtle pinkish cast. Next, she saw Bill, Marie and little Billy walking beside her while she pushed a baby buggy all the way to John Bogda's house where they were gathering with others for church service.

She awoke with a start. There had been talk about establishing a new church in the small town of Wilmette, but there was no building. Evanston was where they had gone to church ever since they had arrived from Germany. The community of Wilmette was growing and could certainly support a new church.

In only a few minutes, Tilly's energy had been restored, and she put it into immediate action. She checked the clock, pulled the roast out of the oven, set the table for four adults and four children and put the finishing touches on the cake.

With her work completed, she took off her apron, picked up her sleeping child and stepped out the front door. She walked, almost ran, to John and Whinny's house. It was three o'clock when she left the house and only five minutes later when she arrived to see Whinny through the window still reading the morning paper, with no thoughts or plans about dinner. A loud rap on the front door distracted Whinny from the editorials.

"Well, hello, mine gut sister," Whinny greeted Tilly as she opened wide the door.

As Tilly entered with a smile, she didn't bother to sit down but began talking to Whinny right inside the door. The baby was still asleep in her arms.

"Whinny, will you put your dinner plans aside tonight and you and your family come join us for dinner? I have a large pork roast and would just love to have you come and share it with us. What do you say?"

"Oh, my goodness, Tilly, you are such an angel! I have been feeling poorly, you know, it's that time of the month. My family was having nothing more than cold sausage and bread for their dinner. You know we will come. Peter and Agnes love your cooking — oh, well, so do I. What time shall we be there?"

"Whenever John arrives from work, come on over to our house, and then we shall have dinner." Tilly forced a smile as she felt another cramp. She was not going to let this distract her from her newfound mission.

On the way home, she walked into the backyard, laid Billy in one of the laundry baskets filled with dry towels and finished taking down the sheets and underwear, folding them neatly. The wind had blown in some clouds from across the lake, and suddenly it looked as if it could rain.

John and Whinny huddled close, sharing the umbrella while Peter and Agnes ran ahead. Agnes ran like a girl, skipping almost over the puddles on the street. Peter ran fast and deliberately jumped full force in the middle of the puddles, trying his best to splash his sister. This great game left both children soaked to the bone by the time they arrived at Uncle Bill and Aunt Tilly's house. They were both commanded to stand by the oven until they dried off or at least warmed up a bit.

Steam was rising from the plate and bowls that were filled with pork roast, sauerkraut with caraway seeds, fluffy mashed potatoes, fresh applesauce with a pinch of cinnamon, hard rolls as big as a fist, fresh butter, cold beets and gherkins in sour cream. The cake was waiting in the kitchen as the after-dinner surprise. As soon as the blessing of the food was given, Peter dove for the bread and butter.

"I could eat every roll on that plate," he announced with pride.

"You mind your manners — there are other people eating here, too!" his mother scolded her eldest.

"Ah, Ma, I was just foolin'," he said, sounding defeated.

Not a scrap of food was left in the bowls or on the plates, and even though everyone was more than satisfied, they all looked forward to cake. Every guest was offered ice-cold milk, and later, coffee was served to the adults. Peter begged for a taste of the adult-only drink, and when his father caved and gave him a sip, Peter retreated to the living room to join the girls with a look of disdain upon his face. He began spitting to get rid of the lingering aftertaste from the bitter brew.

"John, honestly, you just encourage that awful behavior. Make him stop spitting. He can be so rude. John, did you hear me?" Whinny had that no-nonsense tone in her voice.

"Peter, be nice," John yelled in the direction of the living room.

After the uncomfortable moment passed and the children were quietly playing, the grownups remained at the dining room table sipping their second or third cup of coffee. Tilly returned to the dining room after nursing the baby and putting him to bed. It was now that she revealed her agenda.

"Whinny, John, Bill — I want to share a dream, a thought, an idea with all of you. Before Marie and I settled here in Wilmette, we met a pastor and his wife named Matthias in Hamburg. It was such a pleasant surprise to learn they had relatives in the ministry here in America, and one of them is Rev. J. D. Matthias. He would come from time to time to this community from Bethlehem Lutheran in Evanston. He has since moved on to another town. There is no Lutheran church building in our community. Hmm, how shall I put this without sounding too outlandishly bold? Well, here it goes. Since you, John and Whinny, have a large house with a bigger living room and dining area adjoined, why don't we all have church at your home? That way, we can begin to save money, have some fundraisers and then take the funds and build a church building in our little town of Wilmette."

John and Whinny looked at each other and began to grin from ear to ear.

"Tilly," John began, "my darling wife and I were just having this conversation and have been praying about it. I felt impressed that we needed a confirmation to see if this was just our idea or if it was really the will of God."

Whinny broke in, "Tilly, this is that confirmation we have been seeking!"

Bill looked at everybody and said, "Let's talk with the pastor." All agreed.

By November 1903, 12 men had organized a new congregation named St. John's Lutheran Church. They raised money, and by 1906, the church members had purchased two empty lots on the corner of Prairie and Linden Streets. These men signed a contract to construct the building for $2,300.

There were 242 members and 40 Sunday school children. A

245

theological student, Mr. F. H. Kretzschmar, served as pastor. Marie took confirmation classes and joined the Lutheran church while services were held at her uncle's home. When the congregation had outgrown the homes of John Bogda and Fred Whitt, they moved to Jones Hall on Wilmette Avenue near Green Bay Road, where they continued to hold worship services and church functions until the new church was built.

***

Tilly Bogda enjoyed cleanliness and order in her life. It made her feel closer to God. She had heard since birth from her own mother that cleanliness was next to godliness. Cleaning her own home gave her a deep-down comfort and contentment that she could not express in words.

Having clean hair and a fresh-scrubbed body after a hot bath, and then slipping into clean sheets that smelled of sunshine, produced a feeling of safety and peace way down within her spirit.

To say she was a fastidious cleaner would be an understatement. She lived and breathed the rule: "Everything has a place, and everything should be in its place." She became somewhat of an evangelist with her gospel of cleanliness. Everyone in her household was expected to pick up, wipe up and sweep up any personally committed messiness. Tilly made sure Marie knew this from an early age. Bill, on the other hand, had years of training still ahead of him. He was not slovenly or purposefully inattentive to her wishes, but he just did not share the passion his wife held for cleaning. He enjoyed a clean and orderly home and was so very happy she was willing to keep it that way for him. He was not so thrilled that she had volunteered their family to clean and set up Jones Hall every Sunday. He was cooperative but not thrilled.

Tilly just didn't understand this, and she felt it was beginning to interfere with the way she felt toward him. She would pray countless times for her feelings of disgust to leave her, but then he would do something and that tiniest annoyance would set her right back into an attitude of grumbling. Tilly saw this opportunity as a good thing that the whole family could be involved with, and everyone would be blessed. *How can Bill not see this activity as a good thing and have fun doing it with his family?* she wondered.

One early morning while Marie and Bill were still sleeping, Tilly went to the dining room table and started reading her Bible. She was instantly convicted of her attitude of withholding love and respect for her husband. She quickly asked for forgiveness.

"Lord, I don't want to be harsh and critical toward Bill, or toward anyone for that matter. Why am I so angry with Bill? He is nothing but loving and kind to me. John was not a neat person. He would leave his boots covered with manure right outside the window where our table sat, producing an unappetizing stink. I didn't think he was horrible when that happened. I just moved the table rather than grumbling at him to change. Oh, Father, I am at a total loss in what to do in this matter. What should I do?"

The Holy Spirit breathed a cool and gentle thought into her hot and troubled mind. "I know!" she said aloud. "I will visit his mother and ask her. She has known him as a little boy and now as a man. Today, I will plan a visit and ask if she would like to go for a walk. This day promises to have good weather. That's it! Thank You, my Lord and my friend!" Up she jumped from her chair and put her whole attention into making breakfast and lunch for her husband and daughter.

Bill rolled over in bed to find Tilly's side of the bed empty. He yawned and stretched, kicking off the covers. He listened and grew very still as he heard his Love singing in the kitchen.

Every man should wake up to a happy wife singing and to delicious smells of coffee and bacon, he thought. Quickly he dressed for his daily work and tiptoed into the kitchen. Tilly had her back to him and was filling his soup pail with warmed-up goulash from last night's supper. She was still singing as he approached her, but she paused to hold the last note of the song. When she finished, he quickly put his arms around her waist and gave her a kiss upon her neck. Tilly jumped in surprise and turned to face Bill, gently nuzzling into his chest.

Tilly's Song

After Bill was on his way to work and Marie off to school, Tilly washed and put away the breakfast dishes. Putting on her hat and placing Billy in the baby buggy, she walked to Aunt Whinny's house. She left Billy with his aunt and cousins. Not wanting to waste any time, she then went down the street to visit her mother-in-law.

"Gut morgen!" she greeted Grandpa and Grandma Bogda. He was still sipping coffee and reading the paper, while Grandma Bogda was kneading rye bread dough. She stopped and wiped her hands and offered Tilly a hot cup of coffee.

"Nein, danke," she answered.

"Please, now, dear, we must use our English," Grandma Bogda chided.

"Very well, I came to see if you would like to go for a walk this bright and beautiful morning. I would like to talk with you and perhaps go to the bakery for some Strammer Max*; I know they don't make it like they do in Berlin, but perhaps some Brotzeit* like they have in Trier?"

Grandma Bogda happily agreed upon the outing and gave strict instructions to punch down the bread dough if they were gone more than two hours. Grandpa agreed as a dutiful husband who, in his opinion, was helpful to his wife in every way.

Grandma Bogda was a master at reading faces and moods and quickly got right to the point.

"So, my dear, you wished to talk with me alone?" she asked, trying to keep in step with Tilly.

"Oh, yes! You do know I love you and your good husband, and you are my family in my heart, not just because of legal binding due to marriage?" Tilly asked to determine a safe foundation for the following conversation.

"Yes, yes, you may speak frankly with me without fear of harsh judgment. I, too, have been married and had children, moved to a foreign land and share much of the same things you have in life. What is it, my daughter — what has you troubled?"

Tilly stopped and spoke to her from her heart, fighting back tears. "Much to my shame, I have become a critical wife to my husband, your son. I crave order and cleanliness; as I see by the way you keep your house, you also do. How is it that Bill's little habits are becoming so annoying to me? I feel angry as I pick up his clothes left on the floor just where he took them off. He carries dishes all over the house and never returns them to the kitchen. I will make a dessert for an occasion, and when I go to present it, a piece is missing. When I scold him, he smiles at me as if it is funny. Marie now thinks it's funny to do it, also. I feel my affection for him is threatened by all these little careless antics. Even when it is time to go to the building to set up for church, he stalls and thinks up every excuse to be excluded from our duties. I love Bill, but I am at a loss as what to do, how to think. It is something I have committed to prayer, and yet God chooses to make this my personal trial."

Grandma Bogda kept looking into Tilly's blue eyes as she spoke and gently touched her shoulder and nodded her head with compassion.

"Oh, yes, I know this one very well. But let me explore a little further, for in my years I have found that often what appears to be the trouble is not the real problem. May I ask about your relationship with your husband who died in Germany?" she asked respectfully.

"Oh, you may ask. What is it you wish to know?" Tilly offered amiably.

"Was this issue a problem with John?" she queried.

"His behavior was not so different from Bill's. He was not as neat and tidy as I hoped him to be, but the difference was that it didn't bother me as it does now."

"Do you know why?" she probed.

Tilly thought for a moment. "We lived on a farm. Our home was small and full of children. I was always picking up and cleaning after them and, and ..." Her voice trailed off.

Grandma Bogda remained silent, but took both of Tilly's hands into her own and shared the companionship of silence.

Tilly's eyes filled with tears, and in a whisper she spoke.

"Is it that my home needs more children, and I am angry that it has not happened yet? Is that my true frustration and annoyance with Bill? Is that what you think? Can that be what is really happening with our marriage? Can I be somehow blaming him for this unfulfilled dream?"

Grandma Bogda did not give her an immediate answer. They continued to walk until they arrived at the bakery. Tilly's mind was lost in thought, so Grandma Bogda ordered two coffees with hot milk and sugar. She looked at their simple meal and said, "Gesegnete Mahlziet" (Blessed be your meal). Together, they shared a roll with butter and jam. Neither was hungry, and they only nibbled at a small portion of their rolls.

On this outing together, they saw almost everyone they knew from church and their neighborhood. They were able to keep outside appearances happy and light, although they both felt the pain of Tilly's discovered truth. Tilly offered to pay, but her friends who owned the bakery shook their heads no. After thanking them profusely, the women started back home.

"Tilly," Grandma Bogda broke the thoughtful silence, "I don't think it matters what I think. It only matters what you think about all of this in your life."

"But what do I *do?*" she asked, a little more loudly than she intended. "Sorry, I don't know what I can do to remedy this feeling, this way I react to Bill. I feel horrible. He has been such a blessing to me, and I love him. He told me before we got married that he felt like he somehow failed Helenea and that somehow she also failed him. I do not want to fail him or him me." She stopped walking again and gave out a big sigh.

"There is no soft way to tell you, but what you are going through right now is how faith is made. Faith doesn't mean never doubting or feeling frustrated or angry. It just means that no matter what the circumstances are, you continue to believe that love will always win." Grandma Bogda turned away from Tilly and silently prayed for strength and wisdom.

"Faith means that no matter what, love always wins?" Tilly was drinking this statement into her parched spirit as she repeated Grandma Bogda's words. "I was so filled with faith when I was assured everything would be better once Marie and I came to America. My friend, Beatrice, spoke a word of knowledge to me that God would restore what the locust had eaten. I believed her then, and I must believe her now. Bill lost more than I did. He lost his wife and child. I still have Marie, and she is a good girl." She tapped Grandma Bogda on the shoulder and as she

Love Goes On

turned to face her, Tilly reached out and hugged her mother-in-law. As she held her, she said, "I must not give up believing that God will work all this out to be good. I am not going to be so worried about having another baby. If I do or do not, it will not keep me from praising God for my life or from loving those that God has already given me to love."

"Oh, Mathilda," Grandma Bogda said, weeping, "Ei, du lieber Himmel (Ah, merciful Heavens!). Oh, my darling, darling, you have the answer. You have found the truth of all this with God's help. He makes everything beautiful in its time. My dear, there are the highs and the lows in life, but there is a time for everything. Now go home and love my son and my grandchildren! And Tilly, remember to do so with joy! Life is short, as we both know."

Together, they walked arm-in-arm back to Grandma Bogda's home with a new spring in their steps. They found Grandpa Bogda asleep in the chair and the bread dough oozing down the bowl onto the counter. Without a word, they looked at each other and began to giggle.

Tilly kissed Grandma Bogda goodbye, and again they giggled. She hurried home to start supper for her beloved Bill and children. Marie opened the back door, pushing Billy who was crying for "Mama." Marie had fallen at school and had skinned her knee and torn her new leggings. Bill was late for supper because the train was late. Tilly washed the dinner dishes and hummed one of her favorite tunes, realizing her life was normal.

Months passed with normal everyday living. Summer had come and gone, and another harvest season occupied Tilly's world. Added chores included putting vegetables away for the winter, making jams and sauerkraut and pickling beets and cucumbers. After all this was completed, it would be time to start baking for the holiday season. Christmas presents needed to be made and socks to be knitted. Her children seemed to wear out their socks or outgrow them faster than she could knit them. Bill's socks had been darned to the point they didn't seem to have any of their original yarn left in them.

There was cooking, cleaning, sewing, knitting, gardening

and occasionally helping her friends in the bakery for extra cash. This extra money never seemed to be used for herself; it always seemed to be used for someone she knew who was in need.

Tilly was helpful as a midwife assistant, a cook for those who were sick, a laundress for a new mother who was overwhelmed with her new workload, a visitor to her elderly neighbors and a gardener willing to share her vegetables and her seasonal roses with others. Life had taken on its own familiar rhythm with the normal high and low notes of living in this world. Tilly's life was a love song in harmony with others. Only occasionally did she come across a person who was tone-deaf to her lovely music.

One such occasion was while Tilly and Marie were walking in the native forest in the early springtime where the wildflowers grew in profusion. They followed a trail that started at Elmwood Avenue and 10th Street. Bill and little Billy were at Grandpa Bogda's house visiting while the girls spent the afternoon enjoying a walk, picking flowers. Out of nowhere, an old woman pounced on Tilly and began bullying her.

"What do you think you and your little girl are doing in my woods?" the old woman demanded in a gravelly voice.

"My dear madam, my daughter and I are having a refreshing walk, picking flowers and bothering no one," she answered as calmly as she could, fighting back her feelings of being insulted.

"This is my spot in these woods, and no one is welcome here, so GIT out of here NOW before I hit you with my cane!" she yelled at Tilly and then at Marie, who came to her mother's side, looking scared.

"Oh, now I recognize you. You were at the Women's Club eating the refreshments before it was time. I know because I made those pastries at the bakery and stayed for the meeting," Tilly announced, taking the upper hand.

"So you're the one who made them vile eats at the meetin'. I'm here to tell you they weren't fit for mule fodder! And you and your child here are not fit to be standing on my ground. Be gone with ya, or I'll run you off of here."

She lifted her cane as if to strike Tilly.

Tilly reached up and grabbed the cane away from the old woman. She turned to Marie and said, "Go get Papa or anyone you know to come here and help me with this trouble." Marie said nothing but ran as fast as she could.

Tilly was so angry she could have used the cane to beat the woman, but a little voice inside her said, "That's enough!" Instead, she spoke to her sternly.

"Shame on you for trying to scare me and especially my daughter! Don't ever do that again! I have as much right to walk in these woods as you do. I don't want to be frightened that someone will jump out with a cane to do harm whenever my daughter and I decide to walk here. Now, do I make myself clear to you?"

Tilly was visibly shaking. The old woman no longer looked angry, but instead had a look of bewilderment upon her face and in her eyes.

Meanwhile, Marie had found Edward Kanitz from church and asked for his help. When they both ran to where Tilly and the older woman were, they saw them sitting with their backs to a tall elm tree, talking very quietly and acting very civil. Mr. Kanitz looked at Marie and said, "Young lady, it appears there is no trouble here after all."

Marie agreed, "Yes, sir, thank you for coming. Sir, I prayed I would find someone to help me, and then I saw you. I also prayed that Mama and this old woman would not fight and would become friends; as you see, Jesus heard and answered both prayers. I guess I'll see you at church this Sunday."

Edward Kanitz knelt down on one knee, looked Marie straight in the eyes and said, "Little lady, if you ever need help, I will be more than happy to assist you in any way. It is a good thing what you did this day: pray for God's help. I trust you always remember to do that first in any type of emergency. Will you remember, my dear?" he pleaded tenderly.

Tilly had seen them run up and stop short. She had heard their conversation and now gave Mr. Kanitz a friendly nod and smile. He tipped his hat to the ladies and turned and walked out of the woods and then on to his home.

Tilly's Song

One thing Marie admired about her mother was she was nobody's pushover, but her gentle spirit was always quick to forgive and make peace with others. Marie never knew what really happened that day. When she asked her mother what happened, all she said was, "Marie, if we all live long enough, we, too, will be old someday. We need to be kind to everyone, no matter how old we are."

* *Weihnachtsgebäck.* This is the term used in Germany for the time of Advent when housewives bake all the Christmas stollen, strudels, breads and cookies.

*Dreikonigsbend. The feast of the Magi, celebrated on the 6th of January.

*A special thank-you goes to Pastor James G. Bauman and his congregation for giving me information during their centennial in 2003 about the early days of St. John's Lutheran Church.

*Stammer Max. This is a snack eaten around 10 a.m. consisting of very thinly sliced fatty pork, known to us as bacon, on a slice of sour rye bread to make an open-faced sandwich, usually served with a glass of Kirsch, a cherry liqueur.

*Brotzeit. In northern Germany, this is what they call the 10 a.m. snack, which is usually sweets and coffee or a small cheese sandwich with fruit.

Chapter 14
In Everything Give Thanks

Marie celebrated her 16th birthday with a house full of young girls her own age and one 6-year-old brother.

"Mama, I wish Billy would go visit some of his friends and leave us alone. He thinks he is being so cute in front of my friends, but all he is really being is a show-off. Please, Mama, he is going to ruin my Sweet Sixteen party. We have games to play, and he has already hidden most of the pieces to the games."

"William Bogda, Jr.!" The sound in her voice was "No Nonsense," and the tone had the demand that meant, "Come here NOW!"

Billy's head popped up from behind the couch where he was lurking to surprise the girls as they arrived. He now realized his plans had been foiled by his tattletale sister and his mother, who seemed to always know his whereabouts.

"I'm right here, Mama. I haven't done anything wrong."

"You haven't done anything wrong *yet*," she scolded, wagging her finger in his face. "Come into the kitchen with me. We need to have a talk." He stalled for time until she yelled at him again. "Now, William!"

"Oh, all right!" He hurried into the kitchen, closing the door behind him.

"Sit down. Billy, your sister is a young woman now, and she doesn't want you embarrassing her in front of her friends. If you were 2 years old, it would be different, but you are 6 years old now and — well, uh, can't you go and visit Peter while the party is going on?"

"No, I can't. Peter went fishing with Papa and Uncle John," he replied, hanging his head low.

"Oh, yes. I forgot for a moment. You could have also gone fishing with them, but, no, you didn't want to get up so early. Well, I guess you can just go to your room and take a nap during the party."

"Oh, Mama, do I have to?"

"Billy, your father is gone, we have a very important birthday party that Marie has planned for a long time, and I am not feeling very well right this minute. I realize you are 6 years old and teasing your sister and her friends is the highlight of your life right now."

"It really is, Mama. That's the true reason I didn't want to go fishing with Papa, that and the cake. I have caught every spider I could find to scare the girls, and I have hidden all the pieces to the games, just to see their reaction. I want to stay. It should be fun."

"Fun for you maybe, not fun for Marie. I am not going to let you ruin her good time. We make your birthdays special, and I know you would be more than upset if someone came along and tried to do things to ruin your party. Be nice to your sister," she added half-heartedly, feeling suddenly nauseated. Right at that moment, in through the back door entered Grandma Bogda, Aunt Whinny and Elsa, all loaded with presents.

"Hi, Grandma! May I help you with all those packages?"

"Why, my dear, what are you doing here? I thought you went with the men folk fishing early this morning. You shouldn't be here — these girl parties will just bore you and lead you to create mischief. Ask your mother if you can go and keep Grandpa entertained for the afternoon. He decided at the last minute he would rather sleep in than go catch big fish. I really think he thought you, Billy, were going and there would not be any room for him in the boat."

She leaned over and whispered in his ear. "If you will do that and be a good boy, I'll save you a big piece of cake. How does that sound?" She stood up and gave him a wink.

"That sounds great! May I, Mama?"

"Yes, yes, of course!" she answered, not even looking in his direction. Tilly was overcome with dizziness and turned to grab a chair so she wouldn't fall.

Without any hesitation, Billy ran out the door. In the heat of the July afternoon the cicadas were singing loudly in the tall elm trees that lined the street and the park near the shore of

In Everything Give Thanks

Lake Michigan. He ran yelling with the sole purpose of hearing his own voice. He made it to the front steps of his grandfather's porch with record-breaking speed.

Back at the birthday party, Aunt Whinny looked at her mother-in-law with amazement. "How do you do that?"

"Do what?" Grandma Bogda said, not really paying any attention to Whinny. All her focus was on Tilly.

"Tilly, you don't look like you feel well."

"I have been nauseated for a while. Not all the time; it just comes and goes," Tilly explained.

"Well, my dear, you are either entering into the change of life a bit early, or you're pregnant," she stated matter-of-factly.

Whinny gasped. "Oh, Tilly, could it be so?"

Tilly sat there dumbstruck. Grandma Bogda, Whinny and Elsa moved to the living room where Marie and her friends were starting the guessing games. Marie waved at her grandma and aunt and motioned for Elsa to come and join in. The sound of happy girls filled the house, and all the activities pulled the attention away from Tilly as she went to her bedroom to lie down. The girls didn't actually miss her at all until it was time to cut the cake and open presents.

"Where's Mama?" Marie asked, looking at her grandmother.

"Don't worry, she doesn't feel well right now. May I cut the cake for you?" she asked.

"All right, but Mama is missing the party."

Marie was quickly distracted by girls calling for her to open their present first. Teenage-girl giggles filled the room.

***

The next day, Bill came home with a letter in his hand for Tilly.

"Your friend has sent you mail. The postman ran about two blocks to catch me and give me this letter. I hope the pastor and family are well. Some men at work said things are not looking good in the mother country. There are rumors of war again, and the people are suffering from another depression. Many of the men are sending food and clothing back home to their relatives. Shall we do this for our friends in Hamburg?"

He handed her the letter. Tilly ripped it open and began reading it as fast as she could.

My dearest friend,

I must write this quickly so as to not use up too much lamp fuel. My heart is about to burst, and I must come before my God and my friend and confess what is festering within my spirit.

My husband, who is also my pastor, has become increasingly taken in by the ever-growing need of our flock of believers. Please understand, I am not trying to minimize each and everyone's great need and constant pain, but, Mathilda, I need your added prayer to my prayers for my family.

My good husband stays up into the early morning with no sleep at all. I have gone to him endless times to invite him to bed. He eats so little and sleeps so little, I dare say his body should by now be dead. He is deaf to my enticements and will not tolerate my scolding. Our children hardly know him, and I am left lonely in our marriage bed.

But now, my friend, what I confide in you I feel I can tell no other. Today as I was pulling the cart to bring food to our dear widows, I stumbled and fell on my knees, wounding them and causing them to bleed. A man stepped out from somewhere to help me. To my shame, I began to weep. I seemed to be frozen. This stranger knelt down and held me as I cried, and I leaned into him with such affection and longing. I have never until today known such feelings were within me. An eternity passed between us in those few moments that now place him forever within my heart.

When I came home with my stockings ruined and bloody, my husband either did not notice or did not care to comment on my plight. Tonight I turned my hurt feelings into a scolding and accused him of staying up too late at night. I blamed him for using too much lamp fuel. With an angry voice, he told me he would leave and go out-of-

doors to read the Holy Word by starlight. I do not remember how I responded, but it was equally foolish.

At this moment, I feel a wedge and hammer breaking our stony hearts apart. Tonight is Fastnacht, and my husband needs no costume to seem foreign to me.

Mathilda, the man I love, who loves God as I do, is changing into someone I do not feel as close to as I did the stranger who came my way. My faith seems so weak right now as I have wandered into that dry place, the desert of my soul. Good sister, hear my plea and pray for me! Tomorrow is Fasching, and I, too, share some of the agony our dear Lord felt as He was led into the desert of temptation.

Beatrice

Tilly sent more care packages and letters of encouragement to help Beatrice, her family, the widows and the orphans. She continued to pray for her friends and ask for prayer from those in the church who also had loved ones living in Germany. She was inspired to send Beatrice some of the sermon notes she had taken during church services; poetry, lyrics to songs, anything she could think of to help her dear sister in her time of spiritual attack.

Bill's sister continued to write, but shared little news about the political climate in Berlin. The letters sent to Germany seemed to take longer to arrive. Often German postal workers opened the packages and removed much of the contents. However, letters of gratitude always came back, conveying how happy the recipients were to be loved and remembered in prayer, as well as to receive something from their family and friends in America.

Talk among the German workers in the Chicago area increasingly reported trouble from the homeland. Each Sunday, more and more time was spent praying for the loved ones that still lived in the motherland. Germany was headed for more trouble, and there was nothing they could do about it other than pray.

***

Bill knew that Tilly was pregnant as he noticed the increased weight and the nausea. Although he felt sorry that Tilly was so miserable, he was overjoyed that they were going to have a baby in the house.

The next few months went by quickly. Finally, Tilly could no longer keep the news a secret; her belly filled out her clothes, and her walk soon became more of a waddle. Papa Bill had a perpetual smile on his face as others looked at his wife's belly and then at him. They would give encouragement with words like, "This baby will keep you young," or "Now you will have someone to take care of you in your older years." He always beamed with satisfaction at these comments.

Tilly seemed to be the only one who heard the snide words like, "Isn't Tilly a little too old to be having a baby?" She decided not to let anything steal her joy in this moment. She had longed for this baby for many years.

Other changes were taking place at this time. Mrs. Carlisle had found a job for Marie as a domestic worker. It paid well because Eleanor Carlisle had given such a sterling recommendation as to the quality of Marie's working habits. Bill and Tilly were proud of Marie and her newfound financial independence; however, they were sad she was leaving home.

"Tilly, let's look at this realistically. Marie is not far from here. We can see her any time. She can even stay here on her days off. This is a wonderful opportunity to enter the work force and gain experience. This is a good thing, Tilly, really, it is!" Bill stated as much to reassure himself as he did Tilly.

"I know, she is so gifted and such a good help. I know she will do a good job. What you say is true. This is another big change in our lives, and soon we shall have a baby in the house. Oh, isn't life wonderful and strange all at the same time?"

Tilly looked at Bill and spied him wiping his eyes. She called to Marie, "My Love, your ride shall be here soon. This will be your first day at work without me. Oh, you shall do such a good job. Come, Papa and I want to pray with you before you leave."

They all joined hands, prayed blessings upon Marie and

sent her off into the world. Tilly felt a different kind of birthing pain that day as Marie emerged into a new and bigger world.

Marie had been away from home working for one month before she came home to visit. Sitting around the dining room table, she began telling her family about her new work friend, doing her best to capture the pronunciation of the words and the physical antics that endeared Miss Prissy to Marie. Tilly and Bill sat listening intently to Marie share her stories.

"Aunt Prissy is one of 14 children. She had her 21st birthday last Thursday and has already given birth to five children, but only three have lived past infancy.

"In the kitchen it seems children are always coming in and going out the back door. All day long, Aunt Prissy yells the same words over and over to her children and her younger brothers and sisters: 'Don't be slammin' dat door, ya hear?' Well, obviously nobody ever hears those words except for me, because 'that back door is always a slammin'." Marie's eyes were sparkling as she leaned in closer toward her parents and continued her story.

"Eva is Aunt Prissy's youngest child, and she is a real mama's girl. She practically lives on Aunt Prissy's hip. That child just loves to be held, and whenever her mama is tired of holding her, I carry Eva. This little tiny girl can talk just like an adult; she calls me her 'Misa B' friend. Eva must be 3 years old by now, because she talks and is old enough to wear panties, and she can feed herself.

"It was so funny." Marie stopped and giggled. "I was holding Eva when she noticed the brown freckles on my arm. She took her little finger and touched each one of them and asked, 'Whatz dat?' Finally, she asked her mama, 'Mama, why Misa B have pock-a-dots on her arms?' I listened intently to hear what explanation Aunt Prissy had to give so her little girl would understand.

"'Oh, darlin' child, da good Lard jest loves variety. Why, I have heard tell that in Africa, they's gots horses with stripes all over their bodies. I's heard tell that God has even made some tall ol' birds that stands on one leg and has pink feathers. Even more, in the sea, there's creatures the shape of stars. My sweet baby, God jest loves doin' interestin' thangs, so if He wants to put pock-a-dots on Misa B's arms, I suspect He has a right to do it, Him bein' God 'n all. You understand, baby?'"

Marie looked at her parents as they started to laugh. She kept telling the story while they smiled and giggled. "Aunt Prissy told that whole story to her little Eva in the time it took her to roll out a pie crust, crimp it and put it into the oven to bake. That was funny, but what made it so funny to me was she was not trying to be funny.

"When her hands were free, she reached over to me and took Eva and sat her little girl on top of her pregnant belly." Assessing Tilly's belly, Marie stated, "You and Aunt Prissy look like you are going to have babies about the same time. Little Eva asked her mama why her belly was so fat. Aunt Prissy said, 'Cause I got your baby brother inside of me cookin' until he is done and ready to come on out of me, just like da pie crust there. When he's done, he will come on out of me and be jest right. You need to know, child, your baby brother is goin' to be a littl' child, not a sweet to eat. No, but he will be sweet just as all babies is.'"

Marie was doing her best to sound just like Aunt Prissy and using her hands to give all the antics her friend used. Marie continued. "Aunt Prissy reached down and started kissing Eva's cheek, and Eva began to squeal, 'Don't eat me up, Mama.'" Tilly, Bill and Billy again laughed uproariously.

Marie looked at her family and enjoyed sharing her stories with them. New experiences were fun for her to share, and she also had learned some things about life that were different from her own childhood. From Aunt Prissy she had seen unbridled affection and carefree play. Marie made a secret vow to herself that she would play with her children like that when she had babies. Her daydream was shattered by the banging of the back door. Without thinking, she yelled, "Don't be slammin' dat door, ya hear?"

This time it was not laughable. Uncle John stood at the kitchen door, his face white as a sheet. Bill stood up.

"John, what is it?"

"Brother, our father is dead! Mother was making dinner,

In Everything Give Thanks

and he was sitting in his chair reading the paper. She thought he had fallen asleep. When she couldn't rouse him, she ran to our house and, well, I'm here. We need to get help. I knew you would know what to do!" He stood in the doorway, choking back the tears.

All returned to Grandma and Grandpa Bogda's house and found some neighbors had already gone to summon the doctor and the police. Grandma Bogda asked if she could wash his body and help the funeral director dress him before the funeral. Everyone agreed to her request. Three days later, Peter Bogda was laid to rest following a funeral that celebrated his life on earth.

Two months passed. Grandma Bogda sold their house and moved in with John and his family. All her energy was now directed toward the new life that was soon to be born into the Bogda family.

Tilly made plans for the day the baby would be born; everyone had strict instructions as to what they were to do. First, Grandma Bogda would come with some of her friends from church to assist with the birth. The doctor was given notice that he might need to be summoned, if necessary. The layette set had been knitted with love and lots of lace because of the predictions made by the older churchwomen that, according to the way Tilly was carrying this baby, the child just had to be a girl. The rationale used for their prediction was that she had carried Billy in a totally different position.

In Tilly's master plan, she had coached each person about their individual duties. Billy would stay with his cousins at Uncle John and Aunt Whinny's house. Marie would be summoned from her workplace as soon as her mother went into labor so she would be there to assist with the delivery. The plan also included the whole congregation at St. John's praying for a safe and quick delivery, resulting in a healthy baby and mother.

Bill was to put a fresh coat of paint on the cradle he had constructed for Billy's birth. Grandma Bogda and Aunt Whinny were to finish the linens for the cradle made from beautiful white eyelet. Women friends willingly promised to sew and knit baby clothes. With this plan in action, everyone would make ready to welcome this baby Bogda into their lives.

In February 1907, the Chicago area had a record-breaking snowfall. Bill had just come in from shoveling the walkway to the house when he smelled something burning. Bread was in the oven, and dark smoke was billowing out the sides of the closed oven door. Tilly was nowhere in sight.

Bill looked the situation over. The kitchen was a mess, lacking its usual orderly appearance. As he moved toward the oven, he almost slipped because of the water all over the floor.

"Tilly, where are you? Can you smell that your bread is burning?"

"Well, take it out of the oven and throw it away!" she yelled to him from a distance. There was an edge in her voice he had never heard before.

"Bill! The baby is coming." Her voice trailed off.

Bill burned himself as he reached into the hot oven and pulled out the pan of burnt bread, absentmindedly forgetting to use an oven mitt. Billy walked into the kitchen just in time to see his father dance around the kitchen holding his burnt hand, sliding in the water on the floor. When Papa Bill saw his son looking at him, he quickly asked, "Where is your mother?"

"She is in bed and just sent me to come get you. I'm supposed to run to Grandma's house and tell her that ol' baby is finally coming out of her belly today," he said, disgusted by the whole ordeal. Papa Bill frowned at his son's negative attitude about what was happening, but quickly changed his attention to the matter at hand and ran to his bedroom.

"Are you sure it's time?" he asked, kneeling beside Tilly and taking her hand.

"Bill, women know these things. Have you forgotten when Billy was born?" She gritted her teeth as she managed a contraction.

Actually, he *had* forgotten. He remembered the tender moments of holding the baby for the first time and making very sure it was a male child, but the labor was a blur in his memory. He knew very well not to confess his lack of memory to Tilly right now.

"Oh, Tilly, I love you so much. I am so glad you are having

my baby. You are such a good mother," he said as tenderly as he could to his wife, who looked in no mood for much talk of any kind.

"Yes, yes. If this doesn't prove I love you, Bill, I am not sure what would," she said with a bit too much edge in her voice.

"What can I do for you right now?" he asked, trying to be helpful.

"Has Billy left to get your mother?" she asked, making a low guttural sound as she travailed in labor. Bill jumped to his feet and went back into the kitchen. Billy was sitting at the table playing with his top.

"Go, go, go!" he yelled at his son. Billy dropped his top and ran out the door. Bill looked out the window to make sure he was running in the direction of his brother's house. He held his hands behind his back and began pacing and praying at the same time. *Tilly is going to be 40 years old in two months, and this delivery may be difficult for her,* he thought. *No,* he corrected himself, *she is strong and healthy and in God's hands. This baby is a miracle, which in truth all babies are. We are receiving an answer to prayer,* he continued to assure himself.

Another little worry thought wiggled into his mind with the sole purpose of robbing him of his joy of the moment.

"What if she dies?" he spoke out loud. "No, don't think that way. God forgive me."

"Bill, I need you!" Tilly yelled, breaking into his conversation with God. Bill raced to Tilly's side. She was in a panic. She motioned to him to pull the covers away and check to see if the baby was coming. The baby's head had fully crowned. Tilly made an awful sound and began to push. With careful hands, Bill caught the baby by the shoulders as the baby was delivered with the next big push.

The bedroom door swung open, and Grandma Bogda was there to take over. Their baby girl had a strong and healthy cry. Grandma Bogda wiped the baby clean and then presented her to Tilly so she could nurse.

"Oh, my darling, what shall we name her?" Tilly asked Bill.

"There is only one name that fits our baby daughter. I want her name to be Beatrice, if that is permissible," he said, and then he leaned over and caressed Tilly's moist forehead.

"Oh, Bill, I cannot wait to write my dearest friend and tell her. She is the one who years ago told me that God would restore what the locusts have eaten. God has kept His promise to me on this very day. I have a wonderful life with a family that I desired. All in God's timing, all in His will."

"There is a time for everything, Tilly," he said, wiping the tears from his cheeks.

"And a season for everything under heaven," Grandma Bogda added, with a big smile as she reached for her newest granddaughter.

"I think she is too tired to eat right now," Tilly said as she handed the sleeping child to her grandmother. The baby was swaddled in a beautiful white knitted blanket and then gently placed back in Tilly's arms. Bill and Grandma Bogda looked at each other, then over at the baby. Tilly's face was full of light as she hummed a lullaby.

Peter arrived in a buggy to fetch Marie at her workplace and told her the baby had arrived. They raced to her home as fast as the horse could run. Marie prayed for her mama; her prayer was a chant of thanksgiving.

"Oh, thank You. Thank You. Thank You. Oh, I am so happy. I just know Mama is happy. Thank You. Thank You." Without realizing it, Marie had begun to pray the way she remembered her papa in Germany had prayed. She had heard that in everything we were to be thankful.

Marie was out of breath with excitement. She paused at the back door to calm herself. Billy opened the door and was the first to greet Marie with the news that they had a baby sister named Beatrice. Marie hugged her baby brother and then hurried to her mother's room. Papa Bill saw her coming and greeted her with a big hug.

"Is everyone well?" she questioned, still out of breath.

"Perfect. I will take you to see them." He was so pleased he could share his joy with Marie.

As they approached the door, Marie heard her mother singing a German lullaby to her baby sister. Bill and Marie tiptoed and peeked through the slightly opened door to the bedroom.

Tilly was singing, undisturbed by their presence. They looked at each other and both smiled.

"Marie, this song seems to be your mother's life song," he said, feeling deeply touched at the beauty of her voice.

"Papa, I don't know the words; however, the song sounds very familiar to me. It makes me feel safe and loved and I feel … I don't know how to say it." She looked up at Papa Bill's face.

"Complete?"

"Yes, everything feels complete somehow. All in this world is right, just this very moment. I am content. God has restored all that was taken from us. Papa, I am so grateful right now," Marie said, wiping her eyes.

She pushed open the door and stuck her head inside, smiling at her mother and baby sister. Tilly beamed with pride and then motioned for Marie to come closer.

"Oh, how beautiful! May I hold her?" Marie begged. Her mother handed the baby to her. Smiling as she recognized the blanket she had knitted for her baby sister, Marie took the baby in her arms and held her as if she were breakable china. With the tips of her fingers she caressed the baby's tiny cheek, and she kissed the top of her little head. Looking at the tiny eyelashes and little nose, Marie began talking to her new sister as if she were an adult.

"Oh, Beatrice, you shall be called 'Little Bee.' I have so many stories to tell you, my dear, it shall take a lifetime for you to hear them all. We have waited such a long time for you. I am so glad you are here." Marie began humming the melody of her mother's song to her little sister and to herself as well.

One month later: Hamburg, Germany

"Mother, I have a letter from America addressed to you. The handwriting looks like that of the kind woman whom you call your beloved friend, Mathilda," Beatrice's youngest son said, waving the letter for all to see.

Beatrice wiped her wet hands on her apron and rushed to her son to retrieve the letter. Teasingly, he ran from her as she reached for the envelope. She ran after him and snatched the letter from him and quickly tore it open and read it with eager eyes. Beatrice was careful to preview it silently. Once she found there was no sensitive information, she began reading it aloud for her whole family to enjoy.

My Sister in Christ,

What lovely news I have to share with you. The words of knowledge you spoke to me so many years ago have come to fruition. Our Lord is the God of restoration. My old life has been replaced with a new life filled with righteousness, peace and joy. Isn't that what the Lord Jesus told us made up the kingdom of God? He deserves all the praise! I am looking at my sleeping baby daughter, whom Bill and I have chosen to name Beatrice, after you, of course. Outside my window, I can see Billy playing with his boyhood friends, and my sweet Marie is here preparing lunch for us all.

By the time you receive this letter, baby Beatrice shall be christened and dedicated to the Lord. I shall be dressing her in the linen gown my own mother was christened in more than 50 years ago. My grandmother spun the linen thread and wove the cloth to make this very special garment. My hope is my grandchildren and their children will be dedicated to the Lord in this very gown.

Now, my love, let me tell you about our baby! Our adorable daughter has red hair, much like yours, and crystal-blue eyes just like her father's. She is content to be held, fed and kept clean, and does not seem to voice herself with crying, but much prefers to coo and gurgle and suck on her hand. Billy at first was very jealous, but she has won him over, and he loves her every antic. Marie has taken over, and it seems the only time I can hold her is when I nurse her. Bill is a fool for this baby girl, and we all laugh as he tries to keep her constant attention with his funny gestures.

Although my journey in this life is not yet complete, I have reached that good place where I can be content in whatever circumstance I am found. I arrived at this station in life before I found out I was carrying Beatrice.

My Lord has granted me His favor and blessed me with a husband, son and two daughters for this time in my life here in America. Marie is older now, but she is still my great help and companion. She is also very happy with life here in America and deeply loves her little brother and baby sister. She is working for a family that lives nearby, but we see her often, more now that the baby has arrived. Although my other loved ones are at home in heaven right now, I have confidence that I shall see them again. Nevertheless, today is where I am living ... and I am blessed to stay in the present. And you, my dear friend, have been with me through it all: my highs and lows, my doubts and trials, my joys and celebrations.

In Everything Give Thanks

Thank you, my friend. Thank you!

Please, write and tell me what you and your family are doing. I continue to pray for the widows and those who need help in your parish. Give my love to your husband, the good pastor, and to your wonderful children. I am thrilled to hear your eldest son shall be married soon. I ask for blessings for him and his bride.

Oh, good sister, most beloved friend, love goes on even when life as we know it ceases. Thank you for your help, so I could learn that about life!

Love and kisses to you,
Tilly

Epilogue

The life of restoration continued as the years passed. Beatrice, litl' Bee, grew into a lovely young woman. Billy served in the U.S. Army in Germany during World War I. Marie met a stockbroker from Minneapolis, Minnesota, married and had a daughter and a son.

Tilly and Bill had a full life together in Wilmette, Illinois. The Great War to end all wars, as it was called before being renamed World War I, ended the letters of correspondence between Tilly and her beloved friend, Beatrice. Bill never heard from his sister again. Memories lived on and were cherished more and more throughout the years.

The Carlisle family continued to sponsor German immigrants until World War I began in Europe, ending their ministry in the United States. However, this band of believers continued to minister to Uncle Larry.

After Marie grew up and moved to Minneapolis, Minnesota, she received a letter from Mama Carlisle informing her that Lawrence Carlisle had completed his prison sentence at Joliet, Illinois. Actually he had his sentence reduced due to good behavior. The letter stated he was now living in Los Angeles, California, with his wife and seven children. They were pastors of a little church that ministered to alcoholics, drug and gambling addicts. Her letter explained that while he was in prison, Frank, Eleanor and their children continued to visit him.

As their children grew older, they kept their relationship with their uncle through visitations and mail. It was during one of those visits that Uncle Larry met his Savior. From that day forward, he was a changed man. Eleanor made the comment, "He committed his crime and served his 20-year sentence in prison, but what is 20 years compared to the freedom he now has for eternity?"

Mattie and her husband continued to weave in and out of the Bogdas' family life. Many characters in this novel share their stories in the next novel, *For Richer or Poorer; I Take Thee Marie*. It covers the time period from 1907 through the Great Depression and ends after World War II.

Appendix

FAMILY KNITTING PATTERNS

Tilly's Knitted Washcloth

    #10 needles
    Cotton 4 ply   Cast-on 4 stitches

Row 1-Knit 2, yarn over, knit to end of row. Continue the same until 40 stitches.

Decrease row-Knit 1, knit 2 together, yarn-over, knit 2 together. Knit to end of row.

Continue the same until 4 stitches. Then bind off. (This magically makes its own lacy edge.)

Baby Booties-Make 2

Cast on 15 stitches. Use a size 5 needle. Use baby weight yarn that will give a gauge of 16 stitches + 24 rows = 4 inches.

Row 1 (wrong side) Knit 7, place marker (pm), k 1, pm, k7.

Row 2 (right side) k1, make 1, knit to marker, make 1, slip marker (sm) k 1, sm, make 1, k to last stitch, make 1, k1. There should be 19 stitches. To make a new stitch, lift the horizontal thread lying between needles and place it onto left needle. Work this new stitch through the back loop.

Row 3-4 Repeat Row 2. There should be 27 stitches.

Row 5-8 Work even in Garter Stitch, removing markers. Garter stitch is knitting every row.

Row 9 Knit 10, k 2 together, (pm), k 3, (pm), k 2 tog, k 10. There should now be 25 stitches.

Row 10 Knit to 2 stitches before marker, k2tog, (sm), k 3, (sm), k2tog, k to end. There should be 23 stitches.

Row 11 knit to the end of the row.

Repeat Rows 10-11 for 4 more times. There should be 15 Stitches. Work in k1, purl 1 rib for 3 inches. Bind off loosely in ribbing.

With yarn and large-eyed blunt needle, sew back and foot seam. Weave in ends. Cut ribbon into 2 equal lengths and tie into bows. With sewing needle and thread, sew ribbon to the Bootie.

SOCKS — This is only the author's opinion, but nonetheless true. If anyone loves you enough to knit a pair of socks for you, treasure them, both the socks and the loved one. Never machine wash or dry them, for fear they may be lost to that unknown place where socks are kidnapped. Gently and lovingly wear them, wash them and put them in a place of honor because, I am here to tell you, knitting socks is the most difficult job in the entire world!!!

I don't have any patterns of the socks Tilly knitted, but there are many, many patterns available. All I do know is my Nana, Marie, told me her mother seemed to either be knitting socks for her family or darning the ones she had knitted for them until the Lord came for her. I don't know this to be true, but I suspect we all go barefoot in heaven.

RECIPES for Good Eatin'

Part of the riches I inherited was some of the recipes that were actually written down by my grandmother (Grossmutter), whom my sister and I referred to endearingly as "Nana." However, much to my dismay, many of these recipes are just lists of ingredients with no directions as to how to prepare them or how long to cook them or the amount of yield. In place of specifics are such comments as knead until it feels right, cook until done, add more if needed, add a pinch of this or other such cryptic messages that were intended for the veteran cook, but not helpful at all to the inexperienced. It has been my intent to clarify these mysteries so these treasures of the palate may be enjoyed by the future generations. With the help of two cookbooks, *The Cuisines of Germany* by Horst Scharfenberg and *The German Cookbook* by Mimi Sheraton, I have been able to research recipes and find similar dishes that give instruction to the ingredients within my recipes. I dare say most of the cooking my ancestors did was using ingredients that were seasonally

Appendix

available to them, and any of these that required much preparation were only prepared and eaten on Holy Days or feast days. Meat was not eaten daily, but bread was. Sugar was scarce, so the beekeepers not only helped to assure pollination of crops, but also were able to rob the delightful nectar the honeybees stored away for their young. Fresh vegetables were only available during the summer growing months, and root crops were a big part of the family garden because they could be stored and eaten throughout the winter. Whenever there was an abundance of cabbage, sauerkraut was made; extra cucumbers became pickles; fruit, jelly and jams, etc. Grain was always planted as a staple crop that could later be made into bread, cereal and flour for other dishes. It was also planted so the kernels could be fed to the livestock, and the chaff it provided could be used in a variety of ways. Wine, beer, sausage, cheese, butter and bread were almost always made at home, if you lived on a farm. It could be bought from bakers, butchers, brewmeisters or other such vendors, if you were a merchant living in a city.

Most of the dishes listed in this appendix are rich foods that are high in fat and salt. In today's world, these foods are viewed as unhealthy, but let me point out that these high fat dishes were not eaten every day but were usually prepared and eaten on special occasions. The daily meals were sparser than those meals enjoyed on holidays. Daily foods included cereal, soups and hearty bread. At the turn of the 20th century, people walked more and engaged in much more manual labor. Meals were eaten slowly and relished with added servings of fun conversation. There is an old German saying that I think is absolutely scientifically sound: Much laughter improves the digestion! My wish is that whenever your family and friends put their feet under your dinner table, good food and good humor will be shared and the combination will contribute to good health.

Homemade Rolls
    2 pkgs yeast or cakes of yeast
    2/3 cup warm potato water
    1/3 cup sugar
    1/4 cup lard or shortening

1/4 cup butter
1 tsp. salt
2 eggs, beaten
4 cups flour

Dissolve yeast in the warm potato water, add sugar, salt, eggs, fats and 3 1/2 cups of flour. Knead and add remaining flour as needed. Knead until you can hear the dough squeak. Roll into a ball and place it in a buttered bowl. Let rise for 1-1 1/2 hours or until double in size. Place a towel over the dough so it will not dry out. Punch down and then shape into whatever shape rolls you desire. Let them rise again and then put them into a hot oven, approx. 400 degrees F for 15 to 18 minutes. Butter the tops as soon as you take them out of the oven. Yield is about 32 rolls, depending on the size and shape you have made them. (This recipe can be shaped to make nice crescent rolls.)

Hot Cocoa

The secret to hot cocoa is to use the very best imported Dutch Cocoa you can find in the market. If you just have regular cocoa then add a touch of vanilla to the cocoa and milk after it is heated. And this must be the best vanilla made by extracting the vanilla bean into brandy. I am somewhat of a cocoa snob, as you can see.

Potato Rolls

This can either be made into potato bread or rolls.

2 cups water	1/2 tsp. salt
2 medium potatoes, boiled and mashed	2 eggs
	8 Tbsp. butter, cut into 1/2 in. bits
1 package yeast	
1/2 cup plus 1 tsp. sugar	5 1/2 to 6 1/2 cups unsifted flour

Cook potatoes and drain and reserve 1 cup of potato water. Mash the cooked potatoes. You will need 1 cup cooked mashed potato. Use 1/4 cup of lukewarm (110 degrees F) potato water to start the yeast. Add 1 tsp. of sugar to yeast and potato water. (If you ever have leftover mashed potatoes from the dinner before, this makes a great starter for the rolls for this evening's meal.)

Combine 5 1/2 cups of flour and remaining sugar and salt in deep mixing bowl and add all the liquids: mashed potato, potato water, eggs, yeast and 8 Tbsp. butter. Mix ingredients until they form a smooth, soft ball of dough.

Knead until smooth, shiny and elastic, approximately 10 minutes. Put in greased bowl and cover in draft-free area until it rises to be double in volume. Shape into a loaf or into rolls and bake in a preheated oven of 375 degrees F until golden brown and it sounds hollow inside when rapped with your knuckles. Let cool or eat warm after it sets for 5 minutes. Yield: 1 regular loaf or 1 dozen rolls.

Fresh Applesauce

Take 6 tart apples, peel and core them, then shred. Melt about 1/4 cup of butter and sauté the apples in the butter until the apples cook down into applesauce consistency. Sprinkle cinnamon sugar to taste. Serve hot or chilled. Great served with pork dishes or potato pancakes.

Potato Pancakes — Kartoffelpfannkuchen

Potato pancakes the way my grandmother, Nana, made them were more of an art than a science. Most German recipes include onion among the simple ingredients, but she served them for breakfast and with sweet toppings, and the onion did not enhance that flavor, so she left them out of the recipe.

She would take 2 large baking potatoes, peel and shred them into a bowl. She would add a large slightly beaten egg to the shredded potatoes. Next she added a pinch of salt and enough flour mixed into the potato and egg to make a thick batter, but not stiff. On a very hot skillet, she would pour about 2 or 3 Tbsp. of oil or bacon drippings and fry about 1/4 cup of potato batter until golden brown with crispy edges.

To determine if the pan is hot enough, take a little of the

batter and put it on the skillet. If it sizzles, the skillet is hot enough. Sometimes she made these pancakes as large as a dinner plate or small silver dollar size, depending on her mood. She would then drain the pancake on a paper towel or brown paper and while hot, dust them with powdered sugar. They were eaten hot with fresh applesauce.

The poor cook was the last to ever eat, so to avoid this, the first one fed, then became the cook and served others until it was their turn to fry these delicious pancakes. Depending on the number of people who are to be served and their appetites, the recipe was sometimes made two or three times. Cold milk is the preferred beverage with this meal.

Creamed Chipped Beef on Toast

4 Tbsp. butter
1/4 cup finely chopped onion
1/4 cup flour
1 cup milk
2 Tbsp. dry sherry
1 Tbsp. fresh lemon juice
1 cup light cream
4 to 5 oz. paper-thin dried beef

In a heavy skillet, melt the butter, add onions and cook slowly for about 5 minutes, until they are translucent but not brown. Add the flour and blend well. Stirring the mixture with a wire whisk, pour in the cream and milk in a slow, thin stream and cook over high heat until the sauce comes to a boil and thickens slightly and smoothly. Simmer for 2 to 3 minutes and then add the dried beef, sherry and lemon juice. Sprinkle with black pepper and paprika. Serve over toast. Serve immediately while toast is still crisp.

Note from the author: I doubt seriously that at Ellis Island in the medical dormitory any sherry or lemon was added to this recipe. Believe me, it makes all the difference in the world to add it to this meat and gravy dish.

Cucumbers in Sour Cream

Peel and slice very thinly 2 large cucumbers. Put them in a bowl and salt them liberally, and then put crushed ice over the cucumbers and a little water with 2 Tbsp. of tarragon vinegar.

Let them stand in this for 30 minutes. Take them out of the icy water and squeeze out the excess vinegar water. Add to them 1/2 cup of sour cream, 2 Tbsp. finely minced parsley, 1 small onion cut into thin rings, 1 Tbsp. sugar, 2 Tbsp. tarragon vinegar and paprika for a little garnish color. Serve immediately.

Fluffy Mashed Potatoes

The secret to fluffy mashed potatoes is to heat the milk and butter and pour it in after the potatoes have been mashed. Before serving, add some sour cream and salt and pepper to taste. Garnish with chives or green onions and crisp bacon pieces.

Christmas Stolen — Aunt Ada's version
  1 cup scalded milk
  1/2 cup sugar
  1/4 cup butter
  1 yeast cake or 1 pkg. of dry yeast in 1/4 cup of potato water
  (Potato water is the starchy water poured off of boiled potatoes.)

*Note: The secret to good bread is to feed the yeast with a small amount of sugar or potato starch and lukewarm water until you see the yeast bubble and spread. It is the gas formed by the yeast that makes the dough rise.

  2 eggs beaten
  1 tsp. mace or ground cardamom seed
  1 tsp. salt
  4 1/4 cups flour
  1/2 cup chopped walnuts, pecans or almonds
  1/2 cup candied citron fruit (the kind that is used in fruitcake)
  (Most recipes I have read have the dried fruit soaked in a little brandy or rum to soften, but I don't recall my teetotaling Nana ever doing this.)

Mix the cooled milk, sugar and butter together with yeast

and eggs. Add the dry ingredients a little at a time and then the solid nuts and fruit that have been dredged in a little flour. Knead and then let rise. Punch down and let rise again. Shape into a braid or flat folded like traditional stolen. Bake at 350 for 45 minutes, or as my Nana used to say, until done. (In other cookbooks, the braided version is very similar to what is called Bohemian Braid. This bread uses the spice mace rather than cardamom seed or ground cardamom. The same recipe for this type of holiday bread is called Swedish Coffee Braid only if the spice used is cardamom.) Both mace and cardamom give off a fragrant aroma, which I like equally well; the taste is also very similar.

Yield: 1 large stolen or 2 braids.

Pork Roast/Sauerkraut with Caraway Seeds

This recipe is so easy. Take a 3-4 lb. pork roast and brown it on all sides in a heavy skillet that has a tight fitting lid. Pour 1 lb. of sauerkraut and juice over the browned roast, and sprinkle about 1 Tbsp. of caraway seeds over the sauerkraut; then put in an oven at 350 degrees F for 2 hours. In the last 15 minutes, add the slices of one apple and replace the lid. The meat should fall apart when done. This meat goes well with fluffy mashed potatoes.

Stuffed Pork Chops

Determine the number of servings needed. One pork chop is usually one serving. Purchase the thick sliced chops or have the butcher cut them thick for you. This is an easy dish to prepare, and the chop is baked rather than fried. Heat oven to 350 degree F. Prepare your favorite stuffing for chicken, goose or turkey. Add your choice of dried fruit to the stuffing, such as dried apricots, raisins, cranberries, pineapple or fresh apple. Walnuts or pecans are also a welcome addition. Make a slit in the pork chop to the bone, forming a little pocket, and place some stuffing inside the opening. Four chops take about an hour to cook. Cook covered the first half hour and then without the cover for the remainder of the cooking time so the meat will have an attractive brown color. Take the pan drippings, add hot water and thicken with cornstarch for a nice glaze over the meat.

Cream Puffs and Vanilla Cream Filling

The cream puff shell can be used for any type of stuffing you wish, from shrimp or any other meat salad, creamed chicken or pudding. Our family usually enjoyed them as desserts. There is a trick to making good cream puffs and it is adding one egg at a time and mixing thoroughly before adding the next egg. It does not tolerate any distractions, so plan a time when you can make this dessert from start to finish, uninterrupted.

1 cup water	4 large eggs
1/2 cup butter	*Vanilla Custard filling
1/4 tsp. salt	confectioner's sugar
1 cup sifted flour	

In a saucepan, heat water, butter and salt to a rolling boil. Reduce heat and quickly stir in flour, mixing vigorously with a wooden spoon until mixture leaves the sides of the pan and forms a ball. Remove from heat. Using a wire whisk or preferably an electric mixer, beat at medium speed adding one egg at a time, beating approximately 30 seconds after each addition. Scrape bowl and beater. Mix at highest speed for 15 seconds. Depending on the size of the cream puffs, use a small spoonful or a larger one, or place batter into a pastry tube and squeeze onto a greased cookie sheet. Bake at 400 degrees F in a preheated oven for 10 minutes, and then lower the temperature to 350 degrees F and continue to bake for 25 minutes. Puffs are ready when they are double in size, golden brown and firm to the touch. Remove puffs from oven and cut the side of each with a sharp knife. Put them back into the turned-off oven. The puffs must be cut so the inside can dry. If not, the puff will collapse in on itself and the whole effect is ruined. Keep the door ajar and let them stand for 10 minutes. Cool puffs on a rack. Slit top; fill with Vanilla Custard filling. Sprinkle with confectioner's sugar.

*Vanilla Custard filling — may be made up ahead of time and chilled until ready to fill the cooled puffs:

1/3 cup sugar	1 1/2 cups milk
1 Tbsp. flour	1 egg yolk, slightly beaten
1 Tbsp. cornstarch	1 tsp. vanilla — the real stuff!
1/4 tsp. salt	1/2 cup whipping cream (whipped)

In a saucepan, combine sugar, flour, cornstarch and salt. Gradually stir in milk. Cook and stir until mixture thickens and boils; cook and stir 2 to 3 minutes longer. Stir a little of the hot mixture into the egg yolk, returning it all to the hot mixture. Cook and stir until mixture just boils. Add vanilla; cool. Beat smooth; fold in whipped cream.

(Note: As the custard cools, to avoid a scum forming on the cooling surface, sprinkle a little sugar over the surface.)

<u>Wilted Lettuce</u>

This is a quick and easy side dish and can actually be used with any summer green, not just lettuce.

1 head of leafy lettuce or greens, such as kale, collards or cabbage (Note: Iceberg lettuce doesn't work for this recipe.)
2-3 strips of bacon
Wine vinegar, to taste
Sugar, to taste
1/2 tart apple shredded (optional)

Fry bacon until crisp. Remove crisp bacon and cool, then break into pieces to be added to the dish as a garnish. Shred lettuce or greens. Stir into the hot bacon drippings, and stir until the greens are wilted. Add wine vinegar and sugar to taste. Sprinkle bacon bits and shredded apple, if you like, on top. Serve hot.

Appendix

Red Cabbage

This is a dish where the purple cabbage magically turns red (the secret is the chemical change that occurs whenever the vinegar is added to the cabbage). There are many different ways to season this dish, and everyone is welcome to add their own herbs or spices, but it is basically stir-fried cabbage in some type of fat with sugar and vinegar added and cooked until tender, but not mushy. My Nana said the best red cabbage was cooked in goose fat drippings with currant jelly to sweeten rather than just sugar. She insisted on always using red wine vinegar rather than apple cider vinegar. I have used bacon drippings with olive oil and even butter and just plain old vinegar. I'm here to tell you, it's all good.

White Cake w/Raspberry Jam and Glaze

Cook in a moderate oven — 350 degrees F. Grease generously and flour 2 9" layer pans or 13 x 9" oblong pan.

Cream together until fluffy	2/3 cup soft butter or shortening
	1 3/4 cups sugar
Stir together	2 2/3 cups sifted flour
	3 tsp. double action baking powder
	3/4 tsp. salt
Stir in alternately with	1 1/3 cups of thin milk (half water)
	2 tsp. almond extract or vanilla
Fold in	4 egg whites (1/2 cup), stiffly beaten

Bake layers 30 to 35 minutes or oblong pan 35 to 45 minutes until tested done with toothpick or cake tester. Carefully cut into layers to make a four-layer cake. Spread the bottom three layers generously with raspberry jam. Drizzle top with glaze made from 1 cup of confectioner's sugar and 1/4 cup of lemon juice with one tablespoon of lemon zest.

Tilly's Song

Pickled Beets

Cook 2 pounds of fresh beets. Cool and cut into round slices or use peeled baby beets. In a saucepan, bring to boil 1/2 cup vinegar, 1/2 cup water off the boiled beets, 2 Tbsp. sugar, 2-4 whole cloves, 1/2 tsp. salt, 3 peppercorns and 1 bay leaf. Pour hot liquid over cooled beets. Cover and chill. These beet pickles seem to be best in 3 days to 1 week.

Real Meatloaf

This dish was originally made by mixing beef, pork and veal together. Mostly today, it is made with only ground beef. If you try it with sage-flavored pork sausage, it will turn this ho-hum meat dish into a family favorite.

- 1 lb. lean ground beef
- 1/2 lb. Pork sausage with sage seasoning
- 2 cups bread crumbs
- 1 egg, beaten
- 1 cup of condensed milk
- 4 Tbsp. minced onion
- 1 Tbsp. minced garlic
- 2 tsp. salt
- 1/2 tsp. pepper
- 1/4 tsp. dry mustard
- 1/4 tsp. cardamom (optional)

Bake this mixture in a 9"x5"x3" loaf pan in a moderate oven of 350 degrees F for 1 1/2 hours. Serves 8 people and is best eaten with brown gravy and mashed potatoes. Some prefer it served with catsup rather than gravy. Either way, it is good, and it is also great for sandwiches the next day. This is the same filling my Nana used to make her cabbage rolls, but instead of cardamom, she used cinnamon.

Pie Crust-Lard

- 2 cups flour
- 1 tsp. salt
- 2/3 cup lard
- 5 to 7 Tbsp. ice water

Appendix

Sift flour and salt in bowl. Cut lard into flour mixture until the pieces are the size of peas. Add very cold water a few drops at a time. Press into a ball. Divide in half. Roll 1/8 inch thick. Place in pie pan and prick with a fork. Bake at 450 degrees F for 8 to 10 minutes. This is excellent for any cream pie. In today's thinking, this is not a healthy choice, but if you occasionally make this as a treat, you will discover it is the flakiest pastry you have ever eaten!!

Potato Salad

Potato salad is like meatloaf: every family has its own version. This is not a hot potato salad, which is usually thought of as German. This is a cold potato salad with mayonnaise, but it is always good to the last bite. Exact measurements are not written down. My Nana always said to do this until it looks right! HA!! So this recipe is *about* this amount of ingredients; a little more or less is up to your individual taste. Enjoy.

> 6 medium-size red potatoes (This is the best type of potato to make potato salad.)
> 1 medium onion, chopped fine
> 5-6 inner tender stalks of celery with the yellowish-green leaves, chopped fine
> 1/3 cup sweet pickle relish or 3 large sweet pickles, chopped fine
> 2 hard-cooked eggs, chopped
> Salt and pepper to taste
> Enough mayonnaise to cover the vegetables as a dressing

Cook the potatoes and eggs together for convenience. Cool. Shell and chop the eggs. Cut up the potatoes into bite-size chunks. Potatoes may be peeled or not. Chop up all the other ingredients, and mix together with the mayonnaise. Cover and chill overnight for flavors to mingle. This dish is great with ham or barbeque. If you prefer macaroni salad, the only difference is to substitute 4 cups of cooked, cooled elbow macaroni instead of the potatoes. Yum!

Roast Goose

Like our Thanksgiving turkey, the goose has his day on November 11th, St. Martin's Day; also, it is traditional in many countries on Christmas Day.

1 plump young goose, about 12 lbs.
6 medium-large tart apples
1/2 cup of plums or prunes, partially cooked
3 pints of stock
Salt and pepper to taste

Select a nice young goose, and allow it to hang for several days. (What this means today is that if you don't start out with a live goose that you have to kill and dress, make sure the frozen goose is thawed and drained of all blood.) Wash and clean the goose and wipe dry. Rub both the inside cavity and the outside with salt and pepper. Pare and chop the apples and plums, and stuff the cavity with the fruit. Sew up the goose, truss it and roast it at 425 degrees F for about 2-2 1/2 hours, basting very frequently with its own juices. When goose is browned, add the stock. Continue to cook until goose is done. You can tell the goose is done when the meat pulls away from the bone.

Shortly before the goose is done, pour off the gravy, replacing with 2 cups of hot water. Set the gravy for a few minutes for the fat to rise, then skim off all the fat possible and save it.*

Place the goose on a heated platter and garnish with baby new potatoes and parsley. Serve with red cabbage.

*Place the goose fat in a skillet with a medium chopped onion and an apple; simmer until the fat has taken on their flavors. Strain the fat off into a jar, and chill to use later as a spread for dark bread. (I do believe this is an acquired taste).

Cabbage Soup

This is the famous soup made out of whatever is leftover and needs to be used up. It basically starts with cabbage, onion, carrot or parsnip and chicken stock; cook until vegetables are tender enough to eat. Feel free to add green beans, celery, mushrooms, tomatoes, garlic, zucchini squash or new potatoes as well. It is great on a snowy day with hot fresh bread and plenty of creamery butter or garlic-flavored olive oil.

Pot Roast with Oven-roasted Vegetables

The standard pot roast is made with a shoulder cut or a rump roast, since these are the tougher cuts on the animal. (NEVER, NEVER, NEVER use the pot roast method of cooking roasts on beef tenderloin or rib roast, or my Nana will descend from heaven and smack you!)

In a large skillet, brown roast (3 to 5 lbs.) in a little bacon grease or oil. Place in a roasting dish that has a lid that fits tightly, or continue to cook in the skillet that has a heavy lid. Cover just to the top of the meat with water. Add several pieces of garlic and 1/2 an onion, cut up into chunks, 2 bay leaves and a teaspoon of mustard seed (optional). Cook the roast for 1 1/2 to 2 hours. Remove lid and add to the roast enough peeled and diced potatoes and carrots to feed your family a generous portion. Continue to cook until the vegetables are tender.

This may be cooked on the stove top, in the skillet, or in a roasting dish in the oven at 350-375 degrees F. Pour the juice off and thicken with a roux of flour and fat to make the brown gravy. Slice and arrange meat onto the platter with the vegetables garnishing the meat. Any leftover meat and gravy makes for great hot open-faced roast sandwiches.

White Cake with Peaches and Cream

This can either be a plain white cake or shortbread cut into a square, then topped with freshly sliced sweetened peaches and drizzled with heavy cream. (A more modern way to prepare this dessert is to use either canned peaches or thawed frozen peaches and top with vanilla ice cream. However you put it together, this is a great summer dessert.) Peaches can be replaced with any seasonal berry.

My Nana's shortcake with strawberries, or blackberries, or peaches was more like a big sweet biscuit. The cake or biscuit was a normal biscuit with 1/4 cup more butter cut into the flour and 2 Tbsp. of sugar added to the recipe. It was baked in a pie plate. When crispy brown, it was cut into wedges, buttered and filled with sliced, sweetened fresh strawberries. Strawberries were also ladled over the top of each slice. It was served in a bowl with either whipped cream or vanilla ice cream served on top. It is especially good if the shortcake is still a little warm.

Deviled Eggs

This is not an exact recipe, but more a how-to recipe. Hard cook the number of eggs you wish to serve. Peel and cut into halves. Remove the yolks and add mayonnaise, finely minced onion, sweet pickle relish and capers. Spoon the yolk mixture back into the center of the halved eggs. Sprinkle with paprika or caviar.

Christmas Cookies — Pfeffernusse

    4 cups sifted flour   1/2 tsp. black pepper
    1 tsp. salt   1/4 tsp. powdered anise
    1 tsp. soda   1 tsp. mace
    1 tsp. baking powder   1 tsp. allspice
    3/4 cup molasses   3/4 cup shortening
    3/4 cup honey   1 egg

Sift all the dry ingredients together. Place honey and molasses in a saucepan and warm (don't boil). Add the shortening and stir to melt in the warm liquid. Cool and add beaten egg. Stir in the dry ingredients, being careful not to over mix the dough.

Let the mixture stand for 15 minutes, then form into little balls the size of a walnut. Place on greased baking sheet. Bake 12-15 minutes at 350 degrees F. Roll in confectioner's sugar while still warm. I have found people either really love these little cookies or don't like them at all. They look like Mexican Wedding cookies, so forewarn people ahead of time.

Sugar Cut-out Cookies

    3/4 cup butter (no other fat will do, only real butter)
    3/4 cup granulated sugar
    2 large eggs
    1 tsp. vanilla or rum extract

2 2/3 cup flour
2 tsp. baking powder

Preheat oven to 400 degrees F. Cream butter and sugar together. Beat in eggs and extract. Add baking powder and flour, one cup at a time, mixing well after each addition. The dough will be very stiff. Divide dough into two balls. DO NOT chill dough.

Roll dough out onto a floured cookie sheet; cut out cookie right on sheet. Remove excess dough. (Secret: Place a dampened towel under the cookie sheet to prevent slipping as you roll out dough.) Dough should not be more than 1/4 inch thick. Dip cutter into flour before each use. Press on dough and then remove the excess dough. Bake cookies on the top rack of the oven. Bake the sugar cookies for 8-10 minutes or until lightly brown. Remove cookies from cookie sheet immediately after removing from the oven onto a rack. Before the cookies are cool, dot mark cookies with designs or writing with a toothpick to make decorating easier. Let cookies cool on a rack before decorating them with icing and candies.

<u>Quick-pour Icing Recipe</u>

This is the perfect icing to delicately coat cookies. It dries to a smooth, shiny surface, unlike ordinary icings. Use for frosting the surface of cookies only.

6 cups confectioner's sugar, sifted
1/2 cup water
2 Tbsp. light corn syrup

1 tsp. almond extract
liquid food color, as desired

Place sugar in a saucepan. Combine water and corn syrup. Add to sugar and stir until well mixed. Place over low heat. Do not allow temperature to exceed 100 degrees F. Remove from hear, stir in flavor and food color.

If you wish to decorate the holiday cookies using a pastry bag and pipe on the designs, this is the best recipe for decorating frosting.

Snow-white Butter Cream Icing

Decorations made with this icing or frosting may be air-dried. These decorations are a pretty, translucent quality, are good tasting and do not require refrigeration or freezing.

2/3 cup water
4 Tbsp. Meringue Powder
12 cups sifted confectioner's sugar (approx. 3 lbs.)
1 1/4 cups solid white shortening
3/4 tsp. salt
1/2 tsp. clear vanilla flavoring
1/2 tsp. almond flavoring
1/4 tsp. butter flavoring

Combine water and meringue powder; whip at high speed until peaks form. Add 4 cups of sugar, one cup at a time, beating after each addition at low speed. Alternately add shortening and remainder of sugar. Add salt and flavoring; beat at low speed until smooth. This all used to be done by hand, but then God invented the electric mixer. Thank You, Lord! Yield is 7 cups.

It can be cut in half if you are only making cookies for your own home use, but if you are giving them away as Christmas, Valentine's or Easter presents, you will probably need to double the recipe.

Gingerbread Cookies w/Icing

Sometimes called Gingies, known to help alleviate motion sickness.

Mix together thoroughly	1/3 cup soft shortening
	1 cup brown sugar
	1 1/2 cups dark molasses
Stir in	1/2 cup cold water
Sift together and stir in	6 cups flour
	1 tsp. salt
	1 tsp. ground allspice
	1 tsp. ground ginger

Appendix

	1 tsp. ground cloves
	1 tsp. ground cinnamon
Stir in	2 tsp. soda dissolved in 3 Tbsp. of cold water

Chill dough. Roll out very thick (1/2"). Cut dough with 2 1/2" round cutter. Place far apart on lightly greased cookie sheet. Bake until when touched lightly with finger, no imprint remains. Bake in a moderate oven 350 degrees F for 15 to 18 minutes. Yield is approximately 2 1/2 dozen cookies. These may be iced when cooled using the following simple white icing.

Simple White Icing

Blend together 1 cup sifted confectioner's sugar, 1/4 tsp. salt, 1/2 tsp. vanilla extract and enough milk to make it easy to spread, about 1 1/2 Tbsp. This is good to glaze donuts or sweet bread.

Thanks to a dear friend, Cathy Smith, I was able to borrow her mom's recipe for cake frosting. The recipes I had for cakes either didn't include a frosting recipe or else they just didn't eat many of their cakes with regular frosting, but instead used whipped cream or fruit topping. The following are three never-fail recipes. Thanks, Cathy.

White Frosting

1/2 cup shortening
1/4-1/3 cup milk
1 Tbsp. almond extract
4 cups (1 lb.) confectioner's sugar

Mix together shortening, a little milk, flavoring and 1 cup of the sugar with a wooden spoon or electric mixer. Gradually add more milk and sugar until all the ingredients are added and well mixed. Increase the speed of the mixer to the highest speed, and whip the frosting for 5 minutes until light and fluffy. Yield: 3 cups

Butter Cream Icing
    1/2 cup shortening   1 tsp. almond extract
    1/2 cup butter   4 cups confectioner's sugar
    2 Tbsp. milk (add 2-4 Tbsp.
    more if frosting a cake)

Cream together the shortening and butter. Add extract. Gradually add sugar, scraping the sides well. Add milk between 2nd and 3rd cups of sugar. Beat until light and fluffy, approximately 5 minutes. Yield: 3 cups.

Chocolate Butter Cream Icing
Add 1/2 cup of cocoa or 2 1-oz. unsweetened squares of chocolate and an additional 1-2 Tbsp. of milk to the above recipe, once it is made. Mix until well blended.

Orange Cookies
    1 cup butter or lard
    1 cup sugar
    1 cup brown sugar
    1 egg
    2 1/3 cups all purpose flour
    1 tsp. baking soda
    1/2 tsp. salt
    2 Tbsp. orange juice
    1 Tbsp. orange peel

Cream the sugar and fat and add egg. Beat until smooth and creamy. Slowly add the dry ingredients and at last add the orange juice and peel. Form into small balls the size of a walnut. Bake at 350 degrees F for 10 minutes. You will want them to be chewy with crisp edges. Yield approx. 2 dozen cookies. Attractive with orange sugar sprinkled on while hot. These keep well only if they are hidden. These are my favorite cookies, and I have never seen them in any cookbooks or at any parties.

Fastnacht
    Makes about 2 dozen doughnuts.

Appendix

In America, these were called Spudnuts and were made with potato flour rather than boiled potatoes. Other than that, they seem to look and taste the same.

In Germany, these doughnuts were eaten the Tuesday before Ash Wednesday because Lent season was supposed to be void of any sweets or desserts. Hot Cross Buns broke the fast from sweets on Easter morning.

2 cups water	1 pkg. or cube of active yeast
1 medium boiled potato	1 tsp. plus 2 1/2 cups sugar
4 Tbsp. butter, plus 2 tsp. softened butter	6 to 6 1/2 cups unsifted flour
	2 eggs
1 tsp. salt	
Oil for deep fat frying	

Cook potato until it can be easily mashed with a fork. Drain and reserve 1 1/2 cups of the cooked potato water. Mash the potato. You will need 1/2 cup. Beat the 4 Tbsp. butter into the mashed potato. Cover and keep warm.

Cool the potato water to lukewarm (110 degrees F). Dissolve yeast and 1 tsp. of sugar in 1/4 cup of the potato water. Let stand for 2 to 3 minutes to see if the yeast is actively growing to double in size.

Combine 6 cups of flour, 1/2 cup of the sugar and the salt in a deep mixing bowl. Make a well in the flour and drop the potato, eggs, yeast and remaining 1 1/4 cups of potato water. Using a wooden spoon, mix ingredients together until dough forms into a soft ball. Place the dough on a lightly floured surface and knead for about 10 minutes, until the dough is smooth and elastic. Add more flour to hands as needed to handle the dough without it sticking to hands or surface.

Use the remaining butter to evenly coat the bottom and sides of a large bowl. Cover and let rise for about 1 1/2 hours, or until the dough is double in bulk.

To shape the risen dough, cut into squares, or if you prefer, use a doughnut cutter and let rise in a draft-free place for 30 to 45 minutes or until double in bulk.

Fry at 375 degrees F for 3 minutes or until puffed and

brown. Drain and then drop into a bag of granulated sugar or powdered sugar.

These treasures are best eaten while they are still warm.

Sauerbraten

(I think my Nana made our family Sauerbraten once that I can remember. She said it was an awful lot of work, as you will see. Hardly anyone goes to all this trouble to cook an authentic Rheinischer Sauerbraten. Today, most cooks just rely on bottled marinade or sauce to put on cooked roasted meat. If you want to try this very German dish, plan ahead and enjoy.)

> 5 pounds of rump roast — beef, pork, lamb or wild game
> 3 cups white vinegar or wine (not cooking wine, it is too salty)
> 3 cups water
> 1 large onion, sliced
> 2 bay leaves
> 8 cloves
> 8 peppercorns
> 1 Tbsp. pickling spice
> 1 large carrot or parsnip, scraped and sliced
> 4 slices of bacon
> 2 Tbsp. butter
> 2 large onions, sliced
> 1 bay leaf
> 6 cloves
> 8 to 10 gingersnaps, crushed to make the gravy in the last half hour of cooking

If the meat is very lean, it will need to be larded with bacon, either by you or a butcher. Some prefer to tie the roast with string so it will hold its shape better throughout this process. Rub the roast well with salt and place in a deep, close-fitting glass or earthenware baking dish. Combine the vinegar or wine and water with onion, bay leaves, cloves, peppercorns, pickling spices and carrot in a saucepan and simmer for 5 minutes. Cool marinade and pour over meat. Keep in a refrigerator or below

40 degrees F, but do not freeze, for 3 to 5 days. It needs to be turned a couple of times a day. Remove the meat from marinade, and dry off the meat.

Cook the bacon until fat is rendered, and then add the butter. Use this fat to brown the meat on all sides. DO NOT use too hot of a flame or it will make the fat break down and produce smoke, which will also blacken the meat and destroy the flavor of the dish. Strain the marinade and reserve. Remove browned meat, add onions and cook until deep golden brown.

Place meat on top of the onions, and add strained marinade over the meat with fresh bay leaves and cloves. Cook by bringing the marinade to a boil, then reduce heat and simmer very slowly for 3 1/2 to 4 hours.

This is a good dish to cook in a crock-pot, but it may take longer than 4 hours. The meat is done when it can be easily pierced with a fork or skewer. Remove meat; strain the liquid. Pour liquid into a pan, and bring to a boil. Add the crushed gingersnaps to the liquid, and cook until thickened. Slice meat very thinly and ladle some of the gravy over the meat; pour the rest into a gravy boat. Serve garnished with cooked carrots, parsley and pickled pearl onions. Serve with mashed potatoes or spraetzels and fresh hard-crusted bread or rolls.

NOTE: Nana used leftover gingerbread cookies to thicken the gravy. I noticed a note to herself on one of the recipe cards to remind her to strain out the raisins in the gravy after the cookies part had dissolved in the meat juices.

*Thanks to *The German Cookbook* by Mimi Sheraton, 1965, Random House, New York, for the directions on how to make this dish!

Spraetzels

This is basically a standard egg noodle: egg, flour, salt. What makes it a spraetzel is that the dough is forced through a sieve into boiling water to make a crazy curly sort of noodle. Everyone has her own version of this recipe. Some use just a little oil or butter to make a soft noodle dough. Others may add just a hint of nutmeg, cardamom or lemon zest to liven up the plain pasta. However, nothing needs to be added to the dough recipe when it is to be served with sauerbraten, because the rich gravy is absorbed into the noodle and makes for not only a filling dish but one that delights the taste buds.

Homemade Egg Noodle

2 to 2 1/2 cups flour	3 eggs
1/2 tsp. salt	1 Tbsp. cold water

On a pastry board or countertop, place the flour and salt. Make a well in the center and add the eggs and water. With fingers or a spoon, gradually mix the flour and salt with the eggs and water. Gather it all together to form a ball. Knead until you incorporate 1/2 cup more flour until it makes a firm ball. You will need to mix and knead this ball for approximately 15 minutes.

When the dough is smooth, use a rolling pin and roll the dough to the thickness you want your noodles to be. Cut in long 1/4-inch wide pieces.

You may cook them at once in salted boiling water or wrap them in plastic and keep in the refrigerator for a day or the freezer for several months.

Wiener Schnitzel

No single cut of meat is more beloved in Germany than the schnitzel, which literally means a slice or cutlet from the veal leg. In Italy, it is called *scaloppini* and in France, *escalope*. Weiner schnitzel is actually from Vienna, Austria, but the Germans claim it as well.

6 veal cutlets, pounded	2 Tbsp. salad oil
lemon juice (optional)	1 generous cup dry, fine
1/2 to 1 cup flour	breadcrumbs
2 eggs, beaten with 2 Tbsp. cold water	4 to 5 Tbsp. butter, lard or oil

Veal cutlets may be marinated in a sprinkling of lemon juice for 30 minutes before breading. Whether or not they are marinated, sprinkle with salt on both sides before breading.

Measure flour onto a sheet of waxed paper or a flat plate. (I use a pie plate.) Beat eggs and water in wide flat bowl; beat in oil if you are using it. The oil is supposed to hold breading on securely and help to make it crisp. Measure breadcrumbs onto a sheet of waxed paper or plastic wrap. Dip salted cutlets into flour on both sides, then into beaten egg mixture. Let the excess egg drip off, and dredge cutlet with breadcrumbs. Let stand at room temperature 15 to 30 minutes. Heat the fat in large skillet. Do not crowd cutlets into pan. Fry first side very slowly until golden brown. Turn and brown the other side with a spatula, but do not pierce with a fork. Cook at least 4 to 6 minutes on each side. Keep warm in an oven, 250 degrees F, until all the cutlets are cooked.

*The secret to perfect schnitzel is to pound it to 1/16 to 1/8 inch thickness and cook crispy and serve crispy. If it is allowed to get soggy, it is considered inedible.

<u>Krummelkuchen (Crumb Cake)</u>

This is not the type of crumb cake that many make or buy today. Those are made with a sweet biscuit-type baking powder cake and have a streusel topping. This cake is more of a pastry-yeast leavened product with a streusel topping. The dough is basically rich, sweet bread dough.

Dough:
 3 1/2 cups all purpose flour
 1 cup lukewarm milk
 1/2 cup sugar
 2 1/2 tsp. yeast or 2 cakes of yeast
 1/4 cup real butter
 2 eggs

Streusel Topping:
 1 1/4 cups flour
 1/3 cup sugar
 1 Tbsp. crushed almonds or nuts that are available, such as walnuts or pecans
 1/2 tsp. ground cinnamon

5 Tbsp. real butter, melted
confectioner's sugar

Sift flour into a large bowl and make a crater in the center. Into the crater, pour one-half of the milk; add in the sugar and sprinkle the yeast over the top. Sprinkle some of the flour over the yeast. After the yeast begins to foam (15 to 20 minutes), add the butter, eggs and salt and slowly work in the remaining milk to make an elastic dough. Knead by hand for 15 minutes until it no longer sticks to the table or hands. Place in oiled bowl and cover to rise for 1 to 2 hours until double in size, depending on the warmth of the kitchen. Roll dough into a rectangle shape and place on a large baking sheet. Stoneware is the best for this recipe.

To make the streusel topping, start by combining the flour, sugar, crushed almonds and cinnamon. The melted butter should no longer be hot, but still fluid; sprinkle the butter over the other ingredients, coat your hands with flour and rub the mixture back and forth until you have little clumps (streusel) topping.

Sprinkle over raised dough and bake for 35 to 45 minutes in a preheated oven of 325 degrees F. Sprinkle with confectioner's sugar while still warm.

Sun Perch with Grated Horseradish Red Sauce

This pan-fried preparation of fish can be used for any freshwater or saltwater fish. The fish must be cleaned. This means washed, scaled and gutted. Roll the whole fish in half flour and half fine breadcrumbs seasoned with salt and pepper. Pan-fry slowly in enough oil or drawn butter to keep the fish from sticking to the pan. Turn the fish only once, and then put a lid on the pan and continue to cook until the thickest portion of the fish is completely done. Test for doneness by pricking with a fork or toothpick to see if the meat is flaky. Transfer to a serving dish that is garnished with fresh dill weed and lemon and/or limes. The red sauce is nothing more than the sauce used to make shrimp cocktail, which is an equal part of horseradish and catsup. The most delicious red sauce is made by using fresh grated horseradish root instead of the commercial bottled type. This is usually very potent and hot, so add catsup to horseradish at a ratio that best pleases your own taste.

Apple Dumpling

An apple dumpling is a baked apple within a rich pie pastry. The more traditional way to prepare these is to core and peel a baking apple, leaving it whole. Stuff the hole with cinnamon, brown sugar and raisins. Cover the entire apple with piecrust and bake in a 375 degree F oven until the crust is golden brown. The dumpling is served warm with a chilled custard sauce or cold heavy cream.

The less traditional way is to use a cooked apple pie filling, spoon a small amount on a square piece of piecrust and seal the edges with fork marks or finger, pinching the dough together. These look more like fried pies, although they are baked and not fried. Rather than custard or heavy cream, serve with the frozen form: ice cream!

Making apple dumplings is more of a science than an art. The best pastry has flour, lard, salt, egg, vinegar and water. It must be rolled thin enough to be delicately flaky but thick enough to hold together and stay on the apple while baking. If it is too thick, it will not cook evenly and will taste doughy; if too thin, it will be too crisp or it will not hold in the apple juices as it bakes. It takes years to perfect this dish and, alas, some of us never have!

Bread and Butter Pickles

Makes about 4 quarts of pickles.

This is one of those recipes that I only found the list of ingredients and no instructions. If you decide to try this recipe that has been in our family for generations, consult a canning manual for proper home canning methods first. It is not difficult, just time consuming.

> 5 lbs. firm ripe cucumbers (about 10 medium-size cucumbers), scrubbed and cut crosswise into 1/4-inch thick rounds

3 medium onions, cut into 1/4-inch thick slices
1 large green bell pepper
1 large red bell pepper, washed and halved, cut into 2 by 1/4-inch strips
1 cup salt
6 cups sugar
3 cups distilled white vinegar
1 Tbsp. celery seeds
1 Tbsp. mustard seed

Combine the cucumbers, onions and peppers in a large colander set over a bowl. Sprinkle the vegetables with salt, turning the vegetables about with a wooden spoon to coat evenly. Let these stand for 2 to 3 hours to allow the excess liquid to drain. Place the colander under cold running water and wash off salt. Let these vegetables drain.

In an 8-quart enameled or stainless steel saucepan bring sugar, vinegar, celery seed and mustard seed to boil over high heat until sugar dissolves. Add vegetables and boil briskly for about 2 minutes. Remove the pan from the heat and ladle pickle mixture into hot sterilized jars, filling them to within 1/4 inch of the top of jar. Process the jars for 15 minutes in a boiling-water bath with lids on the jars.

Stewed Chicken and Dumplings

This recipe is not difficult, just time consuming. Making the broth ahead of time really saves on the preparation time. Even cooking the chicken ahead of-time is a smart thing to do if you like this dish but have limited time to prepare it.

The secret to good chicken and dumplings has to do with the good chicken stock used to cook the chicken.

First you must cook one chicken with celery, onion, garlic, thyme, fresh parsley, carrot, sage, 1 or 2 bay leaves and a small amount of turmeric just to get the rich broth. Add salt to taste after the flavors have had a chance to cook out into the broth. Take that chicken and use it for chicken sandwiches or some other dish that needs a cooked chicken.

Now take another plump chicken and cook in the drained chicken broth as follows.

3 1/2 to 4 lb. chicken, cut into 8 serving pieces	1/4 cup white wine
	1 stalk of celery, including the green leaves
1/4 cup flour	
1/3 cup oil	1 medium bay leaf
1 large onion, chopped	2 tsp. salt
6 cups fresh chicken stock	freshly ground pepper

Cut the chicken into pieces, dredge in flour and fry until lightly brown. Remove to plate and now slowly cook the onions until soft and translucent but not brown. Add liquid and herbs to the onion, and add the partially cooked chicken to the broth. Reduce the heat and simmer for 45 minutes until the meat is so tender it will fall off the bone. Remove the bay leaf and make the dumplings.

<u>Dumplings</u>

2 cups unsifted flour	1/4 cup finely chopped parsley and/or chives
4 tsp. double acting baking powder	
	2 Tbsp. butter, cut into 1/2-inch bits
1 tsp. salt	
1 cup whole milk	

Cut the butter into the dry ingredients until it looks like coarse meal. Add milk to make a batter. Drop the batter into simmering broth by the tablespoon. Cover the pot and simmer undisturbed for 10 minutes longer. Uncover and cook an additional 10 minutes. The dumplings are done when they are puffed and fluffy and a toothpick inserted into the center of the dumpling comes out clean.

We like to eat our chicken and dumplings served in individual bowls so there is plenty of broth to eat with a spoon.

Disclaimer: Neither of these cookie recipes have their origin in German cuisine. However, all true Germans love good food, and when all is said and done, it really doesn't matter who invented the dish just as long as they can eat some of it and have the recipe to make more of it!!

My Nana liked these cookies. She made them for us, and we liked them, too. It is my hope you will also like these easy-to-make and delicious-to-taste cookies with tea or coffee or straight out of the oven with a glass of cold milk.

Brownies

Melt together 2 squares of unsweetened chocolate (2 oz.) and 1/3 cup butter.

Beat in 1 cup of granulated sugar and 2 beaten eggs. Add 3/4 cup of flour, 1/2 tsp. baking powder, 1/2 tsp. salt and 1/2 cup of broken nuts (optional). Bake at 350 degrees F for 30 to 35 minutes.

Coconut Macaroons

1 3/4 cup shredded coconut
2 Tbsp. flour
3 egg whites
1/2 tsp. almond extract
1/3 cup sugar
1/8 tsp. salt (commonly called a dash of salt)

Combine coconut, flour, sugar and salt. Stir in egg whites and extract. Mix well. Drop from teaspoon onto a slightly greased baking sheet. If desired, top with half a maraschino cherry. Bake at 325 degrees F for 25 minutes or until browned around the edges. Remove from baking sheet at once or it will become a permanent part of the pan. HA! This recipe makes about 2 dozen cookies. These are great at Christmas time with green tinted coconut and red cherry. Very festive!

These treasures require time, energy and fresh, wholesome ingredients. There is no such thing as fast food when it comes to this type of cuisine. It is a labor of love to cook and serve these dishes. Food cooked with love is a nutrient that many are finding deficient in their lives nowadays. Try sitting down together as a family with all your feet under one table and eat, talk, laugh and enjoy one another.

Appendix

I promise you will want second helpings of this kind of fun!

Blessings to you and good appetite,
Carol Welty Roper

Bibliography

Bushnell, George D. *Wilmette: A History.* Wilmette, Illinois: Village of Wilmette, 1997.

Paton, John Glenn. *German Lieder: An Anthology of German Song and Interpretation.* Van Nuys, California: Alfred Publishing, 2000.

Scharfenberg, Horst. *The Cuisine of Germany.* Poseidon Press, 1989.

Sheraton, Mimi. *The German Cookbook.* New York: Random House, 1977.